Spur of the Moment

Books by Theresa Alan

WHO YOU KNOW

SPUR OF THE MOMENT

Published by Kensington Publishing Corporation

Spur of the Moment

Theresa Alan

KENSINGTON BOOKS
http://www.kensingtonbooks.com

KENSINGTON BOOKS are published by

Kensington Publishing Corp.
850 Third Avenue
New York, NY 10022

All Kensington Titles, Imprints, and Distributed Lines are available at special quantity discounts for bulk purchases for sales promotions, premiums, fund-raising, and educational or institutional use.

Special book excerpts or customized printings can also be created to fit specific needs. For details, write or phone the office of the Kensington special sales manager: Kensington Publishing Corp., 850 Third Avenue, New York, NY 10022, attn: Special Sales Department, Phone: 1-800-221-2647.

Kensington and the K logo Reg. U.S. Pat. & TM Off

ISBN 0-7582-0480-9

First printing: July 2004
10 9 8 7 6 5 4 3 2 1

Printed in the United States of America

*For my sister, Sara Jade Alan, who is my hero
and the kind of person I aspire to be.*

Acknowledgments

The adage goes: Write about what you know. However, all I know is how to sit on my ass and read and write books. Thus, I'm grateful to several people who have lives that are more interesting than my own and were kind enough to tell me about them.

First there is my sister, Sara, who is a stand-up and improv comedian and the inspiration for this book. Thanks also go to the fellow members of Sara's New York-based troupe, The Lords of Misrule—Perry Daniel, Brian McManus, Matt Love, and Tim Vierling—for always making me laugh.

For insight into the wild world of acting for television, thanks go to Jim Thorp.

For information on working as a firefighter, thanks go to my father Don Alan, a former firefighter, and to Corey Davidson, a current one.

I am extremely grateful to the following people whose comments and suggestions on early drafts of this book helped improve the manuscript considerably: Melissa Herb, Jennifer Daumler, Sue Arndt, George Wheeler, and Sara Alan. Many thanks also to my agent, Alison Picard, and to my editor John Scognamiglio.

Thanks to Heather Frank, Amy Wilson, Garian Vigil, and Burt McLucas for their unflagging support, and to Mike Homyack, for everything.

Finally, thanks go to my mother, Evelyn Alan, who brags about me so much it is a wonder she has any friends left. But her untiring championing of me and my work means more than I have the words to express. Thank you.

1

The Tampon Safari

Ana sprinted around the five-bedroom brownstone she and her friends rented, racing up and down the stairs, darting into the kitchen just long enough to chug down a cup of coffee like a beer at a frat party, then scurrying into the living room to grab her shoes and linen jacket. She looked like a time-elapsed video, the kind people use to show a flower blooming or a baby chick being born, except a video of Ana wouldn't need to be sped up. She rushed through life in a blur of activity, making her quite the anomaly among her friends. She'd been living with them since college, but neither Jason's and Scott's attitudes, which could best be described as serene, nor Marin's and Ramiro's attitudes, which went beyond calm to just shy of coma, had rubbed off on her. And certainly Ana's go-go-go sense of urgency had in no way influenced her friends.

She jumped along the wood-floored living room on her left leg, pogo-stick like, trying to slip on her shoe, clutching her other shoe and jacket in her other hand. She only got four hops before her stockinged foot slipped under her and she collapsed to the floor in a flailing heap of limbs like a bug splattered against a windshield. She promptly sprung up off the floor and continued getting ready for work.

When she finally got her shoes and jacket on, she grabbed her purse and hurried to the street where her car was parked. She wanted to get to work early so she could leave early to get to the theater well before the show started. Tonight the event planner from Qwest, the largest employer in Denver, was coming to see the performance. If she and her fellow improv actors—her four roommates and a woman named Chelsey— could dazzle him, he might hire them to perform at company parties and retreats. If they could get enough corporate gigs, they could eventually quit their soul-sucking day jobs, and Ana would never have to deal with her boss, The Big Weasel, again.

As soon as she got to the office, she went to the bathroom to void the two cups of coffee she'd had that morning. This was when she learned that her period had started two days earlier than usual. Ana always kept an emergency supply of tampons on hand, except after tearing through her purse, she discovered that there were no tampons to be found. Shit. Marin. Marin was always doing stuff like this, stealing sanitary products from Ana's purse so that Ana found herself at the office, early in the morning before any of her premenopausal coworkers were in, bleeding profusely with nothing to stanch the flow.

Ana exited the bathroom stall and looked at the tampon machine on the wall. She put her 25 cents in the machine and turned the handle. Nothing happened. Great. Great. Super. It was out of tampons. Lovely.

Ana returned to her cube, turned on her computer, and considered her dilemma.

Surely a female co-worker would get to work soon, right? Ana decided to take a little stroll around the office until she found a woman who was packing.

She walked down the hall past the kitchen, past Ryan Brenehy's desk. Ana occasionally thought about hooking up with Ryan. She thought he might be interested in her, if his drunken happy-hour flirtations meant anything. And he was cute and funny and all that; he just wasn't Jason.

She'd been in love with Jason since she met him in her first week of her first year of college six years ago, and she suspected that ever getting over him was probably hopeless. Sure, she'd dated other guys since she met him, but she'd never gotten serious about anyone. Most of her dates were disappointing. Like biting into a cookie expecting to find a chocolate chip, only to find a raisin. No other guy came close to Jason in intelligence, humor, or kindness. And, okay, it must be said, stunning good looks. Jason had the most astonishingly beautiful pale green-blue eyes that looked magically delicious against his olive skin.

It was because of Jason that Ana had become an improv comedian and completely changed her plans for her future. She'd never wanted to be a performer (she'd had fantasies, sure, of becoming a bad-ass musician or a famous comedian or a breathtaking actress, she'd just never actually wanted to get on a *stage*, in front of actual *people*). But when she saw him putting up signs in the dorms, advertising for actors to audition for the college improv comedy group the Iron Pyrits (the logo was of a winking, humorous-looking pirate, but the name was a play on pyrites, as in iron pyrites, as in fool's gold), she decided to go to the audition, just for the chance to see him again. She had no expectations of making the troupe. She'd always been able to make her friends laugh, but that was it, just her close friends, the people she felt comfortable with. She'd never considered for a second getting in front of a room full of strangers and trying to make them laugh, let alone trying to be funny with no script to work from, no net to catch her if she failed.

Her audition was far from flawless, but the members of the team—Jason, who was a sophomore at the time, Ramiro, who was a junior, and Scott, also a junior, liked what they saw and asked her if she wanted to join them. She was so stunned, she didn't know what to say, so she said yes.

That same day, they asked another freshman, Marin Kennesaw, to join the team.

Ana had liked Marin right away. Marin was the kind of woman it was impossible not to like. She was very beautiful—tall, thin, with brown eyes and blond hair—but she was so funny that you didn't think of her as some unattainable beauty, but as your buddy, your pal. Marin had a way of making everyone around her feel comfortable. While she had a secretly acerbic side to her personality, ready to make scorching commentary on humanity's eternal predilection for stupidity and/ or unfortunate fashion choices, Marin saved that side of herself for her friends. To outsiders, she always said the right thing. She had a gift for making even the dullest person feel like the life of the party.

The Iron Pyrits practiced three days a week, and the more Ana had gotten to know Jason, the more she was convinced he was the most amazing guy she'd ever met. He was one of those rare people who didn't just complain about the world, he actually did something about it. He recycled and went to protest rallies and volunteered his time speaking to fraternities and other groups on campus about domestic violence and rape. He sent what money he could spare to various charities. He always brought his own bags to the grocery store and wouldn't use a paper plate or plastic fork for any reason. Ana occasionally got into kicks about being a good citizen, but inevitably she soon grew weary and lazy. Her good intentions were like the first guy she'd slept with: brief and highly forgettable.

After a few weeks of rehearsing together, they'd gone out for drinks after practice, and that's when Jason told Ana that he was head over heels for Marin, and did she think he had a chance?

"She's the most amazing woman I've ever met," he said.

"Yeah, she is," Ana said, feeling like a tire that had run over a nail.

Ana had tried to get over her crush on Jason, but she and Marin had moved in with Ramiro, Scott, and Jason at the beginning of their sophomore year when the guys' other two roommates had gotten jobs in other cities and moved out. How was she supposed to get over Jason when she saw him every day? When she saw how kind and funny and considerate and wonderful he was all the time?

After Scott and Ramiro graduated, they landed jobs at Spur of the Moment Improv Theater in downtown Denver. A year and a half later, two positions on the troupe opened up, and Jason auditioned and got one of them. Several months after that, two more positions opened up. At the time, it had been an all-male troupe, but Ana and Marin took care of that, win-

ning both spots. A year after that, when one of the veteran performers left, Chelsey McGuiness auditioned, got the job, and
became best friends with the rest of them in a matter of hours.

Though Ana had spent the last six years pining for a man
who loved someone else, she'd never regretted going to that
audition. She'd become addicted to making people laugh. She
loved pretending to be different characters. She loved being
creative and thinking on her feet. She never felt as free as she
did when she was on stage. Now, instead of wanting a simple
life with a husband and a nine-to-five job, she wanted to be
rich and famous and win Academy Awards and see her face on
the cover of magazines with headlines proclaiming, "Ana Jade
Jacobs: The woman who transformed comedy." Or "Beauty,
Brains, Talent—Ana Jade Jacobs has it all." What she did not
want was to be marketing software or working for The Big
Weasel.

The office where Ana worked comprised both the eleventh
and twelfth floors of the building, but she couldn't find a single
woman under the age of fifty on either floor. This was what
she got for getting to work early. Screwed.

She took the escalator to the public women's washroom on
the first floor. When she went to the tampon machine, she realized she was out of change.

"Bloody hell." Literally.

She needed to do something to tide her over, so she took
three paper towels and folded them into her underwear. The
scratchy, bulky paper towels made her waddle. She told herself
suffering was good experience for an artist. It would bring her
closer to her cave-dwelling foresisters who used twigs and
straw to confine their monthly flow. But after walking just a
few steps from the bathroom to the elevator, Ana realized that
the cheap, abrasive paper towels were like sandpaper. If she
didn't get a tampon soon, her clitoris would be sanded right
off.

Ana waddled along, Buddha-bellied with bloat. She'd put
on eight pounds in the past few months, and it was all the fault
of hanging out after the shows and drinking too many beers.
She always said she would have just one, but as the hour be-

came two and then three, how could she seriously nurse a single beer for all that time? Once she'd tried drinking citron vodka straight instead of beer, but that was the night she'd gotten so drunk so fast she'd accidentally made out with Scott for three hours in the coat room.

The problem was that her two best friends, Chelsey and Marin, were skinny little waifs, and Ana felt Amazonian by comparison. But if she didn't lose at least a few pounds, she was going to have to admit defeat and buy bigger clothes. The prospect was too depressing. Who wanted to spend money on fat clothes? Right now, she could fit into only half of her clothes, and even those pinched her waist and left her struggling to breathe.

Clothes were made for skinny girls like Chelsey and Marin. It took a miracle for Ana to find clothes that fit her, with her ample bust and the muscular thighs she'd developed as a competitive gymnast as a kid. She'd quit gymnastics when she got to high school and became a cheerleader, though her years of cheering were not something she talked about with the general public. Her close friends knew about her sordid, pom pom-ridden past, but as most of the people she hung out with these days had an artistic bent and tended to frown on things like school spirit, she did her best not to bring the subject up outside her immediate buddies at Spur of the Moment.

When she got off the elevator on the twelfth floor, she saw Paula Moore. Ana couldn't stand Paula. Paula had also graduated with a degree in marketing, but she hadn't moved her way up from assistant yet, while Ana was already a manager. Paula had made a bitchy comment over happy-hour drinks one time in which she basically said that the only reason Ana had worked her way up the corporate ladder so fast was because of her friendship with Scott, who was a graphic designer at the company and had helped Ana land an interview there when she'd graduated two years after he did. Ana wasn't always sure she was grateful to him for this, although it was her fault that she had earned her degree in marketing, thinking it was a sensible way to make a living until she and her comedian buddies starred in their own TV show or toured the country for obscene amounts of money. The problem with having a fallback job was that sometimes, you actually have to fall back on it.

Despite hating her job, Ana always worked hard and had been rewarded for it, something the vacuous Paula held against her. Ana always said that you could tell who your friends were not just by whether they were there for you when your life was crumbling down, but whether they could genuinely be happy for you when you succeeded. As much as Ana disliked Paula, she was a twenty-four-year-old female and likely to be carrying, so Ana waddled over to her.

"Do you have a stick up your ass?" Paula asked.

"An entire tree. Could I please borrow a tampon, a pad, anything?"

"I keep two tampons in cases of emergency. If I give one to you, I'll only have one left."

"I'll buy an entire box and pay you back three fold over my break. Today. A few short hours from now."

Paula scowled at Ana like a schoolteacher looking at a student who hadn't prepared for the test and didn't have anyone to blame but herself. But at last, grudgingly, Paula handed over the tampon.

Ana toddled as fast as she could down the long hallway to the bathroom.

For about four seconds after inserting the tampon, Ana felt relief. Then she felt a familiar rumbling in her bowels.

"Oh shit." Which, of course, was the problem.

Or maybe not such a problem after all. She could take a dump without the precious tampon shooting out of her body like a bullet from an AK-47, right? She hadn't done Kegel exercises for all these years for nothing, had she?

So she tried to void her bowels while keeping the tampon in place. And she failed.

She slumped down on the toilet seat, her pants around her ankles, and declared, with deeply felt emotion, "I hate my life."

2

Psycho Murderers, Mold, and Other Lurking Menaces

Chelsey McGuiness' day had not started well. She got home at six in the morning after spending a luscious evening with a gorgeous man she'd met at the club the night before, only to discover that her window had been broken.

"Shit."

She warily unlocked the door to her townhouse, looking around for signs of theft. The TV and the VCR were still there. She didn't have any jewelry that was worth more than ten bucks or so, except the thirty-dollar watch she was wearing, so she didn't have anything to worry about there.

It had been so depressing when she'd gone to get home-owner's insurance on her new home. The insurance agent went through a series of questions that made Chelsey feel progressively worse about herself.

How much are your paintings worth?

Well, let's see, if you count the Scotch tape I use to hang my unframed *posters*, I don't know, maybe fifty cents?

How much is your jewelry worth?

A hundred bucks, she said, overestimating significantly. She figured if her house burned down, she'd at least get a little extra cash to buy a new watch.

Furs?

Nope.

Firearms?

Good God no.

Computer equipment?

She had a 286 PC she'd bought with student loan money in 1990 that she used as a paperweight. If she needed a computer to write a scene, she used the one at Spur of the Moment. Ten bucks, she'd estimated.

When all was said and done, Chelsey had absolutely nothing of value. What did the insurance agent want from her? She was a single, twenty-seven-year-old female who'd used every last shred of her savings to buy this place.

Usually she didn't mind being single. Just now, though, she'd really like to be married. If she were married, she could force her husband to seek out the armed assailants lurking in the closets or under the bed instead of having to do it herself. Really, what else was a man good for but to seek out the burglars and take the bullet wounds while the woman stealthily sneaked out the window and called the police?

But who knew, maybe the Native American she'd spent the night with would actually call. He'd said he would. And maybe things would work out, and one day he would be the one defending her from organ-eating psychos.

She hadn't meant to sleep with Rob, but he'd been so cute and such a good kisser and he'd told her how hilarious and beautiful she was so many times she'd become delirious with compliments. Also, she had a tendency to go through a slutty phase each time she broke up from a serious relationship. Maybe it was a reaction to enforced monogamy, maybe it was simply research she could draw on when she at last became a staff writer for a show like *Sex and the City*, the greatest show ever with the coolest lead actress ever. Sarah Jessica Parker was Chelsey's absolute idol. Chelsey even looked a little like SJP. She was a size two, with well-defined biceps and a perfectly flat stomach. She had long, curly, highlighted brown/blond hair circa SJP seasons one through four. Where she went horribly wrong, though, was that instead of having a nose with character, a memorable nose, a nose with a little kink, a little curve, a little jut, she had a cute, small button nose that was the bane of her existence. It was a nose that made it impossible for her to be the seductive sexpot she aspired to be. She had forever been and would forever be described with heinous words like *adorable* and *cute*. It made her want to gag.

Chelsey went first to inspect the bathroom for would-be attackers, where the shower curtain was pulled closed as always. She always pulled it closed because it looked nicer, and also, if she left it open, all scrunched together at one side, it couldn't dry out and had a tendency to mold. Chelsey had very strong feelings about mold.

Chelsey steeled her nerves, threw the curtain open, and screamed herself hoarse at the sight of the creature lurking there.

"Meow," her long-haired black-and-white cat, Mo, said, looking curious, as if to say, "What's all the fuss, Mom?" Mo liked to sleep sprawled in the cool tub when it was hot out.

Chelsey gripped her chest and tried to catch her breath as her heart rate returned to something like normal.

When she was passably composed, she went to the front hall closet where, assuming there weren't drug-addled attackers ready to leap out and assault her, she would be able to get a tennis racket and patrol the rest of the house. Granted, sports equipment wasn't the weaponry of choice to protect oneself from blood-thirsty psychopaths, but it was better than nothing.

The closet was clear. She grabbed the racket and went to investigate the rest of the house.

Her heart pounded like bongos in a movie set in a remote African village, all scary and ferocious so you just *know* somebody is about to get sacrificed to the gods or otherwise about to bite it in a particularly vicious way.

Chelsey loved her new home, every bit of it, even her dark, unfinished basement. Being a first-time home buyer had been quite an experience. The racists had come out of the woodwork when she'd been looking to buy a place.

"You don't want to live in that neighborhood, black people live there," they'd said.

"I'm not afraid of black people," she'd protested.

"You have to think about resale value," they'd insisted.

"I'm really not worried." But her arguments had fallen on deaf ears. So, too, had theirs.

She'd ended up buying a small house in Baker, a historically Italian and later Hispanic part of Denver. The ad for the place had said, "Be an urban pioneer!" She'd seen that phrase often during her house hunt and had deduced that it meant, "Young white urban professionals, move into this historically black/ Hispanic neighborhood and jack up the housing prices!" She couldn't decide if she felt bad about becoming an urban pioneer. On the one hand, she believed diverse neighborhoods were a good thing, but on the other hand, she felt like she was part of the reason housing prices were skyrocketing in Denver. The truth was, this was what she could afford and she liked the house and the neighborhood, so she tried not to worry too much about it.

She flicked on the basement lights and jumped from side to side, from backhand to forehand stance, as if waiting for a serve, looking from corner to corner. She saw nothing. The coast was clear, at least down here.

Next she went back upstairs to check the two bedrooms. She took every step slowly, painfully, fully expecting her life to be cut short at any moment. She checked out the closest in each room, she checked under the bed. Nothing. No panting, salivating lunatic carrying various sharp implements of torture.

She went back into the living room again, and that's when she saw it. In a very Soylent-Green-is-people moment of horrified discovery, she saw the baseball on the floor in the corner of the living room. There was no psycho murderer lurking in the shadows, waiting to gut and flay her, just an errant baseball of some neighborhood kids. She looked at the window critically. What had she been thinking? No human being could have crawled through a hole that size. Maybe a creature from *The X-Files* could have stretched his arm eight feet like Silly Putty to unlock the door, but otherwise, the only creature she had to fear coming in through that window was a squirrel.

Now that her life wasn't in danger, her emotions turned from fear to annoyance. She was going to be late for her job as a personal trainer, and she didn't even have the excuse that she'd been fighting off murderous perverts. Also, she did not have the money to replace the window, nor did she have any idea how to go about installing one. Maybe Rob would call her and after another sweaty romp session, she could put him to work. Yes, Chelsey decided, it was a brilliant plan.

3

The Cluster Fuck, Part One

"**W**here have you been?" Scott asked when Ana finally returned to her desk. "I've been here since forever."

"I had to make an emergency run to the store. So much for my plans to get my work done early so I can head over to the theater early. Hang on, I've got to call Marin so she doesn't miss work and I have to cover her rent again."

She called Marin. Ana had to call and hang up four times to avoid getting voicemail before Marin finally answered, sounding groggy.

"What?" was how she answered.

"Get your ass out of bed. You have fifteen minutes to get to work. Where are you going today?"

"Met Life I think. Today and all next week at an insurance company. I could do cartwheels of joy."

Ana would have hated Marin if she didn't love her so much. Marin's problem, in Ana's opinion, was that she had rich parents. Who else but a rich kid would major in something as impractical as theater? A person's chances of getting a job after college with such a degree were the same as their odds of going on *Survivor* and making it out with a shred of dignity intact. Rich kids also knew that when they messed up, as Marin frequently did, Mom and Dad would swoop in just in the nick of time, checkbook in hand, pen at the ready.

"It's called being a grown-up. It's called being responsible," Ana continued.

"I hate being a grown-up. I hate being responsible."

"Yes dear, we all do, but them's the breaks."

"Well I'm up. Mission accomplished."

"No way. Not until you're actually up and have consumed at least one cup of coffee."

"I do not have the energy to make coffee."

"Of course you don't. That's why I made extra and there will still be some waiting for you. You can nuke it for thirty seconds to warm it up."

"I hate nuked coffee."

"Right, but it's either that or make a fresh batch. What's it going to be?"

"Nuked." There was something reassuring to Ana about her friend's consistently lazy behavior. Ana knew she could always count on Marin to take the path of least resistance, and she appreciated her friend's unerring predictability.

Marin got up and shuffled to the kitchen. She got a cup down, poured the coffee, and drank it, cold.

"I drank my coffee. I'm officially up. I'll get to my stupid temp job. Thanks for your help, Mom."

"Did you really drink the coffee? I didn't hear the beeping of the microwave."

"I drank it cold, all right? Geesh. I just didn't have the energy to mess with the microwave."

"Okay. Have a good day at work. See you tonight."

"Smooch smooch, babe. See you later."

The second Ana hung up the phone, she heard her boss say, "Scott, Ana? Can I see you in my office?"

Scott and Ana followed him to his office, a short little trek from their microscopic cubes down the mottled-gray carpeted corridor, which had been designed to look stained and trampled so that by the time it actually was stained and trampled, it wasn't noticeable, to The Weasel's palatial corner office with actual windows and a view of the world outside. Well, a view of the parking lot anyway. At least he knew what the weather was doing and didn't come to work on a bright sunny morning only to emerge nine hours later into a strange blizzardy world like a mole blindly making its way through life. As soon as they sat down, Scott said, "So what's up?"

"I wanted to know where we stand on the collateral for the tradeshow," said The Weasel.

"I'm very glad you asked," Ana said. "I just need you to review the copy for the brochure and approve the graphics for the tradeshow murals, and I actually need you to approve it today, because otherwise we won't be able to get it back from the printer in time for the tradeshow." Ana's least favorite part of her job was having to project manage her boss.

"Not getting it done on time is not an option."

"Of course not, but I can't go to the printer until you approve the copy."

"I haven't seen the copy yet."

"Actually, I gave it to you three weeks ago, both electronically and in hard copy." *And I've asked you about it four times since then, remember, you Big Stupid Weasel?*

"Why don't you make some copies of the brochure and graphics and bring them to me."

"I actually have copies right here." She'd been carrying the copies around with her for the last week, most of which she'd spent stalking her boss, hoping to trap him in a hallway somewhere and get him to approve the damn copy already.

Ana handed it to him. "Doesn't the artwork Scott did look great? It's so eye-catching and colorful!" It was true she thought Scott was a talented artist, but she was gushing to sell The Weasel on it, not to bolster Scott's self-esteem. Ana often called upon her years as a cheerleader and her training as an actress at the office. Cheerleading had been great practice for Ana's future as a performer. She hated sports and didn't give a hoot about who won, who made a basket, or if Danny did in fact sink it after she encouraged him to "Sink it, Danny/Sink it!" Ana just liked tumbling and leaping around. The whole pesky business of encouragement and whipping crowds into a froth of excitement she could have done without.

The Weasel's phone rang.

"Wayne, Wayne! Good to hear from you. Missed you on the golf course this week. Is that right?"

Ana looked at her watch. She hadn't gotten a single thing done and it was already after nine. She glanced at Scott, who made a facial expression that probably nobody else would have even noticed—raising his left eyebrow ever so slightly, his lips pursed in an old-lady smile—that made Ana bite her lip to keep from laughing. Scott was the king of facial expressions, but it wasn't just his elastic ability to contort his face, it was also that Ana knew exactly what he was thinking, exactly how he would mock The Big Weasel's car salesman-fake conversation voice at lunch later that day.

After The Weasel had been on the phone for another three or four minutes, Ana stood up and pantomimed that he should call her when he was free. He shook his head and put his hand out, palm facing her, indicating that she should stay. So she sat down again and studied her watch, careful not to look at Scott lest he crack her up and get them both fired, as the longest five minutes of her life passed. Of course *her* time wasn't valuable. It wasn't like what *she* had to do was important.

At last he hung up the phone. "Where were we?"

"You were reviewing the brochure and tradeshow graphics so I could get them to the printer today," Ana said.

"Right, right."

He skimmed over what she'd handed him.

"You know what this needs? We need to offer them a gift. Have a whole theme. Really grab their attention."

"Huh, that's interesting, because when we first talked about this project, I suggested we say on the postcard that if they bring the postcard to the booth, we'll give them some kind of gift, and you said you were concerned that would make us look desperate."

"The thing is, every marketing campaign needs to have a measurable ROI (return on investment). If we have a card that they can turn in, we can gauge the success of the campaign, and make sure we're getting our money's worth."

"Okay then. What sort of gift are you thinking of? What sort of price range?"

"Something classy, but not that expensive. Ten dollars each, say."

What kind of miracle worker did he think she was? You couldn't get anything classy and logoed for ten dollars each. Twenty maybe, but ten dollars meant a very mediocre grade of pen or desk clock. "So we're sending out a thousand cards. At the high end we can expect a ten percent return, which means we'll have to get at least a thousand dollars of premium items. We have that in the budget?"

He waved his hand as if to say, sure, of course. But Ana knew that when The Big Weasel actually calculated how much he was spending on this tradeshow, he'd be way over budget and looking for scapegoats, and he would never remember this conversation with her.

"Anything else? Is the brochure copy good to go other than adding the bit about the gift?" Ana asked.

"The copy needs more pizzazz. And the artwork needs to be more vibrant. We really need to grab their attention. These are busy executives. They get so many pieces of mail, so many phone calls, so many emails, that we really need to wow them."

Thank you for the marketing 101 lesson, asshole. "Um, Scott and I thought our graphics and copy did have pizzazz. Do you have any *specific* suggestions for how to improve things? Is there anything *specifically* you don't like or would like to see added?" *Because if you think you're fooling me into thinking you're competent by spouting off clichéd rules for marketing, you're not.*

"You and Scott can fix it. You're almost there."

"Okay, we'll make some changes. Can you mark me in your calendar for this afternoon? We have to be sure you can approve the copy today so I can get it to the printer today."

The Big Weasel looked at his Palm Pilot. "I'm really booked up. I've got an opening between four and four-fifteen. It'll have to be quick."

"I'll be here at four sharp."

Ana and Scott returned to their desks. She vowed silently

not to change any of the text. She knew he hadn't really read it. Her text was good. She'd add the bit about bringing the card in and getting a gift, she'd change a few words in the headline, Scott would change a few graphics around, and that would be it.

Ana's phone rang. "Hello?"

It was Marin. "Guess what my parents spent eighty-thousand dollars for me to get a college education to do? To hit Control, F7, Print, Next. Control, F7, Print, Next. For nine dollars an hour. This is a new low."

"Lower than when you dressed up as a hotdog to lure small children into Top Dog Hotdogs?"

"At least then my identity was concealed."

"I feel for your plight, but I have got to get this stupid project done by four o'clock today. Think of it this way: you can turn all this pain into comedy on stage."

"I don't see any humor in this situation. I can't believe they're making me print all this stuff out. I mean I'm killing a zillion trees today so they can have hard copy backups. Jason would have a heart attack."

"Look, I've got to go so I can keep my job so *someone* in the house can have a steady paycheck."

"Don't go! Don't go! I'm going to *die* of boredom."

"Hold on." Ana transferred the call to Scott, telling him, "It's Marin."

"Hey girlfriend," he answered. Ana looked across the make-shift hallway at Scott, who sat in a cubicle facing hers. Ana was glad she worked with him. She didn't like her job, her boss, and most of the people she worked with, but Scott did a great job of keeping her from jumping off the deep end, keeping her laughing and reminding her not to get so worked up over the management practices that drove her batty.

Scott was tall, 6'3", a full foot taller than Ana. He had curly hair that was long enough to spring all over the place, giving him the absent-minded-professor, I'm-an-artist-with-too-many-things-on-my-mind-to-be-bothered-with-getting-my hair-cut look. He was good-looking, but his goofy grin made it difficult to see him as anything other than the giant goofball that he was. Ana had enjoyed making out with him one drunken night at Spur of the Moment, but there was no way she could date someone so tall—there were neck-cramping issues to consider. (She never took their little romp seriously. The occasional smooch session between cast members was practically a prerequisite of the job. Sometimes their skits called for them to crawl around on each other, or to kiss or to be married couples or teenagers just falling in love for the first time. There was bound to be some sexual tension released occasionally, particularly when aided by alcohol.)

Ana couldn't help but laugh as she listened to Scott talk to Marin, having a conversation with himself, pretending to alternately be an employee who had a voice like a Muppet and a boss who talked like Cameron in *Ferris Bueller's Day Off* when he posed as Ferris' dad.

Boss: "But does it *live the brand?*"

Employee: "But, but . . . we don't have the *bandwidth* to make it *live the brand.*"

Boss: "Well, we'll have to *interface* with the *key players* to make sure we have the *buy-in.* Let's make sure we've *covered all our bases.*"

Ana wiped the smile off her face and forced herself to stop listening to Scott and get back to work.

4

Adventures in Temp Hell

Marin had put off going into work for as long as possible, and as soon as she got there she called Ana and Scott so they could entertain her. She kept Scott on the phone for as long as she could, but when her boss for the next week, Shirley, started lurking behind her, with a perm that even extended to her bangs, making her look like she had a fringed orange stuck to her forehead, Marin figured she should probably let him go.

"I really appreciate you calling me with the offer, sir, but even though it's more money than I'm making here, I can't leave this company in a lurch," Marin said.

"Boss standing there?" Scott said.

"Yes. Thanks again. And do keep me in mind if any full-time positions open up after I've fulfilled my obligations here." She hung up the phone. "Well, hello Shirley."

"Just to keep things exciting, I have another important job for you to do," Shirley said. "We need to get two hundred packets together for the sales training on Monday. Here's the original. The binders are in the copy room. Make two hundred copies, hole-punch them, and put them in the binders. You can alternate between this and printing the documents to keep things fun!"

"Printing things out or making copies. It's like Christmas every day here, just one big party!" Marin didn't say this sarcastically, she said it like it genuinely was the best news she'd heard all day, but Shirley tittered weakly, like she wasn't getting the joke. Shirley strode off purposefully, and Marin went to the copy room. She put the stack of paper in the tray and hit the copy button. It pulled the first few pages through and then got stuck.

Marin looked at the copier as if waiting for a fit of inspiration. She had worked very hard to never learn how to fix a jammed copier or copy machine. If someone ever tried to explain it to her, she promptly made sure she forgot everything they said. There were some things it just didn't pay to know.

Every now and then, like when she had to spend her days printing out documents and making copies, being acutely bored out of her mind, she wondered if perhaps she should try to get a real job. She'd been asked to stay on by more than one of the places she'd temped at, but she'd always said no. She knew she'd get too depressed going to the same dreary job day after day. At least as a temp, each day had possibility for something good. You never knew what could happen.

It was obvious to Marin that she was either going to have to become a famous comedian or marry rich, because this working-at-an-office shit was clearly not for her.

Marry rich. Marriage. Yeah right. She hadn't even had a serious boyfriend since high school. Finding someone she wanted to marry was not going to be easy. Guys were just too easy, too predictable. They always fell head over heels for her. They became simpering idiots around her. She needed more of a challenge. She liked Jason—he was cute and good in bed and all that (they sometimes slept together when they were between relationships)—but his infatuation with her was hopeless. What did he think, she was going to marry a school teacher who made like, what, maybe $30,000 a year? Daughters of prominent New York investment bankers did not grow up to marry high school teachers.

It's not that she thought money meant happiness; she had two parents who proved there was no correlation. But Marin didn't plan to spend her entire life broke. Maybe someday she'd hit the big time and she could marry a guy just based on love without considering anything else about him, but to pretend like money didn't matter was a fairy tale. There was romance and then there was reality—Marin wanted love, but she also wanted a big house, vacations every year, and a blindingly large diamond ring. That might seem selfish or overly pragmatic, but Marin didn't care: It was the stone cold truth.

Until rich Mr. Right came along, a more steady income would certainly come in handy, though, and temping was anything but steady. Every time she called her dad for money she got a lecture about how it was time to grow up, and why couldn't she be more like her older brother, who already had a good career following in his daddy's footsteps and making tons of money, blah blah blah.

Marin couldn't help it. She just couldn't be an investment banker; she didn't have it in her. Since she was a little girl she'd had the performing bug. When you have a father who works hundred-hour weeks and a mother who rarely pays attention to you even if you're the only person in the room, you learn quickly how to be funny and adorable and generally pleasing. You take whatever shreds of attention you can get, any way you can get them.

She would have ended up in a theater department no matter where she went to school, but she was glad for the twist of fate that brought her to the University of Colorado and to her friends that she met there. She was confident that she'd make it as an actress. She didn't want to divert her energies by working on a career at an office.

She stared at the copier. She needed more coffee before she could make any decisions about what to do. Marin went to the kitchen and smiled warmly at the young guy standing there, adding sugar to his coffee. She opened cabinets until she found where they kept the coffee mugs.

"Hi. Are you new here? I'm Trevor."

"I'm a temp. I'm just here for the week. Hey, the copier is stuck. Do you know who I should go to to get it fixed?"

"You're talking to him. I work in technical support," he said, smiling broadly.

"This must be my lucky day.".

In the copy room, Trevor opened a couple of doors on the

copier and tore out a sheet of paper that had been caught. "That should do it." He smiled triumphantly. "What did you say your name was?"

He hit PRINT, and the very next page that went through got stuck. Trevor opened the door and tore out another sheet of rumpled paper. Then another sheet and another. He closed the copier door and still the "paper is stuck here" button was flashing. He opened the door again and pulled out more paper, then he struggled to get the ink cartridge out. It came loose in one quick motion, spraying his chest and face with black ink.

Marin tried very hard not to laugh.

5

Villainous Cattle Ranchers and Spineless Principals

Jason was unusual among his group of friends in that he was one of the very few of them that wouldn't necessarily love to quit their day job. (Scott liked being a graphic designer, but if he could work full time as a comedian or artist and never have to deal with the likes of The Big Weasel ever again, he would give his notice in a nanosecond.) Jason really did enjoy teaching. Most of the time.

The times he didn't like it were times like these, when he'd been called into the principal's office after second-period sophomore biology to confront a red-faced, spluttering cattle rancher, the father of one of the boys in Jason's seventh-period biology class, who was accusing Jason of teaching his child socialist propaganda, encouraging vegetarianism, and spreading lies about the effects of pesticides.

In the lessons the irate man was referring to, Jason had explained to his students the environmental costs of the food Americans consumed. He talked about how fewer and fewer farmers could make a living farming in America anymore, and how as a result, the food Americans ate came from foreign countries that didn't have to follow the same laws regarding pesticides and chemicals that American farmers did, meaning pesticides that had been banned for years here in the States were shipped right back into the country from foreign lands. He had talked about how Americans bought food even when it was out of season, so they could have the fruits and vegetables they liked all year long, which led to produce that was shipped from so far away that to get here in one piece, it had to be picked at the wrong time and plugged up with chemicals, which resulted in tomatoes and apples that tasted like red-colored sawdust. He said that the average food Americans bought at the supermarket had to travel 1400 miles, causing a colossal expenditure of fossil fuels. He reminded them of the lesson they'd had earlier on the ozone layer, and the damage wrought by car emissions as well as the fact that the amount of oil available on the planet was finite, and by some estimates would be gone by as early as 2025. While they were discussing the ozone layer, he also said that one of the worst things for the ozone was the gaseous emissions of cattle. "Their flatulence," he'd added, which made the class giggle. He'd pointed out to his students that to produce one pound of beef, ten pounds of grains were required. He said that if everyone ate a vegetarian diet, no one on the face of the earth would have to go hungry.

The solution to these problems was to shop locally, eat less meat, and, if possible, grow some of your food yourself. He talked about his own small garden, and how amazing the food tasted, and how rewarding it was to share the food with friends when it was fresh and in season.

"Sir, I in no way try to influence the eating habits of my students. I just believe in telling them the facts and letting them make informed choices," Jason said to the cattle rancher father.

"You don't let an impressionable child make choices on his own. You think you hand a twelve year old the keys to a car and hope they make a good decision?"

"Sir?" Jason wasn't clear how this analogy in any way pertained to the discussion they were having. Normally Jason was calm and laid-back, which was part of the reason his students loved him. That, and he cracked them up regularly. In the classroom, humor came naturally to him. The downside to being an improv-er was when people found out that he did improv, they inevitably demanded that he say something amusing to them, and he was no good at being funny when ordered to.

He wished he could bring some levity to the current debacle he found himself in, but he couldn't see anything funny about it.

"I'm going to the school board on this, I'm going to the superintendent, I'm going to the newspapers. I don't send my daughter to school so she can get filled up with a bunch of communist malarkey." The cattle rancher shook his thick finger in Jason's face.

The enormous man stood up, put his cowboy hat on, and turned his waving finger toward the principal. "Don't think you've heard the last you're going to hear from me."

The man stormed out, and Jason looked at the principal. *Thanks for sticking up for me.*

The principal was a thin, sickly looking, watery-eyed man who hoped for nothing more than to quietly get to retirement age and get away from the students who scared him more and more every year.

"So what's going to happen?" Jason asked. "Are there going to be repercussions from this? I mean, I didn't do anything wrong."

"I don't know what's going to happen, Jason, I really don't. In the meantime, just tone it down."

"Tone it down? I'm just telling the kids the way it is."

"You're supposed to be teaching biology, not all this political nonsense."

Political? He wasn't being political; just honest.

"I'm not going to lose my job over this, am I?"

The principal just shrugged helplessly.

Jason left the principal's office and returned to his own tiny office. He had twenty minutes to calm down before he had to teach his next class. This was almost as bad as when the mandate had come down that if a biology teacher dared to mention evolution, they had to be sure to say "it's *only* a theory!" like it was as legitimate as a lose-weight, get-rich, cure-baldness pill from a mad scientist on the Psychic Network.

Jason sat at his desk, put his head in his hands, and took deep breaths.

6

Book Smart

At eleven A.M., Ramiro got out of bed, showered, had his morning cigarette, and caught the bus to the bookstore where he worked in LoDo (Lower Downtown).

Ramiro had graduated *summa cum laude* in Philosophy despite being one of the laziest people his friends had ever known. He had an absolute inability to finish anything he started. He'd started writing dozens of novels, hundreds of essays, several plays, and numerous sketch comedy skits. All of them languished in various stages of incompleteness somewhere in his untidy room.

To his credit, though, Ramiro was the only one of them who'd had a serious relationship that lasted more than a year, and had in fact been seeing Nick for a whopping three years now.

Nick was a certified financial planner, a high-achieving, high-paid type, in contrast to Ramiro's laid-back, go-with-the-flow, I'll-make-just-enough-money-to-pay-for-cigarettes-and-my-share-of-the-rent ideology. Nick had blond hair and a slight build, also a contrast to Ramiro's dark features and broad build, thanks to genetics, to his Portuguese and Mexican ancestors, and not to any commitment to working out. In fact, as far as any of his friends knew, Ramiro had never seen the inside of the gym, and indeed, they were right.

Some of his friends thought maybe he had just way too

many ideas and that was why he never finished anything. In any case, he was the smartest person any of them had ever known—ever. While his mother thought his intelligence was squandered working at a bookstore, he liked his life. He liked having time to write and to act and to hang out with his friends. He suspected that someday he'd go back to school and earn his Ph.D. in Sociology or English literature or something, but taking classes and writing a dissertation sounded like so much work, and he liked his life right now and just didn't have the energy to change anything just yet.

He did dream of being able to write full time, and he'd given the writing thing something of a shot. Chelsey had tried to team up with him once to write a pilot for a new sitcom. He'd had great ideas, but after three weeks of getting together for two hours a week, he'd made up an excuse about why he couldn't see her that week, then the next and the next, and with just fifteen pages written (though they were really, really good), the project had been abandoned. Chelsey knew he had more intelligence and talent than the other members of their group put together, but she also knew that if she wanted something to get done, she couldn't depend on him to do it.

7

Shakespeare on the Moon

Spur of the Moment Improv Theater was located on the second floor of a restaurant/bar called aMuse (it was decorated with paintings and decorations of the seven muses from Greek mythology). Steve Cuddy, the founder and director of Spur of the Moment, had teamed up with a friend to create a perfect date-night destination: Get dinner at aMuse, go see a show at Spur, then go back down to the bar for more drinks afterward. Steve ran the theater upstairs, and John ran the restaurant downstairs. Spur had its own smaller bar in the back of the theater to help people along with their two-drink minimum, and that was the usual watering hole for the comedians after the shows. While the restaurant was decorated with rich maplewood floors and tables and elegant furnishings, Spur was dimly lit and stark, decorated only with pictures of the comedians who'd performed there over the last ten years.

aMuse was already filled with happy-hour office workers as Chelsey McGuiness, Marin Kennesaw, Jason Hess, Scott Winn, and Ramiro Martinez began their aural warm ups upstairs, standing in a circle on the small, scuffed stage.

"Lo-leeeee-ta. Light of my life. Fire of my loins. Lo-leeeee-ta," they all over-enunciated wildly and repeated the phrase several times.

"Balcony," Ramiro called, indicating that they should move on to a different exercise.

"She stood on the balcony inexplicably mimicking him hic-cupping and amicably welcoming him in," they said in unison. "She stood on the balcony inexplicably mimicking him hic-cupping and amicably welcoming him in. She stood on the balcony inexplicably mimicking him hiccupping and amicably welcoming him in."

When they finished warming up their voices, they did their physical warm-ups, which included lots of mock karate chopping and the like.

As Chelsey balanced on one foot, her arms raised up à la The Karate Kid, she asked, "Where's Ana?"

"She had to work late," Scott said as he boxed an invisible opponent. "She's trying to finish something up. She'll be here soon."

"Fuck!" They all turned to see Ana race through to the dressing room. "I wanted to be the first one here and instead I'm the last one and we go on in fifteen minutes. Fuckedy fuckedy fuck fuck!"

"Fifteen minutes? Shit," Ramiro said. He, Jason, Chelsey, and Marin walked backstage. Only five people performed each night, ostensibly to give one person the night off, but almost without fail, whoever wasn't performing sat in the audience to watch the show. Because really, where else do you want to spend your Thursday, Friday, and Saturday nights other than with your best friends? Also, no one wanted to miss out on a single laugh.

Scott walked into the audience to sit next to Nick just as Darren, the host, unlocked the door to start seating audience members.

Ana slammed the dressing room door behind her and threw off her work clothes to change into her Spur of the Moment uniform of black shoes, black jeans, and a black polo shirt with the Spur of the Moment logo on the left side. She retouched her lipstick—her trademark red that, she was convinced, lit up her amber-colored eyes. She threw her long, dark brown hair into a haphazard bun.

Then she ran out of the dressing room to the handful of au-dience members who'd been seated. Ana was sweating from her sprint from the parking lot to the dressing room. Great. Sweaty and smelly was exactly how she wanted to meet the event planner from Qwest. And how had she become the delegate on this deal anyway? Steve Cuddy was the director, he was the one who should be handling this, but he didn't have a day job, he could live off what Spur of the Moment made without getting them a whole bunch of extra corporate performances, so he wasn't nearly as driven to get the group more paying gigs as they were.

Ana addressed the audience with a big smile, covertly wiping the sweat from her forehead with the side of her hand. "Hi, are any of you Guy Moran from Qwest Communications?"

"Yeah, hi, are you Ana?" A man at a table close to the stage stood and offered a hand for her to shake.

"I am. I'm so glad you could make it tonight. Let me introduce you to Steve Cuddy, the founder and director of Spur of the Moment."

Guy followed her backstage to the office where Steve worked. Steve had founded Spur of the Moment ten years ago, when he was in his early thirties. He'd stopped performing when he'd had to begin putting more of his time and energy into running the business side of things. He was the only person at Spur of the Moment who was over thirty, the only married person, and the only one with a kid. The rest of the Spur gang regarded him with reverence and more than a little awe. Someone who was raising a kid? Someone who had real, actual responsibilities? Such a life seemed so abstract and weird to them.

"Steve, this is Guy Moran from Qwest. Guy, this is Steve Cuddy," Ana said. "He handles all the bookings and all that kind of stuff. We can do sketch comedy, improv, a mix of the two, whatever you want. The show will be starting in just a few minutes, but maybe you can join us afterwards for a couple of drinks. Enjoy the show, and thanks again for coming!"

Chelsey was the emcee for the night, the one who explained how the skits worked and took suggestions from the audience. She peered out from backstage. No, there was no gorgeous Native American named Rob in the audience. Damn!

The five performers got on stage and waited for the lights

to go on and for Tom to introduce them. Tom Taylor was the muscular sound-and-light guy who kept the lights shining and enhanced the humor with perfectly timed strange noises using just his voice (when one of the actors would open a door, for example, he would make the sound of a door creaking open). Tom had a bright smile that contrasted impressively against his black skin. He'd had a promising career in football until a knee injury on the field in his senior year at the University of Northern Colorado cut his aspirations short. Now he worked as a radio DJ during the day and the Spur of the Moment sound-and-light guy on weekends.

The five players stood with their backs to the audience. Tom turned on Kylie Minogue's "Can't Get You Out of My Head" and as the performers danced around the stage, Tom boomed in his best mock white-guy announcer voice, "Gooooooood evening ladies and gentleman! Welcome to Spur of the Moment. I'd like to introduce the actors for the evening." At this point, four of the actors would stand still and then Tom would put the spotlight on just one of them, and he or she would dance around goofily for about fifteen seconds while Tom introduced him or her, then Tom would shine the spotlight on the next person until they'd all been introduced. When he got to Chelsey, she did her Irish jig moves, wearing a mock-serious expression on her face, all big eyes and pursed lips. Chelsey loved that the years she'd spent as a kid learning Irish dancing had an applicable skill now that she was an adult. That was the thing about improv—absolutely anything you'd ever done, read, or heard could become fodder for material on stage. When you had to act on the very first thought that popped into your head, reacting to whatever the other actors said, things from the darkest recesses of memory had a way of jumping out. Being a successful improv comedian required an extensive ability to remember pop culture trivia, geography, film, and history. If the emcee asked the audience to yell out a person or a place or an event and they yelled out "Justin Timberlake" or "Bora Bora" or "WorldCom's troubles" and you didn't know what they were talking about, you were quite screwed on stage. This had happened to Ana once when she'd asked the audience for a movie genre, and the first thing someone yelled out was "film noir." Ana had heard of film noir, but she wasn't sure what it was or how to go about acting in the film noir genre. She thought maybe film noir was something that had taken place in the 1940s involving men in trench coats and bowler hats. But she also thought film noir might still exist today. So she just went through her scene acting moody and dark and hoping to hell she wasn't making a total ass of herself.

Chelsey took the microphone. "Hello, hello, hello, and welcome to Spur of the Moment. Thanks for coming down tonight. By a show of hands, how many of you have never been to Spur of the Moment before?" About half the audience raised their hands. "Well we are thrilled to have you—maybe almost as thrilled as you are to be here for the funniest show in town. For those of you who are new, this is how it works. Nothing you're going to see on stage tonight has been rehearsed. You will see scenes never before performed because they are created based on suggestions that you, the audience, provide. The actors act on their impulses, they think on their feet. Are we ready to get started?" Hoots, hollers, and applause indicated that the audience was indeed ready. "To get us going, I need a style of literature."

"Shakespeare!" an audience member screamed out, followed by suggestions for romance and horror.

"Shakespeare was the first thing I heard. Okay, now I need an emotion."

"Anger!"

"Anger it is. One last thing I need is a location."

"The moon!"

"All right, you will now see the actors perform a Shakespearean tale on the moon involving the emotion anger. Actors begin!"

Chelsey ran off the stage and Jason and Marin walked on. Jason had grabbed a red velvet, puffy-sleeved blazer and a blue velvet cap with an enormous blue feather from the large store of wigs and partial costumes they kept in the wings. Marin was wearing a red velvet cape over her Spur of the Moment uniform.

"I knew I shouldst hath divorced ye when we were still on earth," Marin hissed. "Nowest that ye hath sentenced me to a life on this barren rock, I shall never find a lawyer of divorce to sue thine ass off!"

"Alack, my bonnie lass, I knoweth that mine actions hath filled ye with a great fiery rage like that of a thousand poisoned serpents scorned. But judge me not for transporting our cattle operations to this crater-laden orb that doth monthly our earthly home encircle. Our bovineious creatures hath gorged themselves of all the hearty grains of planet earth and only here could we find enough room to raise the synthetic grain and raiseth our cows in peace." Jason rubbed his hands together and arched his eyebrow, making an expression like a cartoon villain. The audience loved it and roared with laughter. "Aye, with mine secret chemicals, I will be able to create super cows."

"Super cows?"

"Super cows! Then, we can returnest to earth and sell more beef to McDonald's than anyone else in the universe!"

"Aye?" Marin showed interest now.

"Fear not my shrewish wife—shrewder than the shrewest shrew—by mine honor, I do vow that we shall soon have riches greater than royalty, greater than Sir Jordon of Michael or Sir Gates of Bill," Jason said.

"Rich? Aye? I darest not suspect that mine ears could e'er hear words more glorious than those which thee have cast into this black, oxygenless night." Marin looked lovingly at Jason and said in a gentle voice, "Oh my dear, you are the rose of mine eye indeed. My heart doth flutter for you like the wings of a butterfly. Well should'st I say an earth-bound butterfly, for surely any such winged creature on this zero-gravity sphere would have the life force sucked clear out of its bodily home, its fragile softness imploding like the skin of Sir Arnold Schwarzenegger in Recall of Total." Marin and Jason smiled romantically and embraced, Marin resting her head on his chest as the lights dimmed.

Ana stood on the sidelines, feeling a sharp pang of jealousy. Of course she'd seen Jason and Marin embrace in dozens of scenes before. She even knew that Marin and Jason slept together occasionally—Jason because he loved her, and Marin because Jason was a convenient fuck buddy when there wasn't another guy around to do the job. But still, every time Ana saw them together, a splinter of resentment ran through her.

Ramiro and Ana went out on stage for the next skit, which was a game called "Forward, Reverse." The way it worked was that they started a scene (in this case located in a mechanic's garage), and at any point in the scene, Chelsey could call out "reverse" or "forward," and they'd go back through the scene backwards or move forward again from whatever point in the scene she yelled out the command. No matter what the basic story line was, the scene inevitably invoked laughter, mostly because the actors tended to forget what came when, and seeing them fail was often more fun than seeing them succeed. (Unlike stand-up comedy, where the audience sat there, arms crossed, with an attitude, of "yeah, we'll just see if you can make me laugh," with improv, the audience was rooting for the actors. When the actors messed up, the audience thought it was pant-wettingly hilarious.) She could also yell out "fast forward," and seeing someone race around on stage was also somehow intrinsically funny.

Ana ran offstage, straining to catch her breath. She poured herself a large glass of water from the pitcher they always brought from the bar downstairs. Improv could be sweaty work, and all that talking, singing, and shouting took its toll on performers' vocal cords. Everyone, except Chelsey, drank gallons of water between skits. Chelsey was addicted to Diet Red Stallion and inhaled it by the case, a fact her Spur buddies teased her about relentlessly. They called her Bullsy, after the alleged fact that one of the ingredients in Red Stallion was synthetic bull piss or some such notion.

Ana had done well, and the audience had loved the scene, but she felt unsatisfied. This was getting too easy. She needed new challenges.

Ever since she, Marin, and Chelsey had flown for a week-long training at Second City in Chicago a few months earlier over the summer, they'd learned about the other things they could do with improv—like long-form improv instead of the short-form they did night after night—she'd become restless. They'd tried several times to talk to Steve about letting them try a few new things, but all he said, over and over again, was that what they were doing now worked, it paid the bills, and you don't fix what's not broken. Ana spent her days at the office getting her ideas shot down, and even here, in her creative space, she was being boxed in. It made her crazy. *Shake it off, shake it off,* she admonished herself. Moments later, she ran on stage as a smiley three-year-old girl accompanying her mother to the zoo.

The five players on the stage knew each other well. Ana knew that with Marin and Ramiro, no matter what she said, no matter what ideas or plot twists she threw out, they would be sure to go with it. Chelsey, Scott, and Jason weren't quite as reliable. If Ana went on stage as a man, Scott and Jason were always turning her into a woman. Once she came on stage wearing a hardhat and flannel shirt. In her mind she was a male construction worker. Then Scott had called her mom, and she had to deal with that, though for a second it was very disconcerting. Improv works because you instantly become a new character. You know what to say next because you know your character and how he or she would respond in such a situation. But when you threw something out only to have it twisted by a fellow performer, it made you feel less safe on stage. Having to deal with a sex change in two seconds flat was unsettling indeed.

The next time Ana went on, it was with Ramiro again. Chelsey had asked the audience for a "thing," and the suggestion she got was "can of spray paint." Immediately Ana and Ramiro began feigning spray painting a wall. Ana was the first to start pretending to chew gum with extravagant gusto, but it only took Ramiro a split second to notice what she was doing and join in.

"Like, I don't know the big deal is. We should be able to,

like, express ourselves. To decorate the world around us," Ana said in an Hispanic accent.

On stage tonight, Ramiro said in a falsetto voice, "You said it, girlfriend. People act like graffiti is all illegal and bad and shit. It's art, man. I mean since the, like, ancient *Sumerians*, people have wanted to make their mark."

What the hell was a Sumerian? Were they in Egypt? Was Sumeria a country? Shit, what was she supposed to say?

This was one problem with doing improv with a walking encyclopedia. Ana had graduated with honors, but it was because she was an awesome essay writer and test taker, not because she remembered everything she read like Ramiro did. Or actually remembered anything she'd read. Promptly after taking an exam, everything Ana had learned disappeared like a guy after a one-night stand. Every time she played Trivial Pursuit, Ana's ass would get thoroughly kicked. She could go for hours without picking up a single pie piece, all the while slapping her forehead saying, "I *know* I learned that in school! The name is on the tip of my tongue . . ." Three weeks later, while she was in the shower or doing the dishes, the answer would spring to mind when it could do her no good whatsoever.

Ana decided to try to steer the scene back around to something she knew about. "Yo, check it out, I'm doing something new with the '*i*' in my name."

"A cat's face. Dig it."

"That'll show Margarita not to mess with Maria!" She rolled her *R's* extravagantly.

"Yo, right on. That cat looks like it'll scratch Margarita Dominguez's eyes out. You are an artiste, girlfriend."

"That's what I'm saying, the police, the teachers, the parents, they want to be all, *arresting* us, punishing us, and we're just making the world a more beautiful place."

"It's, like, a human urge to communicate, to create, to let the world know we were here. Do you think the Sumerians were arrested for their writing, their art?"

She had absolutely no idea whatsoever. "No way, muchacha!"

"Damn straight. They were celebrated. Their cuneiform changed the world."

Cuneiform. It sounded familiar. Did it mean cave painting? Was it an alphabet? A kind of Indian rain dance?

Ramiro went on, working through the ancient Greeks, the Egyptians, the Mayans. He talked about how for all time, people have needed to express themselves. He would pause, making people think he was done, then he'd go on, explaining about the hieroglyphics of the Egyptians or whatever. "Those were the days! I wish I coulda been there. Then I wouldn't be all, like, worried about the cops, worried I'd get carted off to jail." Pause. "And, like, think about the Anasazi. Man. Those were the days. I wish I coulda been there. Now people pay big money to see the designs the Indians painted and carved on cave walls. Those pictographs and petroglyphs, they helped to educate their ancestral Hopi tribes, to bring good luck to their caves, and to let the world know that the Anasazi, they were here!"

"Like a 'you are here' on a map, except . . . different." Ana played dumb to Ramiro's casual brilliance. She didn't have a choice to play it any other way.

"Yeah, kind of the like that. Do you think they got carted off to jail? No way." He paused, then launched in about the art of the art of the Bobo tribe of Burkina Faso, whatever that was. The crowd thought it was hilarious. Ana just "uh-huhed" and "you-go-girl"-ed. When he talked about Egypt, she mentioned that her cat *I* in her name was like her kohl-penciled Egyptian foresisters. Sixteen years of education, and all she remembered about Egypt was that they mummified their dead, built pyramids, outlined their eyes with kohl, and liked cats. Nice to see all those years of writing essays and cramming for exams turned out to be so useful.

The scene ended a few minutes later when Jason came in wearing a cop hat and thwapping a billy club against his open palm and attempting to arrest them. Both Ramiro and Ana covered him with spray paint and ran off.

They performed well that night. In a couple of scenes, they

really killed. A couple weren't quite as good as Ana might have hoped, but nothing that would make the audience fidgety with embarrassment or anything. That was how Ana gauged the success of a show: If they didn't make the audience cringe, the show was a hit.

After the show, the actors went to the bar in the back of the theater to have a few drinks as they always did. Each and every one of them had vowed at one time or another to go straight home to bed after a performance. They vowed to drink less alcohol, get more sleep, cut down on their caffeine intake, and lead wholesome, healthy lives. No one, however, had actually ever done any of this. For one thing, they knew that if they went straight home after a show, they'd miss something hilarious that would be an inside joke to the other actors until the end of time. For another thing, performers got drinks for a dollar. (A dollar!) It was such a good deal that to forsake a few beers after the show was downright fiscally irresponsible.

Before Ana joined her friends, she went to talk with Guy from Qwest. He said he liked their work and he'd like them to perform at the company holiday party in December.

"How about corporate retreats, team-building sessions, things like that?" Ana asked.

"I'm sure you've read in the news that things are difficult in the telecom industry. We don't have much of a budget for those things these days, though we hope things will pick up soon."

"Well, I really appreciate you coming by. We'd love to perform at your holiday party and any other events that come up. Steve Cuddy is the one to call to schedule everything. Do you have his card?"

"Yep, he gave it to me earlier. Thanks for your time."

"No, thank you."

She shook his hand and smiled at him, but as soon as he walked away, her disappointment showed clearly in her expression. Why did he have to go and get her hopes up if he knew he didn't have much of a budget? One lousy holiday party? They might make enough money to buy a few Christmas presents, but they'd hardly be able to quit their day jobs with one stinking holiday gig. Ana went to the table in the back where the other actors were sitting.

"Hey, look you guys!" It was Scott, who rode up to the table on a unicycle. With his long, gangly limbs and curly hair springing out all over the place, Ana thought he looked so cute and boyish, which made sense because he really was just a kid in a 27-year-old man's body.

"Hey, give me a shot at that," Ramiro said. As he, Scott, Jason, and Marin gathered around it with glee, Ana and Chelsey went to the bar to order a beer from Tony, the long-haired bartender. Ana had made out with him in the coatroom a few times before. Marin and Chelsey had both slept with him at one point or another, on and off when the alcohol-to-lust ratio tipped the scales. He was nobody's idea of a good boyfriend, or, God forbid, husband, but his exquisite build and sexy smile made the occasional romp with him pretty much unavoidable.

The two women took their beers and sat down at a table near the back of the theater. "How are things going at the gym? Any new crazy characters to tell me about?" Ana asked.

"Can't think of any. I guess the good news at work is that, what with this being America, there are always fat people who need to work their fat asses off."

Ana nodded, agreeing that this was indeed good fortune.

"Do you ever think that someday we're going to wake up and say to ourselves that we're not actors with day jobs, we're personal trainers and marketing managers and admin assistants who do comedy as a hobby?" Ana asked.

"No, no, of course not."

"We have to go to New York. We're never going to be able to make it big in Denver."

"I know, I know."

They all knew this. They'd had this exact same conversation approximately four million times. "But moving to New York would mean planning and saving money," Ana said. "I mean you, me, and Jason could do that, but could you imagine Marin, Scott, and Ramiro? Planning? Saving money?"

Chelsey laughed. The planning and saving was one reason

they hadn't made the move yet, but it wasn't the only one. The reason wasn't something anybody discussed out loud. But the truth was that in Denver, they were big fish. Colorful, pretty fish that other people oohed and aahed over. In New York, they would be tadpoles. Not even tadpoles, plankton is what they'd be, food for tadpoles.

"I need to get a comedy routine together," Ana said. "Doing the comedy circuits means you can rub elbows with a much larger group of comedians than the incestuous little pool of talent here at Spur. That's how Eddie Murphy, Jimmy Fallon, Jerry Seinfeld—God, it's how loads of people got their start."

"So why don't you?"

"'Cuz I'm terrified."

"Why? You get up on stage every night without a script."

"Yeah, but if a scene bombs in improv, there could be a ton of reasons—the mood wasn't quite right or the players didn't quite click or whatever. But if you bomb in stand-up, it's because they don't like *you.*"

"Chelsey?" It was Rob, the man Chelsey had spent the night with.

"Rob! Oh my god! It's good to see you. Have a seat."

"I hope you don't think I'm a stalker, but I didn't want to have to wait until Sunday to see you again, and I thought that since you had to perform tonight . . ."

"I'm glad to see you again. Very glad. This is my good friend Ana Jacobs. Ana, this is Rob . . ."

"Night. Nice to meet you."

"Night as in night and day or as in my knight in shining armor?" Chelsey asked.

"As in I want to make love to you all night long."

"Hmm, somehow I think we've already done that."

"Okay then, I'm beginning to feel just a wee bit extraneous," Ana said. "I'll just go and slink off to a corner and talk to myself like a homeless person." She waited for a moment, waiting for one of them to argue with her. No one did. She took her beer and went over to where Marin was taking her turn on the unicycle.

"My last name is McGuiness," Chelsey told Rob.

"I know," he said, fanning the program that had the bios of all the performers. "I'm hoping you'll sign this so I can sell it for thousands of dollars someday when you're rich and famous."

"Absolutely."

As she wrote, he said, "So will you go on a proper date with me on Sunday? With food and cocktails and all that?"

"Definitely. I'd like that."

She handed him the program, and he read over what she'd written.

Rob, thanks for the wonderful evening. You are magnifique in bed. Also, your penis is huge. Sincerely, Chelsey McGuiness.

"It's not *that* huge," he said, with exaggerated false modesty.

"I know, but I've found that men like you more if you tell them it is. This has been my secret to success with guys all these years."

"Oh nice. I see how it's going to be. I'm just another in a long line of poor saps who have fallen for your many charms."

"Consider yourself warned. So, Rob, tell me about yourself. How do you spend your days and nights when not giving women you've just met multiple orgasms? How old are you? How many siblings do you have? Tell me every last detail."

"Okay, let's see. I'm twenty-seven—"

"Ooh, a younger man."

"Why, how old are you?"

"Twenty-seven and a half, but I turn twenty-eight next month. Okay, finish answering the questions."

"I have two younger sisters. I'm about twenty semester hours shy of a degree in computer animation from the Art Institute of Denver—at the current rate I'm going, it'll be about fifteen more years before I finish my degree—and I work as a firefighter in Denver. I work twenty-four-hour shifts, then have twenty-four hours off, and I do that two more times and then have four days off. I'm just finishing up with my four-day-off rotation, so I'll have to show up to work at seven tomorrow morning, but if you want a repeat of last night, complete with depriving me of sleep, I'm more than happy to make that sacrifice."

"That's a *very* generous offer." Chelsey bit her lip to suppress her smile. She didn't want him to know how happy she was that he was here. She didn't want to scare him off. "So you're a firefighter, huh? I wonder if last night counts as some kind of Oedipal experience even though I didn't know you were a firefighter at the time I slept with you."

"What do you mean?"

"Both my dad and brother are firefighters. I've always thought it's such a crazy way to make a living. I mean fire scares me to death. Why would anyone willingly go into a burning building? One time, my dad told me how when a firefighter walks through the door to a burning building, he has to very tentatively tap his foot to see if there is any floor there, because arsonists like to cut holes so firefighters fall down to some blazing death in a lighter-fluid-created fiery hell—I couldn't sleep for weeks after he told me that. I was so scared my dad was going to die a horrible death."

"There are a few times when I've been pretty scared, but most of the time, I really love the challenge. I really love being the nozzle man, the first guy in there. I feel powerful. I feel like I'm doing something worthwhile. So where do your dad and brother fight fires?"

"In a suburb of Chicago. That's where I'm from."

"Oh yeah, what brought you to Denver?"

"After I graduated from the University of Illinois, I knew I didn't want to stay in Chicago—it's a great city, but the winters are sooooo cold—so I went to the Greyhound bus station and looked to see how far I could get with one-hundred-and-fifty dollars, and of the possible choices, I liked Colorado the best—I mean, I'd never been to Colorado, but it sounded cool, and as the saying goes, 'Go West, young woman,' or whatever, something like that, so I did, and I ended up at Rocky Mountain National Park thinking it was so beautiful, and I decided this was where I wanted to spend the rest of my life. I wanted to live right in the mountains, but there weren't a lot of openings for kinesiology majors there, so I decided on Denver."

"What's kinesiology?"

"It's when you study how the human body moves, stuff like that. You take a bunch of nutrition and chemistry and human anatomy courses."

"Cool. Wait. I don't get it. What do you do for a living with a kinesiology degree?"

"I work as a personal trainer and fitness instructor."

"Gotcha. So how did you become a comedian?"

"Well, over the years I'd come to shows here and at Second City when I went home to Chicago, and I thought what they were doing up there looked like a lot of fun. Also, for a long time I've had this secret fantasy of being a writer for a sitcom, some TV show or something, preferably anything Sarah Jessica Parker is involved in, so when I saw the ad for workshops teaching improv, I signed up. I thought it might help me with my writing and improve my ability to come up with funny lines quickly, you know, which sitcom writers have to do every week. The first level is an eight-week course. Some people are chosen to make it to the next level, and I was one of them. I was really lucky because soon after I got through the third course, there was an opening for the professional troupe, and Steve Cuddy, he's the director and the one who runs the workshops, asked me to join them. One day I can go the New York or L.A. and become a teleplay writer."

"I thought you wanted to live in Colorado for the rest of your life."

"I'll just go to New York or L.A. long enough to become wildly rich and famous and then I'd come back here to live."

"Why not just work here at Spur for the rest of your life?"

"I've met some of the people who used to work here, and they told me it's really unusual for somebody to stay here for more than a year or two, even though Ramiro and Scott have worked here for a little more than three years, Jason's worked here about two and a half years, and Ana and Marin have been here for two. They're apparently the exceptions to the rule. You get burned out working all these crazy late nights and giving up every weekend. It's hard to be married and have kids and have a day job and do this too. We've talked about hiring more people so we could get more nights off, but we never get around to it. The other five used to be in an improv troupe when they were in college. They've been doing this for years. They can't not do it. The only way they'll stop working here is if they get their own television show like *Kids in the Hall* or something. Or maybe if they get married and have kids, but I don't see it happening."

"Why not?"

"Well, Jason I could maybe see getting married someday, if he ever gets over his crush on Marin. Maybe Scott could get married if he ever matured a little, but I don't know. Ramiro is gay, and as for us women, we've been hit on by so many married men at the club here, it's really hard to hold up marriage as this big goal, the answer to all our prayers. It's so depressing. I cannot tell you how many times men with wedding rings on their fingers have come up to me after the show and bought me a few drinks and flirted like crazy with me. They always say stuff like, 'Oh, my wife and I are like brother and sister, we sleep in separate beds, we're going to get divorced,' yada yada yada. I'm like, okay, so when you're actually divorced, maybe you can give me a call then, but I'm not sleeping with a married man. There is just no way that kind of story can have a happy ending, you know? And maybe some of them really are getting a divorce, but I'm guessing that a lot of them aren't, and it's just so depressing to think about how many men cheat or would cheat on their wives if they had the opportunity."

"Not all guys cheat. I've never cheated on a girlfriend."

"Have you had the opportunity?"

"Sure. Plenty."

"I don't know. I believe in love. I'm just not sure I believe in marriage. Maybe I just haven't met the right guy yet, and when I do, I won't have any fears at all about tying the knot."

"I bet that's it. I bet the right guy will make you decide marriage is pretty great after all."

The other five performers returned from their unicycle adventures to give more serious attention to their beers. After Chelsey introduced Rob to everyone and everyone to Rob, Ramiro asked, "So Ana, how did it go with the guy from Qwest? Can we quit our day jobs yet?"

"Not yet, sorry. He said their budget is really tight now, but he thinks he wants us for their holiday party in December."

"That's it?"

"Steve should really be marketing us heavily to the local business community," Ana said, as she had about nine million times before. "I mean Second City not only has performances every night of the week, they have an entire traveling team going around the country. I know Denver isn't as big as Chicago, but still, we should be able to do a lot better than we're doing. I think we just need to market ourselves. We should put on that sketch comedy performance we've always been talking about, and really aggressively market ourselves to agents and the local media and business community. Scott and I could create the posters and flyers, and I can write up the news releases and hound the press trying to get some publicity. I really think if we could show our sketch comedy skills, it would help us branch out. That's what Second City does."

"It would be fun. I think we should do it. Really do it and not just talk about it," Jason said.

"I don't know. It kind of sounds like a lot of work," Marin said.

"It'll be great. It'll give Ramiro a chance to finish some of the sketches he's been playing around with," Ana said. "We'll get Steve's permission to perform here some Sunday night."

"Just one night?" Chelsey asked.

"We can see how it goes and then repeat it. We'll market it like, 'back by popular demand,' " Ana said.

"I'm in. It'll look great on my résumé for when I go to become a staff writer for a hit series on HBO," Chelsey said.

"Okay, I'm in," Marin said.

"Yeah, I guess. I've got three or four sketches you guys could help me finish up," Ramiro said.

"I have some sketches, too, from when I took that sketch-writing class last year," Chelsey said.

"You haven't written anything since then?" Ana asked.

"No. What's your point, that if I want to become a sitcom writer I actually have to do something about it?" Chelsey joked.

"I think we should do a celebrity boxing skit," Ana said. "Marin could do Britney Spears and she could fight, I don't know, some bad ass woman, a woman who can actually sing maybe." Marin did a killer Britney Spears. She had the same dark eyes and blond hair that B.S. had, and she was a good dancer, but when Marin danced, her exaggerated facial expressions and hammy moves were hilarious. She acted all dumb and air headed, with big eyes and a high-pitched voice. "Ani DiFranco? k.d. lang?" Ana continued. "Oh, I know, Rosie O'Donnell! I'll be Rosie. You and I will kind of argue, and then I'll throw a single punch and knock you flat."

"Yeah, but first I'll dance around doing these fly girl moves to avoid getting hit." Marin stood up to demonstrate, getting into it. The others liked the idea too, and started shouting out ideas all over the place. The Keebler Elf against the Jolly Green Giant! Xena against Barbie! The character of Jack from *Will and Grace* against Arnold Schwarzenegger! Ramiro would play Jack. Ramiro was awesome at talking swish. Whenever he played a limp-wristed gay guy type, the audience roared. They thought it was hilarious that someone they assumed was straight, super-masculine straight, could pretend to be so swish. It was a great big irony sandwich.

"How about this? How about feminist cheerleaders?" Ana said. "We'll wear baggie jeans and t-shirts with varsity letters on them, and we'll explain to the audience how for years, cheerleaders have encouraged male violence and aggressiveness with cheers like, 'You've got to B-E A-G-G-R-E-S-S-I-V-E, got to be aggressive, whoo!' but no more. We're a new breed of cheerleaders who encourage women to excel in their careers and their lives, because everyone needs encouragement. We'll cheer men on to share more of the housework and take care of the kids."

"It's got potential," Chelsey said. "It'll be you, me, Ramiro in drag, and Marin, and instead of being all bubbly, we'll be sedate and talk in a monotone. It'll be fun to write the cheers." Just then, Chelsey realized she'd completely forgotten about Rob. She turned to him. "Rob, you're having a horrible time, aren't you?"

"I'm having a great time. Your friends are fun."

"You'd rather be home fooling around with me right now, wouldn't you?"

"That would be a lot of fun too, but we can do that all Sunday and Sunday night, all next week. I'm not going anywhere."

Chelsey's heart did a back handspring. She hadn't thought this might be a long-term thing when she slept with him three hours after meeting him. Well, okay, she hadn't really been thinking about anything but how cute he was. Did this relationship really have a chance to become something, despite having the fact they had sex on their first date?

"I should probably get home and get some sleep before I have to get to work," Rob said. "But let's do brunch on Sunday. Come to my place, I'll cook for you."

"You cook?"

"Sure."

Oh dear. She could very well fall madly, deeply, and passionately in love with this guy.

"Come by around 11. Is that too early?"

"No, that sounds great. I'll see you then."

After Rob left, the rest of them worked on scripts for the show until 4:30 in the morning. Some of the ideas they worked on were based on characters who had popped up now and then in their improv, like Ramiro and Jason's After-School-Special Hector and Bob, in which exchange student Hector explains his Brazilian heritage, and Bob explains about American culture.

Jason/Bob and Ramiro/Hector stood up and started improvising to get some ideas out while Ana wrote it down.

Ramiro/Hector: "Good international friend, what is this? We do not have such things in my country."

Jason/Bob: "Why, my good international friend, it's called a china cabinet. White people buy dishes that are so expensive, they use them only once a year. And then they buy an entire piece of furniture to display these dishes they only use once a year. Then they buy bumper stickers that say, 'Live simply so that others may simply live,' and put them on all three of their cars and their SUV and their boat." And so on. When they'd gotten all the mileage they could out of Bob and Hector, Scott chimed in with an idea.

"I want to do something on the three-minute dating thing."

"What's that?" Ana asked.

"Ana, what's wrong with you? It was on *Sex and City!*" Chelsey said. "It's where you go to these groups where they have like ten men and ten women and they pair up, two at a time, and every three minutes a bell rings and they switch to talk to someone else. The idea is you'll click with somebody and see if you want to go on another date with them to get to know them better."

"The scene will start at a bar so I can show off my cool moves." Scott demonstrated his Roger Rabbit and Running Man moves. Because of his ganglyness, he was a natural at physical comedy. Just about any move he made was hilarious. "While I'm dancing, Jason or Ramiro can do a voice-over." Scott imitated the voice of the guy that does every movie trailer ever made. "'Chuck tried the bar scene. He took out a personal ad. Nothing worked. He was still just a lonely slob. Then he tried three-minute dating!' Then I'll sit at a table and interview you guys and you'll all just be awful and then the bell will ring."

"What kind of awful?" Marin asked.

Scott looked at her blankly. "I don't know." He thought for a moment. "Um, I need to flesh it out more."

"Just a little," Marin said.

"Why don't we all be in the sketch," Ramiro said. "We could have one person decide she's found her soul mate and she won't let go. Jason could be the object of affection and . . . Ana could stalk him." Here everyone tittered. Ana's long-standing crush on Jason was hardly top secret. The rest of them loved to razz her about it. "She could grab on to his legs like little kids do. We could do a bunch of sight gags with her popping up at different tables when he's got his three minutes with a different lady. She could dress up as a waiter and try to sabotage things. Meanwhile, Scott, you're going through all those horrible dates like you said. In the end, Scott, you and Ana end up together somehow."

"I like it!" Ana said. It was disgusting how Ramiro could take a beginning to a sketch and give it a rough middle and an end in eleven seconds flat.

"So what are we going to call our show?" Marin asked.

"I know," Chelsey said. "I had this dream the other night, involving Britney Spears, Scooby Doo—not the cartoon one, the movie digitally created one—and Satan. Satan traveled in Scooby Doo's body, but we knew he was there, and it was our job to protect Britney. I think I was like one of her bodyguards or something, I can't remember. But don't you think that would make a good name for a show, 'Britney Spears, Scooby Doo, and Satan'?"

Her friends just looked at her like she was a strange foreign creature they'd never encountered before. "I'm pretty sure we'd get our asses royally sued off," Marin said. "I think we'd be breaking a jillion libel laws."

"How about 'The Comedy Hootenanny'?" Ana offered.

"You can't use something that uses words like 'comedy,' 'wit,' or 'humor,' " Ramiro said, rolling in his eyes at the obviousness of his point, like he was trying to educate a country bumpkin on basic concepts such as not wearing white pants before Easter. "Look at the shows Second City puts on or the stuff the Upright Citizen's Brigade does. They do shows with names like, 'Curious George Goes to War' or 'The Ice Cream Man Cometh.' "

"How about 'Shangri-Ha,' " Scott said.

"You know what I think a step above that, Scott, would be 'Don't Come See This Show,' " Ramiro said.

"What are you saying, that you don't like my title?"

"In summary: yes, that's what I'm saying."

"How about, 'The Pirates of Pete's Pants,' " Chelsey offered.

"But there is nobody named Pete in this group," Ana said.

"It's a play on 'The Pirates of Penzance.' Ana, for someone so smart, sometimes you're a little loopy in the head. I think it's best you hear it from a friend."

"Yeah, I get that part, but I don't see what it has to our show or us."

"How about 'Fried Peanut Butter Sandwiches.' You know going for an abstract—" Scott began.

"That. Is. The. Stupidest name I've ever heard," Ramiro said.

Ana started laughing. "It is pretty bad."

The others joined in, and when Chelsey snorted, Ana fell right off her chair, collapsing with laughter. Scott pretended to be hurt, but soon he was laughing, too. Teasing and tormenting one another was their primary form of communication.

When they finally recovered, Chelsey wiped the tears from her eyes and said, "I'm going to get a Stallion. Anybody want anything?"

"Bullsy, just say no," Ramiro said.

"Admitting you have a problem is the first step," Marin said.

"Actually Bullsy, the reason we've called you here tonight is: You have a problem. We've come together to perform an intervention," Scott said.

"I don't have a problem! I don't! I don't!"

"You do! You do!" the others chanted. They swarmed in on her and ended up in a group tickle fight, the usual conclusion to their "interventions."

They laughed until their stomachs hurt and they were so tired they could barely peel themselves off the floor. And so they went home to bed, ideas for the show tumbling through their minds like pebbles in an ocean.

8

Quality Family Time

Ana thought that if she and her four roommates had been around in Renaissance times, Marin would have been the lovely, charming, fabulously wealthy queen, universally loved by all. Scott would have been, of course, the court jester. Jason would have been the king and queen's children's tutor, a simple but respectable role. Ramiro would have been the king's advisor, able to come up with brilliant war-winning, destiny-changing strategies over pints of mead. Ana herself would be a scullery maid, working tirelessly for starvation rations and the first one to die off in a bout of bubonic plague.

Still, she loved her friends, though it wasn't always easy. Living with Marin, Scott, and Ramiro meant that no matter how hard Ana tried, the house was in a perpetual state of chaos. It was like living with the kid from the *Sixth Sense*. You know when the Mom leaves the room for like a second and then comes back to find all the drawers and cabinet doors open? That was what Ana faced every day of her life. With the exception of Jason, her roommates were absolutely incapable of closing a drawer or door. Ana would dutifully close all the cabinets, and then in the span of time it took to blink, the kitchen would become a minefield of bruises and concussions waiting to happen—one quick turn into an outstretched cabinet door and you'd be flat on your back with a bump the size of shot glass on your forehead. Her roommates had never once replaced an empty roll of toilet paper with a full one, and they certainly never did their dishes. In the beginning, Ana had yelled and cried and cajoled, but it was useless. It was easier just to clean up after them.

She and Jason had become the de facto Mom and Dad of this family. Jason loved to garden, and that's what he spent all his weekend days doing in the growing season. He took care of mowing the lawn, and he was the only person in the house who ever cooked. He would cook enormous vats of ratatouille or pasta primavera and salads with fresh vegetables from his garden.

Ana did all of the cleaning. If she left it up to the others, their bathtub would resemble a swamp and the rest of the house would look like it had been ransacked by Russian mafia members looking for the microchip that could destroy the world or what have you. But while Ana was bitter and resentful every moment she spent cleaning up after her roommates, she also loved them, and the good things outweighed the many bad sides of living with them.

Take this morning for instance. Ana made coffee, poured herself a milky, sugary cup and made one for Scott too, then padded barefooted along the hardwood floors to Scott's room.

She noiselessly pushed the door open. He opened his eyes and looked at her.

"You awake?" she asked.

"Yeah, I'm just laying here until I work up the energy to get up."

"I brought you some coffee. That should help."

Ana brought him the cup. "Scooch," she commanded. He scooched. She put her coffee on the bedside table and lay next to him, so their arms touched. Scott, being the giant he was, had the largest bed in the house, and it had become the informal meeting place for the family.

"Thanks, but it's too hot for coffee. It's too hot for anything." Between the sound of the fan in the window and the mini-swamp cooler on the floor, it was hard to hear him.

"You're from Texas. You should be used to the heat."

"Yeah, but in Texas they wouldn't have even considered

building a house without air conditioning. What's wrong with these people in Denver?" Scott didn't speak with a southern accent, though if you dared to say that he was from the south, or was in any way southern, smoke would come out of his ears and his head would spin around a few times. "I'm not from the south, I'm from Texas!" he'd yell, as if Texas was its own sovereign nation, which Ana suspected it might actually secretly be. He was fiercely proud of Texas. On the other hand, he'd moved from there at the first available opportunity, and Ana thought this spoke well of him.

Scott's walls were adorned with paintings he'd done himself. He preferred oils and his work often had a surrealist, tongue-in-cheek theme. One of Ana's favorites was of a family of four sitting at the dinner table. A mother, a father, a little girl, and a little boy—all of whom are naked. The girl is grumpily refusing to eat. She has her elbow on the table and her chin resting in her hand, her expression is beleaguered and long-suffering. The younger brother is making a mess, and the Mom is trying to clean him up. The father is looking absently out the window at the sunset red sky.

Scott didn't paint as much today as he had in college, but he still had an easel in the corner for when he wanted a way to relax.

"What are you guys doing?" It was Marin, who scuffled toward them. Scott and Ana dutifully moved over to make room for her. She lay down next to Ana.

"We are being lazy slugs, mostly," Ana said. "I think we need a theme song for our show. We can do it to the music of the *Beverly Hillbillies.*"

"I can't believe it's daytime already." Ramiro walked into the room and took his place on the bed. "I'm so tired. I need a nap."

"You just woke up."

"But getting out of bed proved to be exhausting, and I need a nap to recuperate."

"We're thinking of a theme song for our show," Ana said. "Hey, do we know anyone who can play the fiddle? A fiddle is really what we need. Maybe we can get the music from *Deliverance*."

"Are you guys having fun without me?" Jason said, joining them on the bed. It was a cozy fit, but they could do it.

"We're coming up with the theme song for our sketch comedy show," Ana said. "Help us."

"Let's think of the great theme songs through the ages, and decide what qualities lead to theme-song greatness," Jason said. "*The Love Boat* is clearly up there, in the top ten maybe."

Marin got as far as "the" before the rest of them joined in, singing *The Love Boat* at the top of their lungs. They proceeded to sing every theme song they knew, moving through *Cheers*, *The Facts of Life*, *Greatest American Hero*, and the *Fresh Prince of Bel Air*, among others. Amid much laughter and discussion over important matters like whether the *L* that Laverne always wore on her shirts really stood for "lesbian" (come on, Laverne and Shirley were just a little *too* close) they whiled away a very large portion of their day. Ana loved it, being wedged in with the people she loved most in the world, singing songs, laughing, and feeling absolutely loved.

9

A Proper Date

Sunday morning, Chelsey went to Rob's apartment, arriving at eleven A.M. exactly. He lived three blocks away from the rest of the Spur of the Moment gang in Capitol Hill, near the library. She had been to his place the other night, but they'd been far too busy tearing each other's clothes off for her to properly inspect the place.

This time, after he hugged her and gave her a long, sensuous kiss, she asked him to show her around.

"It's only a one-bedroom apartment, so it's not like there's much to see, but I'll give you the tour."

His home was sparsely decorated, but clean. She wondered if he was always this neat, or if he was trying to impress her. She couldn't remember if it had been neat the first night she was here or not (she hadn't been concerned with his housekeeping skills at the time). In any case, he wouldn't have had much time to clean between Friday night, working a 24-hour shift on Saturday, and now, so it couldn't have been that bad to start with.

There were only two pictures on the wall, and both were sketches of women. One was an old woman in profile, the other was a younger, though not young, woman, her dark eyes intense yet friendly.

"Did you draw these?" Chelsey asked. He nodded. "Are they of anybody in particular?"

"This is my mom, and this is my grandmother. They are both amazing women. They're very strong women. You'd like them."

Chelsey liked how he spoke of such reverence for his mother and grandmother. Maybe it was an Indian thing. She seemed to remember that Native American culture was more matrilineal than European culture. Then again, her knowledge of things Native American was rather rusty. Or more accurately, nonexistent.

The sketches were beautiful. She told him so. "Any other family?"

"I've got two younger sisters, a few aunts. They're still on the reservation."

"In southern Colorado? New Mexico?"

"South Dakota."

"What brought you out here?"

"My dad got me a job fighting fires in Aspen about eight years ago. Then I got a full-time job at the fire station in Denver a year later and I started taking classes at the Art Institute, so I've been here ever since. I visit my mom and sisters a lot though. I try to go to every sun dance and powwow. It's only twelve hours away. It's a nice drive. Are you ready for breakfast?"

"Sure."

"Mimosa?"

"Sure."

After drinks he brought out the rest of the meal. Eggs benedict plus hash browns and toast. Oh Christ, Chelsey thought, more calories than she usually ate in two days. She just smiled and ate slowly. She tried to let herself enjoy it. She'd just work out a little harder tomorrow and restrict her calories for the next few days. Being a personal trainer meant Chelsey was incapable of not counting calories and fat grams of everything she put into her body. She told her clients that the occasional break from calorie counting was okay, but she herself had a hard time shutting off the habit.

After breakfast, they drove over to Chelsey's side of town and walked along Broadway, going into the used books stores and art galleries and furniture stores, which ranged from gross-used, to cool-used, to super-expensive cool-new.

Chelsey sat on a lime green couch in one of the super swanky furniture stores and Rob sat next to her. The couch's back and arms swooped in a wave. The store managers had decorated the area around the couch to give customers a feel for how they could arrange their own living rooms, so beside the couch was a purple divan, and on the floor was a carpet with shapes of circles, triangles, and squares in black, red, lime green, and purple. A funky glass coffee table was in the center of the rug.

"I would love this look for my house," Chelsey said.

"It's okay. I like classic stuff that never goes out of style."

"I mean if I were rich."

"If you were rich you'd blow $3,000 on a couch?"

"Yeah, wouldn't you?"

"Nah. Do you know how under-funded schools on reservations are?"

"No. I thought the casinos were taking care of that stuff."

He let out a laugh. "Yeah, casinos—the solution to all our problems."

"They're not?"

"Only a few casinos make any money. And yeah, those reservations are doing great now. Employment rates are up, all that good stuff. But most reservations are way off in the boonies and aren't easy to get to. They're not enough of a draw to get people out there. Most just barely break even."

"Oh." Chelsey felt like an idiot. "So you'd give all your money to reservations?"

"Absolutely. I'd love it if I could do that."

"What, um, kind of Indian are you?"

"Oglala Lakota Sioux. Pine Ridge Reservation. You've heard of that, right?"

"It sounds familiar." It didn't.

"Wounded Knee?"

"Um, I can't quite remember, but I'm going to take a wild guess and say a bunch of Indians got slaughtered."

He laughed again. "Pretty good guess."

"Hey, so how come your last name is Night instead of Walking Bear or Eagle Feather or something?"

"My dad's white."

"Your dad's white?"

He nodded. "My parents separated a long time ago. I'm not close to my dad, but he did get me the job out here, so that was cool. I needed to get off the rez, so I'm grateful to him for that."

It explained his lightish skin, but the way he talked and dressed (the long hair, the brightly beaded bracelet) he seemed very into being Indian and didn't seem at all into being part white. Then again, how did one celebrate being a white male? Dressing in camouflage, buying truckloads of semi-automatic weapons, and hiding out in a compound in Montana? Having short hair and wearing suits and ties?

"Why did you need to get off the rez-*er*-vation?" She'd started to say "rez," but then felt like she sounded like some poseur, pretending to be familiar with a world she knew nothing about.

"There's nothing to do there but drink."

"Oh." This line of conversation was making her uncomfortable. "Do you want to come to my place and check out my digs?"

"Sure."

They went back to her place and she showed him around. She saved her bedroom for last, which was good, because once they entered that room, they didn't come out again for several hours.

10

The View from Cloud Nine

When Chelsey got to work the next day, she couldn't stop smiling. She was beaming, and her happiness was contagious. People smiled at her like she was an old friend, like seeing her was the best part of their day. It wasn't like she was grumpy ordinarily, but she couldn't get over how positively people reacted to her now that she was giddy with happiness, with that heady, this-could-be-love sensation.

She didn't even mind her hour with Mrs. Friedman. Mrs. Friedman had been coming regularly to her workouts, and she was getting in better shape, but she hadn't lost much weight.

"How's the diet going?" Chelsey asked.

"Oh, you know dear, I just get so *hungry.*"

For Chelsey, reading Mrs. Friedman's nutritional diaries was like reading a script from a Wes Craven movie. Mrs. Friedman always started out with good bran-cereal-and-a-snack-of-fruit intentions, but by late afternoon she was shoveling in the most nutritionally bankrupt food, having a daily orgy of fat and cholesterol.

"Mrs. Friedman, you know the rules, your body is eighty percent what you eat, twenty percent how much you work out."

"I know dear, there are just so many hours in a day."

And Chelsey did know. That's why she liked being an improv comedian. You could become absolutely anyone you wanted in a split second. A change of a wig and you had a new name, a new personality, new parents, and a completely different history. And all of the mistakes you'd made in your real life? Poof! They were gone. In real life, it wasn't that change was impossible, but it was very, very hard. Maybe you'd lose weight or get sober or get out of a bad relationship, but there are a lot of hours in a day and a lot of days in a year, and maybe someday soon or well into the future you'd gain the weight back or fall off the wagon or get back with your ex or a new person who was even worse. People can change, but lessons are so much more easily learned in a half-hour TV show or two-hour movie than over the many years of a person's life, in which lessons are learned and then, too often, forgotten.

"Okay, don't worry about it. Just get right back on the diet plan. I know you can do it!"

To make up for the extravagant breakfast she had yesterday, Chelsey worked out for an extra hour after work, bringing her workout to two and a half hours. For dinner she had a plate of steamed vegetables with nothing on them. She talked on the phone with Rob for two hours and then went to bed with her stomach growling, feeling righteous and cleansed.

11

The Cluster Fuck, Part Two

On Monday, Ana called Steve to ask if they could borrow the theater one Sunday night. "We want to put on a sketch comedy show."

"Why?"

"Ah, to get practice doing sketch. One more thing to add to the résumé, you know?"

"What day were you thinking of?"

"Um," Ana looked at her calendar. "October fifteenth maybe? I mean we're flexible. Whatever works for you."

Steve didn't say anything, so Ana charged on. "It'll be extra publicity for the club. I'll do all the publicity for it, and maybe the paper will do a story on the actors from Spur and maybe people who've never been to the theater will come."

"I don't think it'll be a problem. You can use the theater."

"Really? Thank you!"

Ana hung up the phone and suddenly felt sheepish. She hoped her Spur of the Moment buddies wouldn't be mad at her for deciding on a date without consulting them.

She sent a group email to the five of them.

To: scottwinn@abbott.com; jhess@denvernorthhs.edu; marinkennesaw@hotmail.com; mcguinesschelsey@aol.com; divineafflatus@hotmail.com

From: anajacobs@abbott.com
Subject: Oops, I did it again

Beloved compatriots in laughs, you've variously called me a drill sergeant, a dictator, and perchance a wee bit bossy. I know you say these things with love in your heart—and a good reason. Please don't hate me, but I called Steve to see if he'd let us use the theater, and he asked what day we wanted it. I glanced at the calendar—the only thought in my mind was that we wanted to hold it before the holidays, and I pulled the date October fifteenth out of my ass. Does anyone have a problem with that? That gives us almost five weeks. Saturday Night Live *puts on a show every week. We can do it!*

I think we should practice three times a week. I'm thinking Sunday night, Tuesday, and Wednesday. I know Wednesdays we're supposed to practice improv, but Steve's never there, and it's only for a few weeks . . .

Let's get together tomorrow night at seven and plan our strategy.

About eleven seconds later, she got a reply from Marin, who, rather than wasting her time working, spent her days hovering over her Hotmail account hitting "Refresh, refresh, refresh" over and over again.

To: anajacobs@abbott.com; scottwinn@abbott.com; jhess@denver-northhs.edu; mcguinesschelsey@aol.com; divineafflatus@hotmail.com
From: marinkennesaw@hotmail.com
Subject: RE: Oops, I did it again

Ana, I love how you apologize for being bossy and then plan all of our practices and demand that we meet tomorrow night. But you know we love you. How would we ever get anything done without you?

The fifteenth is fine with me. And I just happen to have nothing to do tomorrow night, so count me in.

In case any of you were wondering, I am very, very bored. I'm supposed to answer the phone, but it hardly ever rings. So I'm just sitting here, near the phone, so I could answer it if it ever did ring, staring at the engineers as they pass by. I have a question for you: Are engineers taught in school along with math to have no fashion sense? This guy who just walked by has this kind of mullet-ponytail deal (no, I'm not kidding, I only wish I were), a t-shirt advertising some software over a belly like a grain silo, and glasses straight from the 1950s. I ask you: Why? If Tommy or Vera or Ralph stopped by this office, they'd grab the nearest fire pokers and gouge their eyes out in horror.

Did I mention that I'm bored? Please send me lengthy missives to keep me entertained.

Smooch smooch, kids.

A few minutes after that, Ramiro chimed in.

To: anajacobs@abbott.com; scottwinn@abbott.com; jhess@denver-northhs.edu; mcguinesschelsey@aol.com; marinkennesaw@hotmail.com
From: divineafflatus@hotmail.com
Subject: RE: Oops, I did it again

RE: Mullets. Here's my question: do people with mullets not have access to the same media as the rest of us? Do they not see magazines adorning the grocery store check out lines? Do they not see that not Ben Affleck nor Brad Pitt nor Cindy Crawford nor Jennifer Aniston sport mullets? Do they not realize there is a reason for this? Because I'm here to tell you: THERE IS.

Ana laughed. Ramiro was the king of bitchy commentary. Not that he was a fashion maven himself—he clearly couldn't be bothered—but, like Marin, he had a way of putting together jeans, t-shirt, shoes, and a belt and looking like a GQ do. It was probably that he had awesome hair that was sloppy in a sexy way and he exuded an air of I've-got-it-together confidence that made him look MTV VJ oh-so-hip.

Ana went on the 'net collecting the names of agents and reporters in the Denver area. There were exactly three agents, so that wasn't hard, but there were an absolute ton of reporters. There were the three big papers, the *Denver Post*, the *Rocky Mountain News*, and *Westword*—Denver's *Village Voice*—but there were also papers for each suburb, plus two dailies in Boulder. For each paper, there were several journalists who wrote features, plus the editors for the entertainment sections, plus the peons that put together the calendar of events. Ana wanted to contact all of them, by every medium she was able to.

Many of the small papers didn't have websites where she could get all the contact info easily, so she had to call them each individually and beg for fax numbers and email addresses.

By the time she'd compiled her list it was already eleven in the morning. She hadn't ever enjoyed a morning at work more.

Ana, still sitting in her chair, wheeled/walked over to Scott.

"Busy?" she asked.

"Yes."

"Wanna work on ideas for the poster for the show?"

"We don't have a name or theme for it yet."

"What's your point? We can still brainstorm."

He nodded. "That does sound a lot better than work."

They spent the next hour tossing around ideas. She sketched a few concepts, and Scott did rough layouts.

"We need to get pictures of everybody," Scott said.

Ana knew they couldn't just download their pictures from the Spur of the Moment web page because web pictures didn't have a high enough resolution for printed pieces.

"I'll have to scan all of our pictures in," Ana said.

"It would be nice if we had a professional group shot. Maybe I could take the one from Spur and Photoshop Steve out of it."

"He's in the center of it. It will look completely unbalanced."

"Yeah. Good point. But how am I going to make it look

cool when we have separate mug shots? Maybe I could do a mural, with everybody's face cut out and tilted at various angles."

"Or maybe we could do something like the Brady Bunch, with all of us looking down or up or to the side at each other."

"I like it! You think Nick will let us borrow his digital camera?"

"I'm sure he would." They all would have loved Nick even without his finance guru's salary, but it really was nice to have at least one friend who could afford things like digital cameras.

Ana hadn't had so much fun at work since . . . Ana had never had this much fun at work. She loved this. She loved being creative. It wasn't that she intrinsically hated marketing and advertising, it was that, when she created stuff for Abbott Technology, no matter what ideas she came up with, she was overruled. All her creativity and hard work were inevitably for nothing. Her boss just wanted something that he could tear up so he could feel important and managerly. Ana had thought about trying to save up enough to start her own agency, but she knew her clients would just do the same thing to her. It wasn't that she couldn't take criticism, it was that most of the time, her boss wasn't making anything better—he'd made it worse or different, but rarely better.

Worse, it wasn't just The Big Weasel she had to please. Weasel was the VP of marketing, but marketing's main function was to create collateral to help the sales team sell Abbott software, which meant she also had to please Deb Myers, VP of sales.

Ana tried not to be hard on Deb, she being the only female exec at Abbott, but while Deb was nice, charming, cute, fun to talk to, and absolutely amazing at selling things, when it came to actually managing projects and people, she was as hopeless as The Weasel.

Ana had been trying to get The Weasel and Deb together to talk about what she needed to do in preparation for Deb's meeting with Techtronic execs for weeks. Ana knew that weeks' worth of work awaited her and she knew it would end up that she'd only have a day or two to do it, but since she hadn't been assigned anything yet, she might as well work on publicizing the show. No reason to be idle, right?

12

The Word for Today, Kids, Is "Apathy!"

Marin swiveled in her chair, painfully bored. She was working as an operator at a phone message service for small businesses that couldn't afford a full-time receptionist but wanted callers to think they could.

Marin's boss for the day was not the brightest star in the sky. He had thick black glasses that fell down his nose constantly and he was the loudest breather she'd ever heard in her entire life. Saliva gathered at his lips in a manner that was both horrifying and compelling to study—like an animal cleaning its butt, it was oddly intriguing to watch.

Fortunately, he spent most of his time in the back office. But before he left her to answering the phones, he gave her a long list of companies and the corresponding codes that would pop up on her monitor. She was supposed to look at the code, see what company it was for, and answer the phone saying, "Hello, this is Company X, my name is Marin, how can I help you?"

Marin looked at the endless list and it was all she could do to keep from laughing out loud. *Yeah right.* But she simply nodded enthusiastically.

Boredom set in promptly after he left. The phone only rang a handful of times an hour, leaving Marin a good fifty minutes out of sixty to stare at the wall.

I should use the time productively. Work on a script for the show.

She tapped her pen against the desk. Took a deep breath. Made a pensive, sucking noise with her tongue between her teeth.

The phone rang. She was almost jubilant to have something to do.

"Hello!"

"Is this the law firm of Ellis and Gray?"

"Yes!" She had no idea.

"May I speak to Mr. Ellis?"

"He's out of the office right now, can I take a message?"

The woman left this endless message, spelling her name, repeating her number. Marin doodled a picture of her boss for the day, saying "Uh-huh, uh-huh," all the while *as if* she were writing the number down.

She hung up the phone.

Bored. So bored.

Sketch, right, she should write a sketch. What should it be about? How about a bored receptionist who answers the phone in an amusing fashion? She smiled. She was brilliant.

The next time she answered, she said in her most seductive, breathy voice, "This is the Lovely Lady Escort Service, how may I please you?"

"Uh, I was just calling in to check my messages? I'm Morgan McKenna from McKenna Marketing?"

"Oh! I'm sorry Mr. McKenna, I'm new here. I must have gotten the numbers confused. Ah yes, here they are . . ."

She read off his messages, hung up the phone, and laughed hysterically.

Over the course of the day, she answered the phone as "911, what is your emergency?" and various escort, dancing, and massage services. And she wrote it all down, exaggerating the reactions of the people on the end of the line if it aided the comedy of the scene.

At the end of the script, the nerdy boss came in and said she had a great phone voice, would she come again?

In real life, however, her jig was up by 1:30, and she was told never to come back again. No matter, she'd spent the hours in an entirely useful and productive manner.

13

The Tap-Dancing Cult Leader

The only problem with living a double life of soon-to-be-superstar/regular person was that it was exhausting. With performances and practices, they had just one free night a week. Ana had been looking forward to Monday night all week so she could get some rest. She was sprawled on the recliner practically drooling in her stupor of exhaustion. Ramiro and Scott were playing back-to-back games of Hot Shots of Golf 3 on the X-Box. Ana had been sitting there for several minutes, staring absently at the TV screen before it occurred to her that watching people play video-game golf was about as much fun as watching people play real golf, which was to say, not at all.

She glanced into the kitchen. From her seat in the recliner, she could see Jason grading papers at the kitchen table. She didn't know how he did it, performing and practicing six nights a week, working all day, and then somehow managing to create lesson plans and grade papers in the middle of it all.

He looked so angelic, sitting there, working studiously, concentrating intently, his hair mussed adorably from running his fingers through it as he graded his students' papers, as if trying to decipher what appeared to be hieroglyphics but were supposed to be essays on cell division.

Marin was on the phone, laughing with an old friend about something or other.

Ana loved that she lived with these four people. It made her feel like she was able to hold on to all the good parts of college life without the annoying stress of exams and essays. The five of them hadn't moved from Boulder to Denver until both Marin and Ana had graduated, but once the last of them was out of school, there was no more reason for Scott and Jason to commute to their jobs in Denver from Boulder, and they'd rented this brownstone in Capitol Hill. But since they'd taken all their furniture and "decorations," such as they were, from the house in Boulder, it hardly felt like they'd moved at all.

Their furniture could only be described by the word "eclectic." There was the flowered couch that had weathered years of abuse and showed it in every stain of mysterious origin and every tattered cushion. It was enormous, however, and easily as comfortable as a bed for sleeping on. Then there was the kelly green recliner that matched nothing and did so with willful extravagance. It, too, was worse for the wear and had several tufts of yellow foam peeking out from various places. There was the white-and-yellow loveseat that housed the remnants of many a spilled beer. Next there was the cheap Target entertainment stand and a coffee table that had teeth marks on all four of its legs from somebody's brother's puppy who'd visited one day many years earlier. While they didn't mind hand-me-down furniture from their parents or friends, Scott had spared no expense when it came to their enormous TV, top-of-the-line stereo, and X-Box. Also, the room was decorated with several of Scott's abstract paintings. Ana thought having original art in the house was the pinnacle of class.

It was the greatest house in the world to Ana. Ana didn't believe in destiny, exactly—that everyone had a life mapped out for her from fetal cell numero uno—but she did believe that in every life, twists of fate presented themselves, and you said yes or you said no, you grabbed on for the ride or were too scared to take the risk, you let bad luck beat you down or you made the choice to grow stronger, and the richness or the pallor of the life you led was determined based on the choices you made every day. For Ana, she had come to college at a time when she was so thrilled to be free of the iron grip of her mother's grasp, she was ready to try anything. Then she saw a cute boy putting up posters for auditions. She thought, *hey, why not give it a try?* And the rest was history.

On the day of the auditions, Ramiro had explained what improv was. "Even though improv is made up entirely as you go, there are rules, tips, and strategies that will help you succeed. For those of you who make it, we'll teach you all that stuff. Today, we just want to get to know you and see a little bit of what you can do. The one rule I'll share with you up front is *don't try to tell jokes.* Try to tell an interesting story. The humor will come naturally out of a good story. If you don't tell a good story, I don't care how many jokes you tell or how much natural talent you have, your performance will be boring to watch. Improv can only succeed if everyone works together as a team. People who want to hog the spotlight by cracking jokes cause scenes to bomb big time. Just give yourself the freedom to see where things go, don't even think or worry about trying to be funny. Scott, Jason, and I will do a couple scenes for you to give you an idea of what this is all about, but first, are there any questions?"

"How many people are you going to take?" a guy with a dorky salad-bowl haircut asked.

"We're looking for two people," Jason said, "But we'll probably ask about four of five to join us because the dropout rate tends to be pretty high with improv. It takes a while to become good at improv, and some people can live with bombing until they become good at it, and some just can't. For those of you who make it, we'll practice three times a week for the first four months, then we'll drop to twice a week. Improv is just like any sport—you need to practice to get good and you need to practice to stay good."

Ana scanned the room. There were about fifteen people auditioning, all of them male except for the blond woman. She figured that they'd probably only take one woman, and it was going to the blond for sure whether she had any talent or not. She was *stunning*.

"We need a suggestion from the audience. Someone give me a thing," Ramiro said.

"An invention!"

Jason jumped into character and began the scene. "Gentlemen, gentlemen, please take a seat," he said in a Thurston Howell III voice. Ramiro and Scott sat on the floor, looking up at Jason.

"I have seen the future," Jason said.

"Tell us, tell us!" Scott said.

"As you know, the year 1900 is fast approaching. I have invented something that, with your help, will change the future. We'll ring in the new millennium with an invention that will change the world as we know it . . . and will also make us very, very rich. My invention will bring us convenience like we've never known before. There are, of course, some downsides, but not to worry, we can cash in on those too."

"What are they?" Scott asked.

"Oh, it's not really important." Jason started tap dancing, slowly at first. "The important thing is that we'll be rich. Let's . . ."

"Stop tap dancing around the issue! Tell us the downsides!" Ramiro said.

"I'm not tap dancing." He started dancing faster. He was really good at it! But of course he hammed it up, exaggerating and occasionally flying his arms out in a tada! manner.

"You are tap dancing!"

"I'm not tap dancing."

"You are tap dancing!"

"I'm not tap dancing."

"You are tap dancing!"

"I'm not tap dancing."

Ramiro couldn't help it, he giggled. He quickly suppressed his laughter, but it made the "audience" laugh even louder, seeing that even the performers thought Jason was hilarious. "Okay, except you are, and if we're going to help you, we need to know everything."

Jason slowed the tapping down, almost to a stop. He'd stand still, then let out a little ta-tap, ta-tap. "Okay. The invention will enable us to travel anywhere we want, but to do that, it will require that we clear cut acres and acres of land all across these fine United States. I figure we'll open a clear cutting business, and we'll make out like bandits."

Ramiro and Scott looked at each other and nodded approvingly.

"Also, it is very expensive to feed. Currently the only way to fuel it is with oil, but I'm sure that will change soon. We'll figure out something else soon. Until that happens, it will let off toxic gases that will destroy the environment and our health . . ." He shook his head and waved his hand as if this were a trifling matter. Ramiro and Scott looked at each other and did the same thing, shrugging.

"It's very expensive and requires constant maintenance and breaks down regularly and people will need to buy replacement parts and we'll set up our entire society to ensure that we can refuel it constantly, but we'll sell all this stuff, and people will buy it, I'm telling you, they'll buy it! We'll be rich. Me and all my loyal followers, we'll be rich!"

"Excellent idea, sir. What do you call this invention?" Ramiro added.

"An automobile."

Scene over.

They performed three more scenes. In one, Jason was an Australian guide, leading Mr. and Mrs. Blufflekowski through the crocodile-riddled rivers of Australia in search of a rare bug. Next Jason played The Four-Hundred-Year-Old Archaeology Professor and then a Chinese acrobat.

As Ana watched Jason, she couldn't believe how talented he was. He was very funny, but he was also a great actor. She'd thought he was gorgeous the first moment she saw him—that was why she was here, auditioning in this fleabag excuse for a theater—but he was more than hot, he was talented! She was in love!

The character of the Cult Leader was a perfect example of Jason's goal in life of bringing the injustices of the world to light in an amusing, entertaining way. This was why Ana loved him—he was smart, funny, talented, and he really cared about people other than himself. He was always looking out for the underdog.

After the guys performed a few scenes, they started randomly picking out groups of two or three or four wannabe

Iron Pyrits to perform together for three minutes. They did this over and over until each person had performed at least twice.

Marin had felt completely comfortable performing. Ana, on the other hand, wanted to wet herself and throw up as soon as she walked up there. Once she got the first words out, though, she relaxed a little, and she felt like her scenes weren't completely awful, just mostly awful.

Next Scott, Jason, and Ramiro asked all the wannabes to stand up and tell everybody a little about themselves.

Ana watched person after person go up and give their mini-biographies and she realized that most of them were pretty damn boring to listen to. It would be easy for her to be more memorable and entertaining than the other people.

She was the third-to-last person to go up in front of the group and talk about herself. As soon as she was facing the audience, she put her right foot to her left knee, raised her arms overhead like a ballet dancer, and said, "The main thing you need to know about me is that when I'm nervous, I like to dance." She moved slowly into an arabesque. She said everything in a bored monotone, "Also, I like to do gymnastics. I like to tumble. I like to tumble quite a bit. I've been studying gymnastics since I was a little girl, and I find it so relaxing. Of course, I've run into problems with it sometimes." She did deep pliés, with her left arm outstretched to the side, curved gracefully, and her right arm moving in circles from below her waist to above her head as she dipped into a plié and raised back up. These were all warm-up moves she'd done before practices; she used lots of these moves in her floor routines. "Like one time, when I was taking the SAT, the administration chick got all in a huff when I did some summersaults down the aisle." People laughed appreciatively. Ana thought, I *love* this! "Or this summer when I lost my virginity . . . well, not so much lost as threw away. Gave it away. Pawned it off on somebody. Anyway, I'd like to tell you it was romantic and erotic and wonderful, except . . . it wasn't. See, I'd wanted to be in love when I had sex for the first time, but I kept waiting and waiting for the guy of my dreams to come along, and he never showed up. Anyway, I did not want to go to college as the first virgin in the history of the universe. Plus, virgins are constantly fed into volcanoes as a sacrifice to the gods—the health risks of virginity are pretty dire. So I was dating this guy over the summer, and even though I didn't really like him, he had the equipment I needed to be devirginized, so I went with it. It was on a Saturday afternoon, and I didn't think I'd be nervous, but as he was struggling with the condom, I started having a panic attack. I really wanted to do some back handsprings or cartwheels to relax, but before I could he was on top of me, and . . . I don't want to say it was bad, but how do I put this? I was as dry as a desert, and our equipment was rubbing together like two pieces of glass. There was this ee-ee-ee-ee sound, and it wasn't the headboards. And when he pulled out, there was this sound of air being expelled from a vacuum-packed package." Ana made the "Thwock!" sound to uproarious laughter. "Well, so, I guess that's all you need to know about me. Oh, one last thing. My name is Ana Jade Jacobs and I grew up in Broomfield, Colorado, and I have my very own pair of Wonder Woman Underoos that still fit me. Thanks for hearing me out. Catch ya later." Ana waved goodbye and as she walked back to her spot on the floor, the applause surged around her.

Ana felt awesome. This comedy thing? She was *hooked.*

14

The Summer of Elastic Waistbands, Part One

It had been a summer of elastic waistbands for Ana, and if she didn't do something quick, it was going to be a winter of elastic waistbands as well. Already she was having fantasies of tearing the drapes from the windows so she could wear them toga-like to avoid having to wear her pants that cleaved her body in half. If she kept going like this, there wouldn't be enough room for both her and the rest of the actors on the small stage. Action must be taken!

It was a Friday night and she had an hour before she was supposed to leave for the theater. For dinner she had steamed veggies and a small serving of pasta with marinara sauce. It was not even a little bit satisfying.

She'd been overweight for several years now, but lately things had reached a critical point where she simply had to put the brakes on her ever-expanding elephantine bod.

She'd put on the twenty pounds in her freshman year in college. While it was routine for students to complain about the food in the dorm cafeteria, Ana thought it was heaven. It was a big improvement from her mother's cooking, and she could always count on there being something to eat. She loved that, not having to worry about whether there would be something to eat at the end of the month. There had been so many times growing up when she and her mom would have no food in the house. There would be spaghetti sauce but no pasta; peanut butter but no bread; taco-flavor packets up the yin yang but no meat, taco shells, lettuce, or tomatoes. She loved the dorm cafeteria. There was always cereal *and* milk for breakfast. At dinner, there was always an entrée *and* a vegetable. And there was a salad bar at every single lunch and dinner, which she found to be supremely reassuring. The cafeteria buoyed Ana with a sense of calmness and safety.

Added to her voracious appreciation of dorm food was her discovery of beer. Boulder had tough underage drinking laws, so going bar hopping before you were twenty-one was practically impossible, but there were always tons of house parties on campus. Plus, since Ana had befriended Ramiro and Scott when they were twenty-one, she was constantly going over to their house after practices to have a few beers and play epic rounds of video games or darts.

Ana had spent the last three years of college trying to lose weight, but she never lost more than a few pounds. She ate well and worked out regularly, but apparently eating until she wasn't hungry anymore was too much for her to reach her goal of lithe sveltness. So she'd made peace with her weight; she wasn't unhealthily obese. But lately she hadn't been working out as much, so not only had she gained weight, she'd gotten out of shape. It wasn't just an issue of vanity, although if she wanted to make it as an actress, it sure did help to be tiny. It was true that female comedians were held to slightly different standards than other actresses, enabling Roseanne and Rosie O'Donnell to become famous despite their weight, but it certainly didn't hurt to be thin. Ana couldn't remember the last time there was a large woman on *Saturday Night Live*, for example. There was often a big guy, like Chris Farley or Horatio Sans, but no big women.

But her real concern was that she didn't fit into her clothes and she didn't have the money to buy new ones. As she sat at her desk day in and day out, she could feel her thighs spreading out like pancake batter on a griddle. It felt like she was carrying around a sleeping kitten in her lap as her gut spilled onto her thighs. Maybe Chelsey could give her a deal on personal training. Maybe having Chelsey monitor everything Ana ate would help inspire her to work out more and eat better.

Ana brought her dishes to the sink and returned to the table. It was the time of the month that she always hated. No, not that time of the month. The rent-due-on-the-first-of-the-month time of the month. Rent was due in a couple days, and Ana had to get out her whip and flog her roommates roundly until they finally paid their share of the household expenses.

Ana paid all the bills in the house, mostly because she didn't trust anyone else to do it. Jason always wrote her a check without being asked, but Ana had to nag the other three for at least four days straight before they finally paid up. Ana *hated* to nag. Plus, Marin was chronically short of funds, meaning that there was always a lot of last minute "I'll pay you back" negotiations to work out before Ana could deliver the rent and pay the utilities.

Marin's perpetual cash-flow problem drove Ana batty. Marin hadn't had to take out any student loans, while Ana had had to pay for college herself. Ana would be paying off her loans till she was sixty. Marin's parents had bought her a brand-new Explorer for graduation, so she didn't have any monthly car payments either. Ana had bought a used car, but she still had $6000 to go before it was paid off, so her monthly expenses were considerably more than Marin's. Granted, she made more money than her roommate, but not nearly enough to rest easy. Ana couldn't believe how much credit card debt Marin had racked up, but Marin never worried about it. Money wasn't real to Marin. She pulled out the plastic, got what she wanted, and didn't worry about the pesky details of how she'd ever pay it all off.

Ana, on the other hand, worried about money constantly. She'd spent her whole life worrying about it. That's what happened when you had a single mom who worked as an underpaid administrative assistant.

Ana's mother, Grace, was sixteen when she'd gotten pregnant. Grace never talked about Ana's father, no matter how much Ana begged for any detail about him—his nationality, his hair color, his height, anything. Her mother often joked that it was an immaculate conception, and sometimes that's how it felt, like Ana had popped into the world out of nowhere. Ana was desperate to know what parts of her came from him, but it really did feel like she was just her mother's daughter. She looked a lot like her mother. They were both short and voluptuous, they had the same amber eyes and thick brown hair, so Ana couldn't figure out what she got from his side of the family. A history of cancer and heart disease, probably.

Of course what she hoped was that his side of the family was fabulously wealthy. She'd spent her entire life fantasizing about him coming back into their lives somehow to give them bankfuls of cash. She used to hope he'd be alive so she could meet him; now it had been so long she didn't care if he was alive or dead—an inheritance would do just fine, thanks.

The fantasy had many different permutations. There was the one where he'd been penniless when he'd met her mother and didn't feel worthy of her, which is why he ran off. But over the years he'd built some fabulous business empire—most likely in the form of life-saving medicines or medical equipment—and now that he was worthy, he'd return and ask Grace to marry him and whisk them away to a life of ease and comfort.

Then there was the one about how he'd been called off to some obscure, top-secret war, and then had become a prisoner for the last twenty-three years, but when he got out, with a huge payment from the offending government of whatever mosquito-ridden, jungle-bound nation, he'd come back and whisk Ana and Grace away to a life of ease and comfort.

Or there was the one where he was a dashing prince of a little known foreign country, and his parents demanded that he marry the princess from some other little known foreign country to keep the nations from war instead of marrying his true love, Grace Jacobs. But now that the princess had died and peace had been declared, he could return to claim Ana and Grace and whisk them away to a life of ease and comfort. A life where Ana never had to worry about going hungry in the week or two before her mom got her monthly paycheck on the first.

No matter how Grace tried, she always ran out of money by the end of the pay period.

From a young age, Ana had a habit of checking the cupboards and refrigerator daily. For the first couple weeks of the month, the sight of food gave her such comfort. The last couple weeks of the month, the dwindling supplies gave her stomachaches and tension headaches. She'd had a stomachache through most of grade school, and her problems with insomnia had started in kindergarten.

But Ana knew that the reason money was tight was because of her, because she'd come into the world when her mother was only sixteen. Grace was always talking about college, and how the only way to get ahead in this world was to go to college. Then she'd sigh wistfully and say that she wished she could have gone. "If only things had been different." Ana knew that she meant, "If only I hadn't had a baby at sixteen, all my dreams could have come true."

Because Grace's biggest goal in life was for Ana to go to college, Grace hated the idea of Ana doing anything that might divert her attention or time away from studying. Ana had taken gymnastic lessons at the YMCA since she was a toddler (they'd had a program that enabled low-income students to take lessons at no cost). When she'd gotten to grade school, her mother wanted her to quit gymnastics and concentrate all her efforts on academics. Ana had been eight years old when she told her mother that having an extracurricular activity looked good on a college application. Eight years old. How had she even known that then—where had she heard it? Maybe it was because her mother's friends were all in college and Ana absorbed it from being around them. Ana absorbed, too, the way her mother looked on with such jealousy and longing whenever her friends talked about school; even when they were talking about teachers they hated or pulling an all nighter to study for an exam, Grace coveted it all.

"College application" had been the magic words. With that and the promise that if Ana's grades ever dropped, she'd quit gymnastics immediately, she was able to continue practices and competitions. Then in high school, she quit gymnastics to become a cheerleader. She wanted to try out for plays, student government, and the school paper, but her mother worried that if she added another activity on top of cheerleading, her grades would fall and her future would be over. They'd had so many arguments that went along the lines of "I want you to have the opportunities I never had . . ." and Ana saying that she wanted opportunities like being in school plays and writing for the paper. Then Grace would pull the "if only things had been different for me" card, and Ana, though furious with herself for doing so, always felt guilty, literally felt guilty for being born, and her mother almost always won.

Ana had felt like the adult in their small family for as long as she could remember. She'd been there through all the times her mother had cried after another boyfriend had broken up with her. Ana knew that the fact her mom had a kid certainly didn't help in the pursuit of a husband—yet one more thing for Ana to feel guilty about. Ana always dutifully brought home the notes from teachers and didn't let her mother do anything until she'd signed them. Ana always did her homework without being asked. And when her mother had the morning queasies (in her first week of college Ana finally realized these were actually hangovers after she'd experienced her own hangover for the first time), Ana would bring her mother orange juice, a vitamin, and three Excedrins before getting dressed, making her lunch, and getting to school all by herself. Ana learned young not to miss the school bus, ever.

She had the grades and the scores to go to an Ivy League school, but not the money. So she chose the University of Colorado at Boulder. Boulder was just twenty minutes from Broomfield, the suburb where she'd grown up, and where her mother still lived. Even though college was only twenty minutes away, Ana lived in the dorms and then in a house with her friends from her improv group, so at least it gave her some distance from her mother.

Growing up poor had made Ana desperate to *be* somebody. Somebody who never needed to worry about where her next meal was coming from. Somebody who had enough money in the bank that if she lost her job, she wouldn't fall into crushing debt and poverty and be out on the street. Somebody who could own her own home—not a puny condo decorated with '70s-style carpeting and god-awful green drapes like her mom— a house. Somebody with such style and great clothes that when she ran into her classmates from grade school and high school they would feel waves of remorse for having made fun of her Kmart clothes and limited wardrobe when she'd been a kid. They'd kick themselves: *Gosh, I wish I'd been nicer to her way back when.*

Ana pushed the bills aside and looked at her watch. It was almost seven o'clock. Oh what she wouldn't give to be able to stay home tonight and go to bed early. She was exhausted.

"Marin, are you almost ready? We're going to be late for the warm ups!" Ana called.

"Coming! I'm almost ready."

Ana went to the bathroom and fixed her makeup, leisurely redoing her hair. She knew when Marin said she was almost ready she wasn't even close to ready. Ana finished freshening up and went and sat on the couch, idly flipping through an *US* magazine. She, Marin, and Chelsey subscribed to every tabloid rag there was. They were improv comedians, so reading celebrity gossip wasn't a guilty pleasure, but important research.

Ana stopped at an article describing how various celebrities lost weight. They had pictures of the stars going from "Puff to Buff." Ana would have given her left eye to look like just one of these women in their alleged "Puff" stages. Puff her ass. The caption should have read, "From Healthy to Skeletal." Reese Witherspoon had cheekbones that could slice concrete. And hello, when she had been "Puff" she'd given birth about eleven seconds earlier!

She looked at her watch again. Shit, they were going to be really, really late. Ana started getting anxious. "Marin! Get your ass down here!" Ten more minutes passed before Marin deigned to show up, and by then Ana was about to have a coronary. But as soon as she saw her friend, she calmed down.

Marin was just wearing a tight gray t-shirt, frayed blue jeans, and boots that cost half of Ana's monthly salary. Marin wasn't wearing any make-up, but she looked like an absolute knockout as always. Marin's beauty never ceased to be breathtaking.

They drove downtown to the theater. It was only a couple of miles away, but thanks to all the traffic lights, it took a while to get there, or at least it seemed like it to Ana. Thank God performers got free parking in the small lot behind the theater. Otherwise they'd have to budget fifteen extra minutes to find a parking space.

Ana started racing through aMuse upstairs to the theater.

"Hold on, hold on, I need to use the ATM," Marin said.

"I'll meet you upstairs."

"No, please just wait for me."

Ga! They only had fifteen minutes to warm up as it was.

Marin took her cash and looked at her receipt. "Shit, it says I only have $150 left in my account."

"That can't be right, you need $450 by Sunday to pay the rent."

"Yeah, I was sort of going to talk to you about that."

Ana sighed. "Let's just do the show. We can talk about it later."

Ana didn't perform as well as she would have liked. She was too tired to be able to think well on her feet. Also, she felt like the Pillsbury Dough Boy, her marshmallow middle popping out of the top of the tight confines of her jeans.

After the show, some of Ramiro's friends were going to meet them at aMuse, so they went downstairs to the main bar, where it was so crowded there was standing-room only.

She, Marin, and Chelsey huddled around one another, talking about the show. Two good-looking guys approached the three women and started telling them how much they'd enjoyed the show. The two guys only looked at Chelsey and Marin. With every minute of the conversation, Ana felt more and more invisible. She knew it wasn't just because she was the size of a balloon in a Macy's parade. She was also tired and cranky and had such dark circles under her eyes it looked like she'd been the loser in a street fight, which certainly couldn't be a turn-on.

Ana watched Marin drink her beer. Marin ate like a pig, guzzled beer by the vat, and yet still had the perfect body. Marin truly was one of those evil women who never worked out and ate cratefuls of junk food daily. Ana hated the stories of how waifs like Christina Aguilera and stunningly sexy women like J. Lo and Shakira insisted on having silos of Ho Ho's and M&Ms in their dressing rooms at all times. It was fine if they were rich and famous and staggeringly beautiful, but if these women genuinely gorged themselves on Twinkies and Doritos, then Ana wasn't sure she had the will to go on living. She was almost certain, however, that nothing but wheatgrass and carrot sticks ever passed the lips of these women. The alleged junk food indulgences were just another lie from PR people, who wanted to make the fantasy of fame, wealth, and beauty complete with tales of heroic metabolisms and effortlessly fat-free thighs.

Okay, bitterness is entirely unsightly. You lead a blessed life. You have a college education and friends who love you and a mother that never beat you unless you count that time she slapped you, and then you really did deserve it. Don't compare your life to other people's lives. Or if you're going to, get friends who are uglier, fatter, poorer than you.

She knew jealousy was one of the deadly sins and besides, it was unbecoming, but Ana couldn't help coveting her friend's perfect life. *You don't really want to be Marin. You'd be self-absorbed and bad with money. Of course you'd also be rich and beautiful, so who'd give a shit? Certainly not you.*

Marin actually seemed to be hitting it off with the one guy, which was pretty rare. She usually told guys she was an HIV-infected lesbian within four seconds of meeting them. She had this way of saying it so sweetly, like, "Gosh, if I weren't homosexual and dying of a terminal disease, I would be throwing myself on you as you're the most dashing man I've ever seen in my entire life." Marin's mother was from a wealthy family in Georgia, where hospitality and social graces were bred into her genes. Most men bored Marin to tears, but she was never bitchy to them, always polite. Ana hadn't been paying attention so she had no idea what he'd said to keep her talking this long.

Chelsey, on the other hand, looked miserable. Ana caught her saying something about how she was dating someone.

"How long have you been dating?" the guy asked.

"Well, not that long actually, but when you know it's right, you know it's right."

"Can I get your number just in case?"

"Well, you know, I just moved today, and I haven't had the phone installed." She didn't even hesitate as she lied. Training as an improviser had its advantages.

"Let me give you my number then."

"Yeah, okay."

"Chelse, when you're done there, I need you to come with me to the bathroom," Ana said, trying to help her out.

"Why is it that women always need to go to the bathroom in pairs?" the guy said, chuckling as if he were witty. This was a common problem after the shows—other people thought they could be funny too. It was like little boys who came out of a Jackie Chan movie karate chopping each other, over-identifying with the larger-than-life, well-choreographed hero.

"Okay, so call me," the guy said, pressing the piece of paper into her hand.

"Er, nice to meet you."

Chelsey and Ana sped through the crowd as quickly as the undulating mass of bodies would allow.

As soon as they were safely in the bathroom, Chelsey thanked Ana for rescuing her. "No problem. Where's Rob tonight?"

"He had to work."

"How are you two doing?"

"Awesome. I think I'm in love."

"That's so great. I'm so happy for you."

"You don't look happy. Is something wrong?"

"No. Yes. The thing is, I'm feeling like a whale. An elephant. An unfortunately oversized creature, anyway."

"I'm sorry, hon. Is there anything I can do to help?"

"Yeah, I think there is. I was hoping maybe you could kind of do me a favor."

"What?"

"I need to get in shape, I'm hoping you can get me a deal on getting fit."

"You already have a membership to the club, don't you?"

"Yeah, but I was sort of hoping to get on a program. Maybe get a personal trainer."

Chelsey clapped her hands together. "That would be so cool!"

"But how much does it cost?"

"Well, what kind of results are you looking for? Fat loss? Improved energy? Increased fitness?"

"I want to be able to fit into my clothes."

"I see." Chelsey considered this. "So how many pounds do you think you'll need to do that?"

"I don't know, seven?"

"Okay, so it'll take about six weeks, and you'll want to meet with me twice a week, which is normally six hundred dollars, but I could get you a discount . . ."

Ana was hoping she'd say maybe $50 total after all the rebates she'd get for being Chelsey's good friend.

"Say five hundred."

"Um, how about we only meet once a week. How much would that be?"

"Two fifty."

She couldn't blow half of her pitiful savings on a personal trainer just because she didn't have the willpower to lose weight on her own. It was madness. But Ana was far too tired to think straight. And it would cost far more than that to buy all new clothes to accommodate her sprawling girth, right? And she was so sick of the guys always ignoring her. Her self-esteem had been shredded far too viciously for her to make a sound decision.

"Okay, when do we start?"

15

The Weight of Memory

What had Marin been thinking? Why had she agreed to go on this date? Maybe because it had been forever since she'd had a boyfriend. The guy she'd met at the club the other night was cute. He seemed nice enough. And even if it didn't lead to wedding bells, maybe they could sleep together once in a while.

Marin would love to have a boyfriend. She wanted to be in love. It was time already.

She hadn't even had a serious boyfriend since high school. Not since Brent. He was twenty-seven, ten years older than her at the time, and already a successful stockbroker. He was good-looking, he drove an amazing car, and he was charming without being as obsequious toward her as the guys her age were. They met in the clubhouse of her parents' country club. Marin was there with two of her girlfriends. The three girls had gone swimming and hot-tubbing and were sharing snacks and playing pool when he approached them. Her eyes were red and stinging from the chlorine, she wore no make-up, her hair was wet, and she was just wearing a loose sundress over her suit. But the way he looked at her—and he only had eyes for her—made her feel both beautiful and shy. Marin never, never felt shy. He put his quarters down on the table to save the next game for him and his friends.

"Why don't the three of you play the next game against us," he suggested. "Boys against girls."

"Prepare to be dazzled by our pool playing, my friend," Marin said. "You boys will be shamed by our fancy moves."

"Really?"

"No. Really we suck. Seriously."

"We're pretty bad, too."

"I'm sure you're not worse than us. Most of the time we can't even keep the damn balls on the table."

They teased each other and themselves about who was worse at pool. (Turns out it was a draw—they were all pretty remedial.) After an hour or so of playing he invited all of them back to his house.

Marin looked at her girlfriends. They both nodded their eager agreement.

"Sure. We'll follow you."

In the car over to his house, it was all Marin and her friends could do to keep from bursting with excited giggles.

"He's gorgeous," Michelle declared.

"Totally hot," Brandie agreed.

"An older man. That is so sexy," Michelle said.

"And look at that car. He makes a ton of money."

"What if you guys get married? You'll be Mrs. Brent . . . what was his last name? Well, you'll Mrs. Rich Wife anyway."

"You guys, shut up. I've known him an hour. I think wedding plans are a bit premature." But Marin suppressed a smile as she said it. She had to admit that even though she'd only known him an hour, the idea of running off and marrying a rich older man—whether it was Brent or not—would fix a lot. It would get her out of the house. It would liberate her from having to rely on her father's money. She would be free at last.

At his house, Brent offered the trio of girls cocktails.

"You could get into really big trouble," Marin said. "We're only seventeen."

"Really? That's it? You seem a lot more mature than most seventeen-year-old girls. I certainly wouldn't want to lead you innocent girls down the road to debauchery."

The way he said "debauchery"—his grin, the look in his eyes, the tone of his voice—thrilled her. He was so much more mature and self-assured than the guys her age. He was sexy and dangerous and exciting.

"We've already been debauched aplenty. Don't worry. It won't be our first taste of alcohol."

"Somehow I didn't think so. Anyway, I'm a gambler by nature. I'll take my chances."

"A gambler, huh?"

"A risk taker, sure. You have to be if you want to be in business. Hell, if you want to succeed in life."

They talked and flirted for several hours. He took her number before Marin and her friends left, and for five anxious days she waited for him to call. With each day that passed she became more and more intrigued by him. She was used to guys calling her within hours—sometimes minutes—of her giving them her phone number.

When he did call and ask if he could take her out to dinner that weekend, she was thrilled. Going out with him was adventurous, exciting, risky. Not that her parents would ever find out. They never had a clue what was going on in her life, even if she told them. But still, she knew what she was doing behind their backs, and it excited her beyond words.

On their first date, he was a perfect gentleman. He bought her flowers, opened doors, ordered a bottle of wine—she didn't even get carded—and told her why this bottle of wine from Provence, France, was the perfect wine to accompany the meal. She loved that he knew about wine. She loved that the waiter didn't blink when he ordered it for the two of them. Around him she was sophisticated. A woman. No longer just some inexperienced high school kid.

She fell for him, hard. And for the first few weeks, she was delirious with happiness. Everything was perfect.

And then.

The first time he hit her they'd been dating for a month. It was just after New Year's and they'd been drinking and laughing and having fun. She couldn't even remember what they

were talking about, but she'd made a joke about him being secretly gay, and all humor evaporated from his expression immediately. His eyes filled with rage and he punched her in the
stomach.

Marin had been so shocked she burst into tears. She'd
never been hit in her entire life.

"Say you're sorry," he said.

"I'm sorry, are you nuts? I was kidding around and you
punch me? And you want me to say I'm sorry? I'm getting out
of here. Don't ever, ever call me again."

She went to leave his place and he came up behind her and
grabbed her by the arm so hard it left bruises; five purple circles around her arm.

"Ouch! That hurts. Let go of me!"

"You're not leaving until you say you're sorry," he said.

He meant it, she could see that. She could see how much he
wanted an excuse, any excuse, to hurt her even more. She saw
it, in his eyes, what he was capable of. All at once she was terrified.

"I—I'm sorry. I didn't mean anything by it."

She had tried to leave then. He insisted that she stay. She
said she was tired, it was late, she should get going. He wanted
her to stay. She stayed.

For the next several days, she refused to return his calls.
When he showed up after school a few days later and asked her
who exactly she thought she was, ignoring him, not returning
his calls, she said she was sorry, she'd been busy. She was so
scared of him that when he told her to get into his car, she did.
And when he called her the next day, she picked up the phone
and agreed to go out with him.

Marin never told anyone about Brent. Not her parents.
Not her friends. Not a counselor. She was embarrassed. Her
friends all thought Brent was such a catch. She was just doing
everything wrong, making him mad at her. She had to stop
making him mad at her. She could see in his eyes just how far
he'd go.

He never made any specific threats. He never said, "If you
try to leave me, I'll kill you." None of that "if I can't have you

no one will" business. But she knew that if she left, he would hurt her, really hurt her.

They dated for a few more months. She was always on guard with him, always watching what she was saying. She didn't joke around with him anymore. She was careful.

He hurt her twice more, once throwing her against the wall, which had left a terrible bruise on her back for days, once punching her in her stomach. He was always careful to make sure the bruises were hidden. He knew what he was doing, and it terrified her.

She felt trapped. If he got so angry over a comment here or there, what would he do to her if she tried to leave him? Where could she hide? He knew where she lived, where she went to school. He knew what nights she practiced late at the theater, practically alone in the enormous high school.

Then one night after she'd practiced late for the spring play, he asked for a blow job and she said she was really tired. They started yelling at each other. He accused her of sleeping with somebody else, of not loving him, of being with him just for his money.

"You're sleeping with him, that guy from the play."

"No, but maybe I should."

That's when he punched her in the face.

She tore out of his townhouse, hailed a taxi, and, sobbing in pain and embarrassment, she went home, her left eye swelling so much she could hardly see out of it. When she got home, the black eye couldn't be ignored, and her parents wanted to know what the hell was going on. She told them.

She had never seen her parents seem more concerned about her. Marin told them that she was scared for her life. That if she tried to leave him, he'd kill her. She was scared, but this attention her parents were giving her, it felt nice, too.

"I'm calling the police," her dad said.

"Dad, he won't spend any time in jail and then he'll really be mad." If he'd gotten so furious over a blow job, what would happen if she called in the police? "I'll be fine. I'll be going off to school soon, he won't be able to get to me. I've been thinking about it, and I thought that, instead of going to Boston

College or NYU, I'll go to Colorado, and you'll tell everyone, I mean everyone, that I'm going to Boston, and if he calls and asks about me, you tell him I went to college in Boston."

"Honey, all the way across the country? Lying to people? Are you sure all this is necessary? It was probably just a fluke thing, him hitting you. All the hiding and lying, it seems so dramatic," her mom said. "Maybe acting in all those plays has made you find drama where there isn't really any."

"You don't think this is dramatic?" Marin pointed to her eye. "This isn't the first time he's hit me, Mom. I've tried to break up with him, but I'm so scared of him, I'm scared he'll hurt me more if I try to leave him. If he can't find me, I won't have anything to worry about."

So that's what they did. Six weeks before the school year was out, she got approval to finish her classes via correspondence. Her understudy would take over the lead in the play. Marin wouldn't be able to attend any graduation parties or say goodbye to her friends.

Early one morning, when it was still dark out, her mother drove her to the airport. Marin would stay in her parents' house in Aspen until she could move into the dorms at the end of the summer. Just before her plane was about to take off at 9 A.M., she called Brent's voice mail—she knew he'd be at work already. She said she was leaving for college early, something had come up and she was sorry she hadn't had a chance to say a proper good-bye. She said she'd had a wonderful time with him, but she didn't think it would be a good idea to do the whole long distance thing. Oh? Hadn't she mentioned? She'd decided on Boston College instead of NYU after all.

She didn't go home for two years after that.

She hadn't fallen in love since. Not one serious relationship in all these years.

She dated, but she worried she couldn't fall in love.

She'd agreed to meet Andrew, the guy she'd met at aMuse the other night, at the new Chinese restaurant on Sixth Street. Andrew was cute—broad shouldered, with sandy hair and dark brown eyes. He worked at a venture capital firm in Boulder. She'd liked him because he'd seemed so sure of himself. Of course, they'd only talked for about fifteen minutes in a loud, crowded bar, so it wasn't like she knew him well. But it had been a long time since she'd had sex, and this dating crap was the best route to getting some.

She got to the restaurant a little late. He was already there, sitting at a table. He jumped up when he saw her. "Marin! I'm so glad you could make it!"

"Oh, yeah, um, sorry I'm late."

"No problem! So is this okay? Do you like Chinese?"

"Yeah, that's why I recommended this place."

"Right!" he laughed. He hadn't been this geeky and over-eager the other night. What was going on? "God, I've thought about you nonstop since the other night."

"Hmm."

"You're probably hungry. I should let you look at the menu."

She looked it over and the waitress came by. "A glass of plum wine, please."

"Me too!" Andrew said.

When the waitress left, Andrew said, in a mock Chinese voice, "Me lika the mu shoo pork. Me lika it long time."

Marin forced a smile. She could tell that he could tell the smile was forced. He shifted uncomfortably.

"So, tell me more about yourself," he said. "What's a gorgeous, funny woman like you doing being single?"

She shrugged. "I don't know. I guess I haven't met the right guy yet."

He launched into what he may have thought were funny tales of the hazards of dating, but Marin found him dull. He was trying too hard and it made everything worse.

Marin would have to do a better job of screening her dates in the future. What had happened? He'd seemed so cool the other night. Maybe he'd been drunk then and that relaxed him so he wasn't this eager-to-please dork. It was the story of Marin's dating life. It's not that she wanted guys to play games or play hard to get, but she wanted a guy who didn't get so nervous around her. She wanted a guy who didn't declare his love for her within hours of meeting her. Guys that said they were in love with her after so short a time obviously weren't in love with her but her appearance. She would get old one day, and these guys who liked her just for her looks would leave her for a younger, prettier woman. A relationship couldn't be based on attraction alone.

So many times Marin had had to break it off with a guy. She'd left a trail of crying men in her wake. She hated making men cry, but she couldn't go on any more dates with guys who didn't make her laugh. More times than she could count, guys had killed themselves trying to impress her—almost literally. There was Chris, the guy she'd gone skiing with who tried so hard to dazzle her with his skiing abilities that, as he zoomed down the mountain, watching her to make sure she was watching him, he crashed into a tree and broke his leg. Then there was the guy driving her to a restaurant, nervously glancing at her off and on the whole trip there, staring a few seconds too long—long enough to rear end a Jeep and total his car.

Whether they nearly mangled themselves or not, she was sick of going out on dates where every word uttered took awkward effort. She was sick of the endless strain of not connecting with someone, not feeling the fire, that spark. She wanted love, passion, fever. She was ready. It was time.

16

Stop the Clock on Christina's Fifteen Minutes Already

Jason sat at his desk working on lesson plans before his fourth-period class. So far, no mention of the cattle rancher or any sort of punishment had come up. Jason suspected that the rancher had thought he could put the fear of God into Jason and that alone would censor Jason's lesson plans henceforth. The rancher didn't know Jason well at all. If anything, Jason became more political than ever, while still being careful to avoid seeming militant by cracking jokes and keeping a smile on his face much of the time.

Sophomore Sarah Synnesvedt entered his office with a light knock.

"Come in," he said, gesturing to the chair in front of his desk. She started to close the door behind her. "No, no!" he said in mild panic. "Keep the door open please."

Sarah wore far too much make-up and too few clothes. Jason was only twenty-five years old, but he felt like some old fuddy-duddy who was horrified by teen fashion. Christina Aguilera was in cahoots with the devil as far as he was concerned. He wanted teenage girls to know that, in the case of fashion, less was not more, more was more.

He was also in a tricky position because, since he was just a few years older than the girls he taught, many of his female students thought they had a real chance of seducing him. He'd found countless notes that he was sure had been strategically planted talking about how hot Mr. Hess was and what sort of lascivious acts they'd like to engage in with him. He couldn't help but be shocked when he compared their behavior to his own at their age. He never would have behaved like that. He'd been shy with girls in high school and had dated the same girl from sophomore year to their freshman year in college. In his sophomore year they were still at the making-out-and-mild-waist-up-only groping stage. He'd thought about sex, certainly, but in the abstract way you dreamed about becoming a rock star or movie star, something distant and far off that you had no actual intentions of doing anything about to make the fantasy come true. He and his girlfriend waited until their senior year to have sex. Even though that was only two years older than the students he taught, he thought these sophomores seemed so much younger than he had ever been. He wanted them to stay innocent as long as they could. He tried to be a realist and remind himself he had been *exactly* that young when he was a sophomore, but his visceral instinct was to dress these kids in amorphous burlap-sacks and segregate them into gender-divided boarding schools where there was no access to the evils of MTV or teen movies.

"Mr. Hess?" Sarah fluttered her eyes, which were coated in glittery silver eye shadow. Jason knew nothing about make-up, but he knew for a fact that Ramiro would have pointed commentary to make about Sarah's over-the-top look. "I was a little confused about what you talked about the other day with the, um, mitochondria and organelles?"

He happily reviewed the concepts with her, delighted that he wouldn't have to deal with teaching about human reproduction until the spring. Every time she cooed about how smart he was, he deflected her compliments by quickly asking her to repeat back what he just said and how that applied to cells and energy or whatnot.

Sometimes Jason wondered if he could head off his students' flirtations by wearing a wedding ring, but he feared that this might make him even more appealingly unattainable.

When Sarah finally left, he had only ten minutes to get to class, so he closed the folder of papers he was grading, inadvertently knocking over the publicity photo of the members of Spur of the Moment that he kept on his desk. He righted it and paused a moment to look at it. It always made him feel good to have his best friends smiling at him. He focused his gaze to the left-hand corner of the picture where, if he'd had graphic software, he could have cropped everyone else out and it would have just been him and Marin.

They looked so good together—he'd always thought so.

He wished he could get over his crush. It was embarrassing and silly. But he was a guy who, when he fell, he fell hard. His first girlfriend had broken his heart when, a month after they started college together, she left him to date the fourth-floor resident advisor in her dorm. Jason hadn't dated anyone for the rest of his freshman year, hadn't even looked at anyone else, though there had been plenty of interested women. It wasn't until Marin that he'd been able to get over his high school sweetheart.

It didn't help that Jason and Marin slept together every now and then—usually in bursts of three, four, or five weeks at a time, although sometimes not for long stretches in between. Just when he thought he really should make a concerted effort to date someone else, they slept together again. In those giggly moments of making love, giving each other massages, and whispering things of no importance, he knew he couldn't date anyone else—it wouldn't be fair to the woman he tried to date. He loved Marin, wholly and passionately.

He figured that she was just young and didn't want to feel tied down. Frankly, he didn't think he was ready for marriage yet himself. Their lives were still too much in a state of flux. They worked crazy hours and drank too much and stayed up late more often than not. They weren't still in college, but this was also nothing like a life with a mortgage, two kids, steady hours, and a healthy balanced diet that wasn't heavily supplemented by beer and tequila. He liked it that way. For now.

17

The Restorative Powers of Pizza and Beer

After the misery of her date with What's-his-face, Marin needed some serious girl talk. She went into Ana's room carrying a six-pack of beer behind her back. Ana was sprawled across her bed with a vacant coma-like look in her eye.

"Are you hungry?" Marin asked.

"I'm starving, but I don't have the energy to make anything."

"I've ordered a pizza for us, and dun dun dun! Beer!" Marin revealed the beer.

"Mmm," Ana grunted. "That's nice of you. I don't actually know if I have the energy to hold a slice of pizza to my mouth, but it's a sweet gesture."

Marin took the caps off two beers, then lay down next to her friend.

"How did your date with guy from the bar go?" Ana asked.

"Ugh." Marin rolled her eyes.

"What went wrong? He seemed so cute Friday night."

"I don't even remember what he looks like anymore. I've blocked the whole experience out in a post-traumatic-stress-disorder-induced amnesia. I mean, at first I was kind of at-tracted to him because he seemed like the kind of guy who wouldn't nudge his friend in the ribs with his elbow going, 'dude, check her out.' He was really nervous, and I hoped maybe he'd calm down, but he never did. I was waiting for a spark to flame, but it was like the match was wet and it just wasn't going to work. He took me to the new Chinese place on Sixth Avenue, and the drink menus? Get this. For the description of the strawberry daiquiri, it said, 'every sip will bring you closer and closer to successful rolling.'"

Ana tried to make sense of that. "What? Is the place like a casino or something? What does that mean?"

"No, it's not a casino, and I have absolutely no idea what it means. Yes I do, it means they were robbed blind by the translator. So then for the margarita, it said, 'every sip will bring you closer and closer to heave.' "

Ana burst out laughing. "It did not!" The more she thought about it, trying to figure out what it should have said, the more hilarious she found it. Ana's laughter was infectious, and Marin joined her. The women's giggles fed on each other.

"And then? And then? At the bottom it said, 'we have different glasses!' With an exclamation point!"

Ana's laughter exploded in a renewed wave of giggles. "That's their big selling point? Where did they find their copywriter?" Ana thought a moment, then repeated, 'Will bring you closer and closer to heave.' " The two whooped with laughter.

Marin loved the sound of her friend's laugh. Hearing it brought back all the memories of all the great times they'd had together over the last six years. It reminded Marin how much she loved Ana. The sound of Ana's laughter made Marin feel happy and safe.

"I think they meant to say 'heaven,' not 'heave.' " Marin said when she was finally able to talk again.

"Oh, that makes sense. But what about the other one? 'It'll bring you closer and closer to successful rolling.' What were they going for?"

"I have no idea."

"Hey girls, I have some pizza for you." It was Scott. "You got enough for everybody, right?"

"I thought you boys already had McDonald's for dinner," Marin said.

"McDonald's? Where is Jason?" Ana asked. He would never approve.

"He's at the peace vigil," Scott said. "So do we get pizza or not? It's the perfect after-dinner treat."

"You boys can scrounge through our crumbs when we're done. Now scoot, we have important girl business to discuss."

The laughing, beer, and aroma of pizza had renewed Ana's energy, and she sat up and tore into the pizza with Marin.

"I'm really kind of bummed it didn't work out with What's-his-face today. I haven't had sex in about forty years."

"Shut up, it's been a coupla weeks for you. I haven't had sex in a year."

"A year! You're shitting me."

"I shit you not. Not since Matt."

"Damn girl, that is serious."

"It's very serious. It's critical. It's code blue critical. You know how in cartoons, when the guy is hungry, he'll look at his friend and his friend will look like a turkey leg to him?"

"Yeah?"

"That's how I'm looking at every guy I see. They are all just meat for me to ravage. Just last night I was looking at Scott and I was like, *you know, he's actually pretty cute.* He just hides it so well with his goofiness."

"You should go for it. He's always thought you're hot."

"What*ever.* What makes you think that?"

"It's so obvious."

"If he's so hot for me, why didn't he ever try anything?"

"Ana, if you'll recall a certain marathon smooch fest in the Spur of the Moment coat closet, he did try something once, but mostly he keeps his distance because he knows you're all crushed out on Jason. But you should give it a shot, see where it goes."

"No, no, it was just a product of my desperation. I need to get a real boyfriend. What is wrong with us? We're all cute, and except for Ram, none of us have ever had a really serious relationship."

"You were with Matt for seven months."

"Oh whoopee, seven months. Anyway, it was never that serious. He was cute and funny—well, he was sort of funny, but just not as funny as you guys. I just had more fun with you guys and I was always annoyed when I had to go out with him. I kept trying to talk myself into liking him because it seemed like I should like him. Like if I were writing a personal ad, I'd say, 'I want a guy who is cute and smart and kind and funny,' which he was, but, I don't know. Maybe I'm not capable of love."

"You love us," Marin said.

"That's true."

"That's probably what the problem is—we're each other's families, so we're not motivated to go out and start families of our own. We do everything you do in a family. We support each other, have fun together, we love each other. We have everything you'd get from being married."

"Except sex."

"Oh yeah, except sex." Marin sighed.

"Hey, I don't want to hear it from you. You can have Jason anytime."

"No, I'm calling it quits this time."

Ana rolled her eyes.

"No, I mean it this time. It's just too much trouble. He always starts thinking that we have a chance to become something more than fuck buddies. He follows me around all moony-eyed and telling me how much he loves me. It's exhausting."

"Yeah, I can see how it'd be a real drag to have somebody telling you how wonderful you are and how much he loves you."

Marin stuck her tongue out at Ana.

Ana sighed contentedly. "Marin, thank you so much for the beer and pizza. It gave me just enough energy to stagger downstairs to put my laundry in the dryer and then collapse into bed."

"You're welcome. Smooch smooch, babe." Marin and Ana exchanged air kisses and hugged.

It was exactly what they'd needed.

18

The Cluster Fuck, Part Three

When Ana wasn't practicing or performing, she spent every free second publicizing and coordinating the show.

She was ready to drop dead from exhaustion.

Ordinarily, just working the forty-plus hours at Abbott Technology made her want to collapse in front of the TV and be nothing more than a remote-control-changing sloth until she was able to fall asleep. Now she wasn't just working forty-plus hours, as well as working nights at Spur of the Moment, and spending every free night practicing and writing scripts, she was using every moment she could find to coordinate getting the show together and properly promoted.

Tom agreed to work the lights and sound for a beer, the typical exchange rate between underpaid performers. Chelsey would work the ticket booth and Jason would walk people to their seats since neither of them was on until the third scene.

In addition to all the time outside of the office she spent on the show, Ana did her best to avoid work while at work in favor of doing stuff for the performance. She'd spent the morning pounding out a news release that she'd send to journalists in the area a week or so before the show.

Ana's phone rang. It was The Weasel. "Ana, I need to meet with you."

"When?" Ana said, annoyed that he was bothering her when she had much more important personal things to work on.

"Right now."

Ana hung up the phone and sighed a sigh that the entire floor could hear, such was her angst.

"The Weasel?" Scott guessed.

Ana nodded, aggrieved. Scott offered a parting impression of The Weasel.

The name The Weasel came out of an improv scene Ana and Scott had done when they were still in the Iron Pyrits together. At the time, Scott had already graduated and been working at Abbott for a year. Ana had been in her senior year of college.

In the scene, Ana played an office underling, Scott played her boss, and Jason was the president of the company. Ana kept coming up with great ideas for the new product launch, and Scott would take her ideas, run to the president, claim them as his own in a very Dilbert pointy-haired boss way. When Jason would say something like, "Yes, that's a great idea. But what should we call it?" Scott said, "Um, let me get my notes." Then he'd scurry across the stage to Ana, making this "pht-pht-pht" noise reminiscent of Hannibal Lecter's fava bean speech, except in a higher-pitched squirrelly tone. After Scott had dashed back and forth from Ana and Jason a couple times, he paused mid-scurry and faced the audience to at last explain why he was making this strange noise. "Weasels are fast, ferocious, and able to *weasel* our way in or out of tight spaces. Weasels' pelts change color with the season, a camouflage that allows us to blend into changing environments. And, we are deft at stealing from other animals. I am The Weasel! I am invincible!"

Plus, Scott's comical, fast-paced mincing steps across the stage were much appreciated. Making the "pht-pht-pht" noise required him to pull his bottom lip under his teeth, scrunch up his nose, and generally make a face that, in and of itself, made people laugh. The audience loved it. Ana loved it.

After the show that night, sprawled across their couches, imbibing beer with gusto, Ramiro and Jason were discussing the finer points of the latest episode of *The Simpsons*, and Ana, recalling Scott's character, starting chuckling to herself.

"What are you laughing about?" Marin had asked.

"Pht-pht-pht . . ." was all Ana could manage before doubling over in laughter. Scott smiled, pleased that she was reinforcing his view of himself as a comic genius.

Ramiro stopped what he was saying about the inherent hilarity of Homer and Mel Gibson stealing the Mad Max car from the Hollywood Auto Museum and joined the new trajectory of the conversation without skipping a beat. "That *was* pretty funny."

"It's my boss to a tee," Scott said. "He's full of shit but he has this incredible gift for getting in and out of tight spots by lying. I almost admire him for it. He is really just this conniving weasel."

From then on, whenever Scott referred to his boss, it was as The Big Weasel. When The Big Weasel became Ana's boss, too, Scott's impression took on even greater meaning, and it made her laugh even harder.

"Hey boss, what's up?" Ana said.

"I have the changes to the email."

"The email?"

"Alerting clients to the changes in Consensys 6.0."

Oh right, the spam email content with which they would harass their clients around the globe. This was Ana's contribution to society: Writing spam email copy.

The original deadline had been so long ago, Ana had forgotten about the project completely. The Weasel handed her back the draft of the email, barely visible beneath his myriad comments in red ink.

She read his remarks as she returned to her desk and felt her mood wither. He'd said that her intro was weak, she needed a better transition, and in general it needed to be shortened. He'd rewritten parts of it. Ana tried to decide if what he'd written was better. In a couple of cases, maybe it was.

She wasn't really a bad writer, was she? God, maybe she was really terrible at absolutely everything. Maybe she wasn't funny or talented and would never make it as a performer, and she wouldn't even have a marketing job to fall back on, because she apparently sucked at that too.

When Ana got back to her desk, she said to Scott, "I want to jump out of the window."

"Please don't, at least not until after the show. Who will take over your parts?"

Despite herself, Ana smiled.

"Come on. We'll get some sandwiches from the cafeteria and enjoy one of the last pleasant days of the year before it snows and we're stuck at home hibernating under blankets for the next five months."

Ana agreed. They went downstairs and got sandwiches, chips, and Diet Coke (Ana) and Coke (Scott).

Behind their office building there was a small area on a cement patio with picnic tables and, behind that, a small lawn and a sprinkling of trees that, with a little suspension of disbelief, could be considered secluded.

When Scott stopped on the patio, Ana said, "I don't want to eat here. Let's find a grassy knoll somewhere."

Scott followed Ana agreeably as she walked passed the picnic area and across the lawn.

"What is a knoll anyway?" he asked.

"It's a, um"—Ana rolled her free arm in sort of wave motion—"and then there are trees. It's kind of a hill . . . or maybe it's sort of concave?"

"Like a ditch?"

Ana laughed. "Not a ditch, I don't think."

"Are there gravelly knolls? Rocky knolls? Pot-holey knolls?"

"I don't know, maybe, but who'd want to have a picnic on a gravelly knoll?"

Scott nodded sagely, as if this were a wise conclusion indeed. They sat under a willow tree on a spot of grass that wasn't particularly knolly, but the trees' long wispy branches gave them a nice feeling of privacy.

Ana scarfed down her sandwich in minutes and told Scott she'd better get back to work.

"Ana, you've been on break for"—he looked at his watch—"seven minutes. And you wonder why you're always stressed out?"

"But I have so much to do!"

"Girlfriend, you need to slow down. Hang with me a few minutes. Come here. Lie down next to me. Let's look at the clouds."

"Look at the clouds?!" she yelped, as if he'd proposed they strip off all their clothes and streak through the streets of downtown Denver.

"When was the last time you just took a few minutes to stare at the clouds?"

Ana thought for a moment. "Does when I'm flying in an airplane and looking at the blanket of clouds under me count?"

"No, when was the last time you just stared at the clouds and tried to think of what things they resemble?"

"I haven't done that since I was a little kid, what with cloud staring being a quintessentially kid activity."

"Bullshit."

"I haven't played with Barbie dolls since I was a kid either. It's just a kid thing."

"Ana, it's a good exercise for your imagination."

That got her. She was always meaning to work on improving her imagination.

She lay back and looked at the clouds.

"What do you see?" he asked.

"Particles of condensed vapor being pushed around the Earth's atmosphere by the wind."

"Very creative, Ana. I bet they named you that in your yearbook, 'Most Creative.' "

She stuck her tongue out at him. "So what do you see, mister smarty pants?"

"I see a mama duck with three little baby ducks following her."

"What? Where?"

He brought his face so close to hers their cheeks touched. When their eyes were at about the same level, he pointed up. "The clouds that are straight up from that brick building, the one with the Absolut vodka billboard right in front of it. See how in front it looks like a duck's beak and little webbed feet sort of waddling and these cute little guys following it?"

Ana looked really hard. She squinted, as if she were trying

to see an image in one of those Magic Eye pictures that looked like gobbledygook until you were so bored you hallucinated that you saw a hidden image. "If I squint real hard I can sort of get an abstract-painting feel for a duck or two." Once she saw it, abstract though it was, she imagined the little clouds of baby chicks waddling through the sky.

"Have you ever seen baby ducks following their mom?" he asked.

"I'm sure I've seen some on TV."

"No, I mean live. It's so cute. They just kind of march along, stopping traffic, like they are the most important things ever, like they have this super urgent meeting to get to, and of course everyone stops and 'ohhhhs' because baby ducks are these adorable little puffs of black and yellow fuzz that melt everyone's hearts. So one time, I forget where I was, the babies were following their mom, the whole town had come to a standstill to watch them, and one of the babies fell through a grate!"

"Oh no!"

"That's what we all said. The mama duck was squawking her head off, and the other baby ducks fell out of line like soldiers at ease except for like, totally confused and baffled soldiers at ease, and all the people watching, we were having a sort of communal heart attack. We were all just having a fit for like a minute, and then this fearless little girl ran up, squeezed her hand into the little, watchamacallit, sewer drain thingy, and pulled the duck out, wet and a little irritated by the delay, but otherwise unharmed, and the baby duck just joined her siblings and they started marching off again."

"Oh, that's adorable. That's so cute." Ana realized that in only a matter of minutes, she felt infinitely better. Far less stressed out. Almost happy even. "What else do you see?" she asked. "Oh, oh, I see one, I see Tigger hopping on his tail, see?"

"No, that's The Weasel, pulling a bunch of bullshit lies out of his ass."

"Yes! Yes! That's exactly what it is."

Scott did his squirrel doing the Hannibal Lecter fava bean

thing while saying, "I'm good at marketing, pht-pht-pht-pht-pht."

Ana rolled with laughter, so Scott kept dishing it out.

Ana's good mood lasted until it was quarter to six and she was just about to shut off her computer, when Deb Myers came up behind her and said, "I need you to finish this up tonight for the meeting tomorrow morning. I'm afraid I can't stay because I have to pick Reagan up from daycare. If you get there even one minute late, they start charging you a ton of money for each minute after six! All you have to do is grab the information from other presentations and proposals we've done. Just edit it and get it into shape. It won't take any time at all. I emailed you the electronic document. If you could just print out seven copies and put it in the box outside my office before eight tomorrow morning, that'd be great."

Ana took the stack of papers Deb was holding. It didn't look like that thick a proposal. She could probably review it in fifteen minutes or so. She'd still have plenty of time to get to her seven o'clock practice for the sketch comedy show.

"Ta!" Deb called, and, before Ana could even glance at the first page of the proposal, Deb was out the front door.

It was only nine pages. Not bad at all. Then she looked through and found out why it was so short—Deb hadn't done anything except to put instructions for what Ana should add. Okay, well, most of the information had been written before, somewhere. She just had to find it.

She decided to start with the easy stuff. Quickly adding bulk to the proposal would give her a sense of accomplishment.

Executive bios. No problem. They were all handily available on the company website.

Except two of the execs had left the company and had been replaced by two different people. Nuts. It had been on her to-do list to update these on the site. Wait, hadn't she already done this? Maybe the webmaster just hadn't done it yet. She knew she'd written something up about Don Hines and Dick Polish when they'd joined the company. Where, where, where . . .

News releases! She'd written news releases on them.

Now, where on the network had she filed them? She didn't write that many news releases; they usually came from the corporate office in California, so it wasn't like there were a ton of them for her to keep track of. Did she file them under their respective names?

She searched. Nope.

Maybe something from the headline. She searched for "new execs," "welcomes," "management." Nothing, nothing, nothing.

She finally did a search on the entire network for their names within all text documents. Of which there were a lot. So it took forever.

She finally found them under the dates she'd sent the releases out: 082202.doc and 091502.doc. Like that was a handy way to store files. Like she'd magically remember when she'd sent them out.

She created a folder under "Ana" called "releases" and retitled the releases "hines.doc" and "polish.doc."

She culled information from each release and added it to the proposal, reformatting as she went. She looked at the clock. 6:05. It had taken her twenty minutes to do the easiest part of the proposal. She had at least fifteen more sections to do.

At seven o'clock, she was only about halfway done. She was going as fast as she possibly could, but it just took time to track down the information from all the zillions of different reports they put together. This was exactly why she never got all the various Word files in order—because by the time her superiors handed the project to her, it was a mere few hours away from the deadline, and she didn't have time.

The nerve of Deb! This was not the first time she'd pulled the "I have to get my kid at daycare" excuse for leaving the office at a reasonable hour. It wasn't that Ana thought parents should leave their kids in daycare 24/7 so they could work around the clock, it was that NO ONE should be expected to work twelve-hour days. What did Deb think, that just because Ana was single and didn't have kids, she had no life outside of work and thus of course should stay late to finish a project that, Hello! they could have started on three weeks ago when they booked the meeting rather than this afterfuckingnoon? Ga!

Ana flew through the rest of the proposal. She knew she was doing crappy work. Her plan was to come in at six tomorrow morning and pretty it up when she had a fresh eye instead of eyes that were tearing up with anger and frustration. Then she'd print out seven copies of what would likely be a thirty- or forty-page proposal and hope like hell the copier didn't break before the meeting at eight A.M.

This was such bullshit. She was always having to stay late at work. She wouldn't mind if she were an ER doctor who saved people's lives or a NASA research scientist or a biologist researching the cure for AIDS, but she *marketed software*. All she spent her days doing was making a few executives and stockholders rich while working herself into an early grave from depression and anxiety.

19

Inside Jokes

Scott watched Ana come into the room and apologize for being late. As always, he thought she looked beautiful.

"Where are you at? What have you done so far?" Ana asked the group.

"Well, we were waiting for you, so we started talking and we sort of didn't stop," Chelsey said.

Scott watched Ana's eyes light up in horror and he couldn't help but chuckle. Ana got stressed out over the stupidest stuff. But he loved her anyway.

"Well, I mean, I guess I was late, we're even. Okay, so Ram, did you bring the sketches you've been working on so we can start practicing?" Ana said.

"I, I tried to work on them . . . but I don't know. They're not really any good. I don't think there's anything worth salvaging."

"We need to get the scripts done! We have to start memorizing our parts!" Ana yelped.

"It's okay," Jason said, "we'll help him work on the sections he's having trouble with. Together, we'll get it done in no time."

The six of them gathered around the table and read through the first script. It was good. It was really good. There were a few places where Ram had written in notes like "fill this out" or "not funny enough." He was far too hard on himself. His scripts were much further along then he thought. For the next three hours, the six of them tossed around ideas and made suggestions for changes and edits to his first script. Ramiro was the hardest one to please. He didn't think anything was good enough. He would have kept rewriting and rewriting his work if it hadn't been for a universal vote from the other five that said his script was finished and he wasn't allowed to make any more changes. Naturally, all the stuff they were working on would evolve regardless of declared moratoriums on changes—everything was a work in progress right up until the moment they hit the stage in front of a live audience.

"Okay, how about my script," Scott said. He got up and began his dance moves. Jason bellowed, "Chuck tried the bar scene. He took out a personal ad. Nothing worked. He was still just a lonely slob. Then he tried three-minute dating!"

Scott let out one more Roger Rabbit move, and that's when he farted spectacularly. He looked sheepish as his friends started coughing and laughing and covering their faces. To his chagrin, his perpetual flatulence was legendary among his friends.

As he frequently said in times of olfactory crises, Ramiro joked, "Dude, your ass could win an Oscar for best supporting actor it's got so much personality."

Jason rushed to open a window.

"Okay, we have to get back to work," Ana said, her face contorted in agony. "No, forget it, I can't concentrate amid this stench."

"I think we need more alcohol," Scott said. "We can drink our misery away."

All night, they'd been pilfering shots of tequila or a beer here and there from the Spur of the Moment bar. At first, Jason wouldn't have any on moral grounds.

"Jason, why do you always have to be such a stick in the mud?" Ana said.

"What kind of world do we live in that having morals is seen as a character flaw?" he said.

Ana considered this. Maybe he had a point.

Then Scott said, "Come on Jason, have some. We're going to have to buy them another bottle of Cuervo anyway. I'll buy the bottle tomorrow after work and bring it over."

Jason accepted that plan. Now that they didn't have to worry about skimming a small enough amount of liquor that it would go unnoticed, they lost any hesitation to consume Spur of the Moment Theater's alcohol. In less than an hour, they were sprawled in their chairs.

"So," Chelsey slurred—she'd had a beer and two shots, more alcohol than she usually drank in one sitting, "I want to know all of your guy's dirty secrets. Who's going to start?"

"We have no dirty secrets," Scott said. "We're all pristine. Clean slates and all that."

"I'm gay. I figure that covers me on dirty secrets for the rest of my life," Ramiro said.

"Except for the part about how it's not secret," Ana pointed out. "Of course Chelsey, we all know your darkest secret, being a Diet Red Stallion addict who *refuses* help."

Chelsey ignored this. "Ram, so . . . I'm sure you're sick of telling the story about how your parents reacted when you came out?"

"We haven't heard the story," Ana said. "At least I haven't."

"I'll tell you about my dad and you can guess how he took it. He's super macho and super Catholic. So there you go. Mom was okay with it, just worried about Dad," Ramiro said.

"When did you come out?" Chelsey said.

"My senior year in high school. Dad freaked. He barely spoke to me that whole year and is still pissed at me. He only let me start coming to family dinners again because Mom and Yo made him."

"Who's Yo?" Chelsey asked.

"Short for Yolanda, my twin sister."

"You're kidding, you have a twin sister?" Chelsey said.

"You haven't met her?" Ana said.

"She comes to our shows all the time," Ramiro said.

"During this year that I've worked with you?"

"Probably. Or actually, maybe not. She and her husband live in Littleton, and they just had a kid a year ago, so they don't go out as much as they used to."

"You guys keep forgetting that I don't have the history you all do."

Marin: "Sorry hon. Can we win you back over with boot-legged alcohol?"

Ramiro: "Come on, a delicious shot of tequila. We'll bring it to you on our hands and knees because you know how much we love you and worship you and couldn't live life without you."

Jason: "It's true."

"Absolutely," Scott chorused.

Chelsey pretended to continue to seem pouty. "O-*kay*," she finally conceded, doing her best not to smile.

20

Daddy's Girl

Marin hated to do it, but she was short of money again and needed to cover her rent. She inhaled deeply and dialed her father's number at work.

She got Gloria, his secretary, as usual. And was told, as usual, that he was on the other line. "It's very important," Marin said. "I'll hold."

Gloria put her on a hold, then a few minutes later picked up the line. "He wants to know how much you want."

"Can't I talk to him?" The comment stung. When Marin called her father, it usually *was* to borrow money. But that was only because she dreaded speaking to him so much she only did it when it was truly necessary.

"Hold on."

A few minutes later, her father's booming voice came on the line. "How much do you want?" he barked.

"Dad, hi. How are you?"

"I'd be great once you grow up and get a real job." He said it like an order. It was really the only way he knew how to talk. He was a man who knew what he wanted and got it. She was the only thing he couldn't control and manipulate entirely. "I'm a busy man, Marin. Tell me how much you need and I'll have Gloria get you a check. One of these days you're going to have to grow up, but I don't have time to figure out what the solution for you is now."

She wanted to tell him that she and her friends were putting on a show, she wanted to tell him about the bad date she'd gone on with the guy she'd met at the club the other night, she wanted to tell him about her life. But what was the point? The only thing he cared about was money, and it was the one thing she just couldn't figure out. She wasn't stupid, but she didn't have a head for numbers or details. She didn't always remember to write down how much she'd written a check for, and she never could get her checkbook balanced. And when she tried to figure out how much she was making from her temp jobs, she didn't always remember to account for taxes being taken out and didn't always calculate her hours worked correctly. She had no head for mundane things like budgets. She'd just gotten another statement from her bank saying she was overdrawn on her account and she owed them $25 in fees for writing a bad check. She was always receiving these things. She hated herself for racking up so much in stupid bank fees, but she couldn't seem to stop writing bad checks. She didn't mean to do it, it just sort of happened. "Seven hundred would do it," she said quietly.

He snorted in disgust. "I'll have Gloria send it out." Then he hung up the phone without saying goodbye.

Marin hated that everyone in her family thought she was a flake. What she hated even more was acknowledging they were right.

21

Dreams

It was just after midnight, and Ana couldn't fall asleep. Yet another hazard of working crazy late hours Thursday through Saturday—it messed up her sleep cycle. When Sunday night came, and she told her body that it must go to sleep now because it had to get up at six in the morning, it paid her no mind. No matter how lethargic she was during the day, yawning dramatically every few minutes or so, staggering through the hours only by virtue of sheer will, when she went to bed, she was suddenly as alert as a tightrope walker on a high wire. If she tried to read or do anything remotely productive, the weary stupor promptly overtook her again, so she'd close her book, shut her eyes, and be zapped by a lighting bolt of nervous energy, in a vicious circle that kept her exhausted.

So, the only thing left to do was to fantasize. Ana hoped her fantasies would eventually morph into dreams, and she wouldn't have to negotiate with her body and mind to get the hell to sleep already.

After she met Jason, her fantasies about her father waltzing into her life bearing riches, villas in Italy, condos in Hawaii, expensive cars, and a life of leisure were replaced with fantasies of Jason finally realizing that she was the woman of his dreams and not Marin. Other times, she didn't care if he fell in love with her and promptly demanded that they got married—

sometimes, she would be happy to settle for a simple romp in the hay.

The fantasies came in a variety of self-esteem flavors. On the high end of the spectrum, there was the one in which Ana was noticed by a talent scout and immediately flown to New York or L.A. to a) be in a movie, or b) perform live as a stand-up comedian. (Though she'd never done stand-up in her life, in her fantasy, she'd already created a side-splitting hour-long routine and had miraculously avoided having to do open mike nights or bombing in front of a crowd, and had emerged, like a baby from a stork delivered whole and without any of the messy and painful birthing rigmarole, as an astonishingly talented comedian.) Jason would (a) see her movie, or (b) see her performance, and bam! just like that, his Marin-clouded vision would clear and he'd finally see that he and Ana were meant to be together.

On the low end of the spectrum were fantasies that she got Jason drunk and he accidentally slept with her or that he just gave up on Marin and settled for her.

What was wrong with him that he didn't see how perfect he and Ana were for each other?

Her feelings for Jason weren't always overwhelmingly intense. Her lust and love for him seemed to come in waves. She always, always cared for him and admired him, but to sustain that level of passion all the time would have killed her. Sometimes she thought it might be possible for her to find a new guy to occupy her last thoughts before she fell asleep, another guy to fantasize and lust after. But then he would say something or smile just so and she believed him falling in love with her wasn't so impossible after all, she would be filled with fresh hope.

She didn't believe there was only one man on the entire planet who could make her happy. But so far, she hadn't found another guy who fit the bill as well as Jason did.

But even if her unrequited love kept on being unrequited, at least her professional dreams were going to take off. She could feel it. This show would change everything. All these nights of performing for peanuts and getting no recognition were going to change. Granted, preparing for it was exhausting, but it was a good learning experience. And working on it made her so happy. If only she could quit her day job and get paid for what she loved, she was sure she wouldn't be so stressed all the time. She'd sleep well and have a life that was at last fulfilling. She just needed a break . . .

At last, Ana fell asleep, her daydreams blending into her sleeping dreams.

22

Bruising Pinky Fingers on the DELETE Key

Chelsey didn't have to work at the club on Monday, so she spent the day at Spur of the Moment, using the computer in the office to work on a skit. Well, that had been her plan, but for the last three hours, all she'd done was typed sentences and then deleted them. The screen remained obstinately, unimaginatively blank for the better part of the time she'd attempted to labor. She had hit the delete key so many times, she was worried she'd bruised her pinky finger.

First she thought she'd try something making fun of how movie producers are infamous for mangling writer's art into junk. Then she realized she was stealing directly from the movie *The Majestic* with Jim Carrey. DELETE!

That was it. Her only idea. And she'd stolen it.

She could not think of a single thing that was even remotely funny. She knew that getting back to writing was hard when she hadn't been doing it regularly. Once she got into the groove and forced herself to write on a regular basis, it would get a lot easier and the ideas would come flowing out.

This was too damn hard. Telling people how to get the most out of their workouts was so much easier. And she had actually thought she wanted to do this for a living, writing for HBO, Sarah Jessica Parker or no Sarah Jessica Parker? She must have been insane.

Okay, okay, you make up stuff every night at improv. Just make

up a few ideas, vomit out some sentences, and edit the hell out of it
until it doesn't suck.

Chelsey took another gulp of Diet Red Stallion for energy, wrote down a bunch of nouns and verbs on slips of paper, put them into a bowl, and pulled two out at random. What she got was "Mom" and "Drunk."

Instantly, a smile came to her face. She remembered the last time she'd gone out for drinks with a mom. The woman was thirty and had two kids under the age of eight, and she'd hired Chelsey to help her lose the weight from her last pregnancy. The woman, Jennifer, loved motherhood and being a mom, but she'd revealed to Chelsey that it had been *forever* since she'd had a night on the town. She'd pounded back the beers and when eleven o'clock rolled around (Chelsey had a seven A.M. session with a client) and Chelsey suggested they get going, Jennifer looked like a kid who had been told Santa wouldn't be coming this year. Whereas Chelsey went out constantly and this was no big deal to her, Jennifer clearly wanted to milk her girls' night out for all it was worth. Drawing on this memory, Chelsey began to type.

Characters:
Ana = the Mom
Chelsey = Mom's friend
Rest of gang = innocent bystanders at nearby tables

Ana
(Drunk. Walks over to neighboring table. Gives lots of hugs. Pounds fist on table and says, as if she were giving the one most critical piece of advice she'd honed from all her years on the planet:)
Have sex. Have lo'ss and lo'ss of sex, whenever you can, 'specially when you're young . . . I 'ad my kizz young. No time for sex. No energy. Have sex now! Lo'ss and lo'ss!

Chelsey
(Grabs friend away)

I'm sorry. I'm really, really sorry. (whispers conspiratorially) She doesn't get out much. She has *kids*.

(Gang gets back to the conversation they were having)

Ramiro
So, like I was saying, we get out of the car and we smell this horrible odor. We figure, you know, it must be Lake Michigan, the dead fish or something. We spend an hour or so checking out the lake, then we head over to this barbecue joint. We get out of the car and then we smell that horrible scent again. We're like, what's going on? We wonder if we'd hit a skunk or something. So I walk to the front of the car, and there is part of a deer long dead and stuck to the grill—it had been cooking on the hood of our car for god knows how many miles . . .

(Gasps, laughs, and oh grosses! from the chorus. Meanwhile, Chelsey is trying to get Ana to stay put so Chelsey can go to the bathroom. Ana keeps slipping off chair. Chelsey tries to right her, gets her back up finally, then exits stage right.)

Ramiro
So it turns out . . .

Ana (Comes back to their table)
I have jus' one thing to tell ya. Have sex now! (Slams hand on table.) I luv my babies. I luv 'em. But I wish I'da had more sex when I was young . . .

(Chelsey re-enters)
Chelsey
Oh god, you guys, I'm sorry.

Marin
Don't worry about it. She's not bothering us.

Chelsey (Coaxing)
Come on, Ana, leave the nice people alone.

Ana
Okay, okay, okay. I jus' got one more thing to say. Have lo'ss
of sex! (Slams hand on table. This time her breast gets stuck
in Marin's beer glass. As Chelsey pulls Ana away, the glass of
beer, still attached to her breast, gets pulled across the table.
Marin gets wide eyed and tries to rescue it. Grabs it at last
minute before it falls off table. Ana has copious amounts of
foam on her newly liberated bosom)

Chelsey snickered at the image. *God, I'm hysterical! I'm probably the funniest woman in America!*

Chelsey literally patted herself on the back. Ah yes, *this* was
why she'd wanted to be a sitcom writer.

23

Fire

Chelsey had never felt such overpowering lust toward anyone before. Usually, she was too busy tallying up information about a guy to make a pragmatic decision about whether they should date. Did he have the same political beliefs as her? Did he want kids? Had he cheated on girlfriends in the past? Had he stayed at one job for a decent length of time, or was he always job-hopping, never satisfied with what he had? Did he smoke? Do drugs? Did he make her laugh? Did she make him laugh? Was she attracted to him?

Even if he met all her criteria, so often when they'd go out it would turn out that he was a terrible kisser or miserable in bed, or he decided he didn't like her or he wanted to get back with an ex. Or there was always that ethereal, can't-put-your-finger-on-it *get* factor: Did you *get* each other? Some things couldn't be fixed or compromised. They were the immutable laws of lust, love, and desire.

With Rob, she didn't worry about anything. From the moment he'd told her he'd enjoyed the show, she'd wanted to tear his clothes off. He was one of the hottest guys on the entire planet as far as she could tell. So as far as being attracted to him, that was a no-brainer. And as for his kissing talents and ability in bed, he scored a perfect ten. What was weird, though, was how everything Chelsey learned about him made her like him even more. And he wasn't shy about letting her know how great he thought she was. He called when he said he'd call, and he always said things like, "God, I always have so much fun when I'm with you." Or, "Man, it's so great to see you. I've missed you so much." Yet Chelsey didn't feel smothered. She didn't feel like he was some desperate, lonely sap who would date anyone just to avoid another Saturday night at home alone.

It had been hard starting a relationship when she was busy almost every night of the week, but they saw each other as much as they could. Chelsey worked her schedule out at Spur of the Moment so that her days off coincided with when he was off work. Then, breaking tradition, she would skip the show altogether and go out to dinner with Rob, or he would cook for her, or she would order Chinese for them.

Tonight, Rob had the evening off and Chelsey had taken it off to celebrate her birthday. Rob told her he'd made reservations at a special restaurant, and that they absolutely had to wait to have sex until after dinner. They'd had a pesky little habit of tearing each other's clothes off the moment they saw each other, and then missing the movie they'd planned to see or arriving appallingly late to the club where they were going to meet friends.

"We can restrain ourselves," Chelsey said. "Or maybe you can just come a little early."

"I can't. I have to help my friend Tim move, and I don't think we'll get done before five or six."

"We're adults. We can be strong."

It was 6:35 when Rob arrived at her house. "That's not fair," he said when she opened the door to let him in. "You can't dress like that and expect me to be able to keep my hands off you."

She was wearing a super short, super tight black dress and her black sandals with the wedge heels. She wore her curly hair long, exuberant with volume and highlights.

Rob pressed Chelsey against the wall, kissed her hard, parted her legs with his knee, and reached under her dress in a quick flash of movement that left her breathless.

They had sex right there against the wall, and there was something so sexy about Rob and their lust she came in two minutes flat and he followed not long after.

Chelsey struggled to catch her breath. She straightened out her dress. "Oh my," she breathed. "We are so efficient. We won't even be late for dinner."

"Sorry about that, I'll make it up to you later."

"Oh honey, there is nothing to be sorry about."

They got to the restaurant and ordered a bottle of wine. After they'd ordered, Rob said, "I have a present for you."

"Yeah!" Chelsey clapped her hands.

"Let me guess, you were a cheerleader in high school."

"No, actually a jock. Volleyball, basketball, and track."

"So you're into sports."

"I'm into playing them more than watching them, except for pro basketball. But that's only because I'm from Chicago and Michael Jordan is the best athlete in the world."

"What? He's not even close."

"What do you mean?"

"Jim Thorpe?"

"Who's Jim Thorpe?"

"Please tell me you're kidding." She shrugged helplessly. "Didn't they teach you anything in school? Like how the greatest athlete in the world was an Indian?"

"Um, I studied kinesiology. I learned about how the human body works?" She was woefully ignorant. She vowed to go to the bookstore the next day and buy every book there was about Indians. "What was so great about him?" she asked.

"Let's see, he won both the pentathlon and decathlon events in the 1912 Olympics. That same year, he led his Carlisle Indian School team to the national collegiate championship, scoring 25 touchdowns and 198 points."

"No way, that's not possible."

"Then he played six years of Major League Baseball and at

the same time he led a pro football team to championships three years running."

"He played pro football and pro baseball?"

"Yep."

"But Jordan played both basketball and baseball."

"And sucked at baseball and never won any Olympic gold medals."

"True. Okay fine, you win."

Rob had the steak, Chelsey had the halibut with steamed veggies. After the waiter brought their meals, Chelsey said, "You make me feel like I'm really stupid."

"I make you feel stupid?"

"No, that didn't come out right. I feel uneducated about a lot of things."

"Not knowing about a football player isn't a big deal."

"If you want to know about working out and eating right, I'm your woman." She took a bite of her dinner. "So where's that present you were telling me about?"

He reached under his chair and retrieved the small box that he'd stowed there. "Happy twenty-eighth birthday," he said, handing her the box and the card.

She opened the card first. On the front were dozens and dozens of hearts in different colors, but in the center there was a large blank place in the shape of a heart. Inside it read, "You've stolen my heart. It's all yours. Love, Rob." She clapped her hand over her mouth to keep from squealing with delight. She didn't need any gift; she would cherish this card forever. But of course she unwrapped the gift anyway. It was a necklace with a tear-shaped dreamcatcher pendant. It had turquoise and antique silver fluted beads. Turquoise was so in this season! And the ethnic thing had been hot for a while now. She loved it!

"I love it!" She slipped it over her head. The pendant fell just between her breasts. Very hot.

"The dreamcatcher will filter out all the bad dreams and allow only good thoughts to enter your mind. The feather sig-nifies air and how vital it is to life."

"Thank you."

When they got home she led him into the bedroom and sat him on the bed. She stood in front of him, then turned so her back faced him as she slowly undid the zipper down the back of her dress, watching him over her shoulder. Slowly, she slid out of her dress. Wearing just heels and her thong underwear, she walked up to him, stood authoritatively in front of him with her legs shoulder-width apart. He bit his lip to stifle a moan as she slowly unbuttoned his shirt while sucking gently on his neck.

This round, they took their time.

Two condoms later, when they were sweaty and thirsty and exhausted, they lay in each other's arms. Though aching for a glass of water, Chelsey didn't move from his embrace.

She traced her finger over the contours of his chest.

"Aren't you scared to go into a burning building?" she asked.

"Nah. We have good protection and are trained not to get hurt."

"But you could die."

"Most firefighters who die on the job don't die from fire. They die from car accidents or heart attacks or something."

"That's very reassuring. Really, you must have been scared once."

"The only time I ever got really scared was this one time, this was when I was a firefighter in Aspen, I was in this A-frame house. That's where the house has a very steep roof. It's shaped like a triangle. I was on the second floor, and the fire had burned out a lot of the floor, so I was walking just on planks and stuff, trying to get to the fire. I couldn't see anything because there's no light and it's smoky so my flashlight was useless. You always have a partner when you go into a fire, and you're supposed to reach out every few minutes or so and make sure your buddy is there. Well, I reached out, and I couldn't find him. So here I am, I couldn't see a damn thing, I didn't know where my partner was, and I was in this really narrow second floor, walking on planks and shit, and then I got really turned around. I couldn't remember which way the access point was and which way the fire was, and I was running out of oxygen."

"How long had you been in the building?"

"Not very long, but your air tank—it's supposed to have like thirty minutes, but you go through it in twenty-five minutes if you're sitting still. When you're in a fire, you have to break doors and windows and chop holes in the roof so air can escape and the temperature of the fire drops. When you're chopping up buildings, it's a pretty aerobic activity and you go through a lot of oxygen. You use your air tank in about fifteen minutes. I didn't know where I was and I needed to get the hell out of there."

"Couldn't you feel the heat of the fire?"

"Firefighters wear all this protective gear, so it's like when you wear an oven mitt—you know what you're touching is hot, but you're protected so you don't really feel it."

"So how did you get out?"

"I made a lucky guess."

"You're kidding!"

He shook his head.

"Huh." It was insanity, this way of making a living of his. "Have you known anybody who died in a fire?" she asked.

"Not personally. But I heard a story about a guy at another station who arrived on the scene and there was a woman crying that there was a baby still in the house. She said the baby was on the second floor on the northwest corner of the house. So the firefighter ran into the house without all of his protective gear on to get the baby. He didn't have his face mask on and he charged upstairs. When he opened the door, there was a backdraft . . ."

"What's a backdraft?"

"Ah, okay, let's see, Firefighting 101: A fire needs three things. Fuel—something to burn like a log or a house or whatever—heat, and oxygen. The fire will continue to burn as long as there is fuel and oxygen around it. But when a house has all the windows and doors closed, the fire will eventually use up all the oxygen and fuel. The flames die down but the fire is still hot enough to burn, and so there is all this pressure building up. So when the firefighter opened that door, he let in a whole bunch of oxygen all at once, and the fire exploded, devouring the oxygen and washing over him like a tidal wave. The fire only blazed like that for a second, but when it rolled over him, it seared his lungs because he wasn't wearing his protective gear, and he was dead like that." He snapped his fingers.

"Oh my god." Chelsey shook her head. "I can't believe you go into fires. You're so brave."

"Does it turn you on, all my unadulterated manliness?"

She laughed. "Very much." She kissed him. "I love you." The second the words came out of her mouth, she gasped in horror and tried to back-track, talking so fast she tripped over the words. "Ididn'tmeanthatImeanIlikeyoualot."

He chuckled. "So you don't love me?"

"I don't—I just—I mean—Look, I'm a girl, and everybody knows if the girl says the *L* word first, the guy will go running. We've only been dating for a few weeks. I'm probably just delusional from having so many orgasms. Don't pay attention to anything I say."

"You can't love somebody after just a few weeks?"

"Of course not. It's crazy."

"'Cuz I really think I love you."

"What?" Chelsey's stressed expression softened.

"I know it's crazy and we've only known each other a short time, but I've dated a lot of girls in my life and let me tell you, you're really special. I'm crazy about you."

"Really?" She smiled.

"Really."

24

The Summer of Elastic
Waistbands, Part Two

On Ana's first day working at the gym with Chelsey, Chelsey took her into a secluded room to take her measurements. This was a true sign of friendship for Ana to let Chelsey know the most intimate details of her body. Chelsey probably had a body fat percentage of .0004 percent. She was 5'7" and probably weighed less than 120 pounds. Ana knew that Chelsey thought fat was more evil than Satan or Osama bin Laden. There was nothing on earth that Chelsey disdained more. Several times when they'd gone out for drinks, dinner, or coffee, Chelsey would look at a fat person and shake her head, revolted.

Ana didn't share her friend's horror about fat, but she did fear Chelsey's judgment of her when she had all the ugly facts about Ana's girth in black and white.

Ana gulped as she stepped on the scale. Chelsey set the lower scale guide at 100 pounds and slid the upper guide along. Up up up up.

Oh please, stop already.

But no. Chelsey just kept sliding it up.

Okay, this was just silly.

Completely unacceptable.

How had things gotten so bad?

Stop! Stop or I'll shoot! Myself.

Finally, the pointer teetered down, then up, then came to a stop in the middle.

It was worse than Ana thought. It was bleak. Nuclear-melt-down end-of-the-world bleak.

Ana waited for an expression of horror on Chelsey's face, but there was none. Of course, Chelsey was a trained actress.

Next came the measurements. Her arm, her bust, her waist, her hips, her thighs, her calves. Her right calf was a quarter inch fatter than her left, and her left thigh was a quarter inch fatter than her right. Good lord, in addition to being a corpulent beast, she was a mutant.

"Don't worry, very few people are perfectly symmetrical!" Chelsey said cheerfully, noting all the horrifying statistics down on Ana's chart.

As she waited, Ana couldn't help it, but she yawned.

"See, you're tired in the middle of the day. That's because you're not eating right. What we're going to do is give you a form to fill out about the foods you like and don't like, and we're going to plug it into the computer, and it will give you three different complete daily meal plans. You'll eat four small meals a day, keeping that energy up there, keeping that metabolism high!"

Just listening to Chelsey's enthusiasm exhausted Ana. She couldn't wait to take a nap.

"Now we're going to measure your body fat percentage."

"Excuse me, what are we going to do?"

"Your body fat. We're going to measure it. It's the most important measurement we're going to take. The important thing to do is to burn fat. What happens if you don't eat properly or if you starve yourself is that you burn lean muscle, not fat. So while the scale might tell you that you've lost weight, I'll check your body fat percentage and I'll know if you've been doing what you're supposed to and whether you're burning lean muscle or fat."

That sounded threatening. Ominous. It gave Chelsey a god-like ability to peer into Ana's life and behavior.

"It's just about math. We'll figure out what your maintenance calories are to maintain your current weight. Then we'll subtract 500 calories a day from that, and that's the number of calories you'll consume each day. And with regular exercise, there is no possible way you won't lose weight. But if you don't eat a balanced diet, you may lose weight, but you're going to lose muscle, which will make it harder to keep the weight off long-term. That's not what we're trying to do here."

She took a little instrument that looked like an ear-piercing gun and measured Ana's upper arms and stomach.

"Okay, your body is thirty-one percent fat." Chelsey said. "That puts you right here." Chelsey pointed to a chart that grouped body fat percentages in "Excellent," "Good," "Fair," and "Poor." Ana was "Fair." Oh it was grim. "We want to be between twenty and twenty-five percent, ideally."

After Chelsey had marked down all of Ana's measurements, she gave Ana a long questionnaire to fill out. Ana filled in what she did and didn't like to eat in various food groups—what her favorite fruits and vegetables were, what kind of proteins she did and didn't like, what breakfast cereals she preferred over others. Chelsey typed the information into the computer, and, in a few minutes, it spat out a bunch of stuff about metabolic rates and suggested daily meal plans.

"You can swap the food it suggests for other foods. But you have to follow the diet exactly. Let me explain. Look here," Chelsey pointed to one of the sample meal plans. "It says to have a lean meat and two servings of carbs for lunch, plus a serving of veggies. It suggests turkey and two pieces of wheat bread, but if you don't want turkey, say, you look in here"— Chelsey flipped through the small food exchange book that she'd given Ana—"under 'lean meats.' There are several to choose from. You can't swap the turkey for a very lean meat or a medium fat meat, just lean. See?"

Ana nodded.

"Another really important thing is going to be serving size. You have to measure everything. You can't just pour yourself a bowl of cereal and hope it's the recommended serving size. It'll often be twice what it should be. So while you think you're consuming 200 calories, you're really consuming 400. See?"

Ana nodded again, more glumly this time.

"Well, our hour is over today, but we'll hit the machines next week."

Ana felt robbed. Even at drastically reduced rates, she was paying forty-two bucks a session and she wanted to spend the hour working her abs and lifting weights and flexing her muscle, not just getting humiliated and shamed and being told things she didn't want to hear. It was an outrage.

But within moments, her disappointment subsided and she felt relieved. Excited even. Now she could go home and relax and get some sleep. God, it would be *lovely*.

"So now you're going to go do your cardio, right?" Chelsey asked.

Even though thirty seconds earlier Ana had been disappointed not to have been forced to lift vast quantities of weights and race along the treadmill for hours, since the idea of going home to bed had entered her mind, all of her good intentions and her last shred of energy had disappeared completely. How could she go to cardio when a comforting warm bed was at home, calling out to her? But she nodded, trudged over to the elliptical rider, and worked up a serious sweat.

25

Primordial Stew

They decided to call the show "Primordial Stew" based on a skit they'd come up with and decided to use as the opening scene. It began with the theater completely black, and Scott booming out in his movie-trailer voice, "In the beginning, the world was nothing more than a primordial stew of one-celled organisms bubbling around. Then one day, a couple of cells went nuts and became a two-celled organism, then eventually fish showed up, then muskrats and bandicoots, wombats and kangaroos, then gorillas and eventually, dun dun dun . . . mankind. As time goes by, the number of innovations and creations grows every day. Ladies and gentlemen, we're proud to present to you tonight, a short history of modern evolution!"

The first skit showed how humans had evolved. Images flashed against the white back wall of the stage of great heroes and heroines of the past as Scott noted the tremendous contributions to society of people like Harriet Tubman, Abraham Lincoln, and Thomas Edison. Then Scott noted that evolution wasn't always an improvement, it changed in fits and false starts. Then pictures of folks like Tanya Harding, Anna Nicole Smith, and John Bobbitt came on screen. Next Scott mentioned about how, in the olden days, all people had to entertain themselves with were books, talking with their friends and families, or playing music and singing. Today we can stare at a box for hours to watch WWF wrestling, *Fear Factor*, and *The Bachelor!*

There was a long part about the evolution of the potato chip—how it spawned the cheese curl, Doritos, Funyuns, on and on, in all manner of ranch, sour cream and onion, jalapeño, BBQ, and nacho cheese varieties. There was Ana's feminist cheerleaders, surely the next evolution in the feminist movement. Every skit made fun of current American culture, from dating to television to advertising to recreation. The finale was an ode to nuclear waste, and a question, "What will tomorrow bring?"

Ana had insisted on adding "A Comedy Hootenanny" at the end of the name so that people wouldn't think they were putting on some dark performance art thing. She and Scott had made posters that read, *One Night Only! Primordial Stew: A Comedy Hootenanny!* At the bottom it read, *A sketch-comedy extravaganza (like Saturday Night Live, only funny) featuring Denver's very own Spur of the Moment performers. 8 p.m. Sunday October 15. Tickets $12.* It listed the phone number to call and the address, all that stuff. And they had spent hours plastering the posters in coffee shops and lampposts all over town.

Ana got home just before seven. This needing to have a day-job thing was really a drag. She had so many better things to do with her life.

Ana struggled to open the door. Strapped to her body were her purse, her enormous gym bag, and her briefcase/bag swinging around her and colliding into her sides. She could feel her gym bag slipping off her shoulders, but she couldn't grab it because her hands were filled with flyers she'd made for the show. As she battled to get the key in the lock, lifting her shoulder to her neck to keep the bag from slipping off her, she could feel that she was about to drop the stack of flyers any second.

Just before all was chaos, Jason opened the door for her. She was immediately enveloped by the smell of dinner cooking—garlic, onions, and fresh herbs filled the kitchen.

"Thank you so much," she said, setting her keys and the

flyers down on the counter and letting all her bags tumble to the floor. "Are you cooking dinner?"

"Spinach risotto and salad."

"You are a good, good man, Jason Hess. Thank you so much."

"You don't always have to thank me so extravagantly. I like to cook, we need to eat—it's a simple system really."

"It's just that I love home-cooked meals . . ."

"I know, I know, because you never had them growing up. What do you have there?" he asked, indicating the flyers.

"I made posters for our show."

"They look really good. Did you go to Kinko's?"

"Are you kidding me? Color prints like this would cost about four zillion bucks. I used the laser copier at work. Marketing is the only department that has a color printer. So at least one good thing has come of me becoming a marketing slut."

"You used the copier at work? Don't you think that's a little unethical?"

"What do you mean?"

"Using company supplies, don't you think that's unethical?"

"Jason, I don't mean to alarm you, but it's becoming evident you've gone completely mad. Look, I know you work for an impoverished school district and probably buy supplies for the school yourself, but I work for an evil corporate empire. You were the one who told me that the average American executive makes like four hundred and forty times what the lowest employees on the corporate totem pole make. All those execs selling their stocks before the crash, while their employees lost all of their 401Ks, all their savings? Sound familiar? You ranted for like two weeks straight about how unjust it was that GE was paying for their former executive's eighty-thousand-dollar-a-month condo plus his golf club membership and football tickets and God knows what else in addition to his nine-million-a-year-severance pay. If companies are giving execs who don't even work there anymore millions a year, don't you think it's fair that a little person makes a couple copies at work? I mean as if that would even come close to closing the inequity gap."

"Executive compensation is a serious issue," Jason agreed, "but that doesn't mean we should be greedy just like they are. How is your stealing office supplies any different than GE paying for Jack Welch's condo each month?"

"I'll tell you how it's different. Jack Welch gets nine million dollars a year for DOING NOTHING. He can afford to make his own damn mortgage payments. I, on the other hand, get paid squat, and can't afford to buy a house, take a vacation, or, for that matter, buy new socks. But since the big wigs of the world won't share and pay us reasonable salaries, I'm taking matters into my own hands. Think of it as a holiday bonus they were too greedy to give me so I took it myself."

"Don't you see how unethical behavior is like a virus? You're excusing your behavior by saying that other people do it. The Jack Welch's of the world say it's okay to do what they're doing because other people are doing it. See?"

"But other people ARE doing it! EVERYBODY steals office supplies. It's our only sad pathetic way of getting back at the monolithic corporations that underpay us, treat us like crap, and fire us without warning every now and then to improve stock prices for the stock holders." Ana sighed deeply. "I don't want to talk about this right now. When is dinner going to be ready?"

Ana wanted to be a good, ethical person, she really did. But she couldn't start now. Not until she'd gotten some food and sleep. A month or so straight of sleep. Jason's values and morals were one of the reasons she liked and admired him so much, but right now his belief system just seemed too exhausting for words.

26

Personal Ghosts

Nick was throwing his annual Halloween party. The First Annual Halloween party was held at Nick's three years ago, shortly after he and Ramiro started dating.

They had met when Nick was on a blind date. The blind date was a friend of Ramiro's date, Bryan. Ramiro and Bryan had only gone out a few times before, and Ramiro was not at all happy about sharing his night with a couple he didn't know and who didn't know each other. The first few dates were hard enough without adding more tension to the fray.

But it soon became apparent over dinner and the subsequent numerous rounds of drinks that Ramiro and Nick hit it off completely, and their dates hit it off with each other.

All night, Nick and Ramiro were cracking each other up. Ram would have never pegged a finance guy to be so funny, but while Ramiro was sharply sardonic, Nick had a quieter way of observing the humorous things in life.

While they each left with the dates they'd come with, when they parted ways, Nick told Ramiro if he ever wanted to meet to discuss the investments or financial planning that they'd talked about, here was his card. They *hadn't* talked about investments or financial planning as Ramiro had no money with which to invest or for which to plan for, but Ramiro graciously accepted his card.

Ramiro never called Bryan again, and apparently the split was amiable, because Bryan never called him, either.

Ramiro did call Nick the next day, however. "I hoped you could help me make some decisions about my money," Ramiro said. "I'm either planning to invest in a nice restaurant downtown or in a bar on Broadway in the very near future."

"I'd have to recommend that you diversify your investment."

"Sage advice. When would you say a good time for me to invest would be?"

"I think tonight. Say eight. Market's looking good."

"Doesn't it though?"

And they've been happily ever after (mostly) since. Their differences complemented each other well—Nick's ability to plan and save and look to the future was great, but he had a tendency to take things too seriously and get stressed out—Ramiro's relaxed attitude and sense of humor helped Nick relax. But they were similar enough in areas that really counted—they were both intelligent, they both loved to read, they both laughed and/or groaned at the same places in movies and TV shows, and they both were secretly addicted to *American Idol*, and yet had managed to keep each other's shameful secret.

For their Halloween party tonight, Ramiro went as Ponch from CHiPs. Nick was a magician, wearing a black magician's hat and a purple velvet jacket and pants. He'd taken a pink rabbit stuffed animal and cut off its head, then glued the head on his hat so it looked like the rabbit was peeking out the top. Jason and Scott went as pirates, with costumes that were remnants from their days as the Iron Pyrits.

Marin went as Cinderella after she'd killed herself from boredom in her "perfect" marriage. She'd gotten the silver silk gown when she was a bridesmaid in her cousin's wedding. Ana actually thought the dress was pretty, though Marin had a point about the way the dress puffed out at the waist in the voluminous manner of a Southern Belle, which in fact, Marin's cousin was. Marin also had a tiara from a tongue-in-cheek award she'd gotten in her senior year of high school. All the graduating seniors had been given plaques predicting what kinds of roles they'd go on to play. Marin had been named "Most likely to play a beauty queen." (Others had "won" awards like, "Most likely to play a drunken, abusive father"— he'd been given a fake bottle of liquor—and "most likely to play a nerd"—he was given a broken pair of black plastic glasses with masking tape holding them together.) Then Marin had painted her face gray, and tied a rope around her neck, noose-style, with about two feet of extra rope draped over her shoulder like a scarf. She'd pinned a sign on her chest that read, "What happens when fairy-tale endings are so damn boring you lose the will to live."

Ana was a Viking. Her mother was half Norwegian and half Czech. She knew absolutely nothing about the Czech Republic, but she did know about the Vikings' history of raping and plundering. On the plus side of her heritage, Ana thought the Vikings had a remarkable fashion sense. The pointy-metal hats were simply inspired, and Ana appreciated that Halloween gave her the chance to pay homage to the fashion mavens of yore offstage and in something like real life.

Ana and Marin stood by the punch, drinking large glasses of it and people watching. Nick had used dry ice to make it look like steam was pouring out of the punch, which was deathly delicious. It tasted like Kool-Aid, so unwitting party-goers would drink it as rapidly as a glass of water, only to find that after a glass or two, they'd have to be collected off the floor where they'd passed out and carried off to a bedroom so as to keep foot traffic flowing smoothly.

A woman dressed as Frida Kahlo, wearing a black wig and a long strip of black felt for her eyebrows and a shorter strip of black felt on her upper lip, poured herself a glass.

"Your costume looks great," Marin said.

"Thank you. I've always loved her work. It's so visceral and haunting." Frida spoke quietly, in a serious breathy voice devoid of humor, as if every word she uttered was chock-full of intellectual importance. Frida paused to read the sign pinned to Marin's dress. "Ah, you can never run out of material to poke fun at the fallacy of the myth of happily ever after." The woman smiled slightly. Ana pegged her as a graduate student. She probably worked with Ramiro at the bookstore. He was always bringing home these brainy types who talked like old school professors reflecting on the good old days when calculators didn't exist and students were required to take Latin and read Chaucer in its original Middle English. Frida eyed Ana. "What inspired your ensemble?"

"I'm part Norwegian and I enjoy celebrating my heritage of raping and pillaging and eating rotting shark meat."

The slight smile Frida had been wearing disappeared and was replaced with a jaw-muscle-clenched frown and stony gaze.

"I'm Norwegian. The Vikings didn't do anything other races didn't do to survive," she snapped.

What had just happened here? Ana had been trying to crack a joke, and she'd managed to completely offend a perfect stranger.

"Of course they didn't," Marin swooped in. "The Vikings are widely known for dramatically changing Europe. They brought cultures and traditions from one country to the next and their fast ships improved transportation by sea dramatically." Marin had such a gift for always saying exactly the right thing. Ana, on the other hand, was always doing this, sticking her foot so far in her mouth that her toenails scraped up her esophagus. She realized, however, that you never could tell what things people could laugh at about themselves and what things triggered self-esteem code blues.

"Indeed," Frida said. No really, she said, "indeed." It was hard to tell her age because of her costume, but Ana didn't think the woman could have been much older than thirty and certainly in no way old enough to say "indeed" without being ironic about it. "Anyway, I believe you're confusing the Icelandic tradition of eating rotted shark meat—a tradition born out of necessity to survive the long winters, mind you—with the Norwegian lutefisk."

Ana nodded, eyes wide with fear at being in such close

proximity to an evident psychopath. "Yeah. You're probably right."

"I left my friend over there," Frida nodded vaguely. "I'd better be on my way."

Ana and Marin smiled pleasantly until she was out of earshot.

"Hello, I was kidding."

"I'm surprised she has 'a' friend. Holy bitch, Batman."

Their attention was diverted by the sound of what they initially mistook for a cat being shredded by a blender but was in fact Scott, dancing on Nick's very expensive dining room table and singing "She's a Brick House" at the top of his lungs.

"Oh good Lord in heaven," Ana said. "How much punch has that boy had?" Marin shook her head.

Ana, Marin, Jason, and Ramiro jumped into action. "Hey, Scott, come on down," Ana said in the kind of gentle, dumbed-down voice one would use with a suicidal person on a ledge.

But Scott just kept dancing comically. The party-goers were roaring with laughter at his antics.

Ana reached up to help him down. Instead, he yelled, "Dance with me, Ana," and pulled her up on the table with him.

"Aaah!" She screamed as he twirled her around. He spun her around doing the West Coast swing. Ana did her best just to stay upright. Scott kept singing and swinging her around until he misjudged the end of the table, and Ana slipped off, taking him with her. He landed on top of her.

"God, sorry, are you all right?" Scott's face was only an inch or so from hers.

She nodded. "I think so."

She looked into his eyes. All the laughter and noise around her seemed to disappear. She could feel his warm breath on her neck. She was stunned to feel a splinter of desire for him. And that wasn't . . . it couldn't possibly an erection that she felt against her leg?

No no, she couldn't possibly be feeling lust for him. It was just that it had been so long since she'd been close to a man. She wanted sex, not Scott.

"You should probably get off me before you crush me," she said.

"Oh yeah, right."

He stood and helped her up. Ana struggled to get her heartbeat back to normal.

27

Forgive Me, Trainer, for I Have Sinned

It was the Friday night before the show. Tee-minus 45 hours till showtime.

Bartender Tony said he was closing the upstairs bar early and that they'd have to go downstairs to procure their beers, which they dutifully did.

Scott and Marin happened upon a large corner table just as the group that was sitting there was leaving and snapped it up.

Ana went up to the bar to get the first round of drinks. Their orders rarely varied: a light for Chelsey, who got tipsy halfway through her first beer, a stout for Ramiro, and ambers for the rest of them.

Ana waited for the bartender to finish filling an order for a waitress. She was debating about whether she should have any beer. She'd already eaten her maintenance calories for the day, and this would put her over by at least two hundred calories. On the other hand, she'd been doing so good and working out so hard, surely an itty bitty two hundred calories couldn't hurt.

"Hey! I saw you perform tonight. You were really wonderful," a guy standing next to her said.

"Thanks." Ana turned to look at him. He had pale blue eyes, dark hair cut very short, and a jagged scar across one cheek. He might have been just okay looking, except for his smile, which was so welcoming and genuinely cheery, it made him striking. The contrast of the warm smile and ferocious-looking scar was captivating.

"Let me get this round," he said.

"Oh, I'm buying for everybody." She waved to the rest of the gang sitting at the table.

"No worries. A beer for everybody. Man, I nearly fell off my chair in that scene with the flashlight . . ." He was referring to a game called "Radio" where all four players got on stage and asked for a musical style and a thing. The room would be completely dark, and then the emcee would randomly flash a flashlight on one of the players, who would have to come up with a verse in his/her music style on the subject of whatever thing the audience suggested, and the emcee would jump to another player, as if he were flipping the stations on a radio. Ana's style had been rap and her thing had been a toilet seat. "Your song about your homies and your heinie . . . oh man, I nearly died."

Ana smiled. It was never a particular challenge to win the audience's affection with scatological humor, but Ana had done a particularly good job of rhyming tonight. It was always terrifying rhyming sentences on the spot, with no rhyming dictionary to consult, but it had come out well, and Ana glowed under the man's praise.

"Thanks. Hey, let me order the beer because performers get drinks for a dollar."

"A dollar! Right on." He gave Ana a ten. Ana ordered the beers, including one for herself.

"Thanks for the beer," she said.

"Do you mind if I sit down with you?"

"Yeah. I mean no. I mean yes you can sit down, no I don't mind."

Ana brought the drinks to the table and slid into the last open seat in the booth. "Hey everyone, this is some guy whose name I don't know but he liked the show and bought us a round in admiration for our comic genius."

"Hey, I'm Kieran," he said, waving and pulling up a chair next to Ana at the already crowded table.

"Hey, Kieran!" Everyone called in unison.

"Well, thanks for the beer," Ana said. She couldn't think of anything else to say. How could she get on stage and pull entire scenes and story lines out of her ass, but she couldn't think of a single thing to talk about with a stranger?

"No problem. It looks like what you do up there is so much fun. How did you get started?"

"It was a fluke, really. I just saw a sign for auditions my freshman year, and they were willing to train, which was a good thing, because I didn't have any experience with acting at all. My mom was pretty worried about my grades in high school, so she never wanted me to participate in extracurricular activities. When I got to college, I just sort of went nuts. I wanted to try new things, so I tried this. I was terrible, I mean miserable, for the first several months. I was just embarrassingly bad, but for some reason, I kept coming back for more. I guess because I liked the people and I liked how free I felt on stage. Four other people were asked to join the team at the same time I did, and two dropped out after just a couple months." She'd only had three sips of beer, but she was already pouring her heart out. She took a long, large gulp of her beer, then another.

She really wanted to know where he'd gotten that scar. Maybe he had been defending a woman from a would-be assailant or he worked in the FBI or the special forces or something. But she thought it was a little forward of her to ask him about the scar straight away, so she asked him instead what he did for a living.

"I work in insurance."

"Health or home and auto?"

"Home and auto."

Blech. How boring. But maybe he'd taken the straight and narrow after doing whatever he'd done to get that scar. A knife fight at a bar had made him take a good, hard look at his life, and he'd turned his life around. Or maybe he was one of the people who verified that insurance claims were valid, and he got in a knife fight with a mobster trying to defraud the system.

"Is this your full-time job?" he asked.

"I wish. Right now we each get a cut of the profits from however many people show up each night, which basically pays for our beer each month. We're trying to get more corporate performances because those pay a lot better. We can do team-building activities, perform at parties, that kind of thing. We're having a hard time right now because everybody is cutting back with this economy." So. Conversation. Think, Ana, think. "Um, so, where did you go to college?"

"I took some classes at the community college, but didn't finish."

Nuts. That blew a whole line of conversation starters like what did you study, what was the craziest thing you did as a freshman, did you know so and so, and so on.

"So, are you from Colorado?" she asked.

"Yeah. From a small town outside of Durango."

"Oh! I love Durango. That's one of my favorite towns in Colorado." They nodded at each other.

"Want another beer?" he asked.

"What?" she looked at her glass. Ooh, she would be going way over her calorie limit with another. She said yes.

When he left to get more beer, Chelsey leaned over to Ana, "He's cute. Got that bad-boy thing going for him. Very sexy."

"He works in insurance."

"Hmm, less sexy." Just then, Rob kissed Chelsey's neck. She giggled and turned to face him and kissed him in a full-on mouth-crushing, tongue-halfway-down-each-other's-esophagus kind of kiss that went on for about an hour. They were in that all-over-each-other stage of the relationship where they had to be touching constantly. Right now they were so close to each other that Chelsey's leg was draped over his—she was practically in his lap.

Ana eyed them enviously. She wanted to be crazy in lust with somebody. It had been too damn long. Ana missed that feeling of excitement. She missed getting aroused just from a look or a casual touch. She felt like part of her emotions were hibernating, and she was ready for them to wake up already.

Kieran came back with the beers.

"Thanks." Ana took a sip and strained to think of some-thing to say. "Um, so where did you get that scar?"

"I was bitten by a dog as a kid."

Oh. Bor*ing*. "Aah. So do you like to travel?"

"I've never been out of Colorado."

"Oh. Would you like to travel?"

"Uh, sure. Maybe."

Why was having a conversation with him so hard? She kept sending out conversational volleys that he just let slam to the floor. She would just have to keep the conversation going all by herself. "I love traveling. I wish I could do it more. This summer Chelsey, Marin, and me went to Chicago and we had the greatest time ever. I mean we were total dorks and got lost about a zillion times, but it was so much fun, even the debacles we had on an hourly basis were hilarious. Like this one time, we were on the el, and Chelsey and Marin got off, and just as I was about to step through the doors, they closed! I couldn't believe it. I looked at Chelsey and Marin through the glass and they looked back at me and we were all bug-eyed and freaked, and all, 'Oh my god! What are we gonna do?' We didn't have cell phones, and of course we didn't have a clue where any-thing was in the city. I mean Chelsey grew up in a suburb of Chicago, but it wasn't like she knew the city very well. Anyway, I got off at the next stop, which was in an unbelievably terrify-ing neighborhood. I mean in Denver, the worst you ever have to deal with is a drunk peeing in the street and maybe a little graffiti. Chicago has actual *ghettos*, actual places where you're traipsing through sidewalks littered with used needles and ducking gunfire every three seconds, and this is the neighbor-hood I found myself in. So I just followed the train tracks the best I could back to the last stop. It was only a ten-minute walk, but it was the scariest ten minutes of my life. The whole time I imagined myself like I was in an enemy jungle and I was some Green Beret specialist, except for the part about how I didn't have an arsenal of semi-automatic weapons, I didn't ac-tually know any martial arts—still don't, actually—and it turned out nobody even gave me a second glance, so my terror was all just a product of my imagination. As soon as I met up with Chelsey and Marin again, everything was fine and we thought the whole thing was hilarious and we promptly began exaggerating the story to make it more exciting and funny." She sipped her beer, and she and Kieran nodded at each other some more. "Then, just two hours later, it started to rain and we didn't want to miss the bus, it was just up ahead and we were racing along to catch it and of course Chelsey, little miss personal trainer, is way ahead of me and Marin, and she turns around to tell us that she thinks we're going to make it, but she failed to take into account that she'd just gone over a curb, so when she turned to tell us and started running toward us, her foot got caught on the curb and her leg went flying out from under her. She was airborne, just *flying*."

Ana stood and demonstrated what Chelsey had looked like when she was taking the nose dive.

"Thank god she wasn't hurt. All three of us just collapsed onto the sidewalk and roared with laughter. I mean right there, in the middle of the insanely busy sidewalks with homeless people swiveling their heads to watch us like they were at a tennis game."

"You're telling him about Chicago, right?" Chelsey piped in.

"Every time we did this"—Marin stood and assumed the flying-through-the-air pose with her arms frozen like a runner's, her one foot flying behind her—"for the rest of the week we just broke down in hysterics."

"Did you tell him about the time . . ."

The six actors, plus occasionally Rob and Nick, kept interrupting each other, piling one story onto another, their voices getting louder and louder so they could be heard over the din. And they kept it up for several hours, well after the bar was officially closed, and after the bar staff had mopped the floor and put up the chairs and wiped down the counters. The glowering stares of the bar staff were the last thing Ana remembered.

* * *

When Ana woke up, the first thing she thought was, *Oh Christ, my head.* Then a split second later, *Oh god, I'm going to have to confess to Chelsey about last night. She probably thought I stuck to one—she was too absorbed in Rob's gaze to know fully how nuts I went, but when we go over my food diary—and my fat ass—I'll have to tell all.* Ana tried to remember how many beers she'd consumed the night before. She'd had such good intentions of stopping after one, but then she'd had that second one, and after that, all her critical thinking skills evaporated into a blurry haze, and imbibing numerous beers seemed like the best idea she'd ever had. Another? Hell yes!

Ana slapped her forehead with her palm, as if that would clear her hazy memory. *Four? Five? Oh, then there was that one I finished for Marin.* Six maybe. Oh lord, that was 1,200 calories on top of the 1,700 she'd already had yesterday. That was bad. That was very, very bad. Her appointment with Chelsey was tomorrow. What was she going to tell her? *Forgive me, trainer, for I have sinned. I had six beers Saturday night, I didn't work out all weekend, and I am a bloated squealing pig.* Chelsey would give her a penance of two hundred squats, three Hail Marys, and an hour on the elliptical rider.

Oh god, the show was tonight. She could not perform looking like a tired, hungover drunk. A fat girl with huge circles under her bloodshot eyes. Yeah, she'd be whisked away to Hollywood looking like this.

There was so much to do for the show tonight, but the most urgent thing was for her to get some beauty rest. So she closed her eyes and went back to sleep, her exhaustion from drinking too much depleting her of all ambition.

When she woke up two hours later, she felt better but was still tired. She staggered downstairs to drink orange juice and take handfuls of vitamins.

Marin was reading the paper when Ana got downstairs.

"Morning, sunshine. How ya feeling?"

"Like I've been run over by an eighteen wheeler."

"Are you excited about your date?"

"What date?"

"With that guy from last night."

"But I didn't even like that guy from last night."

"You agreed to get drinks with him after the show."

"I did?"

"Yeah."

"Great. Like I don't have enough to be stressed out about tonight without having to go on a first date I don't want to go on."

"You kissed him."

"I did not."

"You did. You were making out like horny teenagers."

"I'm never, never drinking again."

"Yeah, sure you're not."

"No, I mean it."

Marin nodded. "Whatever you say, babe."

28

Showtime

Ana ran off the stage, high from the sound of the audience's laughter. They had loved the scene she'd written about the cheerleaders. The various cheers they made up had the audience in tears; the sight of muscular, broad Ramiro in a short pleated skirt was always a crowd-pleaser; and the stunt that had gone "awry," leaving Ana tangled upside down in a jumbled knot of her fellow cheerleaders' limbs, revealing her Wonder Woman underwear, made the audience howl. But the hit of the scene was the fight song they sang while doing high kicks. The song made various demands, from the reasonable to the not-so reasonable, from asking for things like more women's bathrooms and paid childcare, to mandating forced incarceration of men who liked Howard Stern, and government-funded robots that cooked and cleaned for every home. The chorus of the song was "And an orgasm every time!" "Every time! Every time!" Marin would echo.

Ana loved the sound of it, the sound of people laughing. She couldn't keep the smile off her face. She felt awesome. The endorphins in her body were doing high kicks and "hip, hip hoorahs!"

Ana ran back on stage for her next part. For once, Ana stopped worrying and just felt happy. For weeks, she'd been terrified that the sound-and-lights-guy Tom wouldn't show, or nobody would come, or the lights wouldn't work, or the power would go out. But everything was going exactly as planned.

After the show, the actors gathered in the hallway where the audience exited, ostensibly to wish everyone a good night and thank them for coming, but really to keep getting the compliments. Performers are a very sensitive people, after all.

"You were great!"

"Thank you. Thank you so much for coming. Have a good night."

"You were wonderful!"

"Oh, thank you. Thank you so much for coming."

Then a woman approached Marin.

"Hi. My name is Kristen Vigil. Could I talk to you for a second?"

"Sure."

Ana, curious, watched Marin and the woman walk to the corner of the room.

"You guys were hilarious. Your cheerleader thing was great," a female audience member said to Ana as she left the theater.

"Thank you. Thank you so much. Thanks for coming," Ana said.

Ana watched the mysterious Kristen Vigil give Marin a business card.

"You guys are so talented. You could really be on TV," a woman said to Ana. Ana pulled her eyes away from Marin and looked at the lady.

"Oh, thank you. That's really nice to hear. Thanks so much for coming out and supporting live comedy."

That's when she saw him. Kieran was standing there, waiting for her. Shit, she'd forgotten all about him.

"You guys were great. Mind if I stick around after the show?" he said.

"Oh, yeah, of course. That was the plan. Right?" It wasn't a confirmative, "right?" It was a curious, is-that-in-fact-what-we-talked-about-last-night? kind of a "right?"

"Yeah."

Within another minute or two, the rest of the audience had

cleared out, including Kristen Vigil, and Kieran was left on the sidelines as the six friends came together and gave each other a monster group hug.

"That was so awesome! We killed!"

They kept jumping up and down until they collapsed into a heap. After giggles and tickles and a few more hugs, Scott sprang up and pronounced, "Beer for everyone!"

"So," Ana asked Marin casually, "who was that woman you were talking to?" Maybe the woman wanted Marin to play Cinderella at her daughter's birthday party or something, Ana thought.

"She works for Janet March Talent."

It was one of the agencies that Ana had sent a press packet to.

"She says she has a friend in Hollywood, a producer for the WB who is launching a show about college students who live in New York who aspire to get on *Saturday Night Live*, well, it's not called *Saturday Night Live*, it's called *The Funny Farm*, but it's an obvious cover for *SNL*. So they do improv, stand-up, sketch, all that kind of stuff. She thinks I have the right look for one of the characters. She saw my picture in the press packet you sent and liked my look, and she liked my energy on stage tonight, those were her words, not mine, so she wants me to fly out to L.A. to read for the part."

Ana couldn't breathe. She felt like she had when she'd fallen out of a tree as a little girl, like she'd just hit the ground at a hundred miles an hour. She wanted to join in the congratulations and agree with everyone else that this was in fact awesome and cool, but she couldn't speak.

"There's all this stuff I have to do first. I have to go to her office tomorrow and sign with her so she can represent me, but she said there is no fee, so it's not like I have anything to lose. She wanted to fax over my headshots to him, the producer guy I mean, tonight, and I was like, yeah sorry, I don't have those. She was flabbergasted, but she said she'd call him and tell him she has found his Garrett anyway. That's the character's name. The pilot is a mid-season replacement, and they've already cast everyone else over the last couple months, but the producers and directors can't agree on someone to play Garrett. So basically I'll fly out and see if they like my look. They want to start taping right away. They'll shoot twelve episodes in about two months in Los Angeles and it'll replace some show on the WB I've never heard of in January."

"I thought you said it was in New York," Chelsey said.

"It's set there, but they actually film it in L.A."

"Marin, congratulations, I'm so happy for you," Ana finally managed. She called upon every shred of talent she'd developed as an actress over the last six years to sound convincing.

"It's not like I got the part yet. I'm just going to read for it. The character is supposed to be cute and spunky and funny, obviously."

"Still, it's so exciting!" Chelsey said.

"She wants me to fly out tomorrow. The ticket's going to cost like $1500."

"Won't they pay for it?" Chelsey asked.

"No. Not unless I get the part. Are you kidding? I'm sure there are four million cute spunky girls in L.A.; it's not like they need to ship girls in from across the country."

"Apparently they do. You're totally gonna get it, girl!" Ramiro said.

"This calls for a drink!" Scott said. He ran behind the Spur of the Moment bar and began searching out the appropriate cocktail for such an occasion. "Well, I don't see any champagne. What do you think about Gray Goose?"

As the others talked and laughed, Ana did her best to act like she was happy and interested in what was going on. Luckily, Kieran just sat there and drank and was happy to be entertained by the other five Spur of the Momenters and didn't seem to mind that Ana ignored him completely. Despite Ana's vowing never to drink again, she did three shots of vodka in succession, then sat there in the middle of the boisterous room, not hearing or seeing anything. She tried not to think about how she was the one who had done all the publicity to get a full house and get the talent agent to come, yet it was Marin who had been asked to fly out to L.A. to potentially star in a TV series. Ana was reeling. It felt like there was a black hole in her chest, sucking out all the air in her lungs.

After a couple hours, she couldn't take it anymore, and she staggered to the bathroom, closed the stall door, collapsed to the floor, and wept.

29

Destination Hollywood

Thank god for credit cards. Marin had several, a couple of which hadn't been completely maxed out—just enough to cover her airfare and hotel expenses for the next few days.

As Marin waited for her flight, she flipped through the latest issue of *People*. It was the only thing light enough for her to handle with the constant barrage of announcements about how unattended baggage would be confiscated or it was time to board, or for Mr. So and So, Mr. John So and So to please come to the customer service desk.

"Where are you headed?"

She looked up. A good-looking guy in his twenties had sat down next to her. He looked at her expectantly.

"L.A."

"Oh, I thought we might be on the same flight together. But I'm headed to Arizona. Spring training in the winter."

"Spring training? For like, the military?"

"No, no," he laughed. "Soccer. I'm going to play for the Arizona Sahuaros. They're a professional soccer team."

"Oh cool." Marin thought a moment. "Never heard of them."

"Soccer isn't as big in the States as in other countries, but we're getting there. What are you off to L.A. for? Going to be a movie star?"

"I hope to get there someday, but now I'm just going out there to audition for a TV series. Well, a pilot anyway."

"You're kidding, right?"

"No. Why would I kid? I don't even know your name."

"A TV series, wow. Aren't you nervous?"

"No. If it's meant to be, it's meant to be."

The PA system boomed overhead that her flight was boarding.

"Well it was nice to talk to but not meet you," Marin said, shaking his hand.

"You too. Ahh, I'm Blake Hennsley."

"I'm Marin Kennesaw."

"I'll be able to say I knew you when."

"Don't worry, I won't forget the little people."

"I bet they all say that."

"Yeah. Of course we do."

And truly, Marin wasn't nervous. She arrived in L.A., took a taxi to Burbank, and checked into the Graciela Burbank, the hotel where her agent had told her she should stay. It was an upscale place and even though Marin got the cheapest room they had, the cost was exorbitant. She dropped off her baggage, freshened up, and took another taxi to the studio.

Then she started to get nervous. Driving through the windy parking lot, seeing all the sets and soundstages, she realized suddenly she was *this close* to making her dreams come true. Ever since she'd been a little kid, she'd wanted to be an actress in the movies, on TV, on stage—she wanted it all. She had imagined winning an Emmy, a Golden Globe, and, of course, an Academy Award. She'd practiced her Academy Award acceptance speech about four million times. She'd timed it at about seven minutes, even though she knew the winners were only supposed to have forty-five seconds. It was a fantasy. In her fantasy, she could tell lengthy, poignant stories about all the people who'd helped her along the way, which would make the fact that she left her parents off that list that much more pointed. Every now and then she'd imagine that as she started her climb to success, her parents would finally be there for her, and she'd include them in her acceptance speech, but even thinking that she'd have to get famous to get their attention pissed her off all that much more.

A receptionist—an eighteen-year-old knockout—gave Marin the script she would be reading from. Marin waited in the lobby for about half an hour, reading the script and getting a feel for how she should play Garrett. Then the receptionist brought Marin to a tiny room that was packed with about twenty-five people.

"Hi, I'm Don Gordon, the director of *Roommates*." A man thrust his hand forward for her to shake. He introduced the two producers, and the rest of the people went without being introduced.

"Hi, I'm Marin Kennesaw."

"Great. Can I get a copy of your headshots?" Don said.

"Um, I don't actually have any." A collective gasp splintered through the room. Marin thought quickly and pulled off the last sheet of her script, which didn't contain any lines for her. She drew a round face, gave it eyeballs, a smile, and a few doodles of hair and wrote her name beneath it. She handed it to Don, who laughed.

"Well, it's actually better than a lot of headshots I've seen."

Some guy with zero personality read all the other parts as Marin did hers. The director kept running behind the camera, apparently to see how she looked on camera.

"All right. I'd like you to read with the other characters tomorrow, eight A.M.," Don said.

"Okay, well, thanks a lot for your time."

Marin was confused. That he asked her back seemed a good sign, but he seemed totally unexcited about her performance, and hadn't told her if he liked her or if she sucked or what.

Marin went to her hotel and made some calls asking around about getting headshots. The average cost was four hundred bucks. She might not need them right away, but it looked like she'd need them someday to be in this business; it was best to be prepared. Her birthday was coming up; maybe she could talk her dad into forking over some money so she could get the pictures taken.

She called Ana and dutifully reported all the day's events.

"The entire room nearly exploded with shock when I told them I didn't have headshots. So I drew a stick figure kind of face on the back page on the script and gave it to the director. He laughed, so I guess that's a good sign. But the point is, we have to get headshots."

"How much are they?"

"About four hundred bucks."

"Ouch."

"Uh-huh."

"So when do you think you'll find out?"

"They want to start taping right away, so soon. I guess."

"Break a leg, babe."

"I'll do my best."

30

Going and Going and Never Getting Anywhere

The next day at work, Ana was clearly in a funk. Scott kept trying to cheer her up, cracking jokes and telling stories, but Ana was in her own world, and more often than not, she didn't hear him or only smiled wanly in response.

"You're awfully quiet," Scott said.

It took Ana a moment to realize he'd said something.

"What?"

"I said you're awfully quiet. Are you okay?"

"I'm not feeling very well. I think I may be coming down with something."

All day, Ana felt like a vise was squeezing her heart, tighter and tighter. She went through the motions of working, but couldn't concentrate on anything.

Ana sucked in her stomach. Maybe if she hadn't put on so much weight, she would be the one flying out to audition. She remembered reading an interview with Jennifer Aniston in which the 5'5" tall Jennifer said that she used to weigh 140 pounds and was told by her agent that she'd never get any parts unless she lost thirty pounds. So she did. And then she got the part of Rachel Green.

Which just proved what a brutal business acting was. Women were not only expected to be thin, but underweight. Ana would do whatever it took to make it.

That night, Ana changed into her sweats and lay on the bed

to wait for the phone to ring. She was dreading the phone call from Marin. Whether Marin got the part or had bombed big time, Ana just didn't think she could handle talking to her.

"Have you eaten?" Scott asked.

"Aah!" Ana jumped, yelping with surprise.

"Sorry. I didn't mean to scare you." Scott came into her room and sat down next to her.

"No, it's okay, I'm off in my own little world."

"So have you eaten?"

"I'm not hungry." That wasn't remotely true. She was starving.

"Are you okay?"

She nodded. Scott crawled on to the bed and sat next to her. "'Cuz you don't look okay."

"I'm . . . I guess I'm in a state of shock. I mean it's happening. Our dreams. . . Marin is in L.A. auditioning for a part in a show . . ."

"It's exciting."

"Yeah."

"But you wish it were you."

"Yeah."

Scott took her hand. They stayed there for several minutes, not saying a word. Then the phone rang. Ana's heart raced. Scott picked up the phone that was next to him on her bedside table and handed it to her.

It was Kieran. Ana was completely taken aback. She'd been expecting to hear from Marin.

"Hi," she said weakly.

"Hi. I had a great time the other night."

But Ana had been in the Twilight Zone, unable to do or say a thing. How could he have had fun? "Uh-huh," she said. It was the most noncommittal thing she could think of to say.

"I was wondering if you might want to go out sometime. Tomorrow night maybe."

Fuck. She couldn't believe she had to deal with this right now. "You know, Kieran, I don't know you very well and you seem like a nice guy, but I'm not sure I'm really looking to date anybody, even casually, at least not right now. A lot of stuff has been going on. A lot of things have changed since Saturday. Well, might have changed, I . . . look, you know what, this was just not a good time for you to call me. I have your number and maybe when my head has cleared and the world is back to normal . . . I might be ready to go on a date, just you and me."

"Sure," he said. He sounded disappointed. "You know, I probably just caught you at a bad time. Maybe I'll call you in a couple weeks when things have settled down for you. It must have been crazy, getting ready for the show."

"Yeah, yeah, exactly. I need some downtime. So . . . so I guess we'll play things by ear."

"Talk to you later."

Ana hung up the phone.

"That didn't go too badly for a break up, did it?" Scott said.

"We were never going out. I agreed to go on a date with him under the influence of far too many beers to make a sound judgment."

"Is that true, about you not wanting to date anybody?"

"It wasn't true for the last several months, but somehow, today it's true. Or maybe I just know Kieran wasn't what I was looking for. I want a guy like you or Jason or Ramiro, well, except straight of course. But I mean, a guy who makes me belly laugh all the time. I just want a guy who gets my jokes and who I can talk to without even having to think about it and who makes me laugh so hard I cry. Is that too much to ask?"

"I don't think so," Scott said quietly. "Why don't we get something to eat?"

Ana nodded gloomily, and followed him downstairs to the kitchen.

The phone rang again. Ana picked up the extension in the kitchen.

"Hello?"

"I got it."

"What?"

"I got the part!"

"Oh my god!" Ana and Marin shrieked. "Ohmygodohmy-godohmygod!"

Jason and Ramiro came running when they heard the commotion.

"Did somebody die?" Scott asked.

"I take it Marin got the part," Jason said calmly.

"She got the part! Shegotthepartshegotthepartshegotthepart!!! So tell me everything," Ana said to Marin.

"Today I read with the other actors. There are three guys—Alex, Conrad, and Bennett—and two girls, Devin and Jessica."

"Do you like them?"

"Yeah, I guess. Devin is this cute black girl, and Jessica has this glorious—totally fake, but glorious nonetheless—red hair half way down her back. They are both actually pretty funny. Devin is thirty! And she plays a twenty-one-year-old. Isn't that funny? Conrad is your typical WASPy guy who is arrogant and looks like some Aryan-Nation Ken doll. Alex is very hot, I hope there's a romance written in our future. And Bennett seems, I don't know, really quiet for an actor. Kind of reserved. Maybe he's just one of those types you need to ply with alcohol or have to get to know them for a while before they'll open up."

"So, where are you staying? How much money will you make? When do you start shooting?"

"I'll be out here till just after Christmas. If the series turns out to be successful, I'll have to get an apartment out here."

"No! You can't move!"

"We'll see what happens. For now we're all just staying in a hotel. They'll run the pilot at the end of January."

"Oh my god, are you so unbelievably excited? You don't sound like you're jumping up and down."

"This whole thing is just so surreal. I mean it's happening so fast. It hasn't had time to sink in yet. But get this. They're paying me $60,000."

Ana hadn't been expecting that. She'd been expecting slave wages. "Wow, that's a lot more money than I would have thought."

"They have to pay me a certain amount because to be able to perform, I need to belong to AFTRA, the American

Federation of Television and Radio Actors. It's a union. I had to be offered the contract from a TV show to be able to join, but then to actually act, I have to sign up."

Sixty thousand dollars. It was significantly more money than Ana made in an entire year, and Marin was raking it in for just eight weeks of work. "Wow," she mumbled in a hoarse whisper.

"Listen, you guys were the first people I called. I have to call Chelsey and Mom and Dad and everybody from high school and college and anybody else I can brag to."

"Congrats, Marin. I'm really happy for you."

"Love ya."

"Love you." Ana hung up the phone.

"So? Tell us everything!" Scott said.

Ana repeated what Marin had said, then, while the three of them were talking, she sneaked upstairs to her bedroom, closed the door, and burst into tears.

She fell on her bed and pressed a pillow to her face to mask the sound of her sobs.

Ana awoke the next morning in a dark fog of depression. It took everything she had to get out of bed and into the shower.

She stood in the shower and let the hot water beat down on her for several minutes. She had no idea how long she'd been just standing there, until there was a knock on the door and Scott's voice calling out, asking if she was okay.

"What? Oh, I'm fine."

"It's almost eight. You're going to be late to work."

"I'll hurry." Eight o'clock? What time had she woken up? How could it possibly be so late?

She quickly washed her body and shampooed her hair, skipping the conditioner today. She got dressed in a daze and when she went downstairs, Scott pointed out that she was wearing one black shoe and one brown one. They were completely different styles.

"Are you okay?"

"Yeah, I just . . . I didn't get a lot of sleep last night."

"I made you some coffee."

"Thanks."

This was all backwards. Ana was the mom of the house. She was the one who made the coffee in the morning and asked everyone if they'd slept well and worried and fretted if they hadn't. She was the one who looked out for everybody, not the one who needed looking after. But she was too tired to think about it right now.

At work, Ana was completely unable to focus. Every email she was sent seemed to be written in ancient hieroglyphics; some weird language that she had to battle to translate. Everything took so much effort. It exhausted her.

She stared at her computer screen until it faded into a blue haze. She was a failure. She was kidding herself thinking she had any talent. This was a brutally tough business, and the talentless could not survive. Unless, of course, their father was Aaron Spelling. All these years, she'd just been embarrassing herself, getting on that stage and pretending she could act. She needed to accept that she would not be an Academy Award-winning actress whose face graced the pages of *People* and *Vanity Fair.* She was a marketing manager, and she had to accept that all she'd ever be in her life was a woman who marketed software.

Lots of people were happy with a life mired in the morass of middle management. Why wasn't that good enough for Ana?

So few people succeeded as actors. What were the chances that all six of them would make it? Marin was the beauty, the natural talent. Of course she'd be the one to make it. Ana should stop embarrassing herself by pretending she had a chance.

For the next several days, depression tightened its grip on Ana.

She cried in the car at stoplights, she cried herself to sleep, she cried at the office in the bathroom stall. She cried because she was jealous and because she hated herself for being such a horrible person. She'd always said that you could tell who your friends were not just by whether they were there for you if things were tough, but if they could be genuinely happy for you when you succeeded. And now here she was: She *was* happy her friend was succeeding, but she was also painfully envious.

Ana believed that there were five areas in life that people had to work on to be happy: Love, Friendship, Work, Health, and Finance. She hated her job and she didn't have any money or a boyfriend. Except for friendship, she was bombing big time in everything. And she was depressed because, on top of everything else, she deeply, deeply missed her friend.

She tried to keep her workouts up, but she didn't have the concentration to lift weights. The only thing she could manage was to mindlessly jog on the elliptical rider. Going for miles and miles and never getting anywhere, that was all she could do.

31

The Plight of the Modern Male

One of the nice things about having three gorgeous women as best friends, Scott thought, was that he had all the commitment of a serious relationship with the added bonus of relentless sexual frustration.

After shows at Spur, flocks of men would gather around the women. These were the kind of men that could handle bitter rejection, glowering looks, and pointed comments without notice. They simply went on to the next kill and took what they could get.

Scott was not one of these kind of men.

Women would coo and purr at Jason and even—and this broke Scott's heart—Ramiro, but something about Scott's goofiness and his total inability to put the moves on a woman kept him forever classified as "Buddy." His three brothers and sisters were all married, some were even having kids, and he feared he would forever be the only single person in his family. He'd eternally be the weird artistic outsider who didn't grow up and get married as he had been fervently trained to do. To his nephews and nieces he was incredibly popular. As an uncle he reigned supreme. As a lover, he expected Elmer Fudd fared better.

Scott was more the kind of guy that, at dance clubs, would first try to get noticed as the funny guy by dancing goofily and going all out while doing so. At his height, it was hard not to notice. But once he found a woman he thought looked intriguing, he suddenly tried his best to become invisible, dancing sort of behind her to her side, hoping that she would turn, become instantly smitten, and thus begin a sincere and fulfilling long-term relationship.

He feared, though, that the smoky, drunken atmosphere of a bar was perhaps not the ideal setting to form a meaningful, long-lasting commitment. But what other choice did he have?

Scott put the finishing touches on a painting he was working on. Art was the one area of his life where he'd always felt confident. He was in grade school when he realized he was talented. His class was asked to draw pictures for Valentine's Day cards. He'd drawn, naturally, several hearts, and when his teacher came behind him to inspect his progress, her mouth fell agape.

"Your hearts are perfectly equal on either side!"

Yeah, so?

"You are an artist," she declared. She patted him on the shoulder, shook her head in disbelief, then moved on.

Scott inspected the work of his classmates nearby, and his teacher was right, everybody drew asymmetrical hearts. They would be curvy on one side and then too angular on the other. Or one side would be bigger than the other. Maybe he did have an artist's eye; the ability to translate what he saw in his mind through his fingers onto the page.

Scott became an ardent sketcher-in-the-notebooks kind of guy. He adored comics—they were proof he could draw and then sell what he created. He could actually make a living at this! He managed to do well in his classes despite his endless doodling. So well that his math teacher encouraged him to apply to colleges. His parents had wanted all their kids to go to college. Some of his siblings had gone to community colleges for a while before dropping out, but none earned their degree. Scott would be the first to graduate from a university.

As he researched schools, he came across the major "graphic design." He'd never heard of it before. Certainly in his small town, nobody worked as a graphic designer. When he learned what graphic designers were paid, he abandoned his plans to become a comic strip creator (his passion for the medium was waning as he grew older anyway) and decided to be a graphic designer. He liked his job (except, of course, for The Big Weasel), his friends, his life. He just wished he had someone to share it all with.

32

Acting on Instinct

Saturday morning Ana awoke to a head-splintering hangover. Despite her vow never to drink again and the fact that alcohol was strictly forbidden from her weight-loss plan, she'd been drinking like crazy over the last week. She parted the curtains, hoping the sunny sky would rejuvenate her and give her the will to do something productive. Instead, it was gray and snowing. It looked as bleak as she felt. Winter had finally made its way to Denver.

Ana spent the next couple of hours in bed staring at the ceiling and feeling sorry for herself. She thought of various things she should do to further her career: Work on a stand-up routine and work the open mike night at Comedy Works. Refine the sketches she wrote for the show, tightening them up and making the parts the audience didn't find funny, funny.

She might have stayed there all day except for a phone call she got from Ram, asking her if she could pick him up from work since Nick was in L.A. for business and he just couldn't face riding the bus in this weather.

She thought of having to scrape the ice and snow off her car, navigate the slippery roads, face the brutal cold. It had all the appeal of surgery without anesthesia, but at least it would get her out of bed. Maybe that was all she needed to start feeling better. "Sure, I'll be there. When do you get off?"

"Two-thirty."

That gave her an hour to take a shower and down a pot of coffee, several pain relievers, and a cup of detoxifying tea. "See ya then."

Ana went through her post-drunken-debauchery rituals and still felt like crap.

She got to the bookstore a few minutes early, and since she was able to find a parking space near the door, she decided to wait for Ramiro inside.

Ana knew she should never go anyplace where money could be spent when she was hungover. She had no willpower or restraint in this state. So when she passed by the book about the history of *Saturday Night Live* called *Live from New York*, she picked it up and read about half of the first sentence of the jacket flap copy and decided she simply must have it, even though it was a hardcover and she never let herself splurge on hardcover books. In the point-eight seconds it took her to give herself permission to buy it, she reasoned that it would help her with her career. It would inspire her, give her tips on the biz, and surely help her reach her goals that much faster. Anyway, you were supposed to spend money to make money. That was all she was doing: Investing in her future.

She paid for it and, as she waited for Ram by the door to the employee lounge, she started the book. She'd only gotten a few pages by the time Ram grabbed her in a bear hug, lifted her off the ground, and yelled, "You are the best! You are my hero!" but she was already hooked.

"Whatcha got there?" he asked.

"It's the book that promises to share all the dirty little secrets about the history of *Saturday Night Live* from the writers, producers, performers, execs, everybody."

"You know I could have bought the book at twenty-five percent off."

"I know, but I figured I'll just read it and return it. I don't know. I'm crazy hungover and not able to think straight."

"You're not feeling well? You should take the night off. The four of us can handle a show without you."

"Really? You think?"

"I do."

"Maybe I will."

At home, Ana changed back into her PJs, crawled back into bed, and delved into her 600-page book.

Once she started, she couldn't put it down. She'd always admired performers from *SNL* and Second City. (You'll remember that she cracked a joke about how *SNL* wasn't funny on the poster for Primordial Stew. Her rationale was that it was sometimes true, and damn it, it was a joke, get over it already.) She was particularly in awe of Tina Fey, who was the first female head writer in *SNL's* twenty-five-year history. Marin had gone to Upright Citizen's Brigade theater in New York over the summer when she'd visited her family. *SNL* member Amy Pohler was one of the founding members of UCB, and both she and Tina could be found there some Sunday nights.

Ana read until midnight, mostly because, even though she was exhausted, her heart was racing like crazy from all the alcohol she'd consumed the night before. She was at the part in which Lorne Michaels flies out to The Groundlings theater in Los Angeles to decide whether to hire Julia Sweeney or Lisa Kudrow. Each of them performed three sketches. Julia got it. Lisa said she didn't let it get her down, she just thought about how she didn't get it because she was supposed to get something else. And boy did she ever.

Ana would have been devastated if she hadn't gotten a job on the show that catapulted the likes of Chevy Chase, Gilda Radner, John Belushi, Eddie Murphy, Mike Myers, Joe Piscapo, Jon Lovitz, Phil Hartman, Chris Rock, and Adam Sandler to fame and fortune. But look how Lisa Kudrow turned out. She was making something like a million bucks an episode on one of the most popular shows in recent history. Not bad.

Maybe the same thing applied to her and Marin. Marin got the job in L.A. because Ana was supposed to get something else, something better suited to her personality.

Throughout the book, performer after performer and writer after writer kept repeating that doing the show was absolutely exhausting. They always stayed up all Tuesday night and worked crazy hours the rest of the time as well. They repeatedly mentioned how competitive it was, with all these performers battling to get airtime to show what they could do and all the writers struggling to get their scenes picked to be on the show. Larry David, who would later become the co-producer of *Seinfeld*, only got one or two sketches on the entire year he worked there. Ana thought it was bad when she had to rewrite brochure copy twelve times before going to print; she couldn't even imagine how frustrating it must be to go without sleep for twenty-two weeks only to have her sketches scrapped or cut at the last minute every single time.

Maybe Ana just wasn't tough enough for this business. Maybe she was just someone for whom comedy and performing would be a hobby, something she could talk about at dinner parties when she was married and had left all her lofty ambitions of fame and fortune behind.

Ana shook her head when she got to a part in the book where it said that some of the performers had been "failures" because they hadn't gone on to make zillions of dollars in the movies after leaving the show. Hello, they'd managed to get on *Saturday Night Live*, probably only something like .00000000000000000002 of the population could say that. It was no easy feat. You had to have serious talent to get there. That was the thing, though. If you're a little fish working at Spur of the Moment in Denver, Colorado, and you don't make a movie or the movie you make stinks, you don't have every journalist in the world declaring you a talentless has-been. But if you achieve enough success to get on the popular-culture radar, you opened yourself up to public ridicule for the slightest infraction.

Ana put the book down at last, turned off the lights, and wondered if she had what it took to get on *SNL*. And if she did achieve some degree of fame, would she be able to handle the inevitable hate mail and scathing articles about her that would follow? Or would she do what John Belushi did after reading a negative review of himself for his work in *Continental Divide*, abusing drugs and alcohol after two years of abstinence until he died at the age of 33?

Ana felt suddenly very old, like the window of opportunity

for her to make it was closing. She needed to move to New York and take classes at Upright Citizen's Brigade—get her face known with the powers that be in New York comedy. She needed to be prepared for anything, whether it was to have a store of characters she could draw on if Lorne Michael's decided to stop by at the last minute to see her perform, or to be able to whip out one hilarious sketch after another, week after week. She needed to improve her acting skills. She needed to get stand-up experience. She needed to learn how to sing and play the guitar and write funny songs. She needed to know how to write movie scripts like Adam Sandler. She needed to . . .

As she listed all the ways she needed to improve lest she become a washed-up, talentless old hag before she even turned twenty-five, she finally fell asleep.

Ana wished she were the kind of person who couldn't eat when she was depressed. She got the "couldn't sleep" part down pat, but becoming miraculously skinny without even trying was not hers to be had. She was of the eat-to-feel-better variety.

But she was enjoying her workouts with Chelsey. Chelsey worked muscles Ana didn't know she had, and while Ana was inevitably a little sore after their sessions together, she liked to believe that burning pinching pain in her ass or wherever was the feeling of thousands of calories being consumed by muscles working overtime.

She was eating well during the day, but at night when she came home and her evil trio of skinny male roommates bombarded her with offers of wine or beer or foodstuffs drenched in butter or cheese, it nearly killed her to make a veggie burger (110 calories, 2 grams fat) with a whole wheat bun (120 calories, 1 gram fat) with mushrooms and onions sautéed in Pam (15 calories, no fat) with a bowl of vegetable soup (100 calories). Chelsey said in six weeks, as long as Ana stuck to the plan, she would get over her cravings for fat and calories. But as Ana longingly watch Scott devour a heaping plate of nachos, washing it down with one beer after another, she feared this was a cruel lie. How could she ever not salivate over the sight of nachos and beer?

After the first couple weeks of drinking heavily after Marin had gone to California, Ana was back to abstaining from alcohol. It just sucked watching everyone else have fun after the shows while she drank water with lemon and felt sorry for her fat ass. *This is the price of fame*, she kept repeating to herself. *This is the price of fame.*

Ana washed down three glasses of water to trick her stomach into thinking it was full. Then she went up to bed to feel sorry for herself some more. Self-pity had become her new hobby.

After a few minutes, Scott came in and slid into bed next to her.

"You've been little Mary Sunshine lately."

"Yeah. I know."

"It's because of Marin?"

"It's because I'm fat and untalented and hopelessly ordinary."

"Ana, you are gorgeous and wickedly talented and you couldn't be ordinary if you tried." He turned on his side, propping his head in his hand, his elbow against the bed so he could really look at her. "God, you really believe all those horrible things about yourself, don't you? Let's start at the beginning. You are not fat. You're one of the sexiest women I've ever known."

She rolled her eyes. "Whatever."

"I've always thought you were totally hot. You're busty and curvy and if you weren't my best friend, I'd ravish you. You can ask Jason. I always used to groan to him about how hanging around you gave me perpetual blue balls."

"It's nice of you to lie, but I've been friends with Marin for six years and guys hit on her like mad and ignore me totally."

"Marin is cute, I'll give her that. But she's totally skinny and her tits are way too small. Guys hit on her because she's open and friendly. You always look stressed out about something. You scowl like 98 percent of the time."

"I do?"

"Guys are terrified you're going to claw their eyes out if they try anything with you."

"You really think I'm sexy?"

"I think you're gorgeous. You're beautiful. You're stunning."

"Beautiful? Stunning?"

"Beautiful. Stunning."

Ana thought about this. "I can't believe it, but that actually makes me feel better." She chewed her lip, contemplating this revelation some more. "But if you think I'm so hot, how come you never put the moves on me?"

"Because you've had a crush on Jason for six years. I can't compete with pretty boy Jason."

"I think you're cute."

"Not as cute as Jason."

"I'm over Jason. He's too perfect. It's exhausting."

"So I can put the moves on you?"

Ana considered this. They had made out that one time, and it had been a wonderful time. Plus, it had been such a long time since she'd gotten any. Ana nodded.

"Should we have sex?" he asked.

"I think so."

"I'll get to see your tits?"

She nodded again.

"Yes!" Scott punched the air in victory. "Awesome. I've wanted this for so long."

"Have you ever fantasized about me?"

"All the time."

"But that's so weird. We're best friends."

"Whatever. I'm a guy. I have testosterone. You have enormous luscious breasts and the sexiest legs in the universe. You do the math."

"So how should we do this? Should we get some wine and light some candles?"

"I don't think that's necessary. All we need to do is take off all our clothes and then start fucking like rabbits."

He began unbuckling his pants.

"Scott, you dork, the door is wide open. I'm going to get

some wine and light some candles and we're going to lock the door and we'll go about this like normal adults. Anyway, I don't have any condoms. Do you?"

"I might. But I think they're from like 1979. Do you know how long it's been since I've had sex?"

She laughed. "You were six years old in 1979."

"I'll go ask Ramiro for a condom."

"But then he'll know what we're doing."

"Yeah. So?"

"So that's so weird."

"Ram will be thrilled that my long crush on you will be re-quited."

Ana smiled. "Okay. Meet me back here in a few minutes."

Ana lit several candles and turned off the lights. She got a bottle of wine (she wasn't supposed to drink, but it had been a *year* since she'd had sex and she was going to have a couple celebratory glasses of wine, damn it) and two glasses and brought it all upstairs. Scott was waiting for her on the bed with a box of twelve condoms.

"Think that'll be enough?" she joked.

"For now anyway."

Ana sat on the edge of the bed and drank her wine quickly. Suddenly she felt nervous and awkward. What had she been thinking, agreeing to do this? She'd gone nuts from depression, dieting, and jealousy. What if this didn't work out? They lived together. Their friendship would be over.

Scott sat up and pulled her close to him. Ana took a deep breath, pushed her worries aside, and did what six years of improv training had taught her to do: She acted on her instincts.

Sex with Scott had been amazing. Sex was so much fun! Why hadn't she done it in such a long time? It was awesome!

They made love three times that night and once in the morning, and though Ana was sore, she wanted more, more, more.

All day at work, she looked over at Scott and smiled. She couldn't wait until they went home so they could have more sex. She wished one of them had a van so they could go in the back of it and have sex for their entire lunch hour.

She thought of the way he'd kissed her neck, the way his face had looked with his eyes closed as he strained toward orgasm, the way his fingers felt trailing their way from her cheek, down her neck, across her collarbone, between her breasts, then making their way to her hip bone, where they lingered for quite sometime. Scott had told her she had the sexiest hip bone he'd ever seen. It was an odd compliment, to be sure, but Ana loved that someone thought a part of her body she'd never stopped to consider was the sexiest one of its kind.

Ana crossed her legs. It would do no good at all to get horny at work.

She couldn't believe how a little nookie could improve her spirits so much. She still felt the ache of depression, but the world seemed decidedly brighter today than it had the day before.

There was no question that all the usual clichés about feeling in love were apropos: She did feel like she was walking on air—no, actually she felt like she was skiing on air, down a treacherous, out-of-bounds black diamond mountain at a zillion miles an hour. But in a good way, an exhilarated way. She didn't know what she was doing or where she was going or if there were cliffs and forests coming up, but somehow she had this strange sense of ease, that everything was going to be all right.

A box popped up on her computer screen informing her that she had new mail, and wondering if she'd like to read it now. "Yes," she clicked.

To: *anajacobs@abbott.com*
From: *scottwinn@abbott.com*

You are the sexiest, smartest, most talented, funniest woman I have ever known. I crave you in the most amazing way.

It was crazy, but Ana felt the same way.

Ana hit REPLY.

To: scottwinn@abbott.com
From: anajacobs@abbott.com

> *Dear Mr. Winn,*
> *I'm simply scandalized that you'd abuse work resources in such a manner.*
> *PS: I've been thinking about having sex with you all morning. I'm still thinking about it in fact. Right now I'm imagining taking you into my mouth . . .*

Ana hit SEND. She couldn't stop smiling.

T̲hat night, Ana called Marin at the hotel where she was staying.

"You're never going to believe it," Ana said. "I had sex with Scott."

"God. *Finally.* I've been waiting for you to hook up forever."

"You have?"

"We all have. It's so obvious Scott is madly in love with you and you guys are best friends and are practically joined at the hip."

"He is? We are?"

"So how was it?"

"It was awesome. It was so much fun. I love sex! I'd forgotten how yummy it is."

"Good for you, girlfriend. You deserve some good loving."

"He's a really good kisser, too. And his hands . . ."

"That's enough! There is only so much I want to know about Scott."

"So how are things with you?"

"It's pretty intense. We tape an hour-long show every six days. I think the shortest day I've had here was twelve hours.

Listen to this. In the first episode, I do a stand-up routine at a comedy club, and I do really well, right? Okay, but listen to some of the jokes they have me tell. 'What is the difference between men and women? Men are crabby all month long.'"

"No, not a PMS joke. That's so late eighties."

"I know."

"Anyway, I don't get it. Is that supposed to be funny?"

"They just play the laugh track, so no matter how unfunny I am, I get laughs."

"Can't you make some suggestions for jokes that are actually funny?"

"I tried. I thought I was really nice about it, but the director bit my head off. Apparently they don't much care for nobody actors trying to rewrite their teleplays."

"But you're a comedian."

"Yeah, but they don't want my opinion, just my pretty face reciting their lines."

"You think the series will be a success?"

"Not with writing like this."

"What a bummer. Why don't they get the writers from *Felicity?*"

"I loved that show."

"It was the best. It's so, so wrong that it was taken off the air."

"The world is just not as bright without Keri Russell every Monday night."

"That rhymed. That would actually make a great song lyric. We could do skit where we lament all the TV shows that we liked that were taken off the air."

"Ooh, I like it."

"How do you like the rest of the cast?"

"Devin is awesome. She's hilarious."

"I don't like you making new friends."

"That's very mature."

"Look, I know it's not mature, but you're my best friend and you're not supposed to go off and make new friends and have all these adventures without me."

"Ana, nobody is ever going to replace you. You're my best friend and I love you."

"Yeah, I know, I just want to be sure that everyone else knows it. I want you to wear a T-shirt that says, 'Ana Jade Jacobs is my best friend in the universe and no one can take her place, so Devin, don't even think about it.'"

"Okay."

"Thanks."

"Ahh!"

Ana heard a thunderous crash. "Marin?"

A few seconds later, Marin got back on the phone, laughing hysterically.

"Marin? What happened?" Marin was laughing so hard, Ana couldn't make out what she was saying at first.

Then, "I fell off my chair!"

"You fell off your chair? I don't understand. Have you been drinking?"

"No! I had . . . feet up . . . leaning back . . . tipped over. Ah ah ah!"

Ana cracked up. For a couple of minutes, the only sound over the line was their laughter.

"You are such a loser!" Ana said at last, wiping the tears from her eyes.

"I know."

"I miss you."

"I miss you. Well, I guess I should get going."

"Okay. You should put a helmet on if you're going to do anything dangerous like sit on the couch or pour a glass of milk."

"I will. I love you."

"I love you."

"Smooch smooch, babe."

The best thing about sex with Scott was how much Ana laughed with him and how much fun she had with him. She loved how quickly a simple touch from her could transform his penis from a springy mushroom-looking thing to its full purply veined ridiculousness. Once he was hard, she liked to make him laugh so his penis would spring back and forth like a metronome on crystal meth. This would induce paroxysms of giggles from Ana.

After a couple minutes, Scott stopped laughing and swung his naked body over her so he was straddling her.

"Are you making fun of my manhood?"

"No, I'm making fun of your *throbbing* manhood." She kissed him and then made a thoughtful expression as she considered the term *manhood*. "Manhood—isn't that a funny term? Did you know when I went to cheerleading camp, one of our instructors was from the South and she told us to put our one hand between our 'personalities,' and we were all like, what? It turned out she meant breasts. Can you believe she'd . . ."

He shut her up with a slow, deep kiss. She was ready for him instantly, but he tortured her with light teasing caresses, kissing her on the inside of her thighs even though every thought and synapse in her body was pointing arrows that said, "Psst, over here, just a couple inches higher."

He turned her over on her stomach and gave her a long massage. She couldn't remember ever feeling so relaxed. Then he got to her butt and thighs. He slid his fingers inside her until she was making noises that she was sure were embarrassing and unladylike but she couldn't care less.

Ana didn't know how long they made love. She never once looked at the clock or thought of errands or chores she really should get done tonight before bed. She didn't worry about her day at work or what she'd have to get done tomorrow. She tuned out the world and just focused on how good her body felt. Her mind went to this place where she didn't think at all, it just swirled with colors and sensations.

They fell asleep entwined in each other's bodies, still sticky with sweat.

33

In the Shadows of the Limelight, Part One

Being on a television set was nothing like Marin had imagined it would be. The main thing about it was that it was *bor*ing. Excruciatingly so. She'd have to be at the set at four in the morning, then she'd sit there for an hour doing nothing as the techies fiddled with the lights or whatever, then she'd perform for two minutes and then go sit down again and wait for an hour till she performed again.

Television was a surreal experience, completely different from performing in a play. A play was acted out linearly, so one event triggered the next. Television was completely different. They taped the easy stuff early in the week. The scenes that involved any outdoor lighting or things that couldn't be controlled in a studio sound stage were done last. They worked the taping so that only the people who were in the scenes they were taping that day had to be there. Many of the scenes they'd have to run through two or three times so the camera could capture different angles or cutaways shots. Nothing happened linearly, so in a moment Marin might be yelling at Jessica yet didn't know what it was that had supposedly pissed her off. Or she'd have a heart-to-heart talk with Alex and have no idea what the event they were talking about was.

None of the women were needed on the set on Friday, so Thursday after they got off the set at two, they went home, napped, showered, gussied up, and headed out for a night on the town.

Jessica had done careful research about the trendiest clubs in L.A. She'd created a list and insisted that the three of them hit every one before they finished taping the show, "Just in case it doesn't get picked up and I have to return poor and unknown to Nevada."

The taxi—working on a television show had enabled them to indulge in luxuries like a taxi, and it wasn't like buses were big in L.A., if they even had them—dropped them off at the Good Luck Lounge just before eleven.

They found a circular table, and Jessica and Devin sat on the barstools encircling it.

"I'll get the first round. What do you guys want?" Marin asked.

"Dirty martini," Devin said.

"Diet Coke," Jessica said.

"How are you going to get drunk on a Diet Coke?" Marin asked reasonably.

"I can't afford the calories."

"You weigh about three ounces. You're four calories away from being declared anorexic and shipped off to the hospital. You can get a Diet Coke chaser, but I insist you do a couple shots. You can do an extra hour on the treadmill tomorrow."

"No I can't, really."

"Vodka, rum, J.D. What's it going to be? A couple shots won't kill you. They'll only make you stronger."

"You want us to think you're uncool?" Devin said.

"Peer pressure peer pressure," Marin began. Devin instantly joined her. "Peer pressure peer pressure."

"O-*kay*," Jessica finally agreed with a deep, beleaguered sigh. "Rum."

"Rum it is."

The bar was packed, so Marin walked passed the side of the bar staffed by a female bartender and went straight to the guy, who was underwear-model yummy. As usual, Marin blazed past the other people who had been waiting there. Even in a town in which gorgeous women were as common as bad jokes, Marin stood out.

"What did I miss?" Marin asked when she returned to the table.

"We were just talking about what we did before we got this job," Devin said.

"Which was?"

"I've been in L.A. since I was eighteen," Devin said. "I've done a couple commercials, I've done lots of pretending to be a sick patient for med students to diagnose, lots of stand-up, a few plays here and there, and to pay the bills, I've done it all. I've been a sushi deliverer, a tour guide, a sandwich maker, a nanny. For a while I read books to an old blind guy. I really liked that job but the bugger kicked the bucket and I had to find another job, which just sucked. I was a high-rise window washer for a while, a short order cook, and I've been a clown for kids' birthday parties."

"Damn, girl, you have done it all. Jess, how about you?"

Jessica downed her shot. She scratched her lip. Looked away. "I lived in Nevada till about four months ago. Since I got here I've worked as a lingerie model. We give private shows to guys. It's all totally legit," she said a little too quickly.

"Yeah, whadja do in Nevada?" Devin said, already suspecting the answer. Jessica didn't say anything. "You were a working girl, weren't you?"

"How did you know?"

"I don't get it, we all have to work," Marin said.

"Yes, but we're not *working girls*," Devin said.

Marin mouthed a large "oh" of the "I get it now" variety.

"Did you like it?' Devin asked. "How long were you a working girl?"

"Since I was eighteen, so about three years. Um, did I like it? Um, I made a shitload of money. Sometimes it was kind of fun I guess. I worked at the Bunny Ranch, which is known to be, like, the best brothel in the country. We get tested for STDs once a week, it's all very safe. I'd get a thousand bucks an hour . . ."

"Jesus Christ!" Devin said.

"Well, I mean, I'd get to keep $500."

"You only get half? But you did all the work!" Marin said.

"Um, you know, the house provides the room and all that."

"Who the hell can afford $1000 for an hour of fun?" Devin said.

"You'd be amazed."

"So, tell us everything. Did you do it all? Lick butts and do chicks and stuff?" Marin asked.

Jessica smiled. She was warming up to all the enthralled attention. She nodded.

"Screw a horse?" Marin asked.

"Once."

"Holy shit! I was kidding!" Marin and Devin cracked up. "How do you even . . . I mean . . ."

"You want to know the craziest thing?"

"There was something crazier than fucking a horse?" Marin shot Devin a look of amazement.

"One of my regulars had two ribs removed so he could blow himself."

"No! No! That's not possible! Gross!" Marin and Devin nearly fell off their stools they were laughing so hard.

When Marin and Devin calmed down, Marin wiped the tears from her eyes and said, "No, but seriously, what kind of doctor would remove parts of somebody's skeleton? That can't possibly be legal."

"I had it done. Working at the Bunny Ranch paid for all my surgeries."

"You had ribs removed?" Devin screeched.

"Why? Why?" demanded Marin.

"It makes me look skinnier."

"If you looked any skinnier . . . I mean you look like a prisoner of war."

"What other surgeries did you have?" Devin asked.

"My nose, my cheeks, my knees, my calves . . ."

"Knees like, from a skiing accident?" Marin asked.

"No, I had the fat around my knees removed."

"Knees have fat?"

"The area around them does. What surgeries have you guys had?"

"I haven't any surgeries." Marin said.

"Oh yeah right, you look like that naturally. Devin, how about you?"

"Breasts, stomach, butt . . ."

Marin sat there, open-mouthed with amazement. What insane world was she in? "But doesn't it hurt?"

"Like a motherfucker," Jessica said.

"It's excruciating."

"But you get a ton of Vicadin so you can just sleep for like two weeks. I hardly ate a thing and I lost a ton of weight. It was awesome," Jessica said.

Devin nodded.

"Come on, honestly, what have you had done?" Jessica asked.

"Honestly, nothing. I haven't even had braces."

Both Jessica and Devin gave her a "yeah right" roll of their eyes.

That's when Marin saw him walk in the bar. He was casually dressed in jeans and a silvery-gray, fitted sweater that Marin guessed cost about three hundred bucks. Same for the Bruno Magli black shoes. And the Ulysse Nardin watch? Around fifteen thousand. He had thick, wavy dark-blond hair and pale gray eyes that matched his icy sweater. She liked the way he smiled like he meant it, not that teeth-gritted, put-on, smile-for-the-camera kind of smile so common in people in *the biz*. And a movie person he most definitely was. A producer, she guessed.

She watched him casually as he ordered martinis for him and his friend—a guy, she was happy to note. His friend was also obviously well off. He was good looking, too, but he didn't have the casual confidence of the silver sweater guy. Green-sweater guy was trying too hard.

In Denver, all Marin had ever had to do to get a guy she thought was hot come talk to her was wait until he noticed her. But this was L.A., where beautiful women were like grains of sand on the beach—infinite, everywhere, and invasive. Maybe

Marin would actually have to do something to get a conversation with him going.

Marin, Devin, and Jessica continued talking for half an hour or so. Marin learned that Jessica had slept with six guys and a woman to get the role on *Roommates*. Marin suspected Jessica might not have actually *had* to screw seven people to get the part; she probably gave out sex preemptively just in *case* it could help her career. Marin's thesis was supported because Devin had just given one blow job to get an audition.

Marin finished her drink and tried not to look for the silver sweater guy. Just as she was plotting to "bump" into him on her way to the bathroom, deciding what she should say, the waitress brought her another Tanqueray and tonic. "Courtesy of the guy in the gray sweater," the waitress said.

Marin leaned back on her barstool, turned her head to meet his gaze, lifted the drink as if in a toast, and flashed him a smile. Then she returned her attention to Jessica and Devin. Well, she looked at them, pretending she didn't give a damn about the guy, when in fact, all she could do was think about what she should do next. Maybe she should approach him.

"I'm going to go over there and talk to him," Marin said at last.

"Good luck, girlfriend," Devin said.

She walked across the bar, watching him the whole time. When she reached him, he turned his gaze to match hers.

"Thanks for the drink."

"I figured it was the fastest way to ingratiate myself with you."

The remark was so unexpected she laughed. "I see."

"Let me guess: actress. Are you an actress-slash-something else, or one who actually makes a living at it?"

"Currently I'm in the makes-a-living-at-it camp, but that just started recently. I'm shooting a pilot for the WB. It's a mid-season replacement that will launch at the end of January."

"What were you before you were a sitcom actress?"

"A temp-slash-improv comedian."

"Oh my, a smart girl."

"You sound surprised. Are you saying that actresses aren't smart?"

"Oh they can be, but they're not always. Improv-ers are always smart. They have to be."

"Yeah, that's true, but how do you know that?"

"I have two really close friends at Second City in Chicago. When I lived out there I hung out with improv-ers all the time. They were without exception really bright."

"What brought you out here from Chicago?"

"Come on, sunny L.A. versus chilly Chicago?"

"So what do you do? Let me guess: producer."

He laughed. "The movie business isn't for me. I was an entrepreneur, now I'm retired."

"Retired? But you look like you're about thirty."

"I'm thirty-eight."

"Thirty-eight! Wow, you look good for thirty-eight."

He laughed again. "You must be pretty young to think thirty-eight is old."

"I am not. I'm twenty-four. Hey, stop laughing at me. Anyway, thirty-eight is young to retire."

"I got lucky with the company I built. I sold it three years ago for a very pretty penny. I play the stock market some, but mostly I just like to travel and enjoy life."

"So L.A. is your home base?"

"One of them. I have a place in New York, a place in France, a condo in Hawaii."

"Nice."

He shrugged. "I've been lucky."

He didn't seem like he was bragging. Most guys would try to impress her, going on and on about their cars and their swimming pools and their yachts. He was just telling her a fact about himself. He didn't seem proud, just lucky, like life had dealt him a very good hand, but it could have just as easily gone another way.

"My name is Marin Kennesaw, by the way."

"I'm Jay. Jay Prochazka."

"That's a mouthful."

"So am I."

Marin laughed again. Normally a joke like that would make her squirm.

"Jay, it was nice meeting you. Thanks for the drink. I should probably get back to my friends."

"I'd like to see you again. If you want, you can come over to my place, sit by the pool, and work on your tan."

"Thanks, but I don't go to a guy's house till I know them a little better, enough to get a sense of whether he'll cut me up into tiny pieces and bury me in the floorboards."

"I knew you were a smart girl. How about I take you out for a nice meal?"

"That sounds like a very nice idea."

"Can I get your number?"

"You could if I knew what it was. I'm staying at the Graciela Burbank, room 214."

"You don't have a place out here?"

"I'll get one if the show is picked up. I'm from Denver. Well, New York originally. I've been in Denver since college."

"I'll call you tomorrow."

"Sounds good. Talk to you later."

But he didn't call tomorrow, or the day after that. A week went by, and still she didn't hear from him.

34

Accidents

Chelsey fed her cat, Mo, giving her the usual dry food along with wet food. Chelsey used to buy expensive organic cat food when Mo was a kitty, but back then Mo had been a tiny, fluffy ball of flatulence, darting around the house emitting odors so noxious it was impossible to believe such a small creature could create such a vile smell. When Chelsey had guests over, Mo could take out a room as fast as a tear-gas bomb, everyone staggering around blindly, gasping for fresh air. So Chelsey had switched to the cheaper, chemically saturated stuff. It was the American way, really, and Mo should do her patriotic duty to keep the makers of various preservatives and dye-#-what-ever in business. Anyway, Mo was decidedly less stinky these days, which was always a good thing.

Chelsey walked to the bathroom peeling off her clothes, shedding them as she went as though she were leaving a trail of breadcrumbs. She pulled down her workout pants to sit on the toilet, and she felt a strange, disorienting fuzziness graze her butt. It was Mo, of course, who would use the toilet seat as a stepping stone to get to the bathroom sink, where she would moan plaintively until Chelsey turned on a trickle of water for her to drink. No matter that Chelsey had just poured Mo a fresh, cold bowl of water. Mo seemed to think it adventurous to seek out alternative water sources, which meant that Chelsey hadn't had water in a glass any time in the last two years. She had to have water bottles with lids, otherwise Mo would stick her entire face into the glass and sneeze two or three times for each sip of water she commandeered, despite the rules Chelsey had tried to lay down about not drinking from mom's glass.

Chelsey lifted Mo and carried her to the couch. Chelsey lay down and remained perfectly still for a full thirty seconds so Mo wouldn't run off. Mo considered, considered . . . kneading her paws into Chelsey's chest . . . was this really the best place to nap? Was there someplace better? This *was* warm and this scratching-behind-the-ears business sure did feel good . . . Finally Mo settled down with a general condescending air of "I guess this will do."

Chelsey listened to Mo purr as she scratched and petted her. Chelsey really should go make herself something to eat, but she felt too damn tired. All these late nights of practices and performances or having athletic sex for hours on end—it was good fun, all of it, but she often had early morning clients to meet, and she just wasn't getting the sleep she needed.

She knew that skipping meals wreaked havoc on her metabolism. She was doing absolutely everything she told her clients not to do: She was sleeping too little and irregularly, she was skipping meals and not always making the healthiest choices when she did eat . . . She would become a model citizen of dietary virtue tomorrow. Tonight, she just wanted to get her call from Rob from the station and stagger up to bed and pass out.

She looked at the clock. It was 7:30. He usually called between seven and eight on the nights he was at work.

After a few minutes, she picked up one of the ten books on Indians she'd bought. She'd bought mostly nonfiction books about Indian history and tradition, but she'd also bought fiction by Sherman Alexie, Leslie Marmon Silko, Adrian C. Louis, and Michael Dorris.

Chelsey wasn't sure when she fell asleep, but when phone woke her up, she glanced at the clock. 10:33.

"Hello?"

"Are you watching the news?" It was Ana.

"No. Why?"

Ana didn't say anything for a long moment. "I'm sure it's nothing. Rob isn't . . . he isn't on duty today, is he?"

"Yes. Oh my god. What's going on?" Chelsey struggled to get her eyes adjusted to the light and searched for the remote. She fumbled for it from her perch on the right side of the couch to the left arm rest where it lay and pressed POWER. What immediately popped on the screen was the local affiliate to NBC news.

The voluminously coiffed male reporter stood in front of burning house.

"It's still not clear what started the blaze of this three-story home in central Denver, but . . ." The reporter stopped talking and pressed his finger to his earpiece. "It's been confirmed, two firefighters are dead tonight and a third has been injured. Authorities are not revealing the identities of the two fallen firefighters pending notification of their families, but it appears that they were trapped when the roof collapsed."

"Oh my god," Chelsey whispered. "Oh my god."

"Chelsey, I'm coming over, okay? Chelsey?"

Chelsey nodded, which of course Ana couldn't see, but Ana hung up the phone and raced over anyway.

On screen, the reporter was explaining how a fire weakened the supporting joists and beams, which could cause the roof to collapse. On and on he went, talking about what heroes these firefighters were and how many other firefighters had died this year in Colorado and across the country.

It took Chelsey a long time first to even register the noise, then to understand that it was the sound of someone pounding on her door. Her first thought was: *The police are here to tell me that he's dead.*

That's when the tears came. She'd been in too much of a shocked trance before, but now she understood that Rob was gone. She had never been in love before him—she'd thought she had but she'd been too young and stupid to know what love meant. Now that she had found her true love, a guy who challenged her and always taught her something new and laughed at her jokes and made her laugh and whose hand was just the right size to hold hers, she'd lost him. She'd been too happy. No one deserved that much happiness and God was taking it away from her.

But when she opened the door, it wasn't the police, it was Ana, carrying a large box of Kleenex.

"How are you?"

Chelsey's sobbing renewed with additional force, and she gratefully reached out to take a handful of tissues.

"I have to call the fire station, see if they can tell me the news."

"I'll call," Ana said. She didn't need to say that Chelsey was crying so hard she could barely speak.

"No, I will." Chelsey grabbed the cordless phone. It took her four tries to dial the station correctly. "Shit, nobody is answering."

"They're probably all at the fire."

"Do you think I can call 911?"

"How would a 911 operator know about the firefighters?"

"I don't know. I need to do *something*."

She and Ana returned to the couch, where they kept a silent vigil in front of the TV. When the news was over and *The Tonight Show* came on, Chelsey flipped through all the channels, hoping to catch more news on the fire.

"Shit! What are they doing, putting on a comedy show when people are dying?" Chelsey screamed.

"Chelse, why don't you go back to channel nine and mute it, and then if a special report comes on, turn the volume back on."

Chelsey kept flipping channels frantically for several more minutes before conceding to Ana's plan.

"If he were alive he would call," Chelsey said.

"He's fighting a fire. He can't get to a phone."

"They said they'd gotten the fire out."

"I'm sure there is clean-up stuff. Or maybe he's with the injured firefighters at the hospital?"

"Or maybe he's in the hospital. Or the morgue."

Chelsey tried calling the station again. When no one answered, she held the phone in front of her and yelled, "What kind of public safety establishment are you? Why don't you have anyone to answer the damn phone?"

She slammed the receiver down and jumped up. She began pacing furiously back and forth across the living room floor, frantic with nervous energy.

"Do you think we should go to the station? To the hospital?"

"Did the news say which hospital the injured firefighters had been taken to?"

"I don't remember. I know! We can drive to the scene of the fire! Maybe there are firefighters there who know where Rob is."

Chelsey was running to the get her coat out of the closet before Ana could even answer her. Ana sprinted out the door behind Chelsey, grabbing her coat off the back of the kitchen chair on her way.

"I have a really good idea. Why don't you let me drive?" Ana said.

"No, no. I'll do it."

Chelsey was in no shape to be driving a 2,000-pound machine around. "If I drive, that'll let you keep your eye out in case you see anything."

"All right, all right."

Ana drove Chelsey's car to the scene of the fire. A number of curious neighbors were milling about, several firefighters in partial gear were cleaning up, and a man in uniform stood barking orders into what looked like a walkie-talkie—the fire chief, Chelsey guessed.

Chelsey tried to run up to one of the men in fire gear, but was stopped by the man in uniform.

"I'm sorry, you can't go near there," he said.

"I just . . . I heard about the fire, and I just wanted to make sure my b— my fiancé is okay. He's from station six."

"I know one injured firefighter from station six was taken to St. Joseph's."

"Oh my god. Do you know how bad his injuries were?"

He shook his head. He appeared to be genuinely sorry he didn't know the answer.

"Did any . . . were any of the firefighters who died from station six?"

He shook his head again.

Chelsey grabbed Ana's hand and pulled her to the car. Chelsey got behind the wheel and tore out, tires squealing, before Ana could even get the door closed. Ana yanked her seatbelt into place and said a silent prayer.

"Injured? That's not bad, right? Or maybe it is. Maybe he has severe burns. So his gorgeous face will be ruined—it'll be a horrible tragedy, but everything will still be okay. We'll still love each other and things will work out. Of course, maybe the burns are too severe and after a horrible and painful few days or weeks he'll succumb to the injuries. Or maybe something fell on him and he's paralyzed. It would be hard, but we could get through it together. Right?"

Chelsey kept babbling, talking so fast that soon Ana couldn't hear what she was saying. Ana almost didn't notice when Chelsey stopped talking and started hyperventilating.

When she became aware of Chelsey's panicked breathing, her heart stopped. "Chelsey, pull over. Pull over. Stop. Chelsey, stop."

Ana undid her seatbelt and slid as close to Chelsey as she could, trying to get her foot on the brake to slow them down as well as gain control of the steering wheel.

"Chelsey, put your foot on the break or get your leg out of my way. Shit, shit." They were about to careen right into a parked car. Instead, with the both of them trying to steer the car, they crashed into a tree.

35

Dating Debacles

Across town, Jason was finishing up his grading. The drama teacher had asked him to stay late to help her brainstorm for ideas for the set for the next play she was directing. "I know you've worked in theater," she said.

"I did some plays in high school, but nothing but improv since then."

"Still, you know the crazy world of theater," she laughed.

The woman, Lana, was about his age, with a round face, heart-shaped lips, and thin blond hair cut in a bob. Jason had met her before, of course. She always seemed nice.

"Sure. Let me do some grading and I'll meet you at the theater."

"I have a better idea: why don't I treat you to a burger? We can brainstorm over a burger and fries somewhere."

Jason flinched. "I don't eat meat."

Lana giggled again. "I guess that is healthier, isn't it? You name the place. I'll wait in my office. You know where that is, right?"

He nodded. Lana left him and he picked up his purple pen to begin grading again. He hadn't just been asked out on a date, had he?

Oh god. What a nightmare.

Why? You should be going out on dates. She's cute. Who knows, maybe something will happen. You really should find somebody.

But he took as long as he possibly could to grade his papers. Finally, around nine o'clock, he met Lana in her office. She was just as bubbly as ever.

"Okay, you name the place. Am I driving, or are you?" she said.

"Um, I, I think we should both drive in case, I mean, I don't know where you live."

He gave her directions to a vegetarian restaurant on 13th and Grant and met her there a few minutes later.

They sat down and she looked at the menu as if she'd just noticed a bad odor but didn't know where it was coming from. Then the smile returned to her face. "Oh, is it *all* vegetarian?"

He nodded.

"What's seitan? What's tempeh? They have an awful lot of tofu."

"Seitan is made from wheat gluten and has a rich, meaty taste and tempeh is made from fermented soybeans." She looked frightened. "I guess that doesn't sound all that great, but really, they are tasty, you know, the way they are flavored in soy or barbeque sauce and so on." Still hadn't convinced her. "They have some pastas. Do you like pasta?"

This she could tolerate.

Well, this is going well.

"So, the play. Which production are you doing?" Jason asked.

"*Our Town.* I just think that play has such a good message, don't you?"

"I've never actually read that one."

"What plays did you do in high school?"

"*The Outsiders, Ordinary People, Romeo and Juliet . . .*"

"Oh, wow. How exciting." Neither of them said anything for several seconds. Jason studied his hands intently. He tried to think of something school-related to talk about, but was mysteriously unable to think of a single conversation topic. With his friend Rick, the physics teacher, they never tired of conversation about the students, the administration, or the mandates handed down by the school board. Why couldn't he think of anything now?

"Uh . . . so the sets. You wanted to talk about the sets?" He was triumphant for coming up with this.

"Oh, let's enjoy our dinner before we talk about work."

He nodded and waited for her to say something. She didn't. *Dear god, please let this be over soon.*

But it wasn't. It seemed to drag on for an eternity. Finally they finished their meals and talked about some ideas for the set. But every sentence he uttered seemed like such work.

"Do you want to go for a drink somewhere?"

"I should probably get to bed."

"Yeah. It is a school night!" There went that giggle again. "So, I had a lot of fun tonight."

"Um."

"We should do it again, don't you think?"

"I thought we got the designs worked out?"

"No, silly, I mean like, you know, a date!"

"Oh I, Lana, there's sort of somebody else." It wasn't a total lie, but the look on her face made him want to say, "Ha, ha, just kidding, this was the greatest night of my life. Let's go get married." But he simply could not endure another evening like this.

He went home feeling depressed. God he hated this dating thing. Why couldn't he find a woman to love and be loved by? When would Marin realize he and she were perfect for each other?

The physical attraction they shared was undeniable. The sex they had was always explosive, and he knew she felt the same way. Of course he thought she was beautiful, but it wasn't just her looks like captivated him. The way she carried herself with such confidence—it was intoxicating. And they had so much in common: their sense of humor, their love of performing, the way they understood each other—on stage and off, they could always play off what the other said. Together, they made great comedy, great love, and great friends. Their being together just made sense.

36

Flashover

The sound of the car slamming into the tree was horrible: the thud of impact, the glass breaking, the metal crunching. Ana had hit her head on the dash. She touched her forehead and felt the slippery wet blood. Dazed, her head aching, she tried to focus her eyes and saw that the entire front end of the car was smashed up like an accordion.

The car was totaled. But as she got her head together, she realized that wasn't even important: The important thing was Chelsey. Chelsey didn't look injured, but if she kept hyperventilating, she would lose consciousness, possibly even slip into a coma. Ana scanned Chelsey's car for something Chelsey could breathe into.

"Chelsey, everything is going to be okay, don't worry. Calm down, please? Shh shh shh. Sweetie, everything is going to be fine. Rob is fine, don't worry."

There weren't any paper bags to be found in Chelsey's car. The one time when eating fast food—and leaving the empty bag in the car—might actually have been healthy.

Chelsey did have a water bottle in the cup holder on the consol. Ana tore off the top and commanded Chelsey to breathe into the empty bottle. "Make sure to seal the opening around your face. Chelsey, Chelsey, listen to me."

Chelsey never did breathe into the water bottle. She began

breathing normally on her own. "What happened?" she asked, as if coming out of a trance. "You're bleeding."

"We ran into a tree. I think your car is totaled, but the important thing is that we're—"

"Rob! We have to get to Rob!"

"Chelsey. We got into an accident. We're not going anywhere. I'm going to call the police—"

"I'll run. I'll run the rest of the way to the hospital. It's only a couple of miles away." Chelsey opened up the door and got outside. Ana ran out after her and grabbed by the wrist.

"Chelsey, you're not going anywhere. In the state you're in, you're going to get run over by a car or something. Anyway, we need to file a report with the police and get a tow truck to tow your car. That won't take very long. I'll call Jason or Scott or Ram to come pick us up and take us to the hospital."

"Can't you just wait here for the police by yourself?"

"Chelse, it's your car. You'll need to give them all the information. Listen, I'll call Scott and ask him to go to the hospital and tell us what's going on."

Ana made a series of calls on her cell phone. She wasn't able to get through to Jason or Ramiro, but at least Scott was home. She asked him to go to the hospital and find out what the situation was.

"Can't I just call the hospital and see if he's okay?" Scott asked.

"Oh. Maybe. I hadn't thought of that. But what about confidentiality? They'll probably think you're a reporter trying to get the scoop."

"And if I go to the hospital, they'll tell me everything I want to know?"

"Tell them you're his half brother, I don't know. Just go!"

Ana clicked her phone off, and then she and Chelsey waited. And waited. Chelsey was beside herself. She paced up and down the street. Ana did her best to keep up with her, ready to tackle her if she tried to take off to the hospital.

At last the cops and the tow truck driver arrived, and then the paperwork began. Chelsey felt like the paperwork was lava spewing out of a volcano, and she was trying to stop it by hand. No matter what she did, more slipped through. It just kept coming and coming.

All the while, Ana and Scott kept calling each other with updates. Scott couldn't get any news. He didn't even know if Rob was the firefighter who'd been injured.

"They won't tell me anything."

"Crap. Okay, can you come pick me and Chelsey up and take us to the hospital?"

Finally Chelsey finished with the paperwork and the tow truck took her car off to wherever broken cars go to die.

Chelsey and Ana waited on the curb for Scott. Chelsey barely waited for him to come to a stop before she threw open his car door and jumped inside.

Once at the hospital, Chelsey told a nurse she was Rob Night's fiancée, the firefighter who had been injured in the fire. Was he all right?

The nurse said she didn't know, he was still in surgery. That's how they learned it was in fact Rob who had been injured.

"Surgery. Jesus. Surgery." Chelsey paced and paced. She didn't fall asleep all night. Ana and Scott did their best to comfort her, until eventually they fell asleep at awkward angles in the uncomfortable waiting room chairs.

Chelsey was still awake at six in the morning when the morning news came on.

"Oh my god!" Chelsey balanced on a chair to turn the silent television's volume on.

"Our top story this morning is a fire that took the lives of two local firefighters and injured a third."

The sound of the television awoke Ana. "Ahh," she groaned. Her neck was tense with pain from sleeping sitting up. She tried to focus her groggy eyes toward the noise of the television. Scott kept sleeping.

"The fire started in a three-story home in Denver's Capitol Hill neighborhood on Sixth near Downing when a ten-year-old and his six-year-old sister, who were home alone, tried to make popcorn on the stove. Firefighters responded to the blaze at 8:45 last night. Two didn't make it out.

"Local fire authorities are calling Ken Lopresti, Carol Marklund, and Rob Night heroes this morning after the courageous battle that ultimately took the lives of Lopresti and Marklund and injured Night." Chelsey gasped and reached for Ana's hand. "Lopresti and Marklund died in the fire after the roof collapsed and they were trapped under the debris. Other firefighters were unable to get to them through the flames.

"Night was injured when he jumped out a third-story window in an effort to avoid a flashover that would have certainly killed him. Night survived the incident, suffering a broken ankle and a sprained wrist."

"A broken ankle! A sprained wrist!" Chelsey practically cheered with joy, like it was the best news she'd ever heard.

Just then, a male doctor in his early thirties approached Ana and Chelsey. "Are you Chelsey McGuiness, Rob Night's friend?"

"Yes."

"Rob is going to be fine. He had a bad break to his ankle. We had to operate on it to be sure it didn't set wrong, but he's going to be just fine. He'll be in a cast for six to eight weeks and he sprained his wrist, but with regular cold compresses, he should have the use of his hands in no time."

"Can I see him?"

The doctor nodded. "He's still a little groggy from the pain medication. But you can see him."

"When can I take him home?"

"We'll watch him for a few hours, and if it looks like he's doing well and there's no risk of clotting, I'd say you can take him home this evening. Follow me."

Chelsey followed the doctor down the hall to Rob's room. The doctor left so they could be alone.

"What are you doing here? How did you hear?" Rob asked.

"I heard it on the news last night. I've been crying my eyes out for twelve hours straight and I thought you were dead and I'd lost you." She snuggled next to him. They lay in silence for several minutes. Chelsey just held him tight. Eventually she said, "What happened? The reporter said you were running to avoid a flashover."

"Yeah."

"What is that?"

"A flashover—remember when I told you about a backdraft? A flashover is basically the opposite. It happens when the fire has *lots* of oxygen to consume. All these flammable gases pool up at the ceiling. And when they ignite, the flames roll like a ball across the ceiling but it happens in a flash, bam! Just like that, and intense heat pours down from all around. Like a building collapse, heat drops to floor level. In other words, if you're trapped in a room when this happens, you're gonna be one crispy critter."

"Doesn't your fire gear protect you?"

"Yeah, but it can only do so much. If you're in a room that hot for too long—which is hardly any time at all in that heat—the water in your body turns to steam and you literally cook from the inside out."

Chelsey gasped.

"So I was in the middle of the hallway when I saw the flames rolling across the ceiling toward me, and I just sprinted down the hallway and jumped out the window, and the flames followed me out and rolled out right over me."

"Oh my god."

"When I landed I felt this unbelievable pain in my ankle. But it could have been a lot worse."

Neither of them said anything, thinking about how it had been much worse for Rob's fellow firefighters.

"They were friends of yours?" Chelsey asked in a quiet voice.

"They were from another station. She's just thirty-two. She has—had—two kids. And Ken, he was supposed to get married this spring."

"I'm so sorry." She didn't say anything for a beat. "You're going to look for a new job, right? I mean when you're feeling better."

"Why would I do that?"

"Rob, I love you. I don't want you to get hurt."

He shook his head.

"Please don't go back to fighting fires."

"Chelsey, it's what I do. I love it. I'll have some time off to get my leg fixed up and then I'm going back. It's got good benefits, it's a good job."

"But it's so dangerous. I don't want you to go back."

"Last time I checked you didn't get to make the decisions for me," he snapped.

"I didn't . . . I'm just worried about you. I love you."

His expression softened. "I know you do. I love you too."

Chelsey sat next to him all day until he was cleared to go home. She held his hand the entire time. She had feared she'd lost him; now she never wanted to let him go.

37

In the Shadows of the Limelight, Part Two

Ten days had gone by, and still no word from Jay.

Marin had long days at work to keep herself occupied, but there was so much time she spent on the sidelines, waiting to perform, and she was left with far too much time to think about him.

She tried to spend her time waiting to perform memorizing her lines, but she was having a hell of a time concentrating. Typically they got their lines the morning or the night before they were going to shoot. She did her best to remember her lines and her cues—she had no idea what anyone else was saying. She also had to work hard to remember her marks—twice Jessica had stepped too far forward or too far to one side of her marks and earned the fiery ire of the director and cameramen. There wasn't time to re-shoot a scene several times. You got a rehearsal and then you got in front of the camera and got it right.

Worse than being alone with her thoughts and insecurities and what-ifs (What if he forgot what hotel I was staying at? What if I never see him again? What if he wasn't really attracted to me?) was having to chat with her fellow actors. Devin was cool—she'd been in the business for a while and hadn't let the success of getting on a TV series go to her head. Bennett didn't say much, so he was okay, but Jessica and Aryan-nation Conrad and what she had formerly considered to be cute Alex (his arrogant personality had rid her of any attraction to him) had managed to develop egos of superstars in no time at all rather than the beginners they actually were.

They had no trouble talking about themselves, but any time Marin tried to steer the conversation around to more general topics—the situation in the Middle East, the film and television industries in general, pop culture, or world events—they were at a loss.

The three women had a five A.M. makeup call and had to be on the set by six. By one o'clock when they called a lunch break, Marin felt like she was going to pass out from hunger. The studio had, as usual, brought in a miniscule salad with an ounce or so of various low-fat protein—fish, skinned chicken, turkey breast.

This was ridiculous. The guys got real lunches; the women were given twigs and tomatoes and fat-free flavor-free dressing.

"Is there any way I could get some bread with this?" Marin asked the assistant who'd brought them their lunches. The assistant looked at her as if she'd asked for a platter of baby brains. "A sandwich? A bowl of soup? Another salad? Anything?"

"I'll see what I can do."

Marin would just have to remember to pack her own lunches. She'd meant to do that, but by the time she staggered home to bed every night and checked the phone to see if he'd called, she was too tired and too disappointed to go to the grocery store. Or to do anything more than go to bed, thinking about what she'd done wrong, wondering why he hadn't called. It had been ten days. Ten! She'd never gone ten days waiting for a call from a guy.

The assistant brought Marin a fruit salad. Marin sighed. It wasn't much, but it was something.

"So what did you think of how I played my scene?" Jessica asked. Jessica's character, Marissa, worked as a waitress by day. In the scene that had been shot this morning, Marissa had encountered a group of drunk businessmen who at first hit on her and then when they were rebuffed, started joking with each other, saying things like, "I don't know, Jerry, don't take it too hard, you can do better than a waitress." "Hey guys, I bet she's not really a waitress, I bet she's really an *actress.*" Hearty laughs all around. "Oh no, I'm sure she's working on her master's degree." "Probably studying to be a doctor." More laughs.

It was all very meaningful because earlier in the day, when Jessica/Marissa hadn't gotten the part she'd auditioned for, she was wondering if she really was an actress or she was going to be waiting tables for the rest of her life, and if so, was it time to throw in the towel and start working on a different career?

"I wanted her to look hurt, obviously," Jessica was saying, "but I, um, also thought she would show a certain degree of resolve beneath her hurt feelings. A glimmer of steely determination. Did you catch the way I lowered my voice an octave to suggest both that I was trying to keep from crying, sort of that husky pre-tears thing, and that I was coldly indifferent to their hurtful remarks?"

"You did great," Marin said.

"It was a good scene," Devin said.

"I don't really think Marissa is a victim, you know? I think, um, she's a fighter, and I really wanted to convey that to the audience. It was really such an acting challenge."

Marin and Devin exchanged a look. They were grateful when lunch was over and they had to go back to work.

Marin got home from work at 9:30 that night. The light on the phone in her hotel room was blinking.

Do not get excited. Do not get excited. It was probably her mother. Out of nowhere, suddenly her mother had started taking an interest in Marin. Joan had acted as though all these years Marin had performed in plays with school, with the Iron Pyrits, and even for pay at Spur of the Moment had been a silly hobby of Marin's, something to kill time. Now that her daughter had gotten recognition from real-live players in the industry, it was finally real to her, not some silly side interest. Joan reported how she was bragging to all her friends about Marin's success, and kept telling Marin how proud she was.

Marin called for her messages. "Hi Marin," the message began. Marin's heart seized. It was a male voice. "This is Jay Prochazka. We met about a week ago." *Try ten days. Ten long days, buddy.* "I was wondering if you would like to get together Tuesday. I'm on the road a lot, so let me give you my cell phone number."

Marin wrote down the number and considered. Should she call him right now? She had to be on the set on Tuesday; Friday was her day off. Please dear God, let him be free on Friday.

Before she could decide whether to call him right away or not, her phone rang.

"Hello?"

"Hi. Is this Marin?"

"Yes."

"This is Jay. How've you been?"

"I'm great! How are you?" She was so happy, she couldn't keep the joy out of her voice. She knew she should play it cool, but she was so excited she was practically jumping up and down—well, bouncing up and down on the balls of her feet anyway.

"Did you get my message?"

"I just finished listening to it. I just got home."

"So are you free Tuesday?"

"I have to be on the set Tuesday. Friday is my day off this week." Please be able to get together Friday, please be able to get together Friday . . .

He sounded a little miffed. "I'll have to check my schedule. I'll get back to you. I'll call you soon. Talk to you later."

He'd hung up before she could say good-bye. God she hoped he'd call her back. She couldn't believe what a short, strange conversation that had been.

Marin looked around the room. She was exhausted, but she didn't want to get ready for bed. She didn't want to be washing her face or brushing her teeth when he called.

10:03. 10:07. 10:11. 10:18.

Okay, maybe she should hop in the shower. He'd definitely call while she was in the shower.

So she did. She showered like it was a timed Olympic sporting event. She washed, shampooed, brushed her teeth and was out of the shower in four minutes flat. He hadn't called.

10:46. 11:02. She couldn't sleep. She was too wired. He'd meant he would call her back tonight, hadn't he?

Two endlessly long hours after his first call, he called back. "It's all been arranged. Friday will work out just fine."

"Great. So what have you been up to?"

"You know, I'm on the road and could lose the signal any minute. Do you mind if we catch up Friday?"

"Oh, of course. See you then." Marin hung up. It was 11:30 at night, and she was delirious from lack of sleep and excitement, but that had been such an odd conversation. Some guys just didn't like talking on the phone. That was probably all there was to it.

The next day at work, Joey the cameraman pulled Marin aside as other members of the crew fiddled with the lighting.

"What is it?" she asked.

His eyes scanned the room to make sure no one could overhear them. "Watch your back."

"What do you mean?"

"Just be careful. Jessica . . . I've overheard her a few times trying to talk Don into giving her some of your lines. She's saying stuff like you're not focused and it would be better if her character said these things than your character."

Marin was surprised by how much this stung. "Was she successful?"

"No way. She keeps missing her marks. If anything, her character will get less and less to say."

"Thanks Joey."

"You're a good kid. I know this is all new to you. I'm just saying, you can't trust anybody."

Marin was unsettled. She was used to improv, where everyone was equal and everything was done for the group, not for the individual. It hurt that Jessica would go behind her back like that. This dog-eat-dog world was going to take some getting used to.

* * *

At noon on Friday, Jay picked Marin up at the hotel in an Aston Martin Vanquish.

"Nice car," she said, trying not to gape.

"I like it. I thought we'd do a picnic at a park. What do you think? I've got a basket all packed," he said.

"I'm happy to eat anywhere as long as I get free food."

"It's a deal then."

As he took off down the road he asked if she liked working in television.

"I love it. It's insane and exhausting and there is all this politics and backstabbing and everybody is out for themselves, but I love the acting so much. It's just so exciting. If the series doesn't get picked up, I don't know how I'm going to go back to working a boring temp job."

"It's important to love what you do."

"Did you love doing what you did?"

"I loved it, I really did. But for about four years there, all I did was work. I ate at work, I slept at work more times than I want to remember, I lived for work. I had no life. I kept getting dumped by my girlfriends because they were sick of me spending more time on my job than on them. I enjoyed building a good company, but now I'm happy to just enjoy life."

"Have you always had money?"

"My parents did well. My dad was also a businessman and entrepreneur. My mom came from money, too, and investing it was what she did for a living."

"So they gave you the money to start your business?"

"I started out with $10,000 of my own money and a computer. Eventually some venture capital, including some from my dad, helped me grow the business. I think Dad was a little cautious about giving me money at first because—I wasn't the best student, let's put it that way. I'd gotten into some trouble, a lot of trouble actually, and he wanted to see that I had really straightened myself out. I think working so hard is what straightened me out. I had something to really focus on besides just having a good time. Of course, now I'm back to just enjoying life and having a good time."

He drove to Hancock Park in Los Angeles, a mostly residential neighborhood. He drove down a secluded back road. It had a gate, but the gate was open. They drove quite a ways down the windy road, and Marin noted the tennis court, the enormous swimming pool, and the gorgeously landscaped lawn. He stopped in an out-of-the-way spot filled with trees, sumptuous flower beds, and a small creek. This is where he unfurled the blanket.

"Wow, this is beautiful. Why is there no one here?" she asked.

"It's a private park."

"What do you mean private?"

"I mean this is my backyard."

"You're joking. But where is your house?"

"You know when we came to that gate and the road forked two ways? If you went the other way, you'd come to the house. You can see it if you look over that way."

"You're not referring to that sprawling mansion-castle-like thing are you?"

"Yep. My landscapers worked hard to make it as secluded as possible."

"Yeah, the forest does a nice job, but what with it being, what, 30,000 square feet, it's a tad hard to conceal entirely. Just how much did you sell your business for?"

"Quite a lot. Anyway, the house is only 22,000 square feet."

"Oh, I see, only 22,000 square feet smack dab in the middle of one of the most expensive cities in the world."

"I also made a lot of good investments. I got out at the right time."

"I guess so."

"Wine?"

"Please."

"Do you like caviar?"

"Yeah."

"Pâté?"

"Bring it on."

Her parents were filthy rich, but they lived in New York, and while they owned two floors of a 9,000-square-foot penthouse, they had no yard to speak of. Even on their vacation home in Martha's Vineyard, they had just a little scrap of lawn to call their own. Marin was used to wealth, but not this kind of wealth. She did her best not to let on how impressed she was.

"I said I didn't go to guys' houses on a first date, but I have to say, you've piqued my curiosity. Want to give me a tour?"

"Actually, I have other plans for this afternoon, if you don't mind."

38

The Scoop

"**D**o you need some more water? Are you still hungry? Do you need more pain medication? I know you said you're fine, but you don't have to pretend to be strong for me."

"Chelsey," Rob groaned, "I'm not an invalid."

The phone rang. Chelsey didn't make a move.

"I will live for the length of time it takes you to pick up the phone."

Chelsey decided he was right and crossed the living room to retrieve the phone. "Hello?"

"I miss you," Ana said.

"I know, I miss you guys, too."

"You are coming back to performing next weekend, aren't you?"

"I don't know. I feel so guilty. I leave Rob alone all day when I go to work, I just can't bear to leave him alone at night."

"So I guess meeting for drinks tonight is out of the question. It's just, with Marin in L.A. and you incognito . . . I'm desperate for female companionship. I know I have friends from high school and college, but they're not my bestest bestest friends like you and Marin."

"Oh, I wish I could, but I don't think I can. I need to watch Rob . . ."

"Who is it?" Rob called.

"Ana. She wants to go out for drinks. I told her I can't go."

"Chelsey, are you bonkers?" he said.

"Hold on, Ana." Chelsey covered the phone receiver.

"Go out. I mean it Chelsey, I love you, but you've been smothering me."

"You need me. What if . . ."

"Chelse, I have your cell phone number. If I fall and can't get up, I know who to call."

Chelsey got back on the phone. "Apparently my patient thinks I've been smothering him. It's all lies of course. Evidently the fact that when I'm home I won't let him cook for himself, get his own glasses of water, or fetch pain medication, he thinks I'm being overbearing."

"Is he getting around okay?"

"Yeah, actually, he's doing well."

"Leave. Out, woman!" Rob bellowed.

"All right, I'm being ordered to get out of this house and have drinks with you."

"Excellent. Meet me at the Funky Buddha at nine."

"Actually, why don't I pick you up in my new car?"

"You got a new car?!"

"Yeah. I got six thousand bucks back in insurance from the Honda, which was plenty for a down payment. I bought a Saturn. The insurance is really low because it's one of the safest cars out there, and I figure with my recent displays of driving skills, or lack thereof, safe is probably good. It's not the sexiest car, but still, I'm all excited about it."

"Okay, pick me up at ten to nine. I'll trust that you can get me to the bar in one piece."

At 9:02, they ordered cosmos and promptly began to dish.

"So did ya hear about Marin?" Ana asked.

"What about her?"

"She's in love."

"That's awesome."

"With a good-looking millionaire."

"No!"

"Yes. Listen to what they did for their first date: He took her to his estate for a picnic. He has this sprawling yard that looks like a botanical garden with trees and a creek and a swimming pool and a tennis court, and they have a picnic by this creek with all the kind of expensive exotic foods and fine wines you'd expect from a millionaire. What am I saying, he must actually be a billionaire."

"That bitch."

"My sentiments exactly. So then he takes her up in a hot air balloon. His own private hot air balloon, and they do that for a couple hours and then he takes her on his private plane—"

"Private plane!"

"To San Francisco, where they have dinner at some swanky place, see a play, and then retire to the Palace Hotel where they proceed to make love almost all night long and then he whisks her back to L.A. in time for her shoot at four in the morning. She said it was the best sex of her entire life, and she can really see herself falling for him, because he doesn't fawn over her like every other guy she's known. She says he's really broadening her mind and he makes her laugh and is exciting and impulsive and all this stuff. I mean I know this isn't a profound insight, but God, life is not fair!"

"Completely not fair. I am so jealous."

"I love that you said that. I'm about to combust I'm so jealous of her. I mean I love Scott, but if Scott was a zillionaire who could support me so I could just go to auditions all day—"

"That would be awesome! They're going to get married, aren't they. She'll go straight from her rich dad to her rich boyfriend."

"I'm sure they'll get married," Ana sighed bitterly.

"Disgusting."

"Completely. I mean even if this never turns into anything, just to be able to say you went on a kind of fairy tale date like that? But I'm sure they'll get married. I've never heard Marin talk about a guy like this. She always gets bored with guys in like three minutes."

"Like Jason."

"Exactly like Jason."

"So what does this rich guy do that makes him so rich?"

"Nothing. He sold his business three years ago and made zillions."

"God, this gets grosser by the second. What company?"

"I don't know. Internet something I think. I just hope her being with this guy, Jay his name is—oh! I forgot to tell you. He's an older man. Thirty-eight."

"Ooh, a fourteen-year age difference. Very *One Life to Live.*"

"Yeah, so anyway, I just hope that her being with Jay doesn't mean that she's going to stay in L.A."

"If the show is a success, she'll have to stay out there anyway."

"I want her to succeed, but I also . . . you know the five of us have lived together for years. I went straight from the dorms to living with them, and so even though now we have these nine-to-five jobs, it's not like we're really grown-ups, you know? And if Marin goes off and leaves us . . . soon everybody will run off and get married and we'll have to become real grown-ups, grown-ups who don't have plastic fish decorating their walls. We'll have furniture that matches and we won't be able to have Pop-tarts and beer for breakfast—"

"You do *not* have Pop-tarts and beer for breakfast." Chelsey looked stricken.

Ana realized she'd made a tactical error on that one. "No, no, of course not, that was just a theoretical example. My point is, I like living in this stage of *sort-of* grown-upness. I like feeling like I still live in college with my greatest friends in the universe, except for you of course."

"Well, he's rich and doesn't have to work, maybe he can buy a place here."

"Yeah, let's go with that. It'll be so big that even though they're married, he'll let us all live with them and he won't even notice we're there."

"Good plan. You know, I'm really glad you asked me out for drinks, just the two of us. I've always felt so out of things because I don't live with you and I don't have all those years of history with you."

"You know we love you."

"I always thought you guys were so clique-ish."

"We were?"

"You had all these inside jokes."

"We did?"

"It took me forever to feel comfortable around you guys."

"It did?"

"You guys would crack up at this stuff I just didn't get at all. You still do. Like that whole pht-pht-pht thing with Scott."

"You don't think that's hilarious?"

"No."

"But it is hilarious."

"No, actually it's not."

Ana was shocked by this revelation. "Really? Oh."

"But I get it. You and Scott have always had this really powerful connection. I'm so happy you two finally got together."

"Me too. I love having regular nookie."

"Here here."

"Another round?"

"Is the sky blue? Absofuckinglutely."

They ordered more drinks and Ana thought about what Chelsey had said. Ana and Scott had always gotten along well. She'd always really admired his artistic talent. She'd always wished she could be more relaxed about life like he was. But maybe what had really formed such a strong bond with him was working with him every day for the last two years. In so many ways, when she thought about her days at the office it was like thinking back to being in a war—something that induced post-traumatic stress disorder and was something that one *survived*, made it through by the skin of their teeth, etc. All along she and Scott were able to get to know each other in a way their friends never could.

Sometimes crushes were well and truly crushed. In Ana's case, the overwhelming rush of feelings that had been unleashed when she let herself see Scott as something more than a friend had trampled her old feelings toward Jason into oblivion.

Ana sipped her drink and suddenly a memory from college she hadn't thought of in years came rushing back to her. It was a night after a performance she'd particularly bombed. She'd been too focused on the audience's reaction to her, thinking "Do they like me?" and not "What is going on in the scene and what can I do to progress the story?" or, better yet, not thinking at all and just reacting to the events around her.

She had retreated to her bedroom after the show as her roommates drank and laughed in the living room downstairs. She lay on her bed writhing in shame, her face buried in her hands. Every now and then a distinct memory of something painfully embarrassing would jolt through her and she would spasm and moan aloud at the memory.

Scott knocked on her door carrying two Fat Tire beers and a bowl of cheese popcorn that was a distressing shade of urine yellow.

"What's up?" he asked. "Are you tired? Why did you ditch us?"

"I don't deserve to be part of this group. I suck. You should tie an anvil to me and toss me in a river. I deserve nothing more than total abandonment and a slow, painful death."

Scott stopped midway from transferring a clot of popcorn from the bowl to his mouth.

"Where is this self-flagellation coming from?"

"My performance tonight, of course! How can you even deign to speak to me?"

He chewed thoughtfully and washed the popcorn down with a long swallow of beer. "You have self-esteem issues," he pronounced.

"I'm quitting. I'm never getting on stage again."

"What are you talking about? Your performance wasn't bad."

"Don't humor me!" Ana couldn't help it, she began to cry. She was so embarrassed, exposing herself like this, revealing her frailties and insecurities, but she couldn't help it.

"That bit when you and Jason were at the restaurant waiting for the waitress to bring your check and you said, 'Maybe if we look at her needifully she'll bring it.' Then that expression you made . . . 'Needifully . . . Maybe if we look at her needifully.' That was hilarious." He chuckled at the memory.

"Really?"

"It was hilarious because that's exactly what it's like when you're trapped waiting for the waitress to bring you your check. You can't go anywhere or do anything. You've already eaten and caught up on conversation with your friends. All you can do is sit there and hope and try desperately to catch sight of your waitress to let her know you need her. Then when you went and tackled her—it was perfect."

Ana suppressed a smile and dried her tears. She took a handful of popcorn and tossed it into her mouth, letting the powdery, synthetic cheese melt on her tongue.

"There is no such thing as a mistake in improv, Ana. Whatever happens, go with it. You're a smart girl but you can't be so cerebral on stage, always in your head. With more practice, you'll shake that habit. You've got talent, I promise."

"Yeah?"

"Yeah."

Then he let out a majestic fart.

"Aah!" Ana screamed.

"Much better." He patted his stomach contentedly.

"Much better for you maybe. Putrid for the rest of us. Ghastly! Fetid!"

"You're just jealous you can't make such impressive noises using only your digestive system."

"Um no, I don't think so."

"You can protest all you want, but I know the truth."

Ana giggled, and Scott joined her. When he snorted, the laugh-snort combo made Ana helpless with laughter.

That, she realized, was why she loved Scott. He paraded around as if everything was always fun and games, but when she needed a friend, a confidant, a lover, he seamlessly became those things. And when she needed a little comic relief, when she needed the gods on high to send in the clowns, he was that, too.

She realized she'd had hundreds of the nights like that with her friends from Spur—nights when she'd let her guard down, revealed her dreams and falibilities and truest self. Performing had a way of revealing the rawest, realest emotions. The six members of Spur had all seen each other emotionally naked, vulnerable, exposed, and it created a connection between them that went to depths that were hard to find with other friends.

39

Dining Disasters

"Would you mind if my family came to visit for Thanksgiving?" Scott asked Ana.

"No, of course not. Why would I mind?"

"What I mean is, would you mind if they stayed with us?"

"Your parents?"

"My whole family."

"Don't you have three brothers and a sister, and aren't they all married?"

"Yes and yes."

"I don't understand, you want to have ten people stay in this house?"

"Plus four nieces and nephews."

"Fourteen people!"

"They don't have a lot of money. They won't be able to come otherwise. I thought I could stay in your room, and Jack and his wife Lettie and their two kids could stay in my room, and John and his wife Laura could stay in Marin's room, Mom and Dad and Suzy and her husband Dean and my nephew and niece Felix and Lacey can stay in the camper . . ."

"Where will they park it?"

"I was thinking in the parking lot in the apartment complex down the street. Then Beau and Suzy . . ."

"I thought your sister's name was Suzy."

"It is. It's Beau's wife's name, too. I thought Beau and Suzy could sleep in the basement."

"We have an unfinished, appallingly unorganized basement."

"Yeah, I'd have to straighten up a bit. They can sleep on air mattresses."

"Wouldn't it just be easier if we went to visit them?"

"Yeah, probably."

"How about we do that then."

The phone rang, but Ana felt too lazy to reach her arm out to pick it up. Shortly after the third ring, Ana heard Ramiro's baritone voice carry from the first floor. "Ana, it's your mom."

Immediately Ana felt guilty. She couldn't abandon her mother for Thanksgiving. It had always been just the two of them. What would Grace do without her? It was like she'd known Ana was making holiday plans that didn't include her. Ana picked up the receiver from the phone on her nightstand.

"Hello?"

"Hi sweetie. How are you?"

"I'm good. You?"

"How's your social life?"

"Well, Mom, I actually have news for once. Scott and I have decided to make a go of being boyfriend and girlfriend."

"Oooh!" her mother squealed at such an eardrum piercing decibel that Ana reflexively pulled the phone several inches away. "Ana, I really want to get to know your new boyfriend. Come over for dinner Sunday night."

"Mom, you've known Scott for years. He's been my roommate forever."

"I know, but I only knew Scott as a friend, not a boyfriend."

"*I* hardly know him as a boyfriend. We're just getting started."

"Ana, please. I never get to see you. I'd really like to have you over for dinner. It'll be a free meal."

"What are you going to get? Thai fusion? Paglia's? I love their eggplant focaccia sandwich."

"No, I was thinking I'd cook."

"Dear god, are you nuts? Why would you ever think of doing something like that?" Her mother had almost never cooked anything besides mac and cheese and frozen pizzas for dinner when Ana was growing up. They frequently had breakfasts for dinners: frozen waffles, cereal, or homemade Egg McMuffin sandwiches. Even more distressing were the popcorn-for-dinner nights or the choose-your-own-adventure nights, which meant, practically speaking, that Ana would make herself a peanut butter and honey sandwich or a frozen pasta dinner. The very few times Grace had cooked—for holidays or Ana's birthday—the results were at worst disastrous and at best inedible.

What on earth would inspire her mother to *cook* for Ana and Scott? It was madness.

"Ana, please. I'm trying to get more in touch with my domestic side."

Oh great, when you're forty and I'm grown up and living on my own, then you go and find your domestic side. Nice. But Ana was blowing her mother off for Thanksgiving. If she came to this dinner and promised to stay in Denver for Christmas, maybe she wouldn't have to feel quite so guilty. "Okay. What time should we be there?"

Ana had repeatedly warned Scott to eat before he left for dinner and to expect truly stomach-churning fare.

"It's really, really bad. I mean tasteless and burnt and we'll usually eat the entrée first and then the soup and salad and nothing is timed right so everything will be cold . . ."

"Ana, Jesus, I get it already. I'm not expecting five-star cuisine tonight. You've warned me fifty times in the last three days."

Ana was anxious, and her anxiety was exacerbated by the traffic they were stuck in. Who would have guessed there'd be traffic on a Sunday night? Of course anyone who knew anything about football would know there was a game this afternoon, but Ana didn't follow sports, and neither did her roommates.

To Ana, sports weren't about revelry or fun, they were about traffic that totally messed her up when she had someplace to be. Also, sports were about drunk idiots who started riots to celebrate their team winning a trophy or series or whatever it was called.

Ana loved that the guys in her house didn't watch sports. If they were flipping channels and there was nothing better on, they might keep a game on, but they'd provide a running mocking commentary about the fans, the announcer's haircut, the players, the coaches, and how everyone involved took it so seriously, as if it mattered who won the stupid game.

It wasn't like it mattered all that much if Ana and Scott were fifteen minutes late, but she already knew the evening would be a disaster and this was just the first thing to go wrong in what promised to be an evening of humiliations.

As soon as they walked in to her mother's two-bedroom condo, Ana felt immediately relieved that it was Scott who was with her, and not Jason. If it were Jason on her arm, she'd be embarrassed by the old, dingy carpeting and the wildly ugly and out-of-date cabinets. She'd smart from how much she hated the Kmart table, the ceiling fan circa 1978, and the plebian knickknacks all over the place. She'd be embarrassed that her mother would buy nonorganic vegetables that were completely out of season and tasted like plywood, and the humiliation of the actual meal itself would likely have done her in.

But Jason wasn't here, and Ana was only sort of uncomfortable, the usual uncomfortable she felt around her mother, knowing that something would go wrong and she'd have to fix it while assuring her mother it really was no big deal.

"I'm so glad you could come!" Grace hugged Ana. "I have wine. Do you want red or white?"

"Red please," Ana said.

Grace scurried into the kitchen to get the corkscrew. Ana remembered how jealous she'd been of Marin when she had first met Marin's mom. Ana longed to have a sharply dressed mother who accessorized perfectly, whose makeup always was exactly the right shade for her skin tones, and whose hair was shiny and sleek and always cut so it lay just so, unlike Grace, who, no matter how much she straightened or blow-dried her hair, three seconds after she stepped away from the mirror it would kink and coil in the crazed, jagged loops of a drunk's cursive.

Ana had only met Marin's mother once in the six years she'd known Marin. It was when she and Marin had graduated, and Marin's parents had flown out to see the ceremony.

Not once in the four years Ana and Marin had been members of the Iron Pyrits had either of Marin's parents flown out to see one of their performances. Marin acted like it didn't matter to her, but Ana knew it did. She'd overhead Marin on the phone several times to her mother saying how they had a show coming up in four or five weeks—plenty of time to book tickets—and the shows were really fun, maybe they could come out for a couple days and meet everybody.

Twice her parents had told Marin they were going to fly in for the weekend, and these weekends were preceded by Marin going nuts and actually cleaning the entire house on her own volition, and nearly bursting into tears if one of the roomies left his or her shoes by the door instead of promptly charging up the stairs the nanosecond he or she got home to put them away in his/her respective closet.

Marin would get her hair touched up and would buy new clothes, shoes, socks, and underwear, as if her parents had X-ray vision and would know if she were wearing holey underwear.

She would buy good bottles of wine, put them in the wine rack, and warn her roommates to stay away from them or face her wrath. She bought weird foreign cheeses and exotic foods and spread them decoratively around the kitchen. She banned all frozen pizza or frozen dinners, and boxes of mac and cheese and Raman Noodles were hidden in closets and under beds.

Both times, her parents had canceled on her at the last minute, citing work or sudden illness.

The days preceding graduation weekend had been no different, but this time, instead of asking her parents to visit during a weekend when they had a performance, the Pyrits planned a special performance to coincide with her parents' visit.

Marin didn't come out and say that she'd really like for her parents to see what a talented actress she'd become over the past four years. She didn't say how important it was to her that they get a glimpse of something that was of tremendous importance in her life, nor did she say how much she wanted them to meet her best friends. The five friends had become so close over the years that their mannerisms, sayings, and beliefs had influenced each other so much, they didn't realize what a huge impact they'd had on each other's lives until someone outside their group commented on how Ana's and Marin's laughs were eerily similar, Scott and Jason made the exact same facial expression when they found something to be odd *"You like peanut butter and pickled herring sandwiches? Oooh-kay,"* or how Ramiro and Ana made the same gesticulations when they described something they felt passionate about. The five of them were a tiny melting pot of their own, cross-pollinating their opinions and cultural backgrounds.

No, Marin would never admit that having her parents take an interest in her life was of any importance whatsoever. When her parents had promised to visit and then didn't, she would go on and on about how it was such a relief, she couldn't stand them, they didn't get along at all. But her excitement had been obvious by the frantic way she'd run around trying to beautify herself and the house before they were to arrive, and her disappointment when they didn't were obvious in the quick flashes of sorrow in her eyes that were quickly masked with a too-bright smile.

The graduation ceremony was on a Saturday morning, and Marin's parents were going to take the other four Iron Pyrits and Ana's mother out to dinner that night. Marin's parents' personal assistant had scoped out a swanky restaurant in Denver and made all the reservations from New York. So the Pyrits planned the show for Sunday night, renting space at Old Main theater on campus. They posted flyers around campus, and emailed friends to encourage them to "have a cheap night of cheap laughs."

Marin had planned Sunday out to the minute. First a quick walk through Chautauqua park so her parents could see the beauty of the Flatirons and the mountains, then breakfast at a pricey restaurant on the Pearl Street mall, followed by a stroll along the outdoor mall so they could see the cute shops selling jewelry, artwork, and clothes by local and national artists. That night they'd have dinner at the Full Moon Grill, a small restaurant that served delicious food and whose menu changed daily based on what was in season.

That Friday night Ana and Marin had gone to the airport to pick them up. When Ana saw Marin's mother, Joan, walk off the plane, it was all she could do to keep her chin from dropping to the floor. Marin's mother was resplendent. Marin's father was very distinguished, too, and he also had beautifully tailored clothes, a distressingly perfect manicure (Ana spent the evening furtively sneaking peeks at his nails to determine if he was wearing clear polish or if his nails were just buffed to a dazzling shine—buffed, she determined after much internal debate), and the kind of steel gray, expertly cut hair sported by illustrious patriarchs in soap operas, but it was Joan who captivated Ana. She was *gorgeous*. She looked far too young to have a twenty-two-year-old daughter, let alone a twenty-five-year-old son. She was tall and thin and her clothes were made out of such sumptuous materials, Ana desperately wanted to reach out and stroke Joan's arm.

For the next twenty-four hours, Ana was painfully jealous of Marin. She wanted a mother who was so classy, so well-dressed, so refined. Joan always said the right thing. When Scott and Ramiro got into an argument about the upcoming presidential election, she managed to somehow agree with both of them, making both of them feel like they were right.

Ana had been so embarrassed by her mother's cheap, unflattering clothes and haircut that made her look like the women who were dragged kicking and screaming out of their trailers every week on *Cops*.

Dinner Friday night, graduation, post-graduation brunch, and the celebratory dinner all went well. Fun was had by all, even Ana, even if she did blush just about every time her mother uttered a word.

Then Sunday morning, Marin had showered, blown her

hair dry, and gotten dressed. Just as she was furiously brushing her teeth, the phone rang.

"Marin, it's your mom!" Ana called.

About half a second later, Marin had rinsed her mouth and sprinted to the phone.

"Hello?" she answered, a smile on her face. The smile evaporated instantly. "You're kidding. Really? I had the whole day planned. I was really looking forward to you seeing us perform. No, of course, I understand. Yeah, it was really nice to see you, too. Thanks for coming out."

Marin slipped the phone back into its cradle and stared at it.

"What's up?" Ana asked quietly.

"Dad had to get back to work, something came up at the office, and Mom said she was feeling really tired, she thinks she may have caught a bug on the plane and may be coming down with something."

"I'm so sorry."

"Oh no, don't be. It's a relief really. We pretend to get along but we really don't. It's no big deal."

Marin didn't perform with them that night. She said she had a migraine, probably from all the stress of having her parents visit.

That was when Ana finally realized that when fate or God or whatever was assigning parents, Ana had gotten a much, much better deal. Her mother was boisterous, unfashionable, and unschooled—and she loved Ana ferociously. Every success Ana had achieved, Grace bragged about as if it had been her own. Grace had seen every performance of the Iron Pyrits, every football and basketball game Ana had cheered at, every gymnastic meet that Ana had competed in. Ana was extremely, extremely lucky to have the mother that she did.

All the same, Ana desperately wanted a different life than the one her mother had. She didn't want to be satisfied with living in a too-small condo and working for fifty years at a job she didn't like, just so she could pay the bills. She wanted her life to have meaning, to be a part of something bigger than herself. She wanted to be part of a community of artists and writers and actors and comedians. She wanted to be part of a group of innovative thinkers like the Impressionists—Van Gogh, Degas, Gauguin, Manet, Lautrec, and Rousseau—hanging out, drinking absinthe and changing the art world forever, painting pictures that would be loved across continents, purchased for extravagant sums, and continued to be reproduced widely as posters, calendars, coasters, and note cards a hundred years later. Ana wanted to be as influential to acting as Stanislavsky, to improv as Viola Spolin, to sketch comedy as the founders of Second City and the original *Saturday Night Live* players.

Ana didn't know how she was going to touch the world in her lifetime, but right now, she just needed to survive tonight.

"Need any help, Mom?" she asked.

Her mother gave her a look like a little kid who had broken a vase and knew she had to fess up.

"I thought I had enough blue cheese, but it turns out I hardly have any left at all. Would you be a dear and pick some up? I need four ounces."

"Sure, of course. No problem. Need anything else?"

"Oh no, that's it."

"Okay, I'll be right back. Scott, you wanna come?"

"Oh no, Scott, stay here with me and keep me company," Grace said.

"Scott?"

"Sure, I'll stay here. See you in a few."

The store was only a couple of minutes away, but Ana hadn't shopped there in years, so it took several minutes of wandering to find the blue cheese. She'd spent the entire day doing shopping of her own, cleaning the house, and doing laundry, and having to go to the store now, while not that big of a deal, was just one more task that kept her from being able to just slow down and relax already, and she couldn't help feel a prickle of irritation.

When she got home, her mother and Scott were both sitting on the kitchen floor, searching the bottom cabinets. An array of pots and pans was spread out around them. Her mother looked up at her sheepishly.

"What's up, Mom?"

"I can't find the bottom to my springform pan. I know I have it. Look, here's the top." She waved a pie-sized metal loop. "We've looked everywhere and we just can't find it."

Ana was amazed that her mother owned such a device. She'd certainly never used it when Ana lived with her.

"Do you want me to run to the store and get one?"

Grace sighed deeply. "I guess. Do you mind?"

"No. Where should I go?"

"The grocery store has them, that's the closest place."

"Okay, and if you had all the pieces, what would it look like?"

"It looks like a pie pan. We're missing the silver disk that goes on the bottom. The idea is that you can just unclasp the sides like this"—she demonstrated—"so you don't have to flip the casserole upside down to get it out of the pan."

"And it's imperative that we not flip it upside down?"

"It has all these decorative loops in filo dough on top. Look," her mother stood and pointed to the open cookbook lying on the counter. It pictured a savory looking filo casserole filled with cheese and vegetables. It looked fattening, but, therefore, had the potential to be good. Maybe dinner would turn out to be palatable after all.

"Okay, I'm off. Do you need anything else?"

Grace shook her head.

"You're sure? Okay, Scott, you okay here?"

He lifted his wine glass. "I am *awesome.*"

Ana put on a smile, which was replaced by a look of weary annoyance the minute she closed the door behind her.

She got to the grocery store and wandered helplessly up and down several aisles until she finally came to the cooking utensils. After walking up and down the aisle, her eyes shooting up and down the rows of pots, pans, cookies sheets, measuring spoons, and whisks, she finally found a nonstick springform pan. For twelve dollars! *Twelve stinking dollars! Free dinner my ass! Why couldn't we have just gone out to eat? It would have been so much more relaxing and most likely significantly cheaper as well.*

She returned home thoroughly grumpy. She and Scott had gotten there half an hour ago, and Ana had spent that entire time driving to the store, wandering through the store lost and confuse, and waiting in line.

"Oh god, what is it?" Ana said, as soon as she saw the look on her mother's face.

"I didn't realize the recipe called for cream cheese. I thought I wrote every ingredient down. I just . . . I just didn't see it," she shrugged helplessly. *Yeah right, as if the cookbook were written in ink that becomes invisible every now and then on whimsy, like a book from Hogwarts.* "But don't worry!" she said quickly, seeing the annoyance on Ana's face, "I'll just quick dash off to the store and pick some up. You stay here and have some wine and relax."

Ana sat at the table next to Scott and downed her entire glass of wine in one long chug.

"Impressive," Scott said.

"I am *starving*. Do you see why I don't cook? Because every homemade meal made in this house costs about sixty bucks, takes hours to make because you have to go to the grocery store about forty times because do you think she would ever once actually check to make sure she actually had eggs or enough milk or blue cheese or the right cookware? No. Then it inevitably tastes like burnt snot, then there are always a zillion and a half dishes to do—there's just no point."

"Shh, Ana, it's okay. I'm having fun. Just relax." He poured her some more wine.

Because her stomach was so empty, the wine took effect almost immediately. It warmed her stomach, giving Ana a temporary feeling of—not fullness, but at least not quite such acutely ravenous hunger.

Which was a good thing because when Grace returned from the store she spent fifteen minutes finishing preparations on the dish then squealed, "Oh dear!"

"This can't be good," Ana muttered under her breath.

Grace appeared at the door. "Are you two terribly hungry? I didn't realize it takes almost an hour to bake."

Grace saw Ana's annoyance. Ana quickly replaced that expression with one of sympathy when she saw her mother start to tear up.

"It's no problem, Mom, don't worry. Maybe you could put out some cheese and crackers?"

"Yes! That's a great idea."

"I'll help."

Ana promptly poured herself another glass of wine. If she couldn't eat, at least she could get tanked.

Her mother did put out some Triscuits and American cheese. As American cheese was not the most savory of appetizers, the three spent far more time drinking wine than snacking on crackers, so by the time dinner was ready, they were all feeling very, very relaxed.

To Ana's surprise, the dish wasn't *disgusting*, it was just very odd, which was a huge improvement over her mother's usual cuisine. Ana would take a bite, and it would taste incredibly sweet. The next bite would be piercingly bitter. Every mouthful, though, was packed with cheese and pine nuts. More pine nuts than Ana had ever seen in such a small slice of pie. Every bite must have been at least a hundred calories and a couple dozen fat grams.

"So Mom, what are these sweet and bitter tastes I'm tasting?"

"Apples and brussels sprouts."

"Really? I don't think I've ever had a brussels sprout in my whole life," Ana said.

"I have. They aren't bad as long as they're drenched in butter," Scott said.

"I just thought it would be a good dish for a vegetarian."

"But Scott's not a vegetarian, Jason . . ." Ana stopped herself. There was no point. Her mother was trying so hard.

"This is a great girl you've got here," Grace said, somewhat drunkenly. "I'm always bragging to the girls at the office how proud I am of her. Just the other day I was telling everyone how Ana was thinking about studying for the GED."

"You mean GRE? You said GRE, right?" Ana said.

"G-E-D." Grace emphasized each letter, as if she were explaining the correct term to Ana.

Ana said, "No, Mom, I was thinking about taking the GRE, as in the Graduate Record Exam, for grad school. GED stands for General Equivalency Diploma. The only people at my high school to get them were the kids who were addicted to drugs."

"Ffff," Grace fluttered her hand as if to say, "Bah, it's practically the same thing." Ana crumpled in embarrassment. Her mother was always doing that, trying to brag about Ana but getting all her facts wrong. Usually it wasn't a big deal—Ana didn't care if her mother's friends thought she was a pom pom girl and not a cheerleader, or if they thought she was a stand-up comedian and not an improv-er—but sometimes, her mother's announcements made Ana want to die of shame.

After another glass of wine, Ana didn't care if her mother's friends and coworkers thought she was perhaps the first student from a suburban high school in the history of the universe not to earn her high school diploma by the age of 24. She was feeling *good*.

40

Thanksgiving

Everyone was going his or her separate way for Thanksgiving. Ramiro was going to go to his family's, then over to Nick's for Thanksgiving just with their friends. Jason would be with his family in south Denver, and Marin would hang out in L.A. She had the day off, but only one day, so it didn't seem like there was any point in flying home. Although if she were honest with herself, the real reason she wasn't coming home was because of the possibility she might get to spend time with Jay. He had to visit his family in Santa Barbara that day, but he said he hoped he'd get back to celebrate with her that night. She'd vaguely hoped that he'd invite her to dinner with his family, but she knew that was ridiculous, they'd only been dating two weeks. It was much too early to meet the folks.

Since Rob's foot was still in a cast, Chelsey promised to drive him home for Thanksgiving. She'd spend the night with him, meet his folks, and then head home to Chicago to visit her family. She'd pick him up on her way back.

She didn't want to be apart from him for four days. She wasn't sure how she'd make it without him.

Chelsey took the Wednesday before Thanksgiving off, and they drove straight through to South Dakota. It was dusk when they arrived, and Chelsey had a hard time making out where she was supposed to go once they got off the highway and onto the reservation. The roads were unpaved and had crater-sized potholes.

Rob had told her about the numerous fatalities that occurred between Pine Ridge and the Nebraska border. Alcohol wasn't sold on the rez, so Indians had to *drive* to Nebraska to buy alcohol. Some couldn't wait till they got home; some took off for more after already working on a serious buzz. As a result, the per capita number of drunk-driving fatalities was catastrophic. Crosses marked the sites where individuals and entire families had died, lining the way to the rez like a canopy of oaks might line the streets in wealthier neighborhoods.

Chelsey couldn't help gaping at the homes she saw as she drove through the reservation to Rob's family's house. They were little more than outhouses—cheaply constructed boxes with worn paint.

"That's mine. The brown one there," Rob said, pointing to a small house.

"Where am I supposed to park?"

"Next to the Oldsmobile."

"On the lawn?"

"It's not really a lawn."

He was right. It wasn't. There were little patches of worn grass, but mostly it was just dirt.

Chelsey parked next to the Olds—it looked to be about fifteen years old—and walked up to the door with Rob. Slabs of wood were leaning against the house, garbage littered the area around the place. Rob entered without knocking.

His mom and sisters greeted him with smiles and hugs, but none of the loud shouting that Chelsey received when she went home to her family. Something was cooking on the stove, something fatty and oniony—the smell permeated the room.

"Chelsey, this is A'Marie and this is May. This is my mother, Elise," Rob said.

"It's nice to meet you," Chelsey said.

All three women were chubby, Chelsey noticed; his mother was seriously obese. Chelsey did her best not to be horrified by the small, dirty house or Elise's morbidly unhealthy weight.

"Hey bro," A'Marie said. She was sixteen, a junior in high school. "How's the ankle?"

"Better."

"Dinner's just about ready," Elise said.

"Posole?" Rob said.

His mother nodded. "Posole and fry bread."

"What's that?" Chelsey asked.

"Posole is a stew with hominy and jalapeños and pork. Fry bread is fried bread," Rob said.

"Fried bread?" Chelsey couldn't contain her horror.

"It's good," May said quietly, with a shy smile. Rob had told Chelsey that May was twenty and going to the community college in Pine Ridge. "It's easy to make. Just baking powder and flour and water."

As if white bread weren't enough of a nutritional wasteland, on top of that they fried it? Good Lord!

"Chelsey's a little bit of a health nut," Rob explained to his family.

"You need to put some meat on your bones," Elise said. "You're going to waste away."

Chelsey shrugged. "I'm a personal trainer. I work out a lot."

Rob did most of the talking over dinner. It was obvious that his little sisters looked up to him and his mother adored him. Chelsey tried to get down a little of the Posole to be polite, but it nearly killed her. Pork! It had been years since she'd eaten pork. And the fry bread? As if.

It was only a two-bedroom house, so Chelsey and Rob had to sleep on sleeping bags on the living room floor. A'Marie and May said they'd be happy to give up their beds, but Chelsey and Rob insisted. Chelsey was feeling so guilty, she would have slept outside with nothing to shield her from the elements. She thought about her home in Denver—it was at least twice as big and infinitely nicer than this place, and yet she was a single woman without any kids. She remembered thinking how broke she felt after buying her house. She felt like an idiot that she ever could have thought that. *This* was poverty. This was completely different.

She snuggled up next to Rob that night and held him tight. Somehow, seeing where he'd come from made her love him even more.

Ana and Scott left work early on the Wednesday before Thanksgiving and headed off bright and early for the long drive ahead of them.

As always, Ana had vigilantly prepared ahead of time, packing a cooler full of food and water so they could keep their stops to a minimum. She'd also borrowed a few Bill Bryson books on tape from the library, and his humorous travel narratives kept them laughing all the way to Texas. About the time they got to the border, however, Ana was quite ready to get out of the car. Her butt was sore, she was sick of sitting, and there was something about driving long distances that made Ana feel dirty and queasy. She wanted to shower and eat vats of vegetables to make up for gorging on half of an industrial-size bag of pretzels.

They stopped at about eleven o'clock that night to stay at an overpriced, under-comfortable hotel. Despite the lack of luxury, Ana was ecstatic just be able to get out of the car and stretch her legs.

After a good night of sleep, they took off again the next morning and pulled into Scott's family's driveway around noon. Scott's dad was outside tearing weeds from what was probably supposed to be a garden but was so desiccated it looked like a tumbleweed convention.

Scott rolled down his window. "Is it okay if we park here?"

"Park yonder," he pointed to the far left side of the driveway.

Yonder? Had she really just heard the word "yonder" uttered without irony?

Scott parked and he and Ana got out of the car. Scott gave his father a big bear hug. When they finally broke from the embrace, Ana started to mumble a "hello it's nice to meet you" and extend her hand for a handshake. Instead, Scott's father,

Ron, smothered her with an enormous hug and told her about fifty times how happy he was to meet her and how happy he was that she could come down. Apparently Texans were a little more forthcoming with their affection than Coloradoans were.

When the tsunami of welcome abated, Scott noted that his parents had planted new trees in the front yard. At this point, the trees weren't much taller than Ana and were so skinny they looked like they'd lose a fight with dental floss.

"Me and Jack was gonna put a coupla 'em over dare"— Ron indicated a spot closer to the house—"but me and him wasn't sure if that'd be too close to the house."

Holy improper use of the English language! "Me and Jack was"? "Me and him wasn't . . ." Ana wasn't some grammar snob, well okay, maybe she was, but ouch, it hurt her ears to hear this. *"He* and *I weren't,"* Ana corrected silently. *Note the placement of the "I" after the "He." I didn't make the rules up. I just enforce them. If we didn't follow the rules, all would be anarchy and my ears would commit suicide from the horror.*

They went inside and Ana was introduced to a mob of people, but she forgot everyone's name in seconds, despite her best efforts. Over the course of the day, as everyone bustled around to prepare dinner, she simply could not remember who was Jack and who was John. And Lettie and Laura, honestly, Ana didn't even bother trying to call them by name. She just did her best to get in their line of sight before she asked a question so they'd know who she was talking to. Nobody in Scott's family called his sister anything but "Sis." Ana thought that was adorable. Very Dick and Jane-ian. The whole family seemed like a *Dick and Jane* book.

Ana learned that Scott's dad worked in a meat-packing plant, and his mother worked as a checker in a grocery store. Sis was a stay-at-home mom. His brothers were a cop, a carpenter, and a well digger. Scott was the only one who'd gone to college. The only one who had any artistic interests. The only one without a thick Texan accent. In some ways, he seemed so different from his family, but in other ways, he fit right in. The love they shared was palpable. Everyone cracked jokes and told stories and it was constantly loud, but Ana felt comfortable in the midst of the hubbub. They looked out for each other, in small little ways that Ana probably only noticed because she came from such a different family. At Scott's house, nobody got up from the table without asking if they could get anyone anything. If Ana's glass of iced tea was getting low—they drank vat after vat of tea in this place—it was instantly refilled, usually before Ana realized she was running out.

Ana thought of all the times Scott had made a face and told her a joke to cheer her up. She understood now that he came from a family that looked out for each other fiercely, and if one of them was unhappy, they all were.

Despite having little kids running around and a huge crowd of people to feed, no one got stressed or freaked out or short-tempered. No one got teary-eyed when things didn't turn out exactly like they were supposed to—Ana thought it might have been the first Thanksgiving she'd ever had that didn't end up with somebody (well, her mother) crying.

After gorging themselves silly, they played epic rounds of Taboo, Scattergories, and Cranium. At last worn out, they all retired to the living room to watch TV. It had been five hours since dinner, and still Ana's stomach ached from the food she'd shoveled in. But when everyone else started making their way to the kitchen for leftovers, she started to panic—they'd take the last of the mashed potatoes and candied yams and stuffing and pecan pie . . .

"Can I get you a plate?" Sister-in-Law-With-the-Curly-Blonde-Hair said.

It would be rude to turn her down, right? "Sure." She was just being polite, really.

A couple hours later, Ana and Scott lugged their protruding bellies to the room Scott had grown up in to get some sleep. As they lay next to each other in bed, she asked him when he'd lost his accent.

"I never really had a strong accent growing up, I guess because I was always a national broadcast news junky, and Dan Rather, Tom Brokaw, and Peter Jennings don't have accents. I thought they were so cool, that they knew everything, you know? And I lost any vestiges of a Texas accent when I went to school in Colorado."

"So you could fit in?"

"No, it's just that you start talking like the people around you. If everybody says 'cool' and 'awesome,' it's hard not to start sprinkling 'cools' and 'awesomes' in your speech, you know?"

Ana nodded. What she really wanted to know was, "How did you learn to speak English so well despite spending eighteen years with people who say 'we was gonna put a coupla of 'em over dare'?" But she knew that if she made any kind of remark that could be construed as disparaging his family, he'd hurl her out the window. He was that kind of loyal.

Ramiro's Thanksgiving, like all holidays with his family, was an exercise in method acting. It could have been titled: Gay Man Plays It Straight, Ignores Huge Part of His Life. That was how the charade went—Ram pretended Nick didn't exist, and his father pretended he could tolerate his son.

Ram spent the meal thinking about Nick having a great time partying it up with their friends. If it weren't for Yo, the baby, and his mom, Ram would be right at Nick's side, being able to be himself and enjoy his life.

Yo's husband, Kevin, would have never been accepted into the family if Ram hadn't come out of the closet. After Ram's little admission, though, suddenly a European-American paleskinned non-Catholic didn't seem so bad after all.

"It's so great to have a four-day weekend," Kevin said. Their desserts had been reduced to crumbs, the cups of coffee were getting cold. Ram's mom was off doing dishes, but the rest of them sat around the table, busily digesting.

"You just need to tell your boss you're some kind of unusual religion," Ram suggested.

"Jewish. Jewish people have all kinds of holidays off," Kevin said.

"No, no good. Your boss could figure it out eventually. I told a boss once I was Druid."

"You did not."

"Oh, but I did. He was this white Catholic guy, right? All concerned about not pissing off the Hispanic guy, you know, worried about getting slapped with discrimination charges or something. So he said, 'Oh really? How interesting. What do you believe in?' I was like, 'Yeah, you know, we're all into nature. Arbor Day, that's our big day. The big Druid holiday.'"

Yo and Kevin burst out laughing. "You are not serious," Yo said.

"I am serious. He said, 'Oh, really, that's great. I can see that.'" Ramiro nodded with comic exaggeration, playing the part of the duped boss. "He bought it. I got Arbor Day off, Earth Day, any random day I made up. I'm serious."

Yo and Kevin found this hilarious, and Ram joined their laughter. Their merriment was quickly stanched, however, when Ram's father said, with a serious grimace on his face, "You are Catholic. How can you turn your back on God for a day off from work!"

"Dad, I was just being silly, joking around." *That's what I do. It's who I am. Why can't you understand even a little bit about who I am?*

Silence and tension gripped the room until at last Kevin changed the subject to something safe—football, golf, basketball—the harmless conversation of men.

Eventually, dinner was over, and Ram went to his friend's house for after-dinner cocktails. When he saw Nick, he hugged him tight, then took his hand in his own, and gripped it firmly, as if to prove to himself that Nick was real, their love was real. At last, Ramiro was home.

Marin spent her day locked in her hotel room. At first, she simply reveled in the fact that she could sleep in and be a lazy slob, watching bad movies on cable.

She snuggled under her covers, smiling to herself. She'd

been smiling a lot these days. Since her date with Jay, her life seemed to be a whirlwind of excitement. They both had hectic schedules, but they did their best to see each other whenever they could. Marin was amazed by how busy someone who was unemployed could be, but Jay had the most amazingly eventful social calendar she'd ever heard of, and he often traveled to check on various investments or to go to board meetings of various boards of directors that he served on.

The other night, Jay had taken her to a party at the home of a movie producer. He'd been so casual about it. Just, "Want to come to a party tonight?" Not, "Want to come to a party where a number of Hollywood heavies will be?" She'd seen Ron Howard, Winona Ryder, and Ben Stiller, and there were lots of producers, directors, and behind-the-scenes people who Marin didn't know yet, but knew she would be in awe of when she did. Thank god she'd gotten dressed up for it.

She'd had to buy lots of new clothes since coming to California. For one thing, she'd only packed a week's worth of outfits when she'd come out here. For another thing, most of her clothes in Denver wouldn't fit in here. Denver was a casual town that could never be confused for being a high-fashion hot spot. In L.A., there was a strange fashion code that Marin was still working to crack. Even "casual" outfits seemed expensive and high fashion.

She ordered breakfast from room service at about noon, feeling like a queen, who, with a simple phone call or a snap of the fingers, could summon food and drink and whatever her heart desired.

She took a shower, put on a cute, short white nightie and white silk thong underwear. She did her hair and put on a little makeup, even though she knew it would probably be several hours until she saw him. His dinner was at two, but with dessert and coffee and talking and maybe games, she probably wouldn't see him till seven or eight.

Her boredom started to set in around two o'clock. She kept changing positions on her bed, trying to get comfortable. Her body wasn't used to being so inactive for such a long stretch of time. She should probably go work out, but she'd already showered and the task of changing into sweats and going down to the gym seemed Herculean.

By four o'clock, she was sprawled across the bed, the right side of her face smashed up against the mattress, watching some movie that was so awful she could actually feel it robbing hours off her life—not just the two hours she watched it, but the powerful vacuum of its awfulness was actually sucking months or years away from her time on this planet like cigarettes or chronic heavy drinking.

At six o'clock, she ordered dinner from room service, and this was when depression started setting in. Though at breakfast she'd felt like a queen, now she felt like a loser, all alone on Thanksgiving, holed up in a hotel room, watching terrible movies. She made it a big point to ask for a bottle of wine with *two* glasses, as if it mattered what the receptionist or the waiter thought of her, as if they cared she was waiting for her man to show up and wasn't really a social reject.

She ate her dinner slowly, trying to drag it out to fill the hours until Jay got there. She had a glass of wine with her meal, and though she really had intended to share the bottle with Jay, she had another, then another.

She couldn't believe when nine o'clock rolled around and she still hadn't heard from him. She figured he would have called her as soon as he'd left and was about to drive back to L.A.

When he called, it was almost eleven, and Marin had finished off the wine and was nodding off into a drunken slumber.

"Babe?"

"Jay, where are you?"

"I'm so sorry. We waited a couple of hours after dinner to have dessert, then there was coffee and brandy and dessert wine, and I drank too much to be able to drive home tonight."

"Oh, you're kidding," she whined. "I was really looking forward to seeing you."

"I know, I'll make it up to you. When's your next day off?"

"I'm not sure."

"How about Saturday night after you get off the set?"

"Sure. That sounds great." Even though, in truth, most nights she worked on the set she just wanted to crawl into bed the second she got home and crash. They'd only gone out a few nights when she worked, but twice she'd fallen asleep right after sex, something he loved to tease her about.

"Great. See you Saturday night."

Oh well, every relationship had challenges to overcome. All in all, though, she counted herself the luckiest woman alive.

41

Porno Pop-Up Hell

Ana had finished her sessions with Chelsey. She'd lost four pounds in the last six weeks. Hardly enough weight to star in a weight loss commercial, but she was feeling better. She'd loved working out with Chelsey—Chelsey kicked her ass. Ana wished she could afford a trainer all the time.

Ana would have lost more, but Thanksgiving weekend with Scott's family had blunted progress significantly. She felt like she was at least on the right track now, eating better and working out more. Her pants weren't quite so tight anymore, and that was really the main thing.

She ate her lunch slowly, trying to actually enjoy her entire hour-long lunch break. She liked to surf the 'Net while she ate, but she usually scarfed down her food in about four minutes flat, and then she didn't want to keep reading online publications lest some higher-up walk past her and think she was goofing off, rather than taking a much deserved lunch break. So she was determined to keep her lunch in front of her for an entire hour, even with her stomach grumbling angrily. Eating slowly was supposed to be good for you anyway.

Ana nibbled miserably on her carrot stick. She felt like she'd been starving herself for months and was not yet skinny. She knew that it had taken her several months to become the porker who busted out of her pants, but still, she wanted speedier results.

She went to the *New York Times* and read the news and book reviews. Then she quickly looked at *Denver Post* online. She checked the celebrity gossip at *People* and *Us*. Then she decided to swing by *Bitch* magazine, a hilarious mag that critiqued the bullshit of the pop culture she'd so recently been at pains to study in *People* and *Us*. She typed in www.bitch.com, which, as it turned out, was not the correct URL to the feminist *Bitch* magazine. Quite the opposite, it was a porn site of some sort, which spewed out pop-up ads for other lascivious porn sites like fireworks going off in rapid fire succession.

"Shit! Ahh!" Ana knew, *knew*, that this would the exact moment The Weasel, Deb, or the president of the company would choose to stroll by her cube. Getting caught surfing porn sites was, at best, humiliating, and, at worst, a fireable offense.

She used every skill she'd developed playing video games, using her mouse to click the windows shut like she was zapping down enemy airships. Bam bam bam!

Shit, shit, they just kept coming, multiplying like weeds, rabbits, talentless boy bands, and reality TV shows.

Bam bam bam! Fire! Attack!

At long last, she'd successfully killed off all job-losing porn ads. She quickly changed the address to www.bitchmagazine.com, which turned out to be the correct URL. But Ana was too tired to read cogent arguments about the lack of people of color in television or the use of strip clubs and strippers in guy-guy buddy movies. She was breathless from attacking the equivalent of a fleet of hostile war planes.

42

Surprises

It was a lazy Sunday morning. Ana woke up first and watched Scott as he slept. She knew she should let him sleep, but she couldn't resist the urge to kiss him. Mostly still asleep, he kissed her back. As he woke up, his kisses got stronger and stronger, his groping more fervent. She loved that he could be practically asleep and yet have some instinct so powerful he could grope her with a frenzy.

"We're out of condoms," Ana whispered.

"No!"

"Wait here, I'll be right back."

She hurried down the hall to Ramiro's room.

"Hey Ram, can we borrow some more condoms? I'll buy more when I go to the store today or tomorrow."

He pulled open the drawer of his nightstand and as he tore off a strip of three, Ana noticed a large stack of loose paper on his desk. The top page had the words *"Staring at the Sun* by Ramiro Martinez"* typed on it.

"What's this?"

"It's nothing."

"Is it a story? A novel?"

"No, it's not finished. It's nothing."

"But if it were finished, what would it be?"

"A novel, I guess."

"Oh my god, Ram, I had no idea you were working on a

novel. All this time we thought you were a lazy slob and really you've been secretly toiling away on a great American novel. Your first novel. It's so exciting!"

"It's my fourth, actually."

"Fourth! You're kidding! What did you do with the other ones?"

"They're in the bottom drawer of my desk."

"Did you try to get them published? Did you try to get an agent?"

"Nah. They're not any good."

"How do you know they're no good?"

He shrugged. "They just aren't."

"Have you ever let anyone read them?"

"My first . . . I finished it in high school . . ."

"High school!"

"I'd just come out, and I gave the manuscript to my dad. I thought of it as a sort of peace offering. Like yeah, I'm a fag, but I'm also this prodigy."

"Yeah? So what did he say about the book?"

"He said he was impressed that I could type three hundred pages but I had no talent and never would."

"You're kidding. He wouldn't say that."

"He said it like he was really sorry he had to tell me. Like he was just a doctor who had to tell a patient he had terminal cancer. I think if he'd said it in anger, I might have thought he was just trying to be cruel, but the way he said it, I knew he really meant it."

"Ram, you're a great sketch writer. I'm sure you're a good novelist. Maybe, you know, I mean your first novel, you were still in high school. It takes years for authors to develop their talent. Let me read it, okay?"

He shrugged. "It's your time."

Ana hauled the weighty manuscript back to her room.

"Ram's written a novel. Four of them," Ana said to Scott.

"Ramiro? A whole novel? He didn't get bored with it after a paragraph?"

"I guess not. I want to start reading it right away."

"What do you mean?"

"Do you mind?"

"Are you saying I'm not going to get any?"

"You will. Just not right now."

"Four minutes ago I was going to get nookie. And now, no nookie?"

She nodded, happy he understood this turn of events in their entirety.

"Life is so cruel and unfair."

"It's a lesson best learned when you're young. Now off to visit one of the million Internet porn sites if you must, but leave me to the manuscript."

Ana sprawled across her bed and tore into the story. It was immediately apparent that the story was autobiographical. In the story, a Mexican-American 22-year-old guy has just graduated from college and travels through Mexico one summer, just as Ramiro had when he graduated from college.

What struck Ana was that the book was so serious—not a joke cracked or fashion faux pas mocked. It was filled with breathtaking descriptions of everything from a peasant woman sitting on a blanket selling beaded jewelry to a pack of dogs devouring a kitten (she wouldn't have minded if that last one had a wee bit less detail).

The guy in the story, Tonoch, does a lot of reflecting about his past and his future. Time and again he brings up his father's disappointment in him. He feels alternately angry and guilty about this.

Tonoch is a theater major, and his father, a construction worker who didn't have access to a college education, just like Ram's real-life dad, is furious with Tonoch for pursuing the impractical dream of being an actor. He'd stopped paying for Tonoch's education when Tonoch refused to major in business. (Ramiro's dad had stopped helping him through college his freshman year when Ramiro declared he was going to major in philosophy.)

Tonoch's father had fantasies of his son getting paid handsomely and going to work in spotless white shirts with smart-looking ties. He wanted a son whose face didn't get weathered from working outside his whole life. A son who never had dirt under his fingernails. But just as much as his father wanted him to be a businessman, Tonoch knew he'd be miserable with such a life.

Tonoch was at the Temple of the Jaguar at the ancient Mayan ruin of Chichen Itza listening to the tour guide talk about the ancient Mayan people and thinking about how he didn't understand how he could have gone through his whole life without having heard even a word about what his ancestors achieved.

The Mayans had calendars, sporting competitions, markets, art, and a written language at the same time the Greeks did, but all we ever learned in school was about the Greeks and Romans and Egyptians. Never once had I learned about the Mayans. This temple was beautiful. It made me proud. Why did I have to travel 2,000 miles to learn about my history, my people, my past?

I tuned the tour guide out and simply took in the image of the temple. I wanted to drink in every detail. I wanted to carve a memory that would last forever as if that could make up for twenty years of having no memories to forget.

The temple stood shrouded in a sky that was perfectly blue, uncracked by cloud or threat of rain. Or at least a sky that appeared to be blue. My eighth grade teacher, Ms. Adams, told us that the sky is blue is a lie, like the lie the Mayans never existed and never mattered. The blue color is a trick of light. The sun beams down every color of the rainbow, the reds and yellows' longer wavelengths race down to earth to bake the soil while the lazy blues with their short waves get scattered around the dust and moisture particles, making the sky appear blue. So many things are distorted by color, the way the prisms of the world refract and divide it.

Is it any wonder that the Mayans worshipped the god of the sun? It lit the world, yet only let us see what it wanted us to see. It's best to stay on the good side of something so strong yet so cunning.

When I was little, my father caught me staring up into the sun. He towered over me back then. He couldn't know that someday I would grow to be seven inches taller than his 5'3", that my broad build would eclipse his small frame.

He told me I'd blind myself if I stared too long at the sun. I looked up at his looming black figure, haloed by the sun's rays. My eyes had trouble focusing, adjusting from the light. It's dangerous to look so close at something so powerful. You may not like what you see.

"Tonoch" a.k.a. Ramiro was always doing that. Teaching you simultaneously about things like Mayan history and why the sky was blue while struggling to come to terms with his tumultuous relationship with his father. But Ana thought he pulled it off. She couldn't put the book down, and not just because it gave an insight to Ramiro's quiet pain that he'd always kept hidden from his friends. She genuinely liked the stories of Tonoch's conversations with migrant farmers and shopkeepers and other Americans he met along his journey through Mexico.

She spent the entire afternoon reading, using tissue after tissue crying through the sad parts. "It's your father's own issues! He's just jealous that you are so smart and got the college education he never had! Stop being so sad and drinking too much and sleeping with guys that don't treat you well!" she silently told the character in the book.

In the end, Tonoch did what she advised. He found a wonderful man, a professor from the States who did research on Mayan history. The professor was in Mexico for the summer, but had to return to California where he taught in August. He asked Tonoch to come with him and Tonoch agreed. He decided that when he moved in with Manuel he would look for acting jobs and maybe find a job teaching English to people whose native language was Spanish. Tonoch thought that maybe he could get started with a happy life if he was hundreds of miles from his father's disapproving gaze.

Ana shut the book. It was nine o'clock at night. She was starving. She wiped the tears from her eyes. She felt drained. She wondered if Ramiro fantasized about moving away from his father like Tonoch did. But Ramiro was so close to his family, particularly his mother and sister, she couldn't imagine him moving across the country.

She walked to Ramiro's room and knocked on the closed door.

"Come in," Ramiro called.

"Oh, sorry Nick, I didn't know you were here. Can I talk to Ram for a second?"

Nick was sprawled across the bed. Ramiro sat in his ratty brown recliner. They had been laughing at something when she'd opened the door.

"We've been meaning to get off our asses and go over to Sean's place anyway. Ram, I'll wait for you downstairs."

Nick left, and Ana took his place on the bed.

"Hey, are you okay? Have you been crying?" Ramiro asked.

She nodded. "At your book. It was really good."

"You read the whole thing?"

"I couldn't put it down. I haven't eaten all day. I've just been reading."

"The book made you cry?"

"Parts of it are really sad. The ending was happy, but I cried with sad happiness, you know? You should definitely try to get it published."

"No way."

"What do you mean no way? Why would you want to write a novel if you didn't want to try to get it published?"

"I have all these thoughts in my head. I need to get them down on paper, that's all."

"But don't you want other guys who have gone through this to read this? Don't you want to see if you can get money and awards and stuff? Maybe you could start writing full time. I know you don't want to work at the book store for the rest of your life."

"No. It's not any good."

"Ramiro, I think it's good. Why don't you try and see if an agent thinks it's any good or if a publisher thinks it's any good?"

He shrugged. "It's not even finished."

"It felt finished to me. That's just an excuse. You're just afraid of rejection." As she said it, she realized what a dead-on statement it was. It was why Ramiro was so hard on himself, why he never thought anything was good enough to be declared finished. "That's why you never finish anything.

Nobody can tell you you have no talent if you never finish anything and let anyone see it." He didn't respond. "I'm going to see if it can be published."

"Ana, whatever. Nick is waiting for me. I'm glad you enjoyed the book, but really, don't waste your time."

The next day after work, Ana stopped at the Tattered Cover bookstore and went to the section on writing. She spent half an hour flipping through books and finally selected one that discussed how to get a novel published and another that had a listing of literary agents.

She went home and promptly started reading the book on how to get a novel published. It had a section on deciding whether or not to get an agent and another section on how to get an agent. The book said that you might not need an agent for a nonfiction book, but that most publishing houses wouldn't look at a manuscript if it wasn't represented by an agent.

The way to get an agent, it said, was to type a one-page query letter talking about the book and a little about yourself and what else you'd published. It suggested putting down any literary magazines you'd had short stories published in, if any. Since Ramiro hadn't been published, she focused on his experience writing comedy.

Dear _____,

I've recently completed a 120,000-word novel about a young Mexican-American man's journey through Mexico to discover his history and, most important, to determine what he should do with his future. In Staring into the Sun, *Tonoch has recently graduated from college with a degree in theater, a course of study he pursued despite his father's disapproval. Then again, being a gay son to a fiercely traditional Mexican man means Tonoch may never earn his father's approval—or his forgiveness. As Tonoch travels through the vibrant warmth of the Mexican landscape, seeing beauty in everything from ancient Mayan ruins to a wizened old woman selling jewelry displayed on a brilliantly colored rug on the dusty streets of Mexico City, he begins to understand*

*the history of his people, where his father is coming from, and
what he wants his future to hold.*

I believe Staring into the Sun *would appeal to fans of
Richard Rodriguez, Ian Frazier, and Sandra Cisneros.*

*I've been a writer and performer for the last ten years and
founded the Iron Pyrits improv troupe in 1994. I've been a staff
performer at Spur of the Moment Theater in Denver for the
past four years. This is my first novel.*

Please let me know if I may send you Staring into the Sun
in part or in its entirety.

Regards,
Ramiro Martinez

Ana only sent the query to agents who accepted e-queries
to save money on postage. She created a new Hotmail account
just for Ram's book. Email was better than mail anyway: If the
agents mailed letters replying to her query to Ramiro, he'd
know what she was up to. She'd told him she was going to do
it, so it wasn't like she was lying, but this way, if she couldn't
sell it, Ramiro wouldn't know and he wouldn't have more evi-
dence to use to "prove" that he had no talent. If she *could* get it
published, on the other hand, Ramiro would know that his father was wrong and he had talent after all.

She picked ten agents, a mix of men and women, who said
they represented fiction writers to send the queries to.

The book about getting published had said that it typically
took a week or two to hear if an agent was interested in seeing
the manuscript, then two months to hear back on whether s/he
was interested in representing the book. Then it could take up
to a year for a publisher to decide to buy it.

Ana checked the new email account the next day, and three
agents had responded. One said she wasn't taking new clients,
one said he didn't think the book sounded right for his agency,
but the other one said she wanted to read the manuscript in its
entirety!

Ana was a goddess! In just one day she'd gotten someone
interested in reading the manuscript!

Okay, she'd probably only heard back so quickly because

email was the kind of thing you could respond to instantly, but the important thing was that she'd gotten an agent interested in seeing his book. The agent still needed to agree to represent it, so it wasn't like there weren't more hurdles to overcome, but Ana beamed with pride that she'd written a query letter that had enticed the interest of an agent. *Take that, Big Weasel! Who says I can't write killer copy?*

Over the next several days, she heard from all but one of the agents. Four of those six said they weren't interested, which really pissed her off. She hated that Ramiro was getting rejected when they hadn't even read his book. She was sure they were just being prejudiced against gays. But two others said they wanted to see the manuscript, so she dutifully used the office copier to print off more copies, then she lugged the manuscripts to the post office to mail. It cost nine bucks a pop to mail these puppies, but it was worth it if she could help Ramiro make a name for himself in the literary community.

The postman took the packages she'd put the manuscripts in as if they were just a few more boxes and didn't hold someone's future in their taped-up confines. She, however, watched the manuscripts tossed with the other mail with much more reverence. Like coins tossed in a fountain, they held the contents of a dream.

43

Fairy Tale Middles

The last month of Marin's life had seemed so surreal to her. She still couldn't get over the sound of a director yelling "cut!" It was just like in the movies, except this was her real life! The thing that excited her most about her foray into Hollywood, however, was that she'd finally learned what the hell a gaffer was. She'd always seen gaffers listed in movie credits, but until now their role had been a complete mystery. (They do the lighting on the set.)

No, really, the most exciting thing about her life was Jay. Their schedules were difficult to juggle, but the time they did get to spend together was so thrilling, she etched each minute in her memory, reliving every moment again and again. Her life was like a fairy tale, but it wasn't a fairy tale ending where the story stopped and you could only imagine what happened next. She was right smack dab in the middle of all this happiness and excitement, and there were times it didn't seem real.

She was constantly getting caught on the set smiling to herself in a dreamy and entirely idiotic way. Devin teased her gently; Jessica was bitter with jealousy and, despite calling herself an actress, did a terrible job of concealing it; but it was Conrad's remarks that really bothered Marin. He kept insinuating that what was happening in her life off the set was influencing her work on the set. If she ever stumbled on a line, even if it was just in rehearsal, he pounced, making comments about how her mind was on Prince Charming and not her work.

She knew he was just trying to make her look unprofessional, and she was pretty sure she was doing good work, but there was a part of her that worried he might be right. Her sleep was irregular and it was hard to take her mind off of Jay, but she did her best to concentrate on work, and her lines while at work.

When the director called it a day, Marin called Jay. She couldn't believe it when he actually answered his cell phone. They usually had to leave each other dozens of messages and play several rounds of phone tag before getting through to each other.

"I'll pick you up right now," he said.

"No, no, I'm still at the studio. I still have to go home and shower and change and all that." No deodorant could compete with the relentlessly hot lights of the soundstage.

"You're beautiful just the way you are."

"Maybe, but after twelve hours under those lights, I smell like wet dog. Trust me, you want me to shower."

He laughed. "All right, I'll give you an hour."

Marin flagged a taxi. "Graciela Burbank," she told the driver, briefly pulling the phone away from her mouth. "So what's on the agenda tonight?" she asked Jay. She'd learned it was best to ask him this so she didn't end up meeting Steven Spielberg in a t-shirt and jeans. Among Jay's good looks and ample supplies of cash, he also knew an astonishing number of people in Hollywood, which certainly couldn't hurt her career. Marin thought it was interesting how a businessman who said he wasn't involved in the movie biz knew so many people in the movie and television industry. Then again, having money made you popular in just about any circle.

"It's a surprise, but wear a dress, a long one."

"Hmm, sounds interesting. Okay then, I'll see you at eight." Marin didn't have a long dress here in California, so when she arrived at her hotel, she dashed across the street to a ludicrously expensive boutique. She felt rich these days with the salary she was getting from the pilot. Besides, if she was going to be a star, she had to look like a star.

She bought a long black silk dress that hooked at the back of the neck and left her shoulders, arms and back bare. The fabric was so sheer and light she felt somehow more naked than if she actually were naked. She felt daring, going braless, and she loved the way the dress swirled when she spun.

Buying the dress had consumed half an hour, so she raced through her shower, threw on her makeup and jewelry, and dried her hair as fast as she could. She was pinning her hair up when he arrived.

She unlocked the door and attacked him with a hug and kiss.

When they broke apart, he appraised her carefully. "You look stunning."

"Why thank you. I'm almost ready. Just let me finish my hair and put on some perfume and I'll be ready to go."

He trailed behind her as she strode across the room to her mirror. He hovered behind her. In the reflection of the mirror, she watched him watch her. He slipped his hands in from the sides of her dress, cupping her breasts. He kissed her neck.

"You'd better stop that or we'll never get out of here." Marin said, totally unconvincingly.

"I love your easy-access dress."

"That's how they marketed it at the store, actually, noting how quick my date could feel me up."

"Those retailers, they know what they're doing."

They kissed again.

"So are you going to wine and dine me or what?"

He took her to a restaurant at the top of a thirty-two-story building with a panoramic view of L.A. Over a wonderful meal, Marin took in the beauty of city. She loved this life. There was no time for sleep, or laundry, or playing epic games of Quake with her friends, but she could deal with that.

"How was your day today? Still liking the world of television?" he asked.

"Yeah, love it."

"What do you think of your show? Think it'll be a top-rated program?"

"I can't really tell if it's any good because everything goes so fast and it's all taped in such a disjointed way, I can't really follow the story."

"Don't you read the scripts?"

"I memorize my lines and my cues; everything else is a blur."

"So you'll be as surprised as anyone when you see the first show."

"Probably. What did you do with your day today?"

"Played golf."

"Isn't that what old retired people do?"

"I am retired."

"But you're not old."

"That's true, but I love golfing. Old retired people golf because they have the time. I'm lucky because I'm young and have the time. There's a quote from Mark Twain, I can't remember how it goes exactly, but the gist of it is that whatever you would do if you were on vacation is what you should do for your living full time. If I could have, I would have been a professional golfer for a living, because that's what I like to do on vacation. But I wasn't good enough for that, so I worked crazy hours at a job that I enjoyed, but that I certainly wouldn't have done on vacation, so now I can golf all the time. Think about it, if you were on a vacation for the rest of your life and never had to worry about money, you'd still perform, wouldn't you?"

"Of course."

"That's how you know acting is the career you're supposed to pursue."

After dinner, after he'd paid the check and Marin had finished her cappuccino, she asked, "So, I'm wearing this long elegant dress. Why?"

"Do you know how to ballroom dance?"

"I performed in all the plays and musicals in high school and was a debutante to boot. You bet I know how to ballroom dance."

"Excellent."

He took her hand and led her to the dance hall adjacent to the restaurant. There were dozens of couples, mostly older, dancing away, and Jay pulled Marin onto the dance floor. They danced the waltz, the foxtrot, the quickstep, the lindy hop, and some East Coast swing, and the whole time, Marin felt like Cinderella, a gorgeous young woman with her Prince Charming, living the kind of life that only happens in the movies.

It was one in the morning when they called it a night. Jay took her back to her hotel. She liked his house much better—it was enormous yet cozy—but she'd only been there once. Her hotel was much closer to the studio, and with her appallingly early calls, it just made sense to go back to her hotel, depressing though it might be. When they got home, they weren't much interested in décor anyway.

44

Iceberg Lettuce

Marin couldn't come home for Christmas since they were delayed in taping. She had explained how the studio liked to buy TV series in blocks of six because they liked to have the shows in the can in case the series took off after the first few shows. Then they didn't have to renegotiate with the producers until the next season.

It was about a week before Christmas when Ana got a letter from her. Inside was a Christmas card and a check for $500.

I want you to take this money to get headshots and a new shirt so you'll feel like a total hottie when you get your picture taken. Now here's the deal, you can't say that you can't take this money and you can't be offended that I want to give it to you and here's why: you've lent me money countless times over the years, and anyway, we're friends and friends help each other succeed. You want to be an actress and a comedian, and an actress/comedian needs headshots. Anyway, they are paying me a buttload of money to do this series, and I want to share my good fortune with you and that's that. Now stop protesting and have yourself a Merry Christmas. I miss you so much it hurts.

Smooch smooch,
Marin

Ana got teary eyed at the sweetness of the gesture. Here she was gripped by jealousy toward her friend, and Marin was graciously encouraging her to succeed in her career goals. Ana was an evil person who didn't deserve friends like these.

The phone rang. "Yeah?" Ana answered, abruptly wiping the tears away.

"Ana, you never should have lent me this book," Chelsey said. Since Ana had given her *Live From New York*, Chelsey had spent every moment she wasn't with Rob devouring it. She found that she really liked Rob's schedule. She had built-in alone time and didn't have to feel guilty if she wanted a night alone—every other day she got one. She'd hated the schedule when she was a little girl and her father was the one fighting fires and gone all the time. He'd missed so many recitals and plays, and Santa Claus always came at the strangest times— while they were at a restaurant having dinner on Christmas Eve, or Christmas Eve Eve, so Chelsey and her brother woke up to presents that morning. But now that she was an adult, the schedule worked out just fine.

"Why?"

"It's so depressing. It sounds so hard."

"Well, it is hard, duh. But isn't it inspiring, too? Don't you want to be them?"

"Yeah. I just wonder if I have it in me."

"I know, I wonder too. I listen to Marin talk about her schedule, and I'm like, and I think working in an office is tough?"

"I only want to hear success stories. No more about how hard this business is. But I'm completely addicted to this book. I don't think I'll sleep tonight."

"It is dangerous."

"I'm going to get back to it now, if you don't mind."

"I understand completely."

Scott took Ana out to a nice restaurant for dinner. At first she balked at the cost of the entrées, but then he reminded her that he made $20,000 more a year than she did. Ana would need a number of promotions and raises to get to what he was making.

"What's the occasion?" she asked.

"I want to romance my girl. I want you to know that this past month has been the happiest of my life."

She smiled. "Me too."

"I got us tickets to the Bluebird for a show after dinner."

"Cool! What band is playing?"

"I have no idea."

The band turned out to be one neither of them had ever heard of but both immediately liked. It was loud rock music, but they could actually tell one song from the next and liked the lyrics. Ana and Scott bounced up and down—it was the closest they could approximate dancing in the crowded room. When they left hours later, they were sweaty and horny from the heat and energy of the club. They made out for a few minutes in the car before racing home, intending to tear each other's clothes off the moment they got there.

In the few minutes it took to drive home, however, they'd lost all their energy and felt suddenly exhausted. The fact that they'd stayed out late on a work night suddenly hit their bodies.

Inside, they found Jason at the kitchen table grading papers.

"What are you doing up?" Ana asked.

"Just trying to finish this up."

Ana sat next to him. She collapsed on the table, resting her head on her arms. "What are you working on?"

"I'm calculating my budget for Christmas gifts."

"Christmas? That's way far away in the future," Ana said.

"It's three weeks away."

"That's impossible. Thanksgiving was just a couple days ago."

"It was a week ago, and Christmas is right around the corner."

"Shit. Scott, what were your plans?"

"I have to go back home for Christmas."

"But I can't leave my mom for another holiday."

"I didn't think you would. I'll only be gone for a few days."

"Don't leave me alone with my mother. Can't your family come here?"

"Where would they stay?"

"Ana, why don't you and your mom come to my family's house?" Jason said.

"No, I'm not going to barge in on your family party."

"We'd love to have you."

"Really?"

"Really."

"Ask your mom first. See what she says."

His mom said she'd love to have Ana and her mother. Scott would be gone for five whole days. Ana didn't know how she'd bear it.

His plane was scheduled for the afternoon of the twenty-third. That morning when she opened her eyes, Scott was already out of bed. On his pillow was a single rose and a small brown paper bag with a note stapled to it.

Merry Christmas, Ana
Eat me!

Ana opened the bag. Inside was a muffin, an Odwalla orange juice, and another note.

I wanted to make you breakfast in bed, but you know I can't cook. In an effort to ensure our house wasn't burned to cinder, I figured this was the safest bet. Once you're done nourishing yourself, come downstairs. Santa made a special visit, just for you.

Smiling, Ana took the muffin and orange juice downstairs. The Christmas tree was lit. There was a beautifully wrapped gift the size of an oversized book or painting with a note that said, "Open me." She tore off the wrapping paper and gasped: It was a painting of her smiling. He'd obviously painted it from the publicity photo on the Spur of the Moment website. She'd always liked that picture of herself. In it, she's leaning forward on a table, the right side of her face resting in the palm of her right hand, her left hand resting on her right arm.

She has a comfortable, relaxed expression, an easy-going smile that lit up her face.

"Hey now, no crying," Scott said, crawling out from behind the couch and sitting beside her.

Ana sniffed. "Were you watching this whole time?"

"I was hiding behind the Lazy-Boy. I've been sitting there wrapped up in a cramped ball for like an hour. I thought you'd never wake up."

"Scott, thank you. I love it. It's the sweetest . . . it's the best . . . greatest . . . most wonderful . . ."

"You're going to run out of adjectives."

"I mean, I've been *immortalized.* It's so cool! It's just like those boring paintings of people no one's ever heard of at the art museum except this painting isn't boring and you'll be famous." Ana pulled Scott to her and gave him a long, slow, passionate kiss. "It's the best present anyone has ever given me. Thank you. Let me go get your gift. It's not nearly as good, but, you know, I'm not an artist."

Ana ran upstairs and grabbed the gift, then bolted back down the stairs.

Scott tore the wrapping paper off. Inside was a note sealed in an envelope, but that dropped to the floor as Scott inspected the collage Ana had made using pictures of all of the members of the Spur of the Moment gang over the years.

"Guys are just so bad about things like photos and albums and memorabilia," Ana said "I thought if I made it something you could hang on the wall, you'd have a way to remember all the fun we've had together over the years."

Scott laughed, his gaze still on the framed collage. "I remember that night. God, I'd forgotten about that." He pointed to the picture of him, Ana, Jason, and Marin from the night after a show when they'd had a huge water fight back at their house. Ram took the picture of the four of them dripping with water and laughing, buckets or water guns in hand.

"I love it, Ana. It's great. What's this?" he said, noticing the note for the first time. He opened the envelope and read what she'd written on thick, creamy paper.

Scott,

You and I have been friends for six years now, but every day I learn more about you, more things that make me love you.

Scott looked up from the note and met her gaze. "I love you," he said, pulling her in for a hug.

"I love you. I'm really going to miss you these next few days."

"I'm really going to miss you, too."

On Christmas Eve, Grace, Ana, and Jason drove down together.

Jason's mom and stepdad's house was jaw-droppingly enormous. Ana had met Jason's family when they'd come to Iron Pyrits shows or other functions, but she'd never seen his house in person.

"Grace," Jason said to Ana's mother, "these are my older brothers, Paul and Mike. This is my mother, Camille, and my stepfather, Duncan."

Mike, the eldest brother, greeted Jason with a sharp punch to Jason's upper arm. Paul did the same. Both brothers were built like defensive linemen—enormous refrigerators with guts—compared to Jason and his quarterback build.

"Hey punching bag," Mike said.

"Hey douche bag," Paul added, with another punch.

Jason took the abuse stoically. He obviously had lots of practice.

"It's so nice to meet all of you," Grace said. "Camille, Duncan, your home is gorgeous. Could we get a tour?"

"I'll take you," Jason said. "Follow me." He walked across the living room, which was approximately the size of the Pacific Ocean, to a staircase. "Let's start with the guest wing."

"The 'wing'? You have a wing?" Grace spluttered. She was promptly elbowed by Ana, who gave her a stern look of disapproval.

There were three bedrooms in the guest wing alone. Each bedroom had its own bathroom and walk-in closet.

"Ana, crown molding, do you know how expensive that is?" Grace whispered loudly.

"Shh!"

Jason took them back down the stairs of the guest wing, across the living room, and up to the main wing, where his parents had a bedroom the size of Texas, with his-and-her walk-in closets and his-and-her bathrooms. (Two bathrooms that is. One for each of them. Two bathrooms for *one room*.) The master bedroom had a window that went out to their own private patio with a view of the mountains and downtown Denver.

"Jason, you didn't tell me you were fabulously wealthy," Ana whispered.

"I'm not. Mom didn't move in here until she remarried."

"When was that?"

"I was a senior in high school."

Ana didn't have to ask about his father. His dad had moved to California after the divorced was finalized and rarely saw his kids anymore after that. He'd pop up every now and then when he broke up with his latest girlfriend or got divorced for the second, third, or fourth time and felt like he wanted to pretend to be a dad again, but that was it, only when he didn't have a girlfriend or wife to give all of his attention to. Popping up from time to time was more painful for Jason than if his dad had just left forever. Jason could understand that maybe his dad had decided fatherhood wasn't for him or that the sight of his sons was too painful, but always coming in second after whatever miscellaneous women drifted into his father's life was difficult to take. He'd articulated this to Ana one night after his dad had popped into his life again, and Ana had asked him what was wrong. It was yet another reason Ana loved Jason. He was one of those rare men who admitted to having feelings and wasn't afraid to talk about them.

After the tour, Camille asked them to sit down for dinner. All the food had been laid out in matching bowls and platters. There were crystal wine and water glasses, and china plates so delicate they were nearly transparent.

"Your home is simply wonderful, Camille," Grace said.

"Thank you."

"So, Mike, Paul, do you live in the area?" Grace asked.

"I own a home in Boulder," Mike said. "I'm an applications architect."

She hadn't asked you what your job was, Ana thought. *And she didn't ask you if you were a homeowner.*

"I have a home in Castle Rock," Paul said. "Brand new place, built to suit."

"That's wonderful," Grace said.

"Maybe someday Jason will be able to afford a place," Mike said.

"I hear he's saving up to live in a cardboard box," Paul added.

Ana waited for Jason to say how he loved his job and there were some things—lots of things actually—that were more important than money. But he didn't say anything. She wanted to say something, but she was the guest. What could she say?

"I've made Cornish game hens for everyone," Camille said. "Except Jason, of course. Jase, you can take an extra big helping of potatoes and vegetables and salad, okay?"

"Wussy food for a wuss," Mike said.

"Ah, I don't like to be mean to da animals," Paul said in a little-kid voice.

"The poor little birdies deserve to be able to grow up and get a job and have a family just like us," Mike snorted derisively.

Ana couldn't take it anymore. "Jason, aren't you going to say something? Are you just going to take this?"

That shut the place up. As usual, Ana's foot was so far down her mouth, it was halfway down her small intestine. No one said anything for the longest moment in the history of the world.

"He always was the sweetheart of the bunch," Camille finally said. "While Mike and Paul were plowing down guys on the football field, Jason was sponsoring food drives for the homeless or collecting gifts for poor kids at Christmas time. He always did look out for the little guy."

"If you were abused like this your whole life, I'm surprised you didn't grow up to become a serial killer," Ana said. Everyone laughed at this, though she wasn't kidding.

Over dinner, Duncan talked a little bit about his real estate business. Paul and Mike talked about their cars and houses and vacations in Hawaii. Ana, Jason, and Grace barely said a word the whole time. Ana was thrilled when the meal was finally over and Camille started collecting the plates. Ana, Grace, and Jason promptly jumped up to help.

"I think we should we wait a few minutes until dessert, don't you?" Camille said.

"Uh, definitely, I'm stuffed," Ana said.

"Would you mind bringing the coffee cups out to the table?" Camille asked Jason. "I'll make coffee."

Jason and Ana returned to the table with coffee cups. Mike and Paul were brawling about something. *Brawling.* Grace, Ana, and Jason had only been out of the room for a couple of minutes—what had happened?

Many f-words and c-words and other unsavory language was exchanged. Ana and Grace just stared wide-eyed at their shoes. At length, Ana was able to understand that the argument had something to do with an old car and an ex-girlfriend. Mike was accusing Paul of being a girlfriend-stealing rapist; Paul accused Mike of being a drug-addicted alcoholic larcenous thug.

When Camille came into the room, Ana expected her to get control of her brood. Instead, she started screaming too, yelling about how her sons were such an embarrassment to her, didn't she teach them anything, were they born in a barn? And so on.

The screaming probably only lasted five minutes, but it seemed like hours to Ana. "Um, maybe we should just go," she said quietly to Jason and Grace. "I'm pretty full. I don't need dessert."

Grace nodded enthusiastically.

"Did you see that, you're driving off our guests!" Camille bellowed. There were many insults hurled as Ana and Grace tried to thank them for a wonderful dinner and wish them a Merry Christmas. They could hear the yelling all the way out to the car.

Ana, Grace, and Jason drove home in a mute silence. Ana

dropped her mother off first. Jason jumped out of the backseat of the car to open the door for her. Grace gave him a big hug. "You are such a gentleman. Thank you for inviting us."

"My pleasure." Jason watched Grace until she got inside. He waved goodbye and got into the front seat. He put his seatbelt on and stared distractedly ahead.

"I'm sorry if any of tonight was uncomfortable for you," he said.

"No, it's no problem. Are you okay? Is your family always like that?"

"Always. It was worse during the divorce."

"How old were you when they got divorced?"

"They separated when I was six. The actual divorce took about three years."

"Ouch."

"To put it mildly."

Ana thought for a moment. "You know what, Jason? You're iceberg lettuce."

"Huh?"

"Don't you remember when you told me that I should never eat iceberg lettuce because they plant it around all the other vegetables to catch the run off, so it just absorbs all the pesticides and chemicals farmers use?"

"Yeah?"

"You're the iceberg lettuce of your family. You absorb all the bad stuff from your mom and brothers, take all their shit."

He shrugged. "Maybe." He thought about it. "But you're iceberg lettuce, too."

"I am not."

"You are too. You're the iceberg lettuce of our house, taking care of everyone, making sure everyone's okay."

"That's not iceberg lettuce. That's another kind of produce entirely. You stand up for the little guy. Why don't you stand up for yourself?"

He shrugged again. "I do. Just not with my family. Everything with them is an argument or a competition. I'd just rather not get into all that."

They drove in silence for several minutes. It hadn't snowed

since October, and the roads were clear. There were almost no cars on the road, and they made good time.

"So where did you get your bleeding heart? It certainly wasn't from those people."

"No, actually, I think it was. I remember Mike and Paul always just railed on me, and I was younger and smaller than them and I always thought, how easy is it to pick on the little guy? Why not *look out* for the little guy? *That* would take some effort. And in grade school, I remember learning about inner city schools, how they had school books that were thirty years out of date; Pluto hadn't been discovered yet, so their books taught them about only eight planets circling the sun, that sort of thing. I thought, I can look out for people who are less fortunate than I. I realized just how lucky I was. I've never gone hungry. I've always had a roof over my head. I went to a good school, free of gangs or violence. I wanted to give something back. I started volunteering at a soup kitchen . . . it was such an eye-opener. I don't know, trying to give back, no matter what I do, it never seems like enough, but . . ."

"Every little bit helps."

"Exactly. Every little bit helps. And the more you learn about the injustice of the world, the more you want to do about it. There is so much injustice in the world. So much injustice."

At home, Ana got ready for bed. Scott had only been gone for twenty-four hours, but already she missed him so much her chest filled with a dull ache.

45

New Year's

Jay had to be in Paris for Christmas. One of his cousins was holding a big bash at her estate in France, and family members from all over the world were flying in for it. Marin was disappointed she couldn't join him, but her filming schedule wouldn't allow it. She had to be on the set Christmas Eve and the day after Christmas, so there was no time to make a transcontinental flight. Part of her wished he'd stay home with her, but she knew that was selfish. Anyway, they'd only been dating six weeks, they weren't to the part of the relationship where you ditched family to be together. She was disappointed she still wouldn't be able to meet his family, but he promised he'd make it up to her by taking her to a romantic lodge in the mountains for New Year's.

On New Year's Eve, she and Jay spent the day skiing at Mt. Baldy, then had a quiet night at a lodge, complete with a bearskin rug and a roaring fire.

"I made sure to stock up on lots of strawberries and champagne," Jay said.

"Oh," Marin winced. "I don't actually like champagne. It's too bitter and it always gives me a headache."

"That's blasphemy. You must never have had good champagne before."

"No, I have."

"Come on, just one sip. For me."

"Okay, okay."

He popped the champagne and poured two glasses.

"Happy New Year," he said.

"Happy New Year." They clinked glasses and she took a sip. "Nope, yuck. I just don't like it."

"You need to have your head examined."

"I just don't like the bubbles. I don't like soda pop or sparkling water or any of that."

"You like beer."

"But beer isn't this carbonated. I just don't like bubbles exploding in my mouth. I never have."

"Well, more for me I guess. Shall I get you some red wine?"

"Yes, please."

He got her a glass of wine and led her to the living room, where he undressed her. They made love slowly on the bearskin rug. Cliché it might have been, but it was also damn nice. Marin could get used to living like this.

When they were both sated, Marin picked up her glass of wine, and sipped it slowly, savoring its rich plum taste. She loved the way the rug felt beneath her body; she loved how different the world felt without the barrier of clothing, the soft rug against her nipples, her hips, her thighs.

"So," she said, taking another sip of her wine, "we finish taping this week."

"I know."

Marin wasn't quite sure what to say next. "So what'll happen then?"

"What do you mean?"

"I mean between us."

"What do you want to happen?"

What did she want to happen? Part of her would love it if he proposed, but that was ridiculous. She'd never thought of herself as the marrying type. Why was it suddenly so easy to imagine? Anyway, they hadn't even known each other two months. Nobody but movie stars got engaged after just two months. But her life had been so unbelievable these last several weeks, anything seemed possible.

"My plan was to go back to Denver until we find out

whether the series gets picked up. If it does, I'll move back here. If not . . . I don't really know." *Ask me to move in with you.* She wasn't sure how she'd answer, she just wanted him to say it. But she couldn't abandon her friends, could she? She did miss them. But she probably did need to live in L.A. to work on her career. They'd understand that.

"I love Colorado," Jay said. "I'll fly in and see you whenever I can. We can hit all the ski resorts."

It was one of the best answers she could have hoped for, but she was disappointed anyway. She couldn't believe she wanted to ask him where this relationship was going. It was so unlike her. She did want to know, but she restrained herself.

"Hey, did you notice the time?" Jay asked.

It was one minute until midnight. They watched the final seconds of the year tick away, until the final ten seconds, in which, by tradition, they counted out loud.

"Ten! Nine! Eight! Seven! Six! Five! Four! Three! Two! One! Happy New Year!"

As they kissed, Marin felt a flicker of unease. What was wrong with her? Ana was the worrier of the group, not her. Where was all this confusion and self-doubt coming from? This wasn't like her at all. She was probably just a little apprehensive because the last year had been such an amazing year, this one had a lot to live up to.

One day in the first week of January, the director said, "It's a wrap," and he didn't mean just for the day. He meant that was it, taping was over, he'd gotten the footage he needed. There was a moment of silence as everyone looked around, trying to understand the full weight of his meaning. Then the cheers and hugs came, along with an invitation from the director to celebrate that night at his place.

Marin had planned to get together with Jay that night, so she called him on his cell and asked him if he wouldn't mind a change in plans. She told him about the party.

"I really don't want to spend the night with a bunch of fledgling actors," he said.

"Thanks a lot."

"You know what I mean. I just want to be with you."

"We always do whatever you want to do, whenever you want to do it. We never do what I want to do." She couldn't believe how whiny her tone was. What was wrong with her, where was this coming from? She wished she could swallow the words back. Anyway, they weren't true. Jay always made the plans for their dates because he knew L.A. and she didn't, that was all.

"Look, why don't you go? We'll get together another night. I'll come out to see you in Denver real soon."

"No, no. I want to see you. I can skip it."

Jay met her at her hotel room, and they made love. Marin couldn't get into it tonight though. She kept thinking about whether Jessica was sleeping with the entire crew and writing team, so that if *Roommates* did get picked up by the network, Jessica would have finagled a way to edge Marin out entirely.

Marin couldn't help but feel she was missing out. She'd spent two crazy months with these people; it would have been nice to celebrate with them.

She was being silly. She didn't even like most of the people she worked with and she loved Jay. Of course she should be with him.

Shouldn't she?

Two days later, the Spur gang and their significant others were waiting at the airport for Marin's plane to arrive. They all wore plastic sunglasses. Ramiro and Scott held a big sign that had been covered with so much glue and sprinkles it looked like the words were about to melt right off the poster. "Welcome home, movie star!" it read. The Spur of the Moment bunch had no time for subtlety.

As they waited, they people-watched. A number of teenage girls wearing clothes too tight, too short, or otherwise ill-suited to their bodies walked by, simultaneously puffed up with feelings of omnipotence and importance and beaten down by feelings of self-doubt and self-loathing. When one particularly unfortunate Fashion Don't passed by, Ramiro said under his breath, "So what happened, were all the mirrors in Denver confiscated? What was she *thinking?*" Which made everyone titter gleefully.

Several bitchy comments later, their fashion-patrol duties were halted by the arrival of Marin.

When everyone had been thoroughly hugged and screamed out, Marin introduced the man who been hovering behind her. "Everyone, this is Jay. Jay this is everyone."

Chelsey and Ana exchanged wide-eyed looks. "Hmm-mmm good," Chelsey said under her breath. Ana nodded in agreement.

"We've heard so much about you. All good, natch," Chelsey said, reaching out to shake his hand.

More introductions followed. Ana noticed that Jason was the only one who didn't say anything to Jay.

"Tell us everything!" Ana said, grabbing Marin's arm as they made their way through the airport to the parking lot.

"I've already told you everything."

"Tell us again."

"Should we go to aMuse?" Ramiro asked.

Jason: "We always go there."

Ramiro: "Everyone needs a place where everybody knows their name. This is ours."

Marin: "Okay by me."

So they went to aMuse and drank copious amounts of beer as Marin regaled them with tales of the parties she'd gone to, the people she'd worked with, and the adventures she'd had. They asked Jay lots of questions, too, about his travels and the people he knew and things he'd done.

As they talked and laughed and drank, Marin felt as happy as she'd ever been in her life. She had great friends, a great boyfriend, and a career that was going someplace. Just as she'd always known it would, her life was really coming together.

46

The Color Line

Every Saturday morning Ana scoured the house into shape. She put on workout clothes, pulled her hair back, and sprinted around the house like the Tasmanian Devil, carrying Windex in one hand and Softscrub in the other like a cowboy with a gun in each hand as she blazed through the house firing off bullets of cleanser.

Anyone who got in Ana's way would be knocked to the ground. Poor Scott had the misfortune of filling his glass of water in the kitchen sink at the exact moment Ana had decided to tear through the dishes, and he was nearly knocked unconscious when she hurled him aside into the wall.

Over in Chelsey's part of town, things were considerably more peaceful. She and Rob were lazing in bed.

"I'm starving. What should we have for breakfast?" Rob asked.

"I can make fruit salad."

"That'll make a nice appetizer, but you don't really think a couple pieces of fruit can fuel a growing boy?"

"I can make you an omelet."

"Now we're talking. Hey, what's this?" He picked up a copy of Sherman Alexie's *The Indian Killer*, which Chelsey had been reading and had left on her nightstand.

"It's a novel. Have you read it?"

"Not this one. I liked his book of short stories *The Lone*

Ranger and Tonto Fistfight in Heaven and his movie *Smoke Signals*. How do you like this book?"

"It's well written, but a little . . . disturbing. I mean Indians have so many reasons to be angry at white people . . . In the book there's this Indian, he was adopted and raised by white people, and he feels confused and angry and misplaced and so he lashes out by killing random white people . . . Do you ever feel like that? Like you just want to kill white people?"

Rob glared at her. Chelsey was taken aback.

Finally he said, "I can't believe you just fucking said that to me."

"Rob, I was just trying to see, you know, how as an Indian, you feel about white people and what . . . and what's happened."

"Oh yeah"—he jumped up and started pulling his clothes on—"all us dark, scary savages just want to kill the whities and rape their woman."

Chelsey gripped the blanket to cover her naked body. She didn't know what had just happened. "No, Rob, I didn't mean that."

"I've been called chief, Injun, and people have done that ridiculous woo-woo with the hand patted over the mouth my whole life, but I have never been so offended by anything as what you just said." With that, Rob grabbed his shoes, socks, and coat, and stormed out the door. Chelsey started crying, more out of shock than of sadness.

She called Ana. Scott answered. "Can I talk to Ana?"

"She's cleaning. I really don't think . . ." Then he heard her crying.

"Please?" she asked.

"Yeah, sure, hang on." Ana was scrubbing the kitchen floor with such ferocious intensity it was like she was trying to remove bloodstains or dried paint. Scott was careful to keep his distance as he didn't want to obtain any more bruises or head traumas. "Ana, Chelsey's on the phone. She's crying. She wants to talk to you."

"She's crying?" Ana dropped the sponge she was scouring the floor with. She washed her hands thoroughly, then sprinted up to her room. "I've got it!" she bellowed. "Chelse, what is it?"

"It's Rob. We had a fight."

"What happened?"

"Well, so I've been reading all these books about Indians because, well, I never really learned anything about them in school or maybe I did and I just forgot and anyway, I've been feeling really stupid when Rob talks about all these historical events that were hugely important to Indians but mean absolutely nothing to me, so I've been reading nonfiction and fiction and I'm reading this one book called *Indian Killer* and it's about this angry confused Indian who goes around killing whites for retribution for what we did to them and I asked Rob if ever thought about killing white people . . ." Chelsey gulped for air. She'd said all of that in a single sentence without taking a breath.

"You. Did. Not."

"You think that's bad?"

"Chelsey, you accused him of being a would-be murderer!"

"No I didn't! We all think about what it would be like to kill someone . . ."

"I have *never* thought about killing someone."

"You've never been so angry that you imagine having somebody killed or killing them yourself if you thought you could get away with it?"

"No! Christ no!"

"Oh, maybe I've read too many thrillers. But the point is, I was just trying to bring up the topic of race, you know, start a dialogue."

"Don't say the words 'start a dialogue.' You sound just like The Big Weasel when you say that."

"I'm an idiot. I'm such an idiot. He never brings up race as like, you know, this thing we have to discuss. It's just a fact of life for him like, oh, I'll go to the powwow in Denver next week. I'm the one who makes it this big deal about it. I'm always asking him about his traditions and his background. I mean, I think it's really interesting and different."

"Don't you talk about being Irish?"

"It's not the same thing. I wear a claddagh ring and drink too much and like St. Patrick's Day, but lots of people wear claddagh rings and drink too much and like St. Patrick's Day. Whoopdeedo, I'm so ethnic."

"You used to study Irish dancing."

Chelsey rolled her eyes. "Maybe if I ever go to Ireland I'll start to get all into my roots, but I don't know. Anyway, it's not just about traditions, it's about skin color and how there are only about eleven Indians left in the whole world and he's probably going to want to marry an Indian . . ." Chelsey didn't say anything for a long moment. "And I really love him and I'm scared I'm going to lose him because I'm white. I've never dealt with anything like this before."

"The first thing you should do is apologize your ass off. Then you should tell him your concerns and see what he says."

"What if he says I'm right, and things can never go any deeper than just having fun together?"

"Is that going to be better to hear now or three years down the road?"

"It's going to be better to hear never."

"Chelse, get it together, girl. You have to talk to the boy."

47

The Premiere

Ana hardly saw Marin at all when Jay was in town. Marin got back on the performance schedule at Spur, but otherwise she spent every minute with Jay. Even after performances, she and Jay would dash off someplace else (probably the luxury hotel he was staying at). Sometimes they stuck around the bar, but they only paid attention to each other, so Ana rarely got a chance to talk with Marin. As if Ana hadn't been jealous of enough things, now she was jealous of Jay and the attention Marin devoted to him. Even when he was out of town, all Marin could think or talk about was him. Ana wanted things to go back to the way they'd been, when she and Marin could dream about the future or talk about nothing at all—whether the new lipstick they'd bought was too orange or whether they'd liked the outfits sported by Jennifer or Courtney on that week's episode of *Friends*. Even though Ana spent much of her time with Scott, she missed hanging out with Marin. She felt abandoned.

Marin flitted in and out of their house every now and then to get more clothes or do some laundry. Ana was happy Marin was in love—she'd certainly been alone long enough—but Ana wished that Marin could find more time to spend with her friends.

Even though she was annoyed with Marin, she still planned

a Happy Premiere/Happy Birthday party for her. Marin's show *Roommates* aired its first episode in late January, a few days before her twenty-fifth birthday.

On the night of the premiere, the living room had so many people sitting so tightly together on floor (the couch, recliner, and loveseat had long been claimed) that, sitting cross-legged, their knees overlapped. If somebody wanted to stand up to get another beer, she had to tiptoe across the floor, doing her best not to walk on people and trip over the tangle of limbs. Anyone brave enough to venture out of the thick pack of people was immediately deluged with calls to bring more beer! Bring more chips! Me too! More beer!

Marin got a seat on the couch, obviously, being the guest of honor and all. She was squashed happily next to Jay. She was thrilled he could be here for this, but also a little terrified that he wouldn't like it.

"Shh shh shh!" Ana screamed when the show started. She blared the volume on the TV to get the attention of the last whisperers, then quieted it some so it was still commanding and painfully loud, but wasn't quite so much like she was playing for an entire stadium of people who were miles away.

The theme music started and clapping and laughter and cheers drowned out the noise.

The show opened with five of the roommates sprawled lazily across two couches and a love seat. The sixth roommate, played by Jessica, gets home from work and asks Marin/Garrett how her interview went.

"Terrible. She asked me what I wanted to be doing in five years and I just choked. I knew what she wanted me to say. She wanted me to say that I wanted to be working my way up Burkhardt Consulting, contributing my hard work, and blah blah blah whatever, but all I could think was, oh my god, please don't let me be working at Burkhardt Consulting for the next five years."

"Garrett, you're an actress. Surely you can *act* like you want an office job."

"Anyway, I'm doing stand-up at the Scatterbrain Theater

tonight and I've got an audition for a commercial tomorrow. Something's going to turn up. I *can't* work at an office. I just can't do it."

"It's not that bad," Jessica's character says.

Ana watched the show with a curious detachment. It wasn't bad—it wasn't great, but it wasn't bad—but she'd heard too much about taping the show, about Jessica fucking a horse and the arguments the producers had had with directors and the squabbles between the actors and the writers and amongst the actors themselves to be able to suspend her disbelief and lose herself in the story line. Also, it was so weird to see Marin wearing outfits she'd never wear and saying things she would never say.

During the commercials, fist fights practically broke out as people battled their way into the bathroom. All was chaos as all twenty people began talking at once about oh how exciting this was and god, Marin, you look so great up there, I love your character!

After the show was over, there was a long, loud applause and many more congratulations along the lines of "you're so great!" "I love it!" Things got considerably more comfortable once the show was over because people could spread out all over the house instead of just hanging in their tiny living room. Marin and Jay sat cozily on the couch together, giggling like the annoying newly in-loves they were.

The only two people who weren't bursting with excitement and happiness were Chelsey and Jason. Chelsey was depressed because Rob hadn't spoken to her in four days. She'd left thousands of messages, but he wouldn't return her calls.

Jason sat in the green recliner, looking like his best friend in the world had died. He didn't join in the conversation or joke around like he normally would.

Ana knew his bad mood was because of Jay. But maybe it was a good thing. Maybe now that Marin finally had someone serious in her life, Jason would move on to someone who loved him as much as he loved her.

48

Make-Up Sex

Chelsey had called Rob frantically over the last few days. Each time she left long, apologetic messages. She'd done her best to restrain herself to two or three calls a day. Today she was on message number three.

"Rob, I know you don't want to talk to me, but I think we need to talk about this." Nuts, that doesn't make any sense. "It's just, you're really—"

"Hello?"

"Rob? It's me."

He laughed. "I know."

"I just, I wanted to apologize." He didn't say anything. "I'm really, really sorry—"

"I know. I was mad. I needed some time to cool off. I'm sorry too. I don't know why that hit me the way it did. Some things just strike a nerve, you know?"

"Can I come over?"

"Yeah."

She did. She brought ice cream—she didn't see him as the kind of guy who'd be into flowers.

"Peace offering," she said, handing him the ice cream when he opened the door. "I'm sorry."

"I know. Apology accepted. You're trying to understand a world that's completely different from the one you know. I know you're trying."

Kiss me, she thought nervously. Let everything go back to the way it was. She felt stupid and awkward, unsure of what to say next. "Ah, so, I'll get some bowls."

"We don't need no stinkin' bowls."

Chelsey gave him a curious look. He started walked toward the bedroom. He made the gesture with his index finger that indicated she should follow.

They ate the ice cream off one another then showered together afterward to get rid of the ice cream residue. They changed the sheets and lay on the cool fresh linens together.

Chelsey thought about what Ana had said. God, how she didn't want to have this conversation. "Do you have any wine or beer or something?" she asked.

"I've got some beer. You want one?"

She nodded.

He retrieved it and got back into bed beside her. She drank half of it down in a single gulp. Rob looked at her wide-eyed. "Is something wrong?"

"Yeah. I'll tell you in a minute."

"Oh my god, are you pregnant?"

"If I were pregnant, would I be drinking?"

"Good point."

"What if I were pregnant? How would you react?"

"Well, I guess I'd want to find out how you felt about it. If you were excited, I'd be excited. If you didn't want it, I'd support you."

"You'd be excited if I wanted it?"

"I've always wanted kids."

"With me?"

"I know we're a little young and it would probably be better if we waited . . ."

"I guess what I'm asking, Rob, is . . . is"—she finished the rest of her beer—"I'm wondering if you can see things between us as long term. Serious."

"Definitely. Why wouldn't I?"

Relief flooded Chelsey. "Because I make stupid, insensitive racial remarks maybe."

"You're learning. You're trying. You mess up sometimes, but I think your heart is in the right place."

"Yeah?"

He hugged her. "When it's right next to me, it's in the right place."

49

More Surprises

Ana was at the office, working late as usual. She called home to check the messages before she left for the theater. "You. Have. One. New. Message. Message. Sent. At. 1:42 P.M., 'Hi, my name is Alicia Hestler from the Luna Agency and I'm looking for Ramiro Martinez.' " Alicia Hestler, Alicia Hestler, why did that name sound so familiar? "I've tried getting a hold of you through email, but I haven't had any luck so I thought I'd give you a call. Ramiro, I loved *Staring at the Sun* and I very much want to represent you. I have some editors in mind who I really think will love it. Give me a call at. . . ."

Ana sprung out of her chair and screamed. "Oh my God oh my God oh my God!" Ramiro didn't have a cell phone and he was probably on his way to the theater now. Maybe she could call Marin and have her tell . . . No, it would be better to tell him in person.

Ana grabbed her purse, turned her computer off without shutting down properly, dashed to the hall where she waited impatiently for the elevator to arrive, then sprinted out to her car. She drove to the theater with reckless abandon, nearly hyperventilating with excitement.

Ramiro wasn't at the theater yet when she got there. She was about to explode with excitement. Damn him for being late!

She quickly changed and when she exited the dressing room, she saw him talking to Nick.

"Ramiro, I need to talk to you. It's very important." She pulled him away from Nick when Ramiro was in the middle of a sentence. She didn't care. At this moment, she was not a woman to be trifled with. "You have to hear something." She dialed their home voicemail on her cell phone and gave him the phone.

"I don't understand," he said, after he'd clicked the phone off.

"A couple of months ago, I sent out queries to agents to see if they wanted to read *Staring into the Sun*. Three did. So I mailed it out. Alicia was the first person who got back to me. You. Us. She read it and wants to represent you." He didn't say anything as he tried to absorb this. "Don't you get it? Somebody in the industry thinks your book is good enough to sell. She's going to spend time trying to sell your book because she thinks she can make money off your talent. She thinks you can really write."

"Huh."

"Can I tell everybody else?"

"But what if she can't sell it . . ."

"That's not even the important thing. The important thing is that you're a real writer with an agent. An agent for god's sake!"

"I guess . . . Just these guys. Nobody else."

"Everyone! May I have your attention please! Our good friend Ramiro Martinez has written a beautiful novel, and today a literary agent called and said she'd like to represent him."

"A novel?"

"You wrote a novel?"

"I read it a couple months ago and it blew my mind," Ana continued. "Ramiro didn't think it was good enough, of course, so I took it upon myself to market it, and an agent wants to represent him. A literary agent. A real one. In New York!"

There were the inevitable shouts and hugs and handshakes.

They didn't spend a single moment of the forty-five minutes before the show they were supposed to spend warming up, warming up. There were many questions—like how many millions would he make—but few answers. Ana had only read about getting an agent; she didn't know anything else about the publishing business.

Chelsey: "How long will it take before the agent sells it?"

Ana: "I don't know."

Jason: "When will it be in bookstores?"

Ana: "I don't know."

Scott: "Will you go on a book tour?"

Ramiro: "I don't know."

When the theater opened, Jason left to join Nick in the audience, and the other five ran backstage.

As they waited for the theater to fill in, all of Ana's excitement for Ramiro disappeared. Out of nowhere she started to feel a cold dull ache in her chest. She knew this feeling of anxiety well, she just didn't know why it was hitting her now.

Ana didn't understand how her feelings could surge and plunge in seconds flat. Was everyone as moody and emotional as she was, or had all her training as an actor to be in constant touch with her emotions made her insanely unbalanced?

Shake it off, shake it off, she told herself. *Why am I feeling like this? Maybe because Ramiro is on his way to being published? Marin is on TV series? And where am I? Left behind.*

Ana felt suddenly adrift. Since she and Scott had gotten together, she hadn't focused much on how she was going to accomplish her dreams. For her New Year's resolutions, she'd vowed to lose weight, work out more, and get more sleep. She hadn't put a single thing on there about her career. Maybe she'd been so career-driven before she and Scott got together because she'd had nothing else to spend her free time doing. Or maybe since the show, she knew she could work her ass off and still get nowhere.

It wasn't too late to amend her resolutions. She would write more comedy, practice stand-up, maybe even take some voice and acting lessons . . .

It was her cue to run on stage and be introduced along with

the other performers. For the next several scenes, she was able to stop thinking about her career and her future, but the uneasy feeling didn't subside.

Toward the end of the show, Ana was beginning to feel physically and mentally tired from all that was expected on stage. Then when Scott, the emcee for the night, called out that he needed two actors, it was her and Marin's turn to get onstage. Scott turned to the audience. "What is the relationship between these two women?"

"Sisters!" was the first thing he heard.

"Ana and Marin, you're sisters. Actors begin!" He ran offstage.

"You're just jealous," was the first thing Marin said. It took Ana aback. If that was the first thing Marin had thought, Ana must not be doing a good job masking her real-life jealousy. Ana felt suddenly vulnerable.

"I am not. It's just not fair. You never work for anything and everything gets handed to you on a silver platter."

"Oh, boo-hoo, so life's not fair, big deal, news at eleven. Anyway, it *is* fair."

"No it's not. John was going to ask me to the prom, and then you stole him away from me."

"Whatever. John asked me because I'm gorgeous and you're a fat ass."

Ana inhaled sharply. She felt like Marin had reached out and slapped her. Ana hated her body enough on her own, she didn't need Marin to give her a hard time about it, too, even if this was a made up scene. Ana hated the fact that her weight gain was something so public; she wished she could hide it and deal with it on her own. She certainly didn't want it discussed on stage. "You're a boyfriend-stealing thief and you know it. Everything always goes your way."

"Look, it's not my fault if Mrs. Parsons made me the lead in the play and not you. It's not my fault I'm bursting with natural talent."

"You were not the most talented. You were the only one who auditioned who looked the part."

"I can't help it if I'm naturally more talented, beautiful, and charming than you."

And it was true: Marin was just naturally more talented, beautiful, and charming than Ana was, and always would be. There were some things that could be improved and worked on, but there was innate talent and then there was the endless legion of talentless wannabes, and some people could never crawl out of that category. Which group did Ana belong to? Who was she if she didn't have any talent? She wasn't a teacher trying to save the world or a talented painter or a gifted writer. She wasn't thin and beautiful. She wasn't a wife or mother. She wasn't good at her job, as The Weasel liked to remind her a thousand times a day. She was just a stressed out, neurotic wreck who always said the wrong thing at the wrong time, who hung around talented creative people so she could pretend she was one of them herself.

Ana had all these grandiose dreams of fame and success. Of entertaining masses of people. Of being beautiful and wealthy and loved by all. But that's all they'd ever be. Dreams. Fantasies of a different life to make the life she actually led bearable.

That's what it all came down to. The world was divided into those who dream and those who do, who take their dreams and make them real.

I can't help it if I'm naturally more talented, beautiful, and charming than you. For six years, Ana had lived in the shadows of a woman who was simply more talented, more beautiful, more charming than she. A woman who both men and women noticed right away, gaped at, stunned by her beauty. Ana was lost in the shadows of Marin's charm and good looks, upstaged by Marin's superior comedy and acting skills. And the world was full of Marins. Who was Ana kidding, pretending she could be somebody?

"That's what you really think of me, isn't it," Ana said quietly.

"Absolutely!"

Ana burst into tears.

Ramiro jumped on stage, holding a clipboard. "All right, your auditions for *People Who Are Richer and Prettier Than You* was excellent, but the director wants to see more action. A fight maybe. Okay, let's take it from scene two."

Ana quickly wiped away her tears. "You are such a hussy."

"What did you call me?"

"Face it, you're a hussy slut!"

"You bitch!" Marin pounced on Ana. They fell to the ground and starting rolling around with each other. Now that it had been declared just an audition, both Ana and Marin were able to do a better job of pushing aside their real lives and pretending they were auditioning for a part. The audience roared at the physical comedy.

"You're so fat," Marin said, "they've created a T-shirt just for you that says, 'Body by Pizza Hut.' "

"Uh!" Ana yelled. She untangled herself from Marin's grasp and ran off stage. Moments later, she came back with something behind her back, a contrite expression on her face. She said in a soft voice, "All this fighting is stupid. We're sisters. We should love each other."

Marin looked angrily away. Then she seemed to consider what Ana's "character" had said, and Marin's body language softened, until she shrugged, conceding defeat. "Yeah, I guess you're right."

"Come here, give me a hug."

When Marin got a little closer, Ana pulled the gallon of water they kept offstage to drink between scenes from behind her back and poured it over Marin's head. Marin jumped back and gasped.

Ramiro yelled cut. "Good work ladies. You're both hired!"

With that, Ana and Marin ran off stage.

"What the fuck was that?" Marin hissed. "You know I've got a date with Jay tonight. Fuck. My hair is ruined!"

"I'm sorry, it's just what came into my head. The audience seemed to like it . . ."

"Fuck the audience. What is going on with you?"

"Nothing. I'm sorry. It was just a scene."

"Bullshit. You meant everything you said out there."

"Yeah, well so did you. It's totally uncool of you to bring up my weight in front of everybody. I'm *trying* to lose weight. You don't understand what it's like. You can eat whatever you want. You have no idea how hard it is for me to maintain even this Body by Pizza Hut kind of body."

"You know I didn't mean that."

"If you didn't mean it, why did you say it?"

"I don't know, because I'm an actress, *pretending*. Gosh, is somebody maybe a little bit sensitive about her weight?"

"Try very sensitive. I know I've gained weight. You shouldn't judge me on something you don't know anything about. Your body is just like everything else in your life, perfect, without you ever having to do any work for it," Ana hissed.

"You think I didn't work for that TV series? I've been acting and performing for the last ten years. I've worked my butt off to become a good actress."

"It's not just the series, Marin. It's everything. You don't have to worry about car payments or paying back forty thousand dollars in student loans. You don't have to work a mind-numbing day job because you don't have to worry about money. You get to go spend your summers in Europe because Daddy will pay for you to go. And you're gorgeous, but did you have to do anything to get those looks? Everything has just been handed to you on a silver platter. You have a perfect life."

"Oh, I have a perfect life, huh? Which is why my parents have *never* seen us perform and have come to visit me out here only once in the six years I've lived here. Of course Dad will pay for me to go to Europe; he'll do anything to keep me out of his hair. The Explorer, that was his way of pretending to be a good Dad instead of coming out here to visit me. Ana, you don't know how good you've got it. You're talented—a lot more talented than you know, obviously. You've got a mother who thinks you're the sun and the moon and the sky; she literally bursts with pride every time she talks about you. You're beautiful, you've got a boyfriend who loves you more than anything, you're twenty-four and you're already a manager. You've got more talent in a single fingernail than most people do in their entire bodies. I can't help it that the casting director was looking for a slim blond. It was a great experience. I'm very, very lucky, I know. This business is brutal. Directors and agents are always deciding that your looks are out of style or they think your ear isn't the right shape for the part. Whatever. You've got to build up a thicker skin if you're going to make it in this business."

"I know. I know." Ana blinked, which set her tear rolling down her cheeks again. "That's what I'm afraid of. I'm not tough enough, I'm not good enough. I'm just kidding myself, thinking I have talent."

"Don't be ridiculous. Of course you have talent. I remember sitting at the audition for Iron Pyrits freshman year, looking at you, thinking, 'They're only going to take one woman, and it's going to be her.'"

"That's what I thought about you!"

"And then when you got up there and told us those hilarious stories and were doing all these amazing ballet moves, you blew me away. Then when we both made it and I found out you'd never done any acting or comedy or anything, I couldn't believe it. And don't forget, Ana, you were only one of two chosen out of thirteen who auditioned to make the main stage of Spur of the Moment where you get *paid* as an *actor*. Do you think Steve would have chosen you if you didn't have any talent?"

Ana shrugged. "Maybe I have *some* talent. Just not enough."

"What you don't have is the courage to really go for it."

"What! How can you say that? I was the one who thought of putting together the sketch show and got everything together for it."

"Yeah, but where's your agent? When are you auditioning for parts in commercials and trying out for plays?"

"That's really rich, Marin, considering that you've never done any of that stuff. You just got picked out of Denver and plunked into TV just like that."

"I was lucky, I know, but now that I know more about this business, how hard it is, I'm really going to work harder at it. You know what I think? I think you're just afraid of succeeding," Marin said.

"That's ridiculous. No one's afraid of succeeding."

"You are. You're afraid that if you try really hard, you'll find out maybe you can make it or maybe you can't, but as long as you're here in Denver, putting on a few shows here and there without really having to go out there and audition, you'll never find out for sure whether you have what it takes."

Ana reeled at the accusation. She had been working her ass off, trying to make it. Hadn't she?

"Think about your feminist cheerleaders," Marin continued. "You could learn from them. You cheer everyone else on and support everyone else. You believed in Ramiro so much you cheered about him to all the literary agents in New York until you found him one. You said so many great things about Spur you packed the house and landed me an agent. Why don't you try cheering yourself on instead of always tearing yourself down and thinking you're never going to achieve your goals? Why don't you do all the things you'd tell a friend who wanted to make it as a performer to do? You've always said you wanted to try stand-up. Why don't you do it?"

"Because I'd humiliate myself."

"Even if you don't believe you have talent, pretend you do. You know what they say, 'Fake it till you make it.'"

Ana scrunched up her face in confusion. "Who says that?"

Marin shrugged. She was as perplexed as Ana. "You know, '*they.*' Maybe people in AA or motivational speakers. There are lots of addicts and motivational speakers in L.A. I'm pretty sure there's a correlation. Anyway, the point is, you just do what actors do. You pretend to be the person you want to be until you actually become that person."

Scott appeared backstage. "Psst, hey, we need you on stage. The performance is the thing, ladies. Enough with the girly heart-to-heart stuff."

When he ran back on stage to introduce the next scene, Ana wiped away her snot and tears. She sniffled. "I'm so terrified of being ordinary."

"You're not ordinary, Ana. You're extraordinary."

"No, you are."

"No, you are."

"No, you are."

"Okay, okay. We're both amazing women. That's why we love each other so much."

Ana nodded.

Marin pulled her close, hugging her tightly. "Let's get out there," Marin said.

Later that night Scott was sleeping soundly beside Ana. She couldn't sleep. She just stared at the ceiling. She headed downstairs to make herself warm milk spiked heavily with whiskey. Not on her diet, no, but diets never took into account insomnia, did they?

Jason was sitting at the kitchen table, drinking Maker's Mark. It was extremely unusual for him to be drinking hard liquor, even rarer for him to be drinking by himself.

"Can't sleep either, huh?" Ana said. "Can I have some of that?"

He pushed the bottle over to her. She got a tumbler and filled it with ice. She sat across from him.

"You look pretty glum," she said.

He nodded. "Yeah. I am."

"Why?"

"Because I'm a failure."

"Really? How do you figure?"

"What am I doing with my life, Ana? What am I contributing? I read this article today about poverty in Africa. There's this organization that's over there helping to teach Africans how to farm and install wells, that sort of thing. The writer interviewed this African farmer, who proudly showed the reporter his farm. He won't get rich quick, but he won't go hungry and he'll be able to afford to send his kids to school, so maybe they'll have an easier life. I should be over there, helping. Join the Peace Corps or . . . I don't know what."

"You don't think teaching generations of children about how life works is worthwhile? You have, what, at least a hundred kids a year that you teach, right? Times a career of forty or so years. That's four thousand kids whose lives you've touched. And every night when you get on stage and make people laugh, you don't think that's something? Teaching people about toxic waste and government excess in an entertaining way? You don't think that's a contribution?"

He shrugged.

"Think about Michael Moore. We loved *Bowling for Columbine*, right? Maybe the documentary didn't immediately change the world, but it brought to light some serious issues and made people think about violence in America in a new way. He's just doing what he loves, making movies, but educating and entertaining as he goes. You don't need to join the Peace Corps to make a difference. You can't carry the weight of all of the world's problems on your shoulders. There is only so much one person can do."

"That's not the only thing."

"What?"

"There's Marin. Her being with Jay. It's killing me. She seems so . . . serious about him. She's been with other guys before, but she was never serious. I could keep believing she would eventually figure out we should be together. I'm realizing now we're never going to be together. Even if things don't work out with Jay. We're just not right for each other. I'm not her type, and I never will be." He took a long sip of his drink and poured himself another. "And I'm embarrassed that I'm depressed over a stupid crush. There are so many things wrong with this world, and I've been feeling sorry for myself over a crush, wallowing in depression for the past three weeks."

At "crush," Jason's voice cracked, as if the weight of his feelings for Marin were truly crushing him. It broke Ana's heart.

Ana moved her chair so it was right next to his and hugged him. Then she pulled away so she could face him. "I can't believe you think loving someone is no big deal. Why do you think war and poverty and injustice are so painful? Because people we love die or are injured and their pain is our pain and their loss is our loss. Love is no trifling matter. It's no small thing. It's everything."

Jason looked into her eyes, leaned in, and kissed her.

"What the hell are you doing!" Ana jerked away.

"Sorry, it just came over me."

Ana didn't know how to process this. She kept shaking her head, as if she were having a conversation in her head, "What was he thinking?" "I have no idea." "What was he thinking?" "I have no idea."

"Maybe it makes sense, you and I being together," Jason said. "We've always been the responsible, grown up members of the group."

"Jason, you know I'm with Scott now. I can't believe you just did that."

He stared at her.

"Look, I know you're depressed about Marin, but you can't expect me to be your distraction while you try to get over her," she said.

"That's not it at all. Ana, you've liked me for six years. Everyone knows it."

"Of course I like you, Jason. I love you. I love everyone in this house. And yes, I had a crush on you for six years, but I'm really happy with Scott. I'm really happy. I haven't felt like this with anybody since . . . I don't know that I've ever felt like this with anybody."

"Don't you think you owe it to yourself to give us a try?" He started getting all excited, the way he did when he'd come up with an idea he felt certain would solve all the world's problems, or at least some of them. "Just one date. What could it hurt?"

"God, I don't know, Scott's feelings? My relationship with him?"

"You said I needed to stand up for myself. Take what I want. I want you."

"Jason, you've been drinking. You probably won't even remember this conversation in the morning. You should really go to bed now."

Ana scurried up the stairs back to her bedroom and slid next to Scott. Should she tell him about the kiss? But actors have to kiss each other all the time. What was a kiss among actors, and a drunken one at that?

Scott would be furious with Jason. There was no reason to start a conflict between them.

She wouldn't say anything.

So why did she feel like she was lying?

All day at work, Ana thought about what Jason had said. Of course she was still attracted to him, but she'd come to realize that things between her and Jason could never work out. They were just too different. Anyway, she knew he really hadn't fallen out of love with Marin. He hated dating as much as the rest of them did, and so he went for one of his closest friends—ignoring the fact she was dating his best friend. Still, Ana thought about what he said about giving him one date. She had pined for him for six years. No, no, what was she thinking? She loved Scott.

She couldn't shut off the internal dialogue, the questions about her feelings about Scott and Jason over the years. Could she have been just as happy with Jason as with Scott? Could emotions really be switched on and off so quickly? She'd idealized Jason and imagined a perfect love to have something to dream about, something to distract her from her humdrum reality. Whatever she'd once felt for Jason no longer mattered. She loved Scott. There were no doubts in her mind.

When she got home from work, Jason was at his usual post grading papers at the kitchen table. "Hey," she said. "Where is everybody?" She dropped her bags and slipped her coat off. She went to the fridge to get a glass of Crystal Light peach tea.

"Ramiro's out with Nick, Marin's with Jay, and Scott's in his room."

Ana drank her tea, put the glass in the dishwasher, and gasped when she turned around—Jason was standing right there, she'd nearly run into him.

"Did you think about what I said last night?" he said quietly. He stood so close to her she could feel his warm breath on her cheek. She looked at his full lips. What would it be like to kiss them?

What was wrong with her? She had a boyfriend whom she loved.

"Of course not. It's ridiculous."

"I have. I can't stop thinking about it. I can't believe I didn't think of it before."

"Earth to Jason. Remember Scott? He's your best friend. What are you thinking?"

"He'll understand. You and I, we're meant to be together. I just couldn't see it."

"Jason, until the day before yesterday, you were certain you and Marin were destined to be together. Don't you think it's a little weird that suddenly you think you and I are supposed to be together? Maybe you're going crazy from loneliness or horniness or something. Get it together, man!"

"Just one date. You owe it to yourself to give me one date. Six years you've wanted to be with me. Don't you deserve to see if we're really supposed to be together?"

"I'm going upstairs now. To my *boyfriend*, Scott."

Ana marched upstairs to Scott's room where he was working on an abstract painting.

Ana gave him a kiss. "What's it a picture of?"

"See this, that's a comedian. This is the audience. I call it *Hecklers.*"

"Oh yeah, I can see that. Very cool." Ana stripped out of her work clothes and slipped into her sweats.

She collapsed on the bed and chewed her lip thoughtfully. *Just one date. You owe it to yourself to give me one date. Six years you've wanted to be with me. Don't you deserve to see if we're really supposed to be together?* Did she owe it to herself? What was one date after all?

Should she tell Scott about Jason?

Instead she asked, "If you didn't have to worry about money, what would you do? Be an artist? An actor?"

"Yes. Both."

"What's your dream with your art?"

"What do you mean?"

"I mean do you want your own gallery in New York? To have a show at the Guggenheim? To sell your work for millions?"

"I don't have any goals with my art. I just like to do it. It's how I relax."

"But don't you want people to know your work, know you? Don't you want people to see your stuff?"

"I'm not like you, Ana. I don't need to be rich and famous to feel like I'm a worthwhile person."

That took Ana aback. "Is that what you think of me? That I think only the rich and famous are worthwhile human beings?"

"No, I didn't mean it like that. I meant it for you. You act like if you can't make it big, you're not special. Like your life doesn't have any meaning. I don't think like that. I think if you're a good friend to people, if you're kind and honest and loving, you've led a worthwhile life. You don't have to be a famous artist or a rich comedian. You just need to do your best to be a good person."

Ana started to protest, but then realized he was right.

"Yeah, okay, I see your point. I guess I'll buy that. But I think you should give me some more of your paintings just in case you do become rich someday, I can sell them for truckloads of cash."

"Do you want this painting?"

"Really?"

"Really."

"Awesome. Yes. Ooh, I know just where I'll put it in my room. You'll sign it, right?"

"For you, Ana my love, anything."

For several days, Jason sent Ana a barrage of emails extolling her virtues. She found a note from him in her purse that said:

Ana and Jason. It was meant to be. You mean all the world to me.

-J

Rhyming love poetry. Sharpen the razor blades, it was wrist-slitting time.

When she'd discovered the note, her heart shuddered. She felt like she had when she'd tried shoplifting in fifth grade. She hadn't even wanted the stupid trinket she'd stolen, she'd just wanted to steal something. As she'd raced home on her bike, she was certain the police were in hot pursuit, ready to toss her into jail until she was a brittle old woman. She decided after that that the thrill of seeing what she could get away with wasn't worth the terror of getting caught. And that's how she felt now: Guilty. Worried she would get caught. She was going to have to tell Scott, but she knew it could royally mess up his relationship with Jason. She dreaded having to tell him. But what if he'd found this note? He would be so hurt. He wouldn't know that Jason was suffering temporary insanity; he'd think she was cheating on him.

A few nights later, Jason was making dinner for everyone—vegetable soup, salad, and homemade bread.

"Hey you," Ana said to Jason.

"Hey. Dinner's almost ready."

"Cool."

Ana went to the living room, where Scott was playing golf on the X-Box. Ana plopped down next to him.

"Hey babe," she said.

"Hey." He kept right on playing, staring at the TV screen and ignoring her completely.

"Glad you're so excited to see me."

"I'm thrilled."

Jason came into the room.

"Dinner ready?" Scott asked.

"Almost. Look, Scott, I need to talk to you."

"Right now?"

"It's important."

"More important than golf?"

"More important than golf."

Scott paused his game. " 'S-up?"

"Scott, the other night I kissed Ana."

"Jason!" Ana shrieked.

"Why didn't you tell me this?" Scott asked her.

"Jason was drunk. He was upset after seeing Marin with Jay. He didn't mean it."

"I did mean it. Scott, I know you love her, but I've finally realized that Ana and I are meant to be together. Ana's loved me for six years, and I . . ."

"I can't believe you kissed him. I can't believe you didn't tell me."

"I didn't kiss him. He kissed *me.*"

"Scott, I don't want to hurt you, but I think Ana and I need to give it a shot. Just one date."

Ana: "Jason, do I get a vote in any of this? Were you there when I said I didn't want to go out with you? I love Scott."

Scott: "Do you want to go out with him?"

Ana: "Ah! No, I just said that. No, I don't want to go out with him."

Scott: "So you and Jason have been talking about going out together? How long has this been going on?'"

Ana: "He kissed me on Sunday night. He keeps pestering me to go out with him but I don't want to . . ."

Scott: "Why didn't you tell me any of this? How could you keep this from me?"

Ana: "I kept hoping Jason would snap out it. He's depressed about Marin and he's gone off the deep end."

Scott: "Have you thought about it?"

Ana: "Thought about what?"

"Going out with him."

"No, no, of course not."

"You never even considered it? Wondered what it would be like? I mean recently. Since you and I have been going out?"

"No, maybe. I'm not sure. I'm all confused."

"Confused about your feelings for me?"

"No. I love you . . ."

"Ana, please. One date. I'll take you out right now. If it doesn't work out, at least we'll know."

"You should go," Scott said.

"What?! Are you insane? Scott, I don't . . ."

"Go. Just go."

"Nice. You're not even going to fight for me? Shouldn't you two be dueling it out? Instead you just give up on me like that?"

"I know you've had a crush on him forever. I can't compete with Jason."

"Scott, you don't have to compete. There is no competition. I love you. I can't believe I'm having this conversation."

"Ana, if you don't see where this goes, you'll always hold it against me."

"No I won't. I can't believe my boyfriend is encouraging me to go out with another man."

Scott jumped up. He darted upstairs. Ana followed after him.

He sat at his easel and began painting furiously, attacking the canvas with his brush.

"Ana, I want to be alone. Please go away."

"Why are you mad at me? I didn't do anything wrong."

"You kissed him and you don't think you did anything wrong?"

"For the tenth time, Scott, I didn't kiss him; he kissed me. It was one drunken kiss. Get a grip."

"So you don't think it's a big deal? Anytime I get drunk I can go kiss whoever I want?"

"Look, Jason is the person you should be mad at, not me. Do you really think so little of our relationship that one look from another guy and I'm going to leave you?"

Scott shrugged. "Maybe not."

"I'm going to go out with Jason right now, but NOT on a date. He and I need to talk. He's trying to talk himself into liking me so he can get over Marin."

"Have fun on your date."

"You know what Scott, fuck you." Ana ran downstairs to Jason. "Okay, I'm ready for our date. Romance away. Try to steal my heart. Have at it."

Jason clapped his hands together. "Okay, this won't be as good as if I had time to prepare, but spontaneous, that's romantic right? I have to take the soup off the burner and get the bread out of the oven. Just give me a minute."

Ana couldn't think straight. What was she doing? What had just happened? In five minutes, it felt like her whole life had fallen to pieces. *Get your head straight: You're going to talk with Jason, figure out what's made him go loony, help him realize he doesn't really love you. Or maybe you'll fall in love with him, break Scott's heart, and we'll all hate each other and have to move out of the house and I'll lose all my friends and the world will be over. Something like that.*

Jason took her to the Beehive, a small, elegant, dimly lit restaurant a few blocks away. He ordered a bottle of wine. Then he looked at Ana expectantly.

"This is a little awkward, isn't it?" he said.

"Just a little."

"What should we talk about?"

"How you're a total jerk for hurting Scott's feelings and not listening to me, maybe? What's going on with you, Jason? Normally you're Mister Save the World, and this week you don't care who or what you hurt."

"You told me . . ." The waiter came back with their wine and poured them each a glass. "You told me that I should go for what I want."

"Well you want me, great. Why?"

"Why what?"

"Why do you want me?"

"You're attractive, you're focused, you're talented. What's not to like?"

"Why did you like Marin?"

He looked serious. "She's beautiful and fun . . ."

"She's really beautiful. Crazy beautiful."

He nodded. "Crazy beautiful."

"But you know what? Neither Marin nor I are particularly into saving the world. We wouldn't even recycle if you didn't take it to the recycling center for us. Do you really want to be with someone who doesn't care about things like recycling pop cans and paper?"

"Recycling isn't everything."

"Of course it's not everything. I'm trying to illustrate a point. You should find a woman who shares your interests."

"Why are you so sure that you and I have no future together?"

"Jason, the thing about a crush is that it's not a relationship. You can make up whatever you want about what a relationship with someone would be like, but fictional relationships are a hell of a lot easier than real ones. When Scott and I got together, I realized how different you and I really are. Yes, we're the responsible ones in the house, but I'm ambitious about my career; you're ambitious about your belief you can actually make the world a better place. Frankly Jason, sometimes I find your optimism exhausting. And if I find your optimism tiring, can you imagine Marin?"

"Marin's not really the Peace Corps type, that's true, but . . ." He stopped, not knowing how to finish his sentence.

"It's just been hard on you, having this reality check that you and Marin aren't right for each other. It hurts, I know it does."

He took a sip of his wine. He set the glass down. He ran his fingers across his stubbled chin. He nodded. "It does hurt. I really used to be able to see the two of us together. I just had this picture of my life."

"Marin would have certainly helped make that a pretty picture."

"Are you saying I'm shallow?"

"We all like beautiful things, Jase. I'm just saying you were thinking about this fantasy picture, not how things would be in real life. You have to find somebody who values the same things you do."

"That means I'll have to date."

"Yes it does. But you're getting some practice right now. This very minute. How's it going for you? Are the sparks flying, your heart racing?"

He shook his head. "Not really."

"Yeah. Me neither."

"I should probably go home and apologize to Scott."

"I think that's a very good idea."

"We might as well have a nice dinner though, since we're here."

"You're buying, so by all means, a nice dinner it is."

Ana and Jason got home an hour and a half later. Ana promptly ran up to her room, changed into her PJs, and curled up in the fetal position on her bed. She waited for the tears to come, but she felt confused and angry more than sad.

After several minutes, she heard a light rapping on the door. It was Scott. He came in and lay next to her.

"I'm sorry about how I acted earlier. I kind of flipped out about the kiss."

"Yeah, you sort of did."

"I acted like a jerk."

"Yeah, you sort of did."

"I'm sorry. I was surprised. It freaked me out. How did things go?"

"We talked. I think he'll get a grip on Marin and Jay eventually." She studied Scott. "You know what your problem is? You always try to make everyone happy."

"That's bad?"

"It's bad when you can't make a distinction between who's right and who's wrong. Relationships take work, Scott. They'll run into rough patches and you can't just joke around indefinitely and hope they'll go away."

"So what am I supposed to do?"

"When we have problems we have to *talk* about them."

"You are such a girl."

She couldn't help it, she laughed. "You are such a boy. But you need to be the kind of boy who'll kick the butt of another boy who makes the moves on me."

"I promise. The next guy who smooches you who's not me will get the stuffing kicked out of him."

"Excellent."

50

Fake It Till You Make It

Ana was at the office, not working. She had been thinking a lot about what Marin had said. How would Ana advise a friend who wanted to be an actor/comedian? She'd say get off your duff and perform—get out there!

Unless, of course, the friend was as talentless as she was, and then she'd say, quit now to avoid humiliating yourself any further.

But it was true that she had made the Iron Pyrits without any experience. She had been chosen out of thirteen people to make Spur, where she was paid to do what she loved, pitiful sum though it might be. She was the youngest manager in her department, possibly in the company.

Ana searched online for acting classes and information about auditions. She pulled up the Comedy Works website to read about the amateur night. She wrote down the phone number on a sticky note.

Finally, feeling aggrieved, she got back to work.

All day her eyes drifted to the sticky note with that phone number. It said on the website that first-time amateur night participants got two minutes on stage. Two minutes. It was nothing. She could do that.

But what would she say? She strained her brain. She couldn't think of a thing. But just as soon as she wrote a two-minute set, she'd sign-up to perform.

Or maybe she should sign up. If she was locked in to performing, she'd have no choice but to crank out a routine.

She grabbed the phone and dialed Comedy Works before she could change her mind. They put her on the list for the Tuesday after Tuesday.

Promptly after committing to the line-up, Ana regretted what she'd done. She wanted to make her dreams come true, but that didn't mean she wanted to start *right now*.

She felt sick to her stomach. Oh God, getting up on that stage and having to tell jokes. She would never be able to do it.

For the next ten days, Ana wrote and practiced and timed herself and cut and edited and rewrote and memorized and practiced—in front of the mirror, in the car, and in front of members of the household, together, separately, and in every variation of pairs of her friends mathematically possible.

The night before she went on, she performed for Marin for the eight millionth time. "You didn't laugh!" Ana accused. "I knew it. I'm excruciatingly bad."

"Ana, I've seen this routine thousands of times in the past few days. Remember how I laughed my ass off the first time? Even the best jokes stop evoking laugh-out-loud laughter after a while. I'm still amused though. Thoroughly amused."

For her performance, Ana called in the reinforcements—all her friends from work, the club, college, and high school. Her mom and her mom's coworkers were all there. So were Jason and Ramiro's families.

She had told them all they had to laugh out loud. Smiles and smirks were no good to her. She wanted loud, fall-off-your-chair guffaws of uproarious delight. Nothing less would do.

On the one hand, she had her own personal cheering section for support. On the other hand, if she bombed, everyone she'd ever met in her life would be there to see her moment of shame.

Ana was to go on sixth, close to the end, after people had had enough beer to make it easier for them to laugh. Ana took that as a good omen. Still, she was so stressed out she thought she might be sick. Then, when it was her turn, Ana got on stage and took several deeps breaths. She pretended she was playing a character—one who was a stand-up comedian, and it worked. In character, she was able to control her nerves and pretend she had confidence. She did a bit on the challenges of living in the dorms, like trying to covertly have sex while your roommate slept (at least you *hoped* they were sleeping). Ana lay on her back across a chair, leaning her head and back so far she was horizontal, pretending she was in bed. She kept her leg closest to the audience extended, so it looked like she was lying down. She used her other foot to balance herself and to jostle back and forth toward the pretend bed frame as if she were having sex. The whole time, she was darting her eyes are to see if her "roommate" was privy to what was going on. The audience laughed at her expression and physical comedy. The laughter helped Ana feel more relaxed, more assured. She moved on to her bit about mating rituals in Cancun over spring break. Which is to say that drunk boys leaped upon you on outdoor dance floors, shoved their tongues down your throat, and if you were drunk enough not to protest, you'd found your partner for the night. A few more jokes, bam bam bam, and that was it. It was over. Applause. Laughter. Cheers.

She was so high, she couldn't quite tell, but it appeared she was getting laughs from people she didn't know and hadn't coached nor bribed.

At the end of the night, after the amateurs had finished and a local pro had performed the headlining bit, all of the performers lined up to say goodbye to the audience.

Ana got plenty of comments of the "you were great" variety, but what wowed her was when the owner of the club, said, "So you'll be here next week?"

"Yeah, sure."

"The second time is four minutes."

"Great." What was she saying? Two decent minutes had

been a fluke. She could never come up with four minutes of material. "Next week. I'll be here. For sure."

Fake it till you make it. Fake it till you make it.

Ana suspected she had many years of faking it in front of her. But she could fake it, right? She was an actress, after all.

51

Living Arrangements

Chelsey picked up Rob on her way to the theater. He'd already given her a set of keys to his apartment, but tonight she just buzzed upstairs to let him know she was here—if she went upstairs, they were likely to be very, very late for warm-ups.

"Hello, gorgeous," she said when he emerged from the elevator door.

He gave her a long, deep kiss. *Quite the cruel tease.*

"Let me grab my mail."

He unlocked his mailbox, pulled the mail out, and followed her out to her car.

"So today was my final session with Libby," Chelsey said, "and she got on the scale and she'd lost eighteen pounds, and she cried and I cried and it was so cool. I was so proud of her and she kept thanking me and telling me how she couldn't have done it without me. It was so gratifying. It was *awesome.*" It had been one of the best days she'd had in a long time. It was so gratifying to think that she'd helped someone achieve her goals, get healthier, and feel better about herself. There were days, sure, when Chelsey's job sucked, but today, she loved her work and couldn't wait to go in the next day. Chelsey waited for Rob to respond. He didn't. "So isn't that neat?" she prodded.

"Yeah," he said, staring at a letter, his face crumpled with annoyance.

"What's wrong?"

"My rent. My lease is up at the end of the month and they raised my rent to $800."

"You're kidding. That's terrible."

"It is terrible. I'm never going to be able to afford to take you out to dinner again. And a movie? Forget it."

They sat in silence at the stoplight. When the light turned green and Chelsey accelerated, she said, "You should move in with me."

He looked at her incredulously.

"No, I mean it. My mortgage is $1300 a month. If you could pay half that, you'd be helping me out a ton and you'd still be saving money on your monthly payments. Anyway, we spend just every free second together anyway."

"That's a big step."

"Well, you can think about it." Chelsey thought about it, too. She'd made the suggestion without thinking; it just seemed to make economic sense. But as she imagined making dinner together every night (every night he wasn't at work, that is), waking up together every morning, falling asleep together every night, and never having to worry about rushing home before work the next day to get a change of clothes—it would be heaven! She imagined this tranquil world of quiet domesticity. She would always have her brand of shampoo handy. They would cook dinner together and grocery shop together and the most mundane activities would be transformed into blissfully romantic moments.

But she'd done it again, hadn't she? Rushing things. Guys always shied away from women who wanted to rush the whole commitment thing. What could she do? Retract her offer? Say she had just been kidding? Maybe this whole improv thing had backfired. When you were trained to say the first thing that comes to mind, you forgot how to not to blurt out whatever thoughts popped into your head.

52

The Bad News. Squared.

It was a Friday afternoon and Ana was bored to tears. She had plenty of work to do, but she simply couldn't bring herself to do it. Instead, she booked an appointment for headshots with a photographer for the end of March. That gave her four weeks to take off some more weight. She'd taken off a few more pounds, but her goal was to drop a dress size.

She also went online and signed up for an eight-week acting class. She was terrified, but also excited by the prospect of studying dramatic roles and interpreting the work of other writers. She couldn't wait to improve her acting abilities—she'd master every accent known to humankind, of that she was certain.

Small successes really did wonders. For the first time ever, Ramiro had come to her with a one-act play he'd written and asked her for her opinion. He'd never voluntarily let other people see his work! She loved that he would let people in on his writing at long last. Ana's small victories at the comedy club had boosted her spirits, too. She still overpracticed and overwrote her stand-up to ridiculous extremes, but she figured that maybe if she kept working on it, success wasn't a total pipe dream.

She looked at the clock. 4:35. Good lord, would the day never end?

She'd stayed up late the night before at the theater, and she simply couldn't do a single more thing to market Abbott Technology. It was so unfair that she couldn't just say, "It's Friday afternoon at 4:35 and I'm exhausted and I simply can't do a thing for this company until Monday morning," and then go home and begin the weekend she so dearly deserved. No, she had to make it look like she was working or at least keep her body in the office until the clock struck 5:00. Well, maybe 4:55 if nobody was looking. It was Friday, after all.

She pulled up the *Rocky Mountain News'* entertainment guide online, which she'd followed religiously since *Roommates* had aired. *Roommates* had held steady with a 2.1 rating share, which wasn't bad at all for a new show on the WB. The fifth episode had aired on Tuesday, and today officially closed out the February sweeps. The entertainment writer gave a breakdown of each network's hit and misses; which shows were going on hiatus and which shows were getting the ax. Ana skipped right to the section on the WB.

WB: The WB has much to celebrate. Their series Everwood, Family Affair, *and* What I Like About You *have successfully found audiences. Less fortunate were* Raindance *and* Going for Broke, *which have been put on hiatus. WB is saying permanent goodbyes to the well-conceived but poorly executed* Roommates *and . . .*

Ana kept rereading the words, trying to understand what they meant. They couldn't possibly mean what she thought they meant.

When the first feelings of shock were replaced by a sense of loss, she remembered that it wasn't her loss she was mourning, but her friend's. The friend that she'd been jealous of and horrible to. "Oh God, poor Marin."

Ana shut down her computer, not caring that it was not yet five, grabbed her purse, and went home.

She didn't drive quickly like she normally did. She was having too much trouble digesting the news of what she'd read to be an aggressive driver. On the one hand, Marin wouldn't have to move to L.A. On the other hand, Marin really loved doing this, and Ana wanted her to be happy. And, she'd run out of hands, but if she brought in the feet, there was, on the one foot, the fact that it would have been pretty damn cool to have a famous best friend, and having a famous best friend could certainly help Ana make contacts in the biz. But on the other foot, maybe somebody would see Marin on the show and she'd get something even better. It just sucked that it took the combination of good writing, good acting, good directing, and *luck* for a show to succeed, or in the case of shows like *Suddenly Susan*, which was given a remarkable three seasons to catch on (which it never did) crappy writing, crappy acting, crappy directing, and a lot of luck. *Roommates* had only gotten five stinkin' episodes. It wasn't fair!

Ana got home and went upstairs. As she approached Marin's room, she heard what sounded like sobbing. Ana paused in front of Marin's bedroom door. Marin was definitely crying. She must have heard about the show.

Ana knocked. There was no answer. The crying quieted. Ana knocked again. Still no answer. She pushed the door open. Marin was using the back of her hand to wipe the tears off her face.

"Marin, I'm so sorry."

"What are you sorry about? You don't even know why I'm crying."

"I heard."

"You heard? How?"

"I read it online in the paper."

"Oh my God! It's in the paper?" Marin buried her hands and started crying again. "This is so humiliating."

Ana was confused. Did Marin actually think which shows were on television and which ones got axed was top secret?

"I can't believe he did this to me," Marin said. Crying into a handful of tissue. Used tissues encircled her on her bed like a field of pink carnations.

Ana wasn't quite sure who the "he" Marin was talking about was. The producer? The director? Some big wig at the WB? She just hugged Marin.

"I don't understand how the papers could have found out before I did. He must have been out to some show or event with her."

"Who is 'he'?"

"Jay! Jay of course! Jay's cheating on me."

"Jay's cheating on you? How did you know?"

"I found a hair scrunchy on his bedroom floor. You know I wouldn't be caught dead in one of those outside the house."

Ana did know. She loved her hair scrunchies, but was careful to wear them only around the house or when she worked out, lest she become a target for the untiring ridicule of Ramiro and Marin.

"What did the papers say about him?" Marin asked.

"The papers didn't say anything. I was talking about . . ." This didn't really seem like the right time to tell her the show had been canceled. "Something else."

"What?"

"Nothing. So what happened? When did you find it? What did you do?"

"I spent the night with him. Then this morning we had sex again. God, that's the really humiliating thing. I was searching around, trying to find my underwear, and I found the scrunchy. Right away my heart just sank. I asked him about it, and he kind of stuttered, stumbling over his words. He *never* does that. He's always sure of himself. He mumbled something about it must have been from one of the maids. But the way he tripped over his words I knew he was lying. I said something about why would a maid take her hair out of its band unless she was doing something like rolling around in a bed. I don't know, we kind of argued for a few more minutes, and then he stopped trying to pretend like he hadn't slept with anyone and he turned around and said that he hadn't done anything wrong, he'd never promised to be faithful, and life was too short, to sleep with just one woman and his wife didn't mind him . . ."

"His wife!"

". . . sleeping with other women so why should I?" Marin blew her nose and tossed the used tissue with the rest. She grabbed another tissue from the box. "I feel like a prostitute. Just another geisha girl. I didn't matter at all to him and never did. I feel like such an idiot. You know what the worst thing is? The worst thing is that I didn't even break up with him, he broke up with me. He said I was too needy and too high-maintenance, and he was glad I found out. I wish I'd told him off, but I was too shocked. It didn't seem real; it was a nightmare."

"Marin, you are not an idiot. He's a total asshole for not telling you he didn't believe in monogamy."

"I really thought I loved him. What's wrong with me that I can't love the good guys?"

"Nothing is wrong with you. Women fall for guys who cheat on them all the time. It's a learning experience."

"Learning experience. Ha!" she cried out bitterly. "I've had enough of those, thanks."

Ana didn't know what to say or how to help. She felt completely useless. She just held Marin until she stopped crying.

Maybe twenty minutes had passed in a silence broken only by the sound of Marin crying or blowing her nose. Finally, Marin said in a sniffly voice, "What were you talking about?"

"What do you mean?"

"When you first came in here, you said you'd heard and you were so sorry. What were you talking about?"

"Oh nothing. Don't worry about it right now."

"Ana, tell me. I mean it."

"I just can't believe you haven't gotten a call. I don't want to be the one to tell you."

"I was at the cheating asshole's all night and all yesterday. Then I came home and sequestered myself in my room to cry my eyes out. I haven't spoken to anybody but you and the Big Liar for more than twenty-four hours. Tell me what gives already."

"The show."

"*Roommates?*"

"It was canceled."

Marin's reaction surprised Ana completely. She laughed. "Of course it was. Of course. Figures. They gave it a whopping five episodes to find an audience. Shit. That really sucks."

Ana looked at the clock. They were supposed to be at

warm-ups in fifteen minutes. "Marin, I need to get to the theater. I'll bring you a big old bottle of 100-proof alcohol and get Ramiro to fill in for you tonight."

"No, I want to go on."

"You can't be serious. This has to qualify as the worst day of your life hands down."

"Yes, I think it's safe to say that it is. That's why I want to perform. I don't want to be me for a while. I'd like to be anybody else in the world, as a matter of fact."

"Are you sure?"

Marin nodded. "Let me just go wash my face and I'll be ready to go."

At the theater before the show, Ana asked Marin to go refill the water pitcher. While Marin was in the other room, Ana broke the news about both *Roommates* and Jay.

"Unbelievable. What is she doing here?" Chelsey said.

"I can fill in for her," Ramiro said.

"I told her you'd do that, but she wants to go on. She wants to pretend to be somebody else for a while."

As it turned out, Marin was the consummate professional. The five performers put on an exceptionally good show. No one in the audience could have possibly guessed what she'd gone through that day.

After the show they, as always, gathered in the bar.

Ramiro called for a round of shots for everyone.

"Why?" Marin asked suspiciously.

"We heard about the show, and it's bullshit, and I want to drink to the impossibly tough world of being an actor and performer."

His honesty seemed to placate her. "Yeah, I can certainly drink to that."

She called for the next round of shots.

"What are we drinking this round to?" Jason asked.

"To getting over bad jerky men and being open to finding good ones."

They could all drink to that.

After the third round of shots, this one dedicated to getting wasted with your buddies, Ana said, a little tipsily, "Guys?"

She let that hang in the air, as if that was the important thing she had to say. "It's been quite a year. Ramiro has secured a literary agent, Marin has a talent agent, we've found and lost love, and you know what, here we are again, getting drunk after performing at Spur of the Moment Theater in Denver. This is okay, this isn't bad. But I think we owe it to ourselves to see if we can make it in the big city."

"L.A.?" Marin said.

"Chicago?" Ramiro offered.

"New York," Ana said definitively. "We can give it, say, two years. Maybe we'll just lose our shirts and rack up credit card debt and bomb one audition after another, but I think we should really give it a shot. I'm sure we'll have some fun stories to tell the grandkids even if the whole becoming wildly rich and famous thing doesn't work out." Ana affected the voice of an old woman: "Well, sonny, I lived in New York for two years and let me tell you . . ."

"I'm up for it," Scott said.

"You are?" Ana said.

"What do I have to lose? A job at Abbott Technology? Bring out the violins. I'm sure there are a bunch of weaselly bosses I can work for in New York."

"I'm game," Marin said.

"Me, too," Jason said.

"You guys aren't shitting me, are you?" Ana said.

"I say let's go for it," Marin said.

"What'll happen to Spur?" Chelsey said quietly.

"We'll have to recruit several new people, obviously," Ana, ever the project manager, said immediately. "We'll bring a few people up to the mainstage as soon as possible. I don't know, they should be ready to go in maybe six months if we practice with them really hard. I mean I don't want Spur to fall to pieces, but we also have to do what's best for our careers."

"I don't know, you guys. I'm a home owner, and Rob is going to move in with me."

"You can get someone to rent your house for a couple years. You and Rob can share a room in a house we all rent together," Ana said.

"I don't know if Rob will want to move to New York. That's so far away from his family."

"You're not sure *Rob* will want to move to New York or you're not sure *you* want to move to New York?" Ana asked.

"Both, maybe."

"That's fair, you don't have to decide tonight. Talk it over with Rob, think about it, let us know. Ramiro, what about you?" Ana said.

"I don't know, Nick, what do you say?"

"New York? I don't know. I've never thought about it."

"Nick and I will talk it over when we haven't been drinking. We'll let you know," Ramiro said.

"We can't go if you guys don't come," Ana said.

"Sure you can," Chelsey said. "I just don't know if I'm ready for New York."

"Do you want to write for TV or don't you?"

"I think so. I don't know."

Ana was suddenly mad at Chelsey. Moving to New York would be terrifying, no question, but it would also be thrilling and exciting and new. Chelsey was always the one who said she wasn't really a personal trainer, it was only what she did to pay her bills. But if she never took any risks to try to be anything else, how could she ever become the person she aspired to be?

That one performance after the Dark Friday was just about the only time Marin left her room for the next three weeks.

The next day, Marin woke up feeling hung over, though it wasn't from drinking, it was from crying herself to sleep. She had a headache and was too depressed to get out of bed.

She finally got up around three to get something for her headache. She hadn't eaten anything since she'd found out about Jay, but she wasn't hungry. She felt nauseated and queasy. She got a glass of water to wash the Advil down. On the counter was the day's mail, which Ana always arranged in five piles, divided into stacks according to which roommate the mail belonged to. In Marin's pile there were three statements from her bank that she was overdrawn on her account and that she'd bounced three checks. She owed them $75, $25 for each bad check. Who knew how many other bad checks she'd written? She burst into tears. Somehow, seeing her flakiness in black and white seemed proof that she was an idiot. No wonder Jay had ditched her. She was just another pretty airhead who couldn't handle the simplest task of keeping her checkbook balanced.

She went to bed that afternoon and didn't come out for the next few weeks except to go to the bathroom.

She slept up to fourteen hours a day. She wanted to lose herself in sleep. It was the only time she didn't think about what an idiot she'd been. Why hadn't she put the signs together? He'd only ever given her his cell phone number, never his home number. He'd only brought her inside his house once—no doubt his wife had been out of town that weekend. He only met with her when it was convenient to his schedule—and he was unemployed, he should have been able to make his own schedule.

She'd wanted so badly to be in love, and he was so handsome and charming and fun. He was a little bossy, but she kind of liked that. She needed, or at least wanted, someone to take care of her. And he could certainly do that. With Jay, she'd never have to worry about money again. She had so easily been able to see her future with him. She'd so badly wanted to see it, she'd be blind to who he was and the true nature of their relationship.

Her agent called her twice and left messages about an audition for a commercial and for voice-over work. Marin didn't return her calls. She didn't go to any auditions. She stayed in bed, with greasy hair and body odor that overpowered her room.

Ana did her best to get Marin to shower and eat, and to encourage her to perform at the theater.

"It'll make you feel better. Remember how it feels to get on stage and pretend to be somebody else? You love that."

"I can't. Just have somebody cover for me."

"We can't keep covering you forever."

"Have one of the third-level people perform. You said you

needed to anyway. Besides, you guys did fine without me when I was in L.A."

On the Monday after the Friday that marked the three-week anniversary of Dark Friday, Ana decided her friend had been allowed to wallow long enough, and it was time to get serious. Ana brought pizza and beer up to Marin's room.

"I'm not hungry."

"Marin, you haven't eaten anything in three weeks. Have a beer, please? Just a beer." Ana popped the top off and Marin took it grudgingly. She couldn't remember the last time she'd eaten. She took a long swig and immediately felt dizzy.

"Are you sure you don't want a piece of pizza?" Ana said.

"I don't know if I can keep it down."

"Why don't you try?"

Marin had to concentrate on chewing. Her throat was so tight, it was hard to swallow. She only managed a few bites, but it made Ana happy.

"Marin, you've got to snap out of it. Lots of women have been duped by cheating boyfriends. Don't beat yourself up over it."

Marin shook her head. "It's not just Jay. I just feel like a failure. I always pick the wrong guys. There is something wrong with me."

"What do you mean always? You've never dated anybody for more than a couple weeks."

"No, nothing. Never mind."

"Marin, it's me, Ana, you're best friend in the world. Come on, tell me. What other guys?"

Marin took another long swig of beer. "There was this guy. In high school. Senior year. He was older. Good looking. Rich. He . . . he hurt me. He'd punch me sometimes, or shove me. He never took a bat or a knife to me, never hurt me so bad I had to go to the hospital, but I could see it in his eyes . . . he was just, I really thought he was capable of hurting me, really hurting me. Like he wanted to, you know? That's why I ended up going to college in Boulder. I just ran away. The school year wasn't even over. I just hid in our house in Aspen for four months, then went to school in Boulder. When I go home to

New York, I'm still scared I'll run into him. Isn't that ridiculous? In a city as big as New York?"

"Jesus. I'm so sorry. I can't believe you never told me that." Ana digested this news. "Marin, you have to know that none of this is your fault."

"Yes it is. I never like guys who are nice to me. I must secretly be a masochist."

"You haven't had good luck with men. That doesn't make you a masochist. You're being way too hard on yourself."

"That sounds like something I'd say to you."

Ana saw just a hint of a smile on Marin's face. "That doesn't mean it's not true for you."

Ana hugged Marin. They clutched each other tightly for several minutes, Marin's tears falling on Ana's shoulders.

Ana pulled away. "Marin, would you do me a favor?"

"What?"

"Take a shower. I love you, but you're rank."

Marin didn't say anything.

"Please? For me. I'll put some nice clean sheets on your bed while you're cleaning up."

Marin rolled her eyes, but finally relented and dragged herself to the bathroom for a bath.

The next morning, Ana woke Marin up with a voice booming with enthusiasm. "Get up get up get up! Who knows what exciting adventures await you today. Look, I brought you breakfast. Breakfast in bed."

"You are such a cheerleader."

"Yeah, I know. Once a cheerleader, always a cheerleader."

"I didn't mean it as a good thing."

"Believe me. I know. Eat, or else I really will start cheering." Ana stood in the center of the room and started clapping her hands together.

"You/Can do it/You can do it if you try/V-I-C-T-O-R-Y/You can do if you try! What do we want?/For Marin to eat/When do we want it?" Ana's response was cut short when a flying stuffed rabbit struck her squarely in the face. "I'm your best friend in the world and you pummel me with stuffed animals? Nice."

"Give me back Mr. Jeepers. He's my only solace in this dark time."

"Eat some fruit."

Marin rolled her eyes and gave a long-suffering sigh but sat up and balanced the tray across her lap. She forced down a few pieces of fruit, with Ana watching her to make sure she ate. And she did feel a little better after eating something. So much so that after Ana left for work, Marin decided to venture out of her room. She only made it as far as the couch, but it was progress.

Ana harped on Marin every morning before she left for work and every night when she got home.

"Food doesn't cure depression," Marin said.

"Do you want to be depressed?"

"Of course not."

"Do what actors do. Pretend to be the person you want to be until you actually become that person. Fake it till you make it. Sound familiar? What kind of person do you want to be? A depressed anorexic who smells bad? No!"

This particular motivational speech was met by another missile assault piloted by Mr. Jeepers.

Eventually, however, with Ana and the rest of Marin's roommates encouraging her to start eating and performing again, life did start to seem something like normal. Finally Marin mustered the energy to call her agent and apologize for being so difficult to reach. She said she'd had bronchitis. She was feeling better now and would be very interested in going on any auditions she might be right for.

Three days later, when her cell phone rang, she figured it was her agent. She looked at the caller ID and noticed the 310 area code, but didn't think twice about it.

"Hello?"

"Hey babe."

Marin's heart jumped. "Jay? Why are you calling?"

"I missed you."

"Your wife isn't company enough?"

"We've separated. For good this time. Because of you. I want to be with you."

Marin was furious with Jay. Also with herself, the way her heart leapt at the thought that he wanted to be with her.

"Maybe you should have thought of that before you cheated on me. And on your wife I might add."

"That was a mistake. A one-time thing. I'll never do that again. Ever. I promise. Please, let me just see you, talk to you in person."

"No Jay, it's over. Goodbye." She clicked her phone off and struggled to breathe normally.

When she emerged from her bedroom a few hours later, there was an enormous vase of exotic flowers on the table.

"These came for you," Ramiro said. "I wasn't sure if you were sleeping. I didn't want to wake you."

"That fucking bastard. They're beautiful."

"Jay?"

"Yes Jay. He claims his left his wife for good."

"What are these?" Ana asked when she got home minutes later.

"From Jay. The lying bastard."

"Why is he sending you flowers?"

"Claims he's left his wife for good."

"Whatever. Anyway, he's a cheating scumbag. What do you care?"

"I don't." Marin went to the cupboard, got a glass, and poured herself some water. "He says he wants to see me."

"You're not going to see him, are you?"

"No, no, of course not."

"Don't even think about it."

"I won't."

But she did. It was all she could think about. Maybe he did leave his wife for good. Maybe they could get married. She'd never felt anything with anyone else like what she'd felt with Jay. She couldn't just throw that all away because he'd made one mistake, could she?

* * *

A few days later, when Marin got home from an audition for a commercial for a used-car lot, Jay was sitting on the front porch.

"What are you doing here?"

"I told you, I missed you. I haven't been able to stop thinking about you."

"Maybe you should have thought of that before you lied to me, before you cheated on me."

"I know you have every reason to hate me and no reason to ever speak to me, but I really want to talk to you. Let me take you to dinner, okay?"

"No, not okay. Go home to your wife. Leave me alone."

"I told you, it's over with Linda. We have lawyers. The divorce proceedings are moving forward as we speak."

"Jay, I have to perform at the theater tonight. It's over between us. I don't care if you're getting divorced or not."

"You can't mean that."

"I can and I do. Goodbye, Jay."

Marin went inside and pulled closed the door behind her, her heart racing. She'd done the right thing. She knew she'd done the right thing. Then why did it feel so hard?

Be *strong*, she told herself. Jay was like heroin—addictive, and very, very bad for her. But she craved it all the same.

53

White Picket Fences

Sunday night, Rob brought over two videos, *Monsters Inc.* and *Ice Age*, both animated features. Chelsey and Rob snuggled beneath a blanket, eating popcorn.

When the second movie was over, Chelsey said, "Those were such cute movies. I almost wish I had kids of my own just so I had an excuse to go see movies like this."

"When do you want to have kids? Sooner or later?"

Chelsey thought a moment. She tried to imagine herself in New York, trying to go for auditions and working the crazy nights she'd have to work while trying to raise children. "I don't know. Not right away. Maybe a few years down the road." Chelsey changed the subject abruptly. "If I wanted to go to New York, would you come with me?"

Rob expelled a deep breath. "New York, huh?"

"We wouldn't have to go there forever. Maybe three or four years. I could really try to get a shot at writing for television or writing sketch comedy, and maybe even performing sketch comedy. If it doesn't work out, we can come back here and chalk those four years up as an adventure, no harm done."

"Fighting big city fires, wow, that'd be a trip. A total blast. It's pretty far from South Dakota . . . but yeah, I'm in."

"Really?"

"Yeah. If you want to go, I'll support you."

"I don't really know if I want to go. I just wanted to know if you'd go."

"Just say the word, love bug, I'll pack my bags."

Chelsey had wanted to be a writer for television since college. For many reasons. The idea had begun with the thought that she would star in her own workout videos and aerobic workouts aired on television. Then she thought about how cool it would be to entertain hordes of people by writing for the shows she loved to watch. Plus, she had an opinionated streak to her, which she expressed every day in her evangelistic approach to exercise and diet.

But now, suddenly the cut-throat world of Hollywood seemed less desirable. She could easily see sticking around, marrying Rob, and having kids. That was starting to seem like the biggest fantasy she could imagine. Maybe she would end up writing books instead of teleplays. Unlike actors, writers were allowed to get fat, be ugly, and get old. Yes, the pay was crap, but look at the advantages!

54

Potholes on the Road to Happily Ever After

Over the next few weeks, nobody talked about moving to New York, but everyone started looking more closely at the people in the third-level improv course Steve Cuddy taught. There were two or three people with promise. Ana talked to Steve about bringing more people up to be staff performers. He was all for it—he'd been telling them for a long time that their group was getting too small and too comfortable. They needed some new blood to keep them on their toes.

When the current batch of third levels "graduated" from their eight-week course, three were asked to become full-time players. All three agreed.

The now-nine-member team of Spur practiced Sunday and Wednesday nights for several weeks before letting any on the newbies on stage. They started staffing the show so four old-timers played—one always playing the emcee—and two newbies played. It was a painful transition after they'd worked so closely together for so long to have these wild cards, who were sometimes passably okay and sometimes excruciating, but practicing was the only way to get better and it was their own damn fault for keeping the troupe so small for so long.

* * *

"**H**ey Marin, I need the rent for May," Ana said.

"Um, yeah. I sort of am waiting to hear from my agent if I got that voice-over work."

"What are you talking about?"

"If I get the voice-over work, I'll have money for rent. I need to get more work."

"What about all the money you made from *Roommates?*"

"I sort of spent it."

Ana laughed. "Yeah, right."

Marin's grave expression didn't change.

"You're kidding, right?"

Marin shook her head.

"How is that even possible?"

"It was expensive staying in L.A. And I was still sending money back here for my part of the rent. And I needed to buy a lot of nice clothes and everything, you know, so I could look the part. And sometimes when Jay and I went out, I treated. I wasn't worried about money. I figured I was dating a billionaire, it wasn't like the money would ever run out."

"Except it did."

"Except it did."

Ana sighed. "You've got to learn to budget your money, Marin. Especially in a business as crazy as acting. You need to be prepared for long stretches without work. Maybe Nick can help you figure out your finances. Help you budget and plan and all that."

"That's a good idea. Look, I know I messed up. I should have put some money into savings. But I was wondering, just for now, if maybe I could borrow some money, just for this month?"

Ana studied the wall. Considered. Shook her head. "I'm sorry, Marin, I can't. I mean I don't think I should. You know I love you and I want to help you and be there for you, but I think me bailing you out all the time, your parents bailing you out, it's why you haven't figured out how to balance your checkbook and stick to a budget. You need to grow up. You're twenty-five years old. You need to pay your own rent. You're a smart girl. A smart woman. I know you can do it. You just need to learn that you can, in fact, take care of yourself. You *can* make smart decisions."

Ana hugged her, then left the room.

Fuck, what was she going to do?

The phone rang.

"Hello?"

"Babe, it's me."

It was Jay.

"What do you want?"

"I miss you. I want to see you. I want to talk to you. Let me take you out to dinner." She was about to protest. Then he said, "Come on, one free meal."

Free meal. Maybe she could borrow the money from him. Lord knows he had enough of it. He'd probably just give it to her. It wouldn't make up for what he'd done to her, but it would be a start.

"Okay. Name the time and place. I'll meet you there."

Money. It was the only reason she was going. She felt a little nervous, but only because it would be awkward to see him again.

She spent the next two hours getting ready, until she looked drop-dead gorgeous. But only to remind him of what he'd lost.

Marin took a cab and met Jay at Vesta's Dipping Grill. She kept telling herself it was just for a free meal, and to borrow some money. But within minutes of seeing him again, she forgot all about asking him for a few hundred bucks. He had her laughing so hard she cried. He told her about his travels and his parties with Hollywood elite. He told her how much he wanted to take her to his place in Paris.

After dinner, Jay ordered desserts for both of them. He ordered the bread pudding for her, even though she'd rather have had the crème brûlée. Although it was no big deal either way really.

"Have you ever been to France?" Jay asked.

"I toured around Europe one summer. My friend and I were in Paris for, I don't know, about two weeks."

"Did you get to visit Provence?"

"No, though I've heard wonderful things about it. I'd love to go someday."

"I have a house in Provence. It's on a vineyard. The house is very old, but I had it renovated. Of course I had the builders do their best to keep everything looking like the original, except, you know, to make it have working plumbing and electricity."

Marin smiled.

"It took two full years. But I tell you, it's so, so peaceful. I found a stone mason and had him carve a granite table, which I put outside. It's a large table, for big parties of families and friends. But even if you're just out there by yourself—the vineyard, the greenery, the rich smells—it's heaven."

"It sounds lovely. I'd love to see it sometime."

"I'd like to take you to it sometime. I was thinking maybe I could take you there for our honeymoon," he said.

He pulled out a blue velvet box and opened it to reveal the enormous ring inside.

Marin gasped.

"We'll have to wait until my divorce is finalized, of course. It might be a while, I have a feeling my wife is going to do her best to take me to the cleaners and make my life hell. But after that. What do you say?"

She would never have to worry about money again. She wouldn't have to worry about rent, or work, or bugging her dad for a few bucks to tide her over. And if she only got sporadic work as an actress, it wouldn't matter. She'd be fine.

"Jay, I, I'm not like your wife. I believe in monogamy. I couldn't . . ."

"Marin, listen. I think the reason I . . . wasn't faithful to Linda was that she wasn't the right woman for me. I was looking for something—someone—to fill the void. And then I found you, and, to be honest, my feelings for you, they were so intense, they scared me. And that's why I . . . but when I lost you, I realized, true love might be scary, but life without you, it would have no meaning." He took the ring out of the box and brought it toward her ring finger. "What do you say?"

The ring was so beautiful. She wanted it on her finger. She could see a life with him so easily. And it made sense, what he'd said about why he cheated on his wife. He wouldn't have done it if she'd been the right woman for him. Her parents would be so proud of her for snagging such a successful businessman . . . "I say yes."

He smiled and slipped the ring on her finger. She felt like Sleeping Beauty being whisked away into happily ever after. Everything was going to be just fine! Everything was going to be wonderful! And even if it didn't work out, she'd make a killing in the divorce. Unless, of course, there were pre-nups.

Wait, wait, why was she thinking these things? This was Jay, the love of her life, the man who loved her so much it scared him, but who had seen the error of his ways. Of course they wouldn't get divorced. They were meant for each other.

Jay kissed her. "I think this calls for some champagne."

"No, I . . . let's just toast with our wine."

The waiter arrived with their desserts.

"We'd like bottle of your best champagne," Jay told the waiter.

Minutes later, the waiter returned with two glasses and a bottle of Dom Perignon.

"No, really, I don't want any. Thanks," Marin said to the waiter.

"Marin, come on. One glass won't hurt you. We're getting *married.*"

So she drank a glass. It wasn't terrible. But honestly, why couldn't he let her not drink champagne? Why didn't he let her order her own damn dessert?

Was this really what she wanted? She wanted a guy with opinions, yes, a guy who wouldn't let her walk all over him, but did she want someone who made every single decision for her?

But what would she do without him? She was obviously a total financial dimwit. She didn't even have health insurance, for Christ's sake. She needed someone to take care of her; she *wanted* someone to take care of her.

Marin thought about what Ana had said. *You're a smart girl. A smart woman. I know you can do it. You just need to learn that you can, in fact, take care of yourself. You can make smart decisions.* What was the smart decision here? To marry a man who lied to her? Who cheated on her? Who did her thinking for her? Maybe she *could* figure out how to balance a budget. Nick could help her. Ana could help her. Maybe she could even hold down a day job, with paid vacations and sick days, and hallelujah, health insurance. Maybe she was rushing into this. There would be no harm in waiting.

"You know what, I really don't think a champagne toast is necessary," Marin said, slipping the ring off her finger and putting it back in the box. She handed the box to Jay. "I think I need more time to think about this. I love you, but you really hurt me. I need time."

"Marin. Be reasonable. I'm one of the richest men in America. You'll be set for life. This is exactly like you. So flaky and unable to make a decision. Just say yes."

The way he said "say yes" wasn't a plea, it was an order. He sounded, in fact, exactly like her father. Jesus, she did not want to marry a man like her father. Why hadn't she seen it before? Jay was exactly like him, always demanding that they do what he wanted, making the decisions for her, insisting that things went his way.

"You know what Jay, you're right. I should be able to just make a decision. I decide that I definitely don't want to marry you. I don't even want to date you anymore. In fact, I never want to see you again as long as I live."

Jay was speechless as she threw her napkin down on the table and stood to leave.

"What just happened, where are you going?" Jay said, as the gift of speech returned to him. "Okay, you don't have to have any champagne."

"I know I don't. I don't have to do anything I don't want to do. I don't have to be with a guy who lies to me and cheats on me and tells me what to do. I'm a big girl, I can take care of myself."

"Do you know how many women would claw out both their eyes for a ring like this?"

"I don't need big fancy diamonds or lots of money. There are some things—lots of things, actually—that are more important than money." Jason would be so proud, knowing that she actually listened to him once in a while. "Goodbye Jay."

55

The Future

One Monday night, a lovely evening of not having to do anything (except of course for Jason, who was diligently grading papers in the kitchen), Ana, Marin, and Scott lounged in various positions, watching *Corky Romano*, a film that Scott had picked up from the video store and which Ana had started watching accidentally. She'd come home, collapsed on the couch, and by the time she had the energy to open her eyes to see what was on the television, she didn't have the energy to lift herself from the couch.

"I can't believe I'm actually watching *Corky Romano*," she said.

"Oh shut up, you make fun of the movies I like, but I've caught you laughing several times," Scott said.

Damn. She was busted. She shook her finger at him. "That information never leaves this house."

"Hi kids, I'm home," Ramiro's voice interrupted as the door swung closed behind him. "Family meeting! I call an emergency family meeting."

It took a few minutes for them to get off their asses, but after a series of put-upon grunts and groans, Scott turned off the TV, Jason came in from the kitchen, and Ramiro pulled up the footstool so the five of them were in a circle. Even Ana mustered the effort to sit up.

"I have two very important things to tell you. Number one, my agent sold my novel."

"You're kidding! Ram, that's wonderful!"

"Holy crap! Who's publishing it?"

"When will it be out?"

"It's a small press, it'll be out sometime next year," Ramiro said.

"Congratulations. *I told you* you were a good writer," Ana said.

"Ana, I can't thank you enough. I owe it all to you."

Ramiro hugged her.

"So are you a millionaire? Do you get to quit your day job?" Scott asked.

"Not yet," Ramiro said.

"How much did you get?" Ana asked.

"Three thousand."

"Dollars?"

"No, pesos. Of course dollars."

"That's it? Three thousand bucks? You can't quit your job on three thousand bucks," Ana said.

"Actually, my agent gets fifteen percent of that, and the government will get about half of what's left over. So about thirteen hundred bucks all told."

"That's it? You're kidding. How long did it take you to write the thing?"

"About two years."

"But you'll make a bunch of money when it gets optioned for movie rights," Ana said.

"Absolutely."

"I'm so proud of you. I'm so happy for you. A published novelist! At twenty-six!" Ana said.

"So what was the other thing? You said you had two important things to tell us," Scott said.

"We're in," Ramiro said.

"You're in?" Marin asked.

"Nick and I. We'll move to New York."

"Oh my God!" Ana screamed.

"All right!" Marin seconded.

"Wait, wait, there's a catch," Ramiro said.

"Fuck. I hate catches," Ana said.

"We're going to move in together."

"You mean you'll share a room together in our house?" Ana said hopefully, though she suspected that wasn't the correct interpretation of what he'd said.

"No, I mean, we're going to get a place together, just the two of us. I've been wanting to move in with Nick for a long time . . ."

"Why, just because he lives in a palace and we live in a dump?" Ana said, angry and defensive.

"No, because I love him and I want to be with him."

"You'll live close to us and visit all the time and we'll still perform together?" Marin asked.

He nodded.

"At least they want to come," Scott said to Ana. Ana crossed her arms, averted her gaze to the ceiling, and harrumphed dramatically.

"Will we go back to being the Iron Pyrits?" Marin asked.

"Maybe. Or maybe we'll think of something new," Ramiro said. "We'll still be together. So Ana, what do you think?"

"I'm happy you and Nick want to move to New York. And I guess it will be nice to have one less person to clean up after. I'm just . . . I'll miss you. I'm not good with change. But I guess I'll get over it *eventually* . . ." she sighed.

"So we're really moving to New York!" Marin said. "We'll go up against the big dogs. Get on *Saturday Night Live* and have our own HBO specials. We just have to be sure we don't run into my parents. You don't think I have to tell them I'm moving back to New York, do you?"

"I have to call Chelsey." Ana darted up to her room, filled with energy suddenly.

Chelsey was giggling when she answered the phone. "Yes?"

"Chelse, it's Ana."

"Hey."

"Hey. So guess what? Nick and Ramiro are going to move to New York with us. They're not going to live with us, they are going to get a place of their own, but still, it should be cool. You and Rob can move in with us . . . or I guess if you want to get a place together . . ."

Chelsey didn't say anything for a good twenty seconds. "Um, I don't think . . . we don't want to move to New York. *I* don't want to move. I've been thinking about this a lot, and . . . I like it here. I like performing at Spur. I don't think I could do what Marin did working all those crazy hours with all those crazy people and then just, you know, getting nothing out of it."

Ana thought that Chelsey sounded awfully damn defensive, but maybe it was just preemptive defensiveness to knock out any arguments Ana might throw out there. "Chelsey, Marin got $60,000 and an absolutely amazing experience that she'll never forget, no matter what happens. I'd hardly say she got nothing out of it."

Chelsey didn't say anything, so Ana charged on. "So how would you feel if we went without you?"

More silence. "I'd miss you. I'd come visit. You'd come visit, I mean, most of your families live here. And New York will always be there. I can always change my mind and catch up with you guys next year."

"Yeah sure, of course." Ana's anger softened. All at once she felt nostalgic for the good old times they hadn't even left yet. "But will you hate us if we leave you?"

"Of course not. We've been talking about New York forever, I just . . . things are going well at my job. Some days suck, of course, but some days are actually pretty fulfilling. I mean helping people get healthy and feel good about themselves, it's really actually kind of a cool way to make a living. And I have Rob. I want kids and a normal life. I've figured out that those are the things that are really important to me. I think before I was feeling really unsettled and now I just feel . . . I don't feel as restless."

Because you've settled *that's why you're not* unsettled *anymore. You fall in love and let all your dreams fall away.* Ana was back to being pissed. Right now she was riding more of an emotional roller coaster than she normally was, and normally she was on a DEFCON-five kind of emotional roller coaster. "We'll miss you. I mean we're not going anywhere for a while. We still need to bring on a few more actors at Spur. I thought maybe we could patrol the campuses for talent, see if any improv-ers will be graduating in May."

"Yeah, that's a good idea."

"And there are so many things we'll have to do: We'll have to sell our cars and find a place to live and find jobs and save some money . . ."

"I'm happy for you guys, really."

"Well, I guess Rob's there. I should let you go."

"See you tomorrow night at practice."

"See you."

Ana pushed aside the sudden feelings of confusion and ambivalence she felt and spent the rest of the night making detailed lists of everything they'd need to do before they left.

Check blue book value of car

Look into rental vans: better to sell most furniture and buy used in NY? Hire movers?

Get boxes

Check rental prices in various areas of NY

Check job listings in NY—pursue new career?

Prepare victory speech for when I give notice to Weasel

The list went on and on, and even after Ana stopped jotting things down and turned off the light, the ideas clattered in her head like a leaky pipe she couldn't shut off. *Am I making the stupidest decision of my entire life? Am I going to become a broke, abject failure? Will I be raped and mugged and die of some horrible disease?* (She pointedly didn't bother to consider that terrible things could happen to her in Denver as well as New York.) *Will I become famous for only a brief moment, and use my fifteen minutes just like that, and become an impoverished failure, a drug addict who dies a miserable, drawn-out death of shame and misery?*

But what are my other choices? To become magically fulfilled in my job marketing software? To give up on my dreams?

And what kind of life would that be, a life without dreams?

Please turn the page for an exciting sneak peek of

Theresa Alan's next novel

The Girls' Global Guide to Guys,

coming in early 2005!

Boulder, Colorado

"It couldn't possibly have been that bad."

"Oh, but it was. I saw his penis within an hour of knowing him, totally against my will."

"He flashed you?"

"Not exactly. We stopped by my apartment after dinner before we went to the club because we'd gone for Italian, and I had garlic breath, and I wanted to brush my teeth before we went dancing, even though I knew within four seconds of meeting him that it could never go anywhere. I don't know *what* Sylvia was thinking setting us up. But to be polite I had to go through the charade of the date anyway, even though I wasn't remotely attracted to him. So I started brushing my teeth, but I wanted to check on him and make sure he was okay, and he was just sitting there on the couch, naked."

"No!"

"Yes. Naked and, ah . . . you know, aroused." I'm stuck in traffic, story of my life, talking on my cell phone, which is paid for by the company I work for, making it one of the very, very few perks of being employed by Pinnacle Media. "I mean I know it's been a while since I've dated anyone, but isn't the whole point of dating and sex to kind of, I don't know, enjoy this stuff *together?* Like getting turned on by the other person's touch, and not by the sound of someone brushing her teeth in the bathroom?"

"So what did you do?"

"Well, I looked at him like the maniac he was, and he realized that I was appalled and said that he'd assumed that when I said I was going to brush my teeth, that meant I was going to put my diaphragm in."

"I don't . . . is English his native language? I don't see how anyone could possibly come to that conclusion."

"Right, Tate, that's my point. The guy was a loon. So I replied, quite logically under the circumstances I think, my mouth foaming with toothpaste, 'No, I willy was bruffing my teef.' And this whole situation struck me as so wildly funny. I mean in the past six months, I've dated a bitter divorcé, been hit on by a string of lesbians, and now this. How did my dating life go so tragically wrong? Anyway, I just lost it. I crumpled to the ground in a fit of hysteria. I mean I started laughing so hard I literally couldn't stand, and he looked all put out and confused and out of the corner of my eye, as I was convulsing around like a fish out of water, I saw him get dressed, and then he *stepped over* my writhing body and said, '*I don't know where things went wrong between us . . .*' "

"No!" Tate howls with laughter.

"Yes. He said some other stuff, but I was laughing too hard to hear him. I mean, hello, I can tell you *exactly* where you went wrong, buddy."

Tate and I laugh, then Tate says, "Did you tell Sylvia about how the guy she set you up with is a kook?"

"Hell, yes. I called her up and said, 'Hey, thanks for setting me up with a sexual predator.' And you know what she said? She said, 'I knew it had been a long time for both of you, and I thought you might just enjoy each other's company, even if it never got serious.' I don't think you need to be an English lit major to read the hidden meaning in that sentence. I mean, obviously Sylvia thinks I'm such a sad schlub who is so desperate for sex I'll have a one-night stand with a scrawny, socially inept engineer."

"Jadie, look at it this way: You can put all these experiences into your writing. Maybe you'll write a book one day about all the hilarious dates you've been on."

I groan. "I know there is a guy out there for me somewhere. I'm just pretty sure he's not in Boulder, Colorado."

"He's out there. I know he is. Somewhere. Look, I gotta go. I'm going to be late for my shift."

"Have fun slinging tofu."

"Oh, you know I always do."

I click the phone off, and now that I have nothing to occupy myself with I can focus completely on how annoyed I am at sacrificing yet another hour of my life to traffic. Why aren't we going anywhere, why?

I can't wait until the day I can work full time as a writer and won't have to commute in highway traffic twice a day anymore.

I'm a travel writer, though most people call me a "creative director for a web design company." Personally I think this shows an appalling lack of imagination. I *have* published travel articles, after all. Several of them in fact. Granted, all told, in my five years of freelancing I've only made a few hundred bucks on my writing and my travel expenses have come to about ten times more than what I made from my articles, but it's a start.

Finally I see what has been holding traffic up—a car that's pulled over to the side of the road with a flat tire. Great. Forty extra minutes on my commute so people can slow down to see the very exciting sight of a car with a flat tire. I growl through gritted teeth at the sinister gods of traffic who are clearly intent on giving me an aneurysm.

Eventually I make it home, grab the mail, unlock my door, and dump the mail on my kitchen table, my keys clattering down beside the stack of bills and catalogs advertising clothes I wouldn't wear under threat of torture. I sift through the pile; in it is the latest issue of the alumni magazine from the journalism school at the University of Colorado at Boulder, my alma mater. I flip idly through it until I see a classmate of mine, Tina Amundson, who smiles up at me from the magazine's glossy pages in her fashionable haircut and trendy clothes. As I read the article, my mood sinks.

I know I'm not the first person who has struggled to make it

as a writer, but sometimes, like when I get my alumni magazine and read that Tina Amundson, who is my age—27—and
has the same degree I have, is making a trillion dollars a year
writing for a popular sitcom in LA while I'm struggling to get
a few bucks writing for magazines no one has ever heard of,
my self-esteem wilts.

I change into a T-shirt and shorts to go for a run—I need to
blow off steam. To warm up, I walk to a park, then I start an
easy jog along the path that follows the river. It's 7:30 at night,
but the sun is still out and the air is warm.

Boulder has its faults, but it's so gorgeous you forgive
them. No matter how many years I've lived here, the scenery
never stops taking my breath away. Jogging along the Boulder
Creek path, I take in the quiet elegance of the trees, the creek,
the stunning architecture. The University of Colorado at Boulder is an intensely beautiful campus. Every building is made
out of the reds and pinks of sandstone rocks and topped with
a barrel-tiled roof. Behind the campus are the Flatirons, the
jagged cliffs in the foothills of the Rocky Mountains that draw
rock climbers from around the world and help routinely put
Boulder on "best places to live" lists in magazines.

I jog for about half an hour, then walk and stretch until I've
caught my breath. I lie down on the grass, enjoying the feel of
the sun on my skin, cancer be damned.

Three college students are playing Frisbee in one corner of
the field. Across the way, two young people with dreadlocks
and brightly colored rags for clothes are playing fetch with a
puppy.

The puppy makes me smile, but I realize as I watch it that
even after my jog, I still feel tense. My jaw muscles are sore
from clenching them, a bad habit I have of doing when I am
stressed, which is most of the time these days.

I need to get away, to relax. I long to hit the road.

I've always loved traveling. Since I was a little kid I always
wanted to escape, to find a place where I could comfortably
call home and just be myself. In the small town where I grew
up, life was a daily exercise in not fitting in.

The fact that I was considered weird was mostly my parents' fault. They ran a health food store/New Age shop where they tried to sell crystals to align chakras, tarot cards, incense, meditation music, that sort of thing. I'm fairly certain that no one ever bought a single sack of brown rice or bag of seaweed from their grocery store, and the candles and crystals didn't become popular until after I left for college. They got by because of the side businesses they ran in the shop—Mom cut hair and Dad fixed appliances. Yes, I know, a health food store/New Age shop/hair salon/appliance-repair shop is unusual, but when I was growing up, it was all I knew.

My mom was the kind to bake oatmeal cookies sweetened with apple juice and honey. You can imagine how popular the treats I brought to school for bake sales and holiday parties were. About as popular as me. Which is to say not at all.

I sat through years of school lunches all on my own, eating carob bran muffins and apples while every other kid had Ding-Dongs and Pop-Tarts. And I dreamed and dreamed of getting away and seeing the world, going to places where I could be whoever I wanted to be and wouldn't be the weird kid in town.

I found that place in Boulder, Colorado. Boulder is a place where pot-smoking, dreadlocked eighteen-year-olds claim poverty yet wear Raybans. Boulderites believe themselves to be one with nature, but own some of the most expensive homes in the country and drive carbon monoxide–spewing SUVs without realizing the irony. It's a place that manages to be somehow New Age and old school. A place where yuppies and hippies collide and where, inexplicably, people think running in marathons is actually fun.

My life is equally mixed up. It feels like a pinball machine— I'm the ball, getting flung around in directions I couldn't foresee and never considered. Like how I ended up working for Pinnacle Media.

I thought that after graduation I would become this world-renowned journalist covering coup attempts, international corruption and intrigue, the works. But after I got my degree, I couldn't get a job writing so much as obituaries for some small-town newspaper. Frustratingly, papers like *The New York Times* and *The Washington Post* seemed to be doing okay even without my help, and nobody from their respective papers was banging down my door begging me to write for them. They didn't even glance at my resume, just like every other newspaper in America, no matter how small or inconsequential. So I took a job doing Web content at an Internet company during the height of Internet insanity, when every twenty-year-old kid with a computer was declaring himself a CEO and launching an online business determined to get rich quick. We were living large for a while, but then the economy started to turn. I could tell the company was going down, and I felt lucky when I landed the job at Pinnacle.

That feeling lasted, oh, twenty-eight seconds.

I travel to get away whenever possible, taking a handful of short trips each year to cities in the United States, Mexico, or Canada. I've been saving up money and vacation time to go on a real trip, something longer than a four-day weekend, but I keep waiting for some flash of insight that will tell me where the best place to go is, some location that will prove a treasure trove of sales to magazines.

Although maybe it doesn't really matter where I go, whether Barbados is the happening spot this year or if Madagascar is the place to be, whether the Faroe Islands are going to be the next big thing or if Malta will be all the rave. After all, the articles I have sold haven't come from the short trips I've taken but from living in the Denver/Boulder area—stuff about little known hotspots in Colorado and how to travel cheap in Denver. Mostly I write for small local newspapers and magazines. I've gotten a few pieces published in national magazines, but the biggies, the large circulation publications that pay livable wages like United Airlines' *Hemispheres* or Condé Nast *Traveler*, remain elusively, tantalizingly out of reach.

In the past year, depressed about my career, I decided I would try to get another area of my life in shape—my love life. It hasn't exactly gone according to plan.

First, there was the bitter divorcé. I didn't know he was bitter until we went out on our first date. I knew he was divorced; he'd told me. I just didn't know how frightening the depths of his contempt for his ex went.

I met Jeff at the Tofu Palace, where I was waiting for Tate to get finished with her shift, sitting at the table next to him. As another waitress, Sylvia, brought him his shot of wheat grass and his sesame tempeh, he and I got to talking. He cracked me up with little quips and witty remarks. I don't even remember what he talked about, just that he seemed like a nice guy, and when he asked if he could have my number, I told him he could. I started to write it down, and he said abruptly, "Before you give me your number, there is something you should know."

I immediately thought he was going to say that he was out on bail for murder charges or something.

"I'm divorced and have two kids."

I waited a beat. "And?"

"And what? That's it."

"That's your big secret? You're divorced and have kids?"

"Yeah, that's it."

"I think I can handle it."

(Of course that really wasn't his big secret. His real secret was that he was a complete psychopath whose rage toward his ex festered in a frightening and unseemly way.)

The fact that he had kids appealed to me. He told me he saw them every other weekend, a three-year-old girl and two-year-old boy. I imagined Jeff and I getting married, and I would be able to help raise these kids and watch them grow, but on a convenient part-time basis without any of that painful pregnancy and birthing business.

But then I went out on my one and only date with Jeff and that fantasy was blown to bits.

Things started well enough. Then in the middle of a nice meal after a couple of glasses of wine, I asked him something about his ex. Something like if they'd managed to stay friends or why they broke up, I can't remember exactly. Jeff got this maniacal look in his eyes and said, "That lying, money-grubbing bitch. I hate her. Women—all they want is your money. Lying . . . cheating . . . manipulative bitches. But sometimes you get sick of porn and want the real thing." He laughed about that last thing, as if it were a joke, but it very clearly wasn't. And when I looked at him wide-eyed and open-mouthed, he seemed to come out of his trance and our gazes met. I was blinking in shock, and I think he realized that, like an evil villain going around disguised as a good guy, he'd accidentally let the mask slip off and some serious damage control was in order. He smiled. "Just kidding. It was rough going there for a while, but we're friends again." He saw my incredulity. "No really. I love women." *Yeah, to have sex with.* "Sometime you get sick of porn and want the real thing" . . . *unbefuckinglievable.*

So that was the end of Jeff.

Now you'll want to know about the lesbians. Their names are Laura and Mai and they live in my apartment building.

We'd always been polite when we'd met in the hallway or at the mailboxes over the years. Then a few months ago, as I held the door open for them, they asked me what I had going on that night. It was a Friday, yet I had a whopping nothing to do and no place to be. They said they were going dancing at a lesbian bar that night, did I want to go with them? I said sure, it sounded like fun.

Laura and Mai are both big girls and very pretty. Laura looks like Mandy Moore would if Mandy were a size fourteen. And Mai has a build like Oprah—busty and curvy and strong. And they have the cutest style. Their outfits wouldn't be featured in *InStyle* or anything, but I think they have a certain bohemian charm, and can we talk accessories? Clunky, colorful jewelry to die for.

We hit the club a few hours later, dancing our little hearts out. For some reason I didn't think it was strange that they kept buying drinks for me and plying me with alcohol. After all, they knew I was straight, I knew they'd been dating each other forever, what was there to worry about?

It was late when we got back.

"Do you want to come to our place for a nightcap?" Mai asked.

"No. Can't drink no more. Alcohol . . . too much."

"Why don't you come inside and we'll give you some water so you won't have a hang over," Laura said.

I was too drunk to protest—or really even know what was

happening. As I staggered into their apartment, I noticed that the hide-a-bed had been pulled out. I remember thinking, *I didn't know their couch had a hide-a-bed.*

We sat on the edge of the hide-a-bed, the two of them flanking me on either side. In a moment, Laura was blowing in my ear and Mai was kissing my neck and stroking my breast. It took me a moment to process what was happening. My brain was working in slow motion. It was like I'd gotten stuck in a sand trap, and no matter how much I tried to accelerate, the wheels of my brain just went around and around and never got anywhere. But eventually I realized that my breast was being stroked by a woman. I found this information to be very confusing.

Once I finally noticed what was going on, I seemed to sober up instantly. I sprung up off the couch. "I'm . . . I'm . . . I'm straight!" I yelped.

"There's no reason to be locked into these artificial constructions . . . these meaningless boundaries . . ." Mai began.

"Like boundaries! Boundaries good!" My English skills, despite my degree in journalism, had been reduced to the level of a two-year-old. That's when I began backing up toward the door. In moments I was sprinting backwards at Mach-10 speed, a blur of a human at break-the-sound-barrier velocity.

Unfortunately, I hadn't noticed that there was a coffee table between me and the door to freedom.

Another person would have stubbed her leg on it, or perchance been knocked sideways. Me? I was going so fast I became airborne and did a back flip—my head hit the corner of the table on my way down. I knocked myself semi-unconscious.

They say there are two responses to fear: Fight or flight. No one ever said that knocking yourself unconscious was an appropriate reaction to an uncomfortable situation. But there you have it. I'd turned myself into the perfect victim. I had no way to defend myself. I was at their mercy.

Fortunately, Laura and Mai weren't rapists. They'd put the moves on me, been rebuffed, and now they were a flurry of concern, hovering over me and wanting to know if I was okay.

In my half-conscious state, I was dimly aware that the two

of them were dragging me over to the hide-a-bed and hoisting me onto it—managing to knock my head on the metal frame as they did. I quickly fell into a merciful sleep.

In the morning, I didn't remember where I was or what had happened, I just knew my head was in excruciating pain. In addition to a bruise the size of a plum on the back of my head from the coffee table, I had a searing pain just above my ear from where they'd knocked me against the bed frame. On top of all that, I had a blinding hangover.

I groaned in pain. Moments later I heard the patter of bare feet against the wood floor, and I opened my eyes in an attempt to figure out where I was and what was going on.

It was Mai and Laura, who'd run out to check on whether I was all right. They were naked, hovering over me like oversized Florence Nightengales so that when I opened my eyes, all I saw was tit. Four large, ponderous tits, encircling me in a mammary orbit.

I promptly shut my eyes and wondered, how did my life start to read like a *Penthouse* letter? Sure, some people—guys, no doubt—might like a life that read like a *Penthouse* letter. I was not one of those people.

There was another lesbian—that night also involved alcohol and confusing and misguided tit-groping, though thankfully no head trauma—but if you don't mind, it's still too painful and embarrassing to think about, so I'd rather not tell the story in all its gory detail.

Add on the psycho sexual predator from last night, and you have the sum total of my love life in the last six months. And it was no romance novel before that, I can assure you.

I wonder if there is a place where this whole dating and romance thing is easier. Some country where the men aren't as psychotic as the men in America all seem to be. If so, I'm moving there post haste. I just need to find this magical la-la land. I'll search the globe until I find it . . .

I smile at the idea, then I think: if I'm interested in how romance is different in different parts of the world, maybe other people would be too. Maybe that could be my angle when I pitch stories; maybe it would be unique enough to get me in the door of the major magazines.

The ideas zip through my head, and I have internal arguments with myself about where and when I should go. The lazy part of me doesn't want to think about planning a trip, but the other part of me is saying, *Who cares if things are crazy at work; things are always crazy at work. Go! Go before you can change your mind!*

I jump up and run home. There, I strip out of my sweaty clothes, take a quick shower, throw some fresh clothes on, and sprint the four blocks from my apartment to the Tofu Palace where Tate is working tonight.

Tate has just finished taking an order from a table and is heading to the kitchen to give the cooks the order.

The Tofu Palace specializes in food for diners who have wheat allergies, are lactose intolerant, and so on. Vegetarian, vegan, whatever your dietary oddity, the Tofu Palace is here to serve. The Palace does pretty well, what with it being located in Boulder, one of the most health-conscious cities in the universe. Boulder attracts skiers, hikers, mountain climbers, and marathon runners up the yin yang. A Boulderite is as likely to eat red meat as to stir-fry a hubcap for dinner.

The Palace is brightly painted. One wall is purple, one red, one deep blue. The ceiling is pale green, and everywhere work of local artists is displayed for sale at relatively reasonable rates.

When I worked here in college (that's where Tate and I met), I was the only member of the waitstaff without multiple body piercings or a single tattoo. Tate has several of both. Her belly button and nose are pierced. She has a tattoo of a thin blue and white ring encircling her upper right arm that looks like a wave, a rose on her ankle, and the Chinese symbol for harmony on her breast. (Only a special few have seen this one, and one drunken night she flashed me and I became one of them. It was a shining moment in an otherwise disappointing life.) Today she is wearing her long black hair in a loose bun that is held together by what looks like decorative chopsticks.

She's petite, but so thin her limbs seem long and she looks taller than she is, with the graceful lithe muscles of a ballerina. It would be fair to call Tate's look exotic. My looks, with my honey-blond hair and dimples, would be best described as wholesome-Iowa-farm-girl.

I follow her into the kitchen.

"Tate, you're a genius."

"What are you talking about? Lance, leave the onions out of this burrito."

"Just write it down," Lance booms.

"I did. I just don't want a repeat of last time. I lost that tip because of you."

Lance, the cook, just grunts.

"Your idea for the book," I continue. I follow her over to the refrigerator, where she pulls out a couple of cans of organic sodas. "What I'll do is write a book about romance and dating around the globe. I'll interview women all over the world and find out their most hilarious dates ever. I'll find out about differences in dating and marriage in different cultures—the works. I'll be able to sell tons of articles based on my research to bridal magazines and women's rags. You know, stuff like, 'Looking to make your wedding original? Borrow from traditional Chinese or Turkish or ethnic ceremonies around the world to make your wedding an international success.' Or for *Cosmo*, I can write about different sexual rituals around the world, or for *Glamour* I can write something like, 'You think the dating scene in America is grim? At least you don't have to do like the Muka-Muka do—they have to eat worms and beat each other up to see if they're compatible.'"

"Who the hell are the Muka-Muka?"

"Well, that's just to illustrate. I don't know the worst mating rituals in the world yet—that's why I need to write a book about it. I'll collect all of my findings into a single book. I'll be like the John Gray of international relations between men and women. I'll be like an anthropologist studiously researching the most important issue known to humankind: Love."

"And along the way, as you're doing all this important academic research, you might just happen to stumble on Mr. Right."

Damn. Sometimes it's a problem that this girl knows me so well. "Well, you know, if it just so happens that way . . . But you have to come with me. You have money saved."

She pushes the kitchen door open with her butt and delivers the sodas to her table. She drops off a bill at another, then clears off the plates at yet another. I hover at the doorway of the kitchen, waiting for her.

"How much do you have saved?" I ask her as soon as she gets back.

"Order up!" Lance says.

Tate checks the order and starts balancing the plates on her arms. "I'm not sure exactly. Maybe five thousand."

Five grand! And she makes a lot less money than I do. Granted, she doesn't need a car, she lives with four roommates, and she doesn't need to spend a dime on her wardrobe for work, but still, I'm impressed.

"What are you going to do with it? What could be better than traveling the world with your friend? Come with me. Don't you want to see the Eiffel Tower? The Colosseum? The Sistine Chapel?"

She delivers the order, then comes back and pulls me aside conspiratorially. "What about our jobs?"

"I'll work it out with my boss, ask if they can hire a temp for a while or something. And Jack will understand. His waiters are always taking off on road trips for weeks at a time."

"That's true."

"So you're thinking about it?"

"When are you thinking of going?"

"As soon as possible."

"You'll plan everything?"

"Of course. Come on, it'll be the adventure of a lifetime. And maybe you'll find your soul mate. Another free spirit just like you."

She bites her lip. "It might be fun."

"It'll be a blast."

"Do you really think we could do this?"

"Of course we can."

She nods. "This is crazy."

"You love crazy."

She's still nodding. "Tell me when I should show up at the airport."

"Yes!" I give her an enormous hug. "It's going to be the experience of a lifetime," I assure her.

It's a big promise, but there is no doubt in mind that it's a promise I can keep.